IMMORTAL BELOVED

"You seem so real," Marissa said, beguiled by the potent masculinity of Brendan's smile. Her voice held a husky note of bewilderment. "You touched me."

"Oh." Again a look of candor, and that suppressed amusement. "Am I overstepping bounds to do that?"

"Don't you know? I've never been haunted before."

Her fingers plucked at the wool blanket as she glanced up at Brendan. How strong and beautiful he was, the fierceness of his Gypsy features softened by the mystic moonlight. Her skin began to tingle, and she felt an insistent rush of desire move through her body. More than anything in this world, she wanted him.

"I just assumed you'd be a more traditional ghost," she said, lowering her lashes to veil her yearning. "You know—wraithlike and transparent."

"This is a novel experience for me as well. I've dreamed away the years in that house, waiting for your return." He looked at her, a faint smile curving his full, wicked mouth. "Then you appeared again, and for the first time I had interest in assuming my worldly shape."

Marissa felt a shiver of pleasure run up her spine at the tender expression in his eyes. "Brendan, I'm not sure I understand—why me?"

His face turned solemn, though his eyes sparked with intensity. "We're somehow bound together, you and I. Don't you feel it?"

THE BECKONING GHOST

THE BECKONING GHOST

CATHERINE KOHMAN

ISBN: 0-6158-7105-4
ISBN-13: 9780615871059

Cover Designed by Danat'ello, Australia

In memory of generations of Nordstrom women who were gifted with "the Sight," especially Carrie Nordstrom Berg:
For sharing your love of books . . . For all the sweet, halcyon days in your summerhouse on "Arcadia" . . . And for your empathy for our own earthbound spirit . . .
Eternal love and gratitude, Gram

Acknowledgments

I'd like to thank my husband, Victor, and my parents, Leo and Marilyn Williams, for their constant love and support. The rest of my family and numerous friends, scattered far and wide, also deserve a heartfelt thank-you.

To my own Muses, authors Barbara Cockrell, Susan Johnson, and Mary Schultz (Leandra Logan): Thank you for the years of friendship, laughter, and advice. I know I wouldn't have persevered without your confidence in me.

To all the local chapter members of Romance Writers of America who have befriended me in my peregrinations around the country, in particular the Minnesota, Miami, and Utah chapters—a multitude of thanks for your warmth and generosity.

Finally, to my editor, Joanna Cagan, a kind, adventurous soul—thanks for taking a chance on me.

Prologue

Lucknow, India, March, 1857

"Missy, please don't hide from *Ayah*."

From her perch up in a mango tree, Miranda kept a watchful eye on the tangerine silk of Ayah's sari as her nurse wandered mournfully through the grove behind the bungalow. Delighted that her mild tantrum had turned into a game, Miranda smiled, resting her chin on her small fist.

Today was her sixth birthday, and she'd been promised a trip to the bazaar. Yesterday her soldier father had been sent to Delhi on the Honourable East India Company's business, and no one else in the household would take her. In a rare fit of temper she'd fled outdoors, determined to punish the adults who'd deprived her of her favorite excursion. But now she heard a deep, familiar voice on the rear veranda.

9

"Don't worry, Ayah. I'll find Miss Miranda."

The reassuring English voice belonged to her beloved "Uncle" Brendan. A dear friend of her parents, he always played games with her, even though at 22 he was nearer to the vast age of her father. Miranda grasped the engraved gold locket around her neck—her Christmas present from Brendan—and opened it to gaze at his handsome portrait next to her own. Smiling, she clicked it shut and prepared to scurry down from her perch. Then she paused, mindful that she'd be in for a stern lecture from her mother if she went back to the house.

"All right, poppet," said Lieutenant Brendan Tyrell. "You can come out now. I've smoothed your way with your mother, and you needn't worry about a scolding."

With a smothered giggle, Miranda heard Brendan's purposeful steps as he approached her tree. He stopped below her hiding place, and the morning sun shone on the thick, glossy waves of black hair that brushed his collar. She saw him impatiently tap his riding crop against the supple leather of his boot.

"Miranda, love, if you don't show yourself soon, I'll have to find a more deserving little girl to take to the bazaar."

Bothered by his casual threat, she peeked through the dark whorls of mango leaves to gauge his temper. An easy smile lit his tanned face, and his black eyes sparked with a kindred mischief. He wore his usual riding attire, a loose white shirt and cotton jodhpurs.

Without hesitation, she grabbed onto a thick branch and dropped below it. Swinging by her hands, she called, *"Catch me, Uncle Brendan, catch me!"*

Brendan looked up, drawing a sharp breath. The little minx was hanging from a branch, her tiny scuffed shoes dangling almost six feet above his head. If she fell from that height . . .

He quickly positioned himself beneath her and opened his arms. *"Randie-bai,"* he said calmly, using his pet Indian name for her, "let go now, and I'll catch you."

Fearlessly, the little blond-haired girl let go of the branch and dropped into his waiting arms. Once he had her safely in his grasp, Brendan hugged her to his chest while Miranda wrapped her arms around his neck, bussing his cheek. He gave a sharp exhalation of relief.

Miranda's ingenuous green eyes gazed up at him. "That was fun. Can we do it again?"

"Oh, no . . . you're never to try anything like that again," Brendan said, frowning. "Do you understand, Miranda? You could have been hurt if I wasn't right there to catch you."

Secure in his affection, she smiled up at him and said placidly, "But you were."

Brendan gave a deep sigh as he let Miranda down to the ground and smoothed her rumpled muslin skirts. Impetuous and precocious, the child was a handful even at six. How could he begin to explain to her that he—or her parents—wouldn't always be around to rescue her?

Instead, he smiled back at her. "Happy birthday, poppet." He took her small hand in his. "I've heard that there's a troop of Nepalese acrobats performing in the bazaar today. You wouldn't be interested in seeing them, would you?"

11

Catherine Kohman

Miranda's response was a shrieking whoop of joy.

The supple stunts of the Nepalese acrobats delighted Miranda, and after the performance, Brendan led his excited charge through the crowded bazaar. Miranda chattered gaily as they threaded their way between stalls piled high with chased silver vessels, finely tooled leather goods and glittering skeins of gold jewelry mixed with other sparkling baubles. Skillfully draped silks of emerald green, Phoenician purple and crocus yellow snared the eye before it was drawn to the next stall by a flash of celestial blue and gold tissue.

The displays in the spice vendor's alley were a rich, aromatic mosaic: the shallow bowls filled with the bright ocher of saffron and turmeric, the earthy browns of nutmeg and cinnamon, the pale green of cardamom and the fiery orange of dried chilies.

Gnarled, wizened men bent over their mortars and pestles, chattering in Hindi or Urdu, all the while sending an intoxicating potpourri of scents into the air. The rising heat wafted the spicy bouquet upward, blending it with the pungent odors of the market. Noisome stenches and the reek of camels, elephants and oxen vied with the smoked, meaty smells from open cooking fires and the perfumes of jasmine, roses and patchouli.

The brown-skinned, wiry water-carriers screeched over the competing cries of the sweetmeat vendors, who in turn yelled to be heard above the buzzing babel of a dozen different tongues and the constant clanging of bells.

Wondering how well his charge tolerated this assault on the senses, he glanced down at Miranda and saw her enraptured gaze dart from one side of the Hazrat Ganj to the other. As the street widened up ahead, Miranda pointed excitedly.

"Look, Uncle Brendan! A horse dealer!" She tugged on his sleeve to pull him through the milling crowd. "Do you think he has any ponies? Papa says I'm almost old enough—"

"I don't think that's quite the present that your father has in mind for you, poppet." As a bullock cart rumbled by, they came to a stop across from the Arab dealer and his sleek string of gray and sorrel horses. His ears flattened and teeth bared, a silver stallion with a white blaze eyed the lumbering bullock. Before the animal could lunge forward, the Arab jerked hard on the horse's lead and gave him a stern glance. The stallion slipped back into line, ears twitching in sulky annoyance.

Emboldened by the stallion's display of temper, Miranda thrust her lower lip forward in an attempt to pout. "I'm too old to always ride in front of you or Papa."

Her uncharacteristic show of petulance vanished as her curious, skittering glance fixed on the stall beside them, a stall festooned with dozens of cages that each held a brightly plumed bird. "Oh, *Brendan-ji, look!*"

He smiled fondly as she moved from one cage to the next, talking to the squawking mynahs and colorful, nervous finches. From the darkened rear of the stall came a beckoning hiss.

Startled, Brendan stared into the gloomy depths and recognized Vijay Gupta, an informant who'd aided him on a number of his secret missions into the native quarters of Lucknow and the further reaches of the Kingdom of Oudh. Miranda was chattering amiably with the bird-seller, so he

13

slipped unobtrusively into the stall.

The slight Indian looked around, eyes fearful. "Tyrell-*sahib* . . . tell no one you have spoken to me. It will mean my death."

Brendan moved next to him, his voice low. "What is it, Vijay?"

"*Sa'b*, you must go home to England, right away. Take the child with you."

"But you know she isn't mine. Miranda is Captain Seton's daughter. Why should we leave now?"

Vijay's brown, liquid eyes probed his. "If the girl is not yours by blood, she is still the child of your heart, is she not?"

Brendan glanced back at Miranda and saw her gold curls bounce as she deluged the merchant with lively questions. "Well, yes, certainly . . . but—"

"Listen to me, *sa'b*. I know you well—you are an honest friend, a *pukka-sahib*. I also know this to be true—those evil rascals—the *badmashes*—are planning to massacre the British *Raj*. The *memsa'bs* and children too. You must go."

"You've been listening too long to the bazaar gossips, my friend." Brendan smiled grimly, though he knew that Vijay was a faithful and reliable informant, if occasionally excitable. "These rumors of murdering the *Firinghis* have been flying about for months . . . from troublemakers trying to stir things up."

"You are not believing me, *sa'b*?" Vijay hissed through his teeth. "*Tcha!* What of the sepoys? This matter of the defiling rifle cartridges is making the soldiers fear for their caste, that they will be forced to become Christians. It is being said the sepoys will also rise."

Brendan frowned. There had already been trou-

14

ble over the new cartridges for the Enfield rifles. Rumor had spread among the native regiments that the greased cartridge papers, which had to be bitten to load, were soaked in beef and pork tallow.

Though it was untrue, the very idea of such an abomination touching their lips was deeply offensive to Hindu and Muslim alike. The sepoys feared if they used the cartridges, their caste would be broken. Thus defiled, they would be shunned by their families, and denied their proper rewards in the afterlife.

The native soldiers had been reassured that the rumors were false. In any case, they could now tear the cartridges open with their fingers, to avoid touching the papers to their lips. Still, the insidious story spread throughout the ranks that the British were determined to break their caste.

Would the sepoys stay true to the Company's salt? Or would they mutiny, as Vijay was warning him?

"Vijay, you must tell me what you know. Gather whatever information you can, then send word where we may safely meet. I need to know how extensive this disaffection is."

"Yes, *sa'b*. I must go now."

Vijay silently disappeared through the rear of the stall. Mentally debating the seriousness of this latest rumor, Brendan slowly walked back to Miranda and the cages of raucous birds.

"Look, Uncle Brendan. Isn't she beautiful?" Miranda pointed to a ring-necked parakeet preening in a bamboo cage. The greenish-blue bird clung to the bars of the cage and cocked its head to one side, fixing its bright eye on his face.

"That she is, poppet." Smiling to mask his disquiet over Vijay's words, he asked, "Would you like to bring her home?"

The little girl's green eyes grew round, then sparkled. "Oh, may I, Brendan-ji? I'll name her after you!"

Looking askance at the bird, Brendan teased, "She doesn't quite look like a 'Brenda' to me."

Miranda's face fell. "No, she doesn't." She asked hopefully, "Do you have any other names?"

He stuck a finger through the bamboo bars and stroked the bird's smooth poll. "Actually, my middle name is Philip."

"Philip," Miranda said, testing the sound of his name. "That's not right either." Her face lit up. "I know—Pippa! Everyone calls my aunt Phillipa 'Pippa'!"

"Pippa it shall be." He briefly haggled with the merchant, then settling on an agreed price, removed the caged bird from its hook. "Happy birthday, Miranda."

"Thank you, Uncle Brendan," she said with an excited grin. "This is the best birthday I've ever had—except for Papa being away, that is. Wait until he sees my beautiful Pippa!"

Brendan smiled at her enthusiasm, ruffling her shiny curls. "I think he'll be happier to see his little girl."

Bird in one hand and Miranda's hand in the other, he made his way through the riotous confusion of the bazaar. While they waited for a rich litter with silver dragons on either end to pass by, Miranda whispered questions about the occupant of the palanquin, wanting to know what *purdah* was. As they headed back toward the ordered tranquility of the Mariaon cantonment, he ex-

16

plained that it meant seclusion for Indian women of high rank.

Intrigued by this custom, Miranda said, "I guess it's rather like being 'indisposed'—how Mama feels whenever that tiresome Mrs. Grindley calls."

Brendan's shout of laughter made Pippa flutter in her cage, so Miranda spoke softly to the bird to calm her down.

Thus left to his own thoughts, Brendan wondered—were there dangerous days ahead? Perhaps it wouldn't be a bad idea for Miranda and her mother Sarah to go up into the hills at Simla, or down to Calcutta. He'd talk it over with Miranda's father, Anthony, as soon as his friend arrived back from Delhi. In the meantime, he'd contact Sir Henry Lawrence, his superior and the new Chief Commissioner of Oudh.

While he thought deeply about what he would tell Lawrence, Miranda talked happily about her new bird and her pet mongoose, Caesar. From her abrupt silence, he realized that she'd asked him a question. "I'm sorry, Miranda, what did you say?"

She looked up at him with wounded eyes, hurt. by his inattention. "I asked if you minded if I bring Pippa and Caesar with me when I come to live with you."

Though rather confused, he teased, "Live with me? Why would you want to live with a crusty old fellow like me?"

"Well, Mama says that when two people love each other, they get married and live together." She watched his face in grave attention. "I love you, Brendan-ji . . . don't you love me?"

"*Oh, piara*—Miranda darling, of course I do. But it's different." He paused, unwilling to hurt her in his clumsiness. "We can't marry, poppet . . . I'm nearly old enough to be your father."

Impatiently, she said, "That's what Mama said about Sir Mortimer's new wife—that he'd robbed the cradle and could be her *grandfather.*"

Brendan's sudden guffaw silenced her, so he stooped down and hugged her to his chest. "Ah, Miranda, sometimes I think you hear too much, and I *know* you understand too much."

Her pique apparently soothed by his amusement, she asked curiously, "How am I to learn anything if I don't pay attention to what I hear or see?"

Her innocent words struck an apprehensive chord in Brendan's chest. Were Vijay's reports a reality? He hoped not, but he had to check them out properly—to be certain.

To Miranda, he said, "You're right, Randie-*bai.* One *should* pay attention. Now, we'd better get you home and wash all this bazaar dust off you and Pippa or you won't be fit company for your own birthday celebration."

Chapter One

Lake Minnetonka, Minnesota

Except for the two dusty ruts leading off the paved road and into the dense woods, there was no sign that a house existed on the peninsula. Turning her blue Camry into the ruts, Marissa Erickson drove slowly through the lush green woods and felt a rising shiver of curiosity. How would the house look after 16 long years?

The driveway, if you dared call it that, crossed a rough-hewn wooden bridge over a ravine, then wound in between towering maples and luxuriant undergrowth. The scrabbling fingers of a shrub scraped the sides of her car as the late afternoon sun filtered through the thick canopy of leaves.

19

Catherine Kohman

The trees glowed a rich emerald, and the light itself took on an aqueous, greenish hue, like the
light in a Pacific rain forest.

As the drive made a sharp curve around a screen
of basswood trees, Marissa stopped the car and
impatiently brushed her blond bangs out of her
eyes. For a moment, she was ten years old and
seeing the house for the first time. She heard her
grandmother's silvery laughter float across the
deep, cushiony lawn, smelled the metallic smoke
from the Fourth of July sparklers and fireworks.

With a shake of her head, she laughed. "Now,
girl, none of that spooky nonsense of yours!" Her
voice mimicked her friend Kelsey's chiding, affec-
tionate tone.

From across the clearing, she studied the two-
story house—a summer residence that had been
winterized since her last visit. The white clapboards gleamed brightly, the sky-blue trim framed
the windows and doors as neatly as it did when
she was a child. There were some differences—
the burnished sheen of new cedar shakes on the
roof, plantings of dark green yew around the foundation. And the encroaching woods had usurped
a larger portion of the overgrown lawn.

After years in the city, Marissa craved space and
light, and saw she'd have to do some judicious
pruning and trimming to restore the airy sense of
openness she remembered from her youth.

The summers Marissa had spent here with her
grandmother on Arcadia Island were a brief epi-
sode in her life, but they'd always been a stolen,
halcyon time . . . a time away from the stresses of
her parents' troubled marriage. Though her di-
vorced parents had each remarried and now lived
on opposite sides of the Atlantic, her old sanctuary

20

seemed blessedly unchanged. She felt an odd sense of peace and homecoming as she put the Toyota back in gear and parked in the gravel driveway.

The front of the house faced the lake. From the large screened porch or the white-railed veranda above it, you looked down a long sloping lawn to the blue water. During weekend regattas, Marissa remembered, the bay filled with the white sails and rainbow spinnakers of the yacht club racers— a quiet beauty compared to the frenetic buzzing of speedboats driven by yahoos who careened around the busier bays. This part of the lake was more remote, and she welcomed the tranquility to work on her book.

The pressing thought of her book—a biography of the famed 19th-century linguist and author Sir Brendan Tyrell—prompted her to start unloading her car. Her suitcases could wait until the groceries were put away and her computer brought inside.

The key the realtor gave her slid smoothly into the lock, but the French door stuck as she turned the knob. She smiled. Her grandmother had always been after the handyman to fix that very door. Perversely glad that the man had never gotten around to it in the intervening years, Marissa nudged the door open with her foot and entered the house.

Down the hallway, a luminescent red sphere floated in the gloom. *What on earth?* Marissa stopped, clutching a gray grocery bag in each arm. She felt the queer sensation that someone was waiting for her inside, waiting patiently in the quiet darkness.

Of course. The light fixture hanging over the liv-

21

ing room fireplace—that's all it was. She remembered it now—an ornate globe of blown ruby-red glass. An unclosed drapery let in a sliver of the dying sun, making the globe glow on its own.

But that didn't explain away her feeling that there was someone inside the house. A singularly solitary house, surrounded by water and acres of wild, tangled woods. Woods that would muffle any cries for help . . .

"Hello," Marissa called, mustering her shrinking courage, "is anyone there?"

A thick, preternatural silence mocked her nervous query. Holding her breath, she caught a shifting of shadows, and the faint creak of a footfall on the wooden floor.

"If there's someone here, please answer me."

Again no reply. Marissa thought, *Right. I'm sure a burglar or rapist would announce themselves.* Ridiculous—it's just an old, creaky house.

Despite her inner laugh at her attack of the jitters, she set her bags down on the floor and fumbled in her purse for her can of Mace. Spray can in hand, she walked quietly down the hall into the living room, alert for any movement or sound. The palpable stillness taunted her once again.

Marissa reached the large windows facing the lake and drew the draperies open. Rich, honeyed sunlight splashed into the room, chasing the shadows away. No one could hide from the sun's penetrating beams; all the corners of the large, open room and the balcony above it were exposed. She must have only imagined the alien movement, the quiet footstep.

A simple case of nerves, she told herself, setting down the Mace on the coffee table across from the hearth.

The Beckoning Ghost

In front of the two-story fieldstone fireplace, Marissa wrapped her arms around her waist, thinking that this house always reminded her of the Ponderosa.

The living room was open to the peak of the roof, while two bedrooms and the main bath were over the dining room and kitchen. The rustic walls and beamed ceiling were redwood, and even after all these years, the aroma of the wood still lingered. The upper chimney and balcony railings were draped with colorful Navajo rugs, adding to the Western ambience of the house.

Marissa hugged herself—did this beautiful place really belong to her?

She opened one of the sets of French doors bracketing the fireplace and stepped out onto the porch. The fresh scent of the pink peony hedge at the front of the house filled the room. With a tiny thrill, Marissa noted that the white, sofa-sized wicker swing still hung out on the porch. Another flash of memory—all those nights when she and Kelsey talked there, gently swinging in the warm velvet of the lingering northern twilight.

Then she remembered her bags of groceries and came back through the dining room to fetch them. Depositing the bags on the old oak kitchen table, she noted the room looked the same—pale birch cabinets and white countertops, frilly blue and white curtains in the windows. The kitchen made her feel warm and cozy, with its memories of Gran's Swedish pancakes and hot cocoa on cool summer mornings.

As she finished putting away the groceries, she heard a knock on the rear door and went back into the hallway. Through the door, Marissa saw her friend Kelsey grimace as she juggled an unwieldy

Catherine Kohman

potted palm and a bottle of wine. Laughing, she opened the door and took the endangered palm from Kelsey's hands. "Well, Ms. Sheridan! I didn't expect you until tomorrow!"

"What? Leave you alone on the first night in your new home, especially out here in the jungle?" Kelsey sniffed disdainfully, then her blue eyes widened. "I'd forgotten how gorgeous this house is, Rissa. I can see why you got rid of your condo in Boston for this place."

Marissa gently placed the palm in front of the picture window facing the lake and brushed her hands off on her faded jeans. "It's strange, Kelse— that this house was for sale now . . . for the first time in fifty years, and just when I decided to move back to Minnesota."

Kelsey set the bottle of champagne down on the coffee table and pulled up the drooping shoulder of her loose black jersey top. "I thought your grandmother used to own it."

"No, the owners were living in Europe at the time and rented it out for a few years. Gran was reluctant to give it up when they finally returned." Marissa smiled wistfully. "I missed this place. Anyway, it's been in the same family all these years, but the last owners moved to Santa Barbara."

Kelsey finished her cursory inspection of the room and faced Marissa, her hands propped on her narrow hips. "So, you jaded Easterner," she said, her oversized silver earrings jiggling impatiently, "where's my hug?"

Laughing at the good-natured insult, Marissa hugged her tightly. Kelsey was petite and slightly built, and her raven curls tickled Marissa's chin.

Her friend smoothed Marissa's long, thick hair

24

back over her shoulders. "I'm so glad you're back, Rissa!"

Tears pricked Marissa's eyelids. Though the last five years out East had been exciting, they'd also been lonely. When she'd decided to leave Boston, her mother had tried to convince Marissa to come live with her and her second husband, Etienne, in France. But it hadn't felt right. *This*, however, felt very right. She answered, "Not as glad as I am to *be* back."

"So," Kelsey said with a grin, "let's pop this bubbly open and get down to some serious house-warming!"

Marissa headed for the back door, tying the tails of her blue cotton work shirt around her waist. "I'll bring in my suitcases first. We can sip champagne and talk while I get unpacked."

Kelsey sauntered after her. "I should have guessed that you had ulterior motives for inviting me out here. You needed some poor drudge to help you haul in those steamer trunks you usually travel with."

"Steamer trunks? Why, Kelse," Marissa added with a dry smile, "you think I tend to overpack?"

Kelsey ran her fingers through her short black hair and rolled her eyes. "Did Imelda Marcos have shoes?"

"I want to hear all the gory details about why you left Boston. Whatever happened to old what's-his-name—the perennial film student?" Kelsey folded her leotard-clad legs beneath her and took a huge, luscious strawberry from a blue and white Rosenthal bowl, dredging it through a deli container of creamy fruit dip.

Seated next to her on the wicker swing, Marissa

leaned back into the soft floral cushions and pushed off the floor with her bare toes. The porch swing swayed gently back and forth with her movement. "I'm sorry, Kelse—did you say something?"

Kelsey stared at her, noting the faraway expression in her friend's eyes. She always envied Marissa the unusual color of her eyes: a pellucid blend of green and pale gray. Sometimes they were the luminous aquamarine of the Caribbean; at other times, they turned silver, like mist on an Irish mountain. Of an artistic nature, Kelsey always lamented being stuck with such a pedestrian eye color as plain old blue.

"Don't go spacy on me now, Rissa," she chided gently. "Where's Robin? Remember—the love of your life?"

Marissa smiled wryly, the barest hint of discomfort in her eyes. "He was offered a teaching fellowship at U.C.L.A." She sighed and brushed back her loose, tawny mane. "It's just as well; I was going to ask him to leave anyway. He simply saved me the trouble."

"Ah." Kelsey looked at her keenly. She'd never cared for Robin herself; she thought he was too self-centered and not good enough for Marissa by half. "*Not* the love of your life, I take it?"

"Hardly. But it wasn't Robin's fault—I was the one who got restless. He said that ever since I started this second book, I've been moody and distant." She shrugged. "I don't know why."

Then Marissa's pale, oval face flushed with buoyant enthusiasm. "The book is the primary reason I decided to come back. Brendan Tyrell was living here the summer he died . . . or disappeared, some say."

Kelsey's brows raised. "Is the house that old?"

"No, not this house—it was built in the twenties. I meant the old hotel and bungalows that stood here before: Arcadia House."

"I didn't know there was ever a hotel here."

"It burned to the ground around 1900." A shadow touched Marissa's eyes, and the corners of her generous mouth tightened. "The bungalow that the Tyrells stayed in burned earlier, in 1875. Brendan was the only victim. His wife and secretary both escaped, and eventually they returned to England."

Kelsey reached for another strawberry. "What did you mean before—he may have disappeared?"

"Well, they never found his body, or any of his unpublished manuscripts, which he had with him. Of course, the fire was as hot as a blast furnace, so that's understandable. Yet some say Brendan took the opportunity to disappear. Contemporary rumors said his marriage was troubled."

Kelsey leaned back into the soft pillows. "He never surfaced again—nor any of his unpublished books?"

"No, that's another tragedy. The manuscripts lost were the only copies of those particular works. Brilliant translations of Indian erotic poetry, far more sensual than the *Kama Sutra*. Also some ethnographies and linguistic studies. He came to Minnetonka after studying the Shoshone and Lakota languages out in the Rockies."

"What did he look like?"

"I've got a copy from the National Portrait Gallery in London." With her long dancer's legs, Marissa gracefully pushed off the swing and disappeared into the living room. In a moment

27

she was back with the picture and handed it to Kelsey, who leaned forward to study it.

The custom photographic copy was half-size, and showed a tall, dark-haired man leaning against a desk littered with maps and old Sanskrit texts. Behind him, the ornate window of a Moghul palace framed the rose-tinted peaks of the Hindu Kush. The easel next to the desk held a painting of the main gate of Lucknow, India—a wondrous, wedding-cake fantasy in ivory stone.

Though the background of the portrait was interesting because of the content and associations, the man's face drew the eye and held it. Tyrell's face was darkly handsome in an exotic, unconventional way. His high cheekbones, slanting brows and lush, drooping mustache gave his features almost a Magyar cast, though Tyrell was Anglo-Irish by birth. The vitality in those black eyes, in the coiled virility of his casual pose, captivated Kelsey. She grinned in appreciation.

"Tom Cruise, eat your heart out," she breathed in a husky whisper. "Now there's a *real man*. Too bad they don't make them like that anymore."

Marissa smiled in blissful agreement. "I hang this over my computer for inspiration."

"What was his wife like? I bet she had trouble keeping him in line."

Marissa produced two color photocopies of Rosalind Tyrell: one a painting of a finely featured girl in her 20s, the other a photograph of a sour-faced woman in widow's weeds. Only 15 years separated the portraits, yet they hardly looked like the same woman. The girl had rich brown hair and a gay, fragile prettiness, while the woman was drawn and haggard.

Kelsey examined the copies closely. "About the

rumored problems in their marriage—other women, you think?"

"Before he was married, Brendan was something of a rake," Marissa answered thoughtfully. "Yet he seemed genuinely devoted to Rosalind. I think the problem was with his wife. Insanity ran in her family, and she died in a private asylum when she was forty-eight."

Kelsey handed her back the copies. "Sorry, love. Sounds too depressing. I wouldn't want to work on it and stay out here all by myself. Reminds me of *Jane Eyre*: All you need is a brooding Rochester."

Marissa smiled reluctantly. "You make it sound as if I'm in the middle of the Big Woods, Kelse. The island has a bridge now, not a ferry, and there *are* other houses on it."

"Not nearby, with your place stuck out here on the peninsula. And they're mostly weekend people."

"Thanks, friend." Marissa punched Kelsey lightly on the arm. "Are you intentionally trying to scare me or what?"

"Sorry, Rissa." Kelsey grinned. "It's just that you get spooky yourself at times, or you used to."

Marissa's gray-green eyes narrowed in mock censure. "If you're talking about that man I saw in the Walter Library stacks years ago, it was just some student actor in costume on his way to the Rarig theater."

"In an officer's uniform of the Seventh Native Cavalry?" Kelsey raised her brows skeptically. "What was playing—*Clive of India*?"

Marissa's smile wavered, and she idly played with the lace tucks of her camisole. "Did I say that?"

29

"You looked it up in an encyclopedia of uniforms."

"I don't remember the details, yet it's odd. . . . " Marissa's brow puckered, and her eyes clouded as she struggled to recall the incident.

It was so long ago, when she was an undergraduate at the university. In the midst of research for a term paper on the Indian Mutiny, she was prowling the stacks at Walter late one evening, searching for Edward Lecky's 1859 volume, *Fictions Connected with the Indian Outbreak of 1857 Exposed*. She'd looked up to see a dark-haired man standing in the gloom at the end of the aisle, a man in a familiar, old-fashioned white uniform. His face was shadowed, but from the glint of light touching his black eyes, she knew he watched her intently. Until she turned chicken and ran.

"The Seventh, you say?" She gave Kelsey a funny half-smile. "That was Brendan's regiment in India."

Kelsey stared at her for a moment, then hummed the theme from *The Twilight Zone*. "Hey, now you're scaring me! I have to sleep here for two nights, you know."

Marissa tried to shake off her feeling of eeriness, though something elusive about that encounter played at the edges of her consciousness. Finally, she gave up and said lightheartedly, "What sort of room would you prefer, madam? Haunted or non-haunted?"

Kelsey scowled at her. "*Non-haunted*, please." Then she laughed. "Welcome home, Rissa—who else can I be this weird with and get away with it?"

A door at the back of the house blew shut with a loud thunk. Both women started, then looked at each other with widened eyes. Kelsey giggled. "Uh-oh, I hope that wasn't a warning that I've got to be on my best behavior."

Marissa didn't reply. She thought that all the windows in the house were closed, as were the doors leading to the porch. There shouldn't be any drafts. Then she caught Kelsey staring at her with a puzzled expression.

"I'm glad you're here, Kelse, best behavior or not," she answered. "Let's get ready for bed, then I'll show you a picture album I found while I was packing. It's full of geeky pictures of us when we were kids." She added with a teasing smile, "You need a humbling experience, my dear."

While the horned moon arced overhead and a saw-whet owl hooted nearby, Marissa burrowed deeper under her covers to avoid the cool breeze wafting in the bedroom window. With a soft sigh, she slipped back into her dreams.

On a sunny summer afternoon, she stood on the wooden dock below the house. Sailboats zipped across the blue water, heeling over in the wind. There was something odd about these boats; they were old wooden cat-boats and yawls, not the fiberglass Cals and C&Cs she was used to seeing. Then she noticed the rowboats anchored out in the bay—filled with women in frilly white gowns and picture hats pinned securely to their heads.

Marissa looked down at her own clothes and saw that she wore a long white dress. She smiled to herself and turned around. On a knoll behind her, the imposing bulk of the Arcadia House rose, a length of white pillars and long, cool verandas below a vast green roof. A faint lucid thought drifted through her mind, *I'm dreaming that I'm*

31

here over one hundred years ago. The old boats, the quaintly clad women all fit now.

She enjoyed watching the sleek boats tack sharply back and forth, and silently cheered on the most audacious skipper. As the sun dropped behind the trees across the bay, the boats scattered to their home docks, and the women in the rowboats followed them. A lone yacht, the winner of the race, sailed for the dock at the Arcadia.

Marissa waited expectantly while the yachtsman deftly berthed the boat alongside the dock. Clad in a loose white shirt and cotton sailing pants, with a scarlet scarf knotted at his throat, he jumped lithely onto the wooden planks and held out his hand to her. She raised her eyes to his smiling, familiar face—Brendan Tyrell's face.

Another lucid thought—of course, she'd talked about him for most of the evening. His face was deeply tanned and more darkly attractive than she remembered. Then she drifted past those thoughts and simply took his hand. His grasp felt sure and strong as he helped her into the boat. The light in his eyes touched her, warm and boldly intimate.

Once she was settled in her seat, Brendan cast off and expertly trimmed the sails. In the late summer dusk, they skimmed over the silver-lavender water, headed toward the twinkling lights across the bay.

As she turned over in her sleep, Marissa was half-awakened by the coolness of the muslin sheets. June evenings could still be cold, she thought. Then her leg found a warm spot on the double bed and she moved over to soak up Robin's lingering heat.

32

The Beckoning Ghost

Her eyes flew open. Robin—in Minnesota? *No way.*

"Kelse?"

No reply. Her friend was sleeping in Marissa's old bedroom, across a small bridge further down the balcony. Marissa had moved into her grandmother's room because it was larger and overlooked the lake. If Kelsey wasn't in the room, then who was?

Suddenly awake, Marissa slid through the warm spot near the edge and got out of bed. A spicy Oriental scent hung in the air. Gasping as her feet touched the chilly wooden floor, she stepped into her fleecy slippers.

She remembered the French door that opened onto the second level veranda and tried the handle. The veranda had no other access, but someone could use a ladder. . . .

Still locked, from within—no one could have come in that way.

Unease bubbling up within her, Marissa went along the balcony and peered down into the gray gloom of the living room. It was hushed, undisturbed. She peeked in Kelsey's room. Even in the dim moonlight, she could see her dark-haired friend sleeping peacefully.

As she moved away to stand by the balcony railing, a thin rush of warm air caressed her cheek, and she inhaled an aromatic whisper of cherry tobacco. Instead of chilling her, the scent touched off a quiver of response deep inside her, making her ache to reach out—to reach for someone incredibly dear to her. Yet she knew instinctively an impossible barrier stood between them.

What in heaven am I thinking? Mystified, she sagged against the redwood rail and her fingers

33

dug into the nubby wool of a Navajo blanket. *I must be imagining all this*, she thought. *Maybe I miss Robin more than I realize—after all, we lived together for five years. Sleeping alone again is something I'm going to have to get used to.*

Though even as those words entered her mind, Marissa knew it wasn't Robin that she longed to reach for in the darkness. Robin didn't smoke a pipe.

She sighed. The stresses of her breakup with Robin, the move and her new writing project must be affecting her nerves. *I need rest*, she decided, *that's all.*

She slowly walked back to her room. From the doorway, she studied the half-darkened room. An old double bed, an antique marble-topped dresser, a mahogany vanity with an Art Deco mirror. In the corner between the bookcase and chimney, an over-stuffed chair of faded chintz—empty. Nothing strange or sinister there.

Marissa climbed back into bed and hugged the covers to her chest. She tried to concentrate on the movers arriving tomorrow with her books and furniture. In her head, she arranged and re-arranged the rooms until her muscles loosened.

Drifting in the netherworld between sleep and wakefulness, she heard a deep, familiar voice whisper, *Go to sleep now, poppet.*

Curiously reassured, she sank once more into her dreams.

Chapter Two

What can a tired heart say,
Which the wise of the world have made dumb?
Save to the lonely dreams of a child,
"Return again, come!"
                                    —*Walter De La Mare*

The next morning, Kirk, an old high school friend, came across the lake in his sleek runabout to help Marissa move in. He toted heavy boxes of books and helped push the furniture vans' big-wheeled dollies up the rutted driveway.

After the vans left, Marissa and Kelsey unpacked her belongings while Kirk rearranged the furniture to her plan. It was an exhausting day, so Marissa didn't have any time to dwell on her weird experience from the night before.

To thank her friends for their hard work on her behalf, she treated them to dinner at Lord Fletcher's, across the bay. After dinner, the three of them returned to her house and talked on the porch, drinking a fruity bottle of Gewurztraminer.

When she took the empty bottle and glasses back to the kitchen, Marissa heard the heavy creak of male footsteps along the balcony above. She smiled. Kirk must have gone upstairs to use the bathroom after drinking all that wine.

She walked back out onto the porch. "Kelse, I thought I'd give Kirk the bedroom across the bridge from yours—"

She stopped. Kirk, broadly muscular and blond, dwarfed Kelsey as they sat on the swing together, conversing quietly. He wasn't upstairs, walking on the balcony.

Kelsey looked up at her. "Is something wrong, Rissa?"

"Ah, no." She stumbled over the words, masking her confusion. "Ah—how about Swedish pancakes for breakfast?"

Half-listening to their reply, she wondered how she could have mistaken the noises of an old house settling for footsteps. Yet they had sounded so clear, so *purposeful.*

"I don't know about you two," she said with a feigned yawn, anxious to get upstairs to find the source of the sounds. "I'm off to bed. Night."

Marissa climbed the stairs up to the balcony, running her hands over the redwood walls and railing, peering into the bedrooms opening off of it. There were still unpacked boxes in the rooms, but nothing that would have shifted or even made a noise approximating the footsteps she'd heard.

Curiouser and curiouser.

She tried to dismiss the footsteps again, blaming it on the age of the house. She wasn't threatened—she felt at home here, and *happy*—a refreshing sensation after the depression and moodiness of the last year with Robin.

Well, she thought with a nervous smile, she wasn't going to give up her dream house. If it occasionally went bump in the night, she'd have to learn to live with it.

Somehow.

After Kirk left on Sunday, Kelsey pulled out a lawn chair to lay on the unroofed part of the veranda and soak up the sun. With her golden complexion, she could tolerate it. Thanks to her parents' Scandinavian genes, Marissa usually burned, so she decided to explore the woods around the house instead.

By early June, the maples, oaks and basswoods were all leafed out. Though the ephemeral spring flowers on the forest floor were done blooming, Marissa found clumps of wine-and-yellow columbine. As girls, she and Kelsey used to pick the columbine—honeysuckle, they'd misnamed it then—and bite off the curled ends of the blossoms to suck out the sweet nectar. Now she left the tiny trumpet-shaped blooms unmolested.

In the slanting, golden light, she wandered through the huge trees, picking her way through the underbrush, enjoying the verdant solitude. Drifts of late-blooming violets—purple, white and yellow—carpeted the lightly shaded areas. Overhead, orioles trilled their liquid songs and warblers flitted in the highest branches, while catbirds called to her from the shrubbery.

Marissa stumbled onto a deer trail and followed it deeper into the woods, away from the house. The trees grew closer together here, and the sun passed behind a roiling, amoeba-like cloud, creating a premature twilight. Without the warmth of the sun, the birds fell silent. She shivered in her denim shorts and white T-shirt as a cool breeze sprang up. Was a sudden storm blowing in?

About to turn back toward the house, she saw what looked like a building up ahead. Compelled to check it out, she saw all that was left was the fieldstone foundation and two partially collapsed walls of peeling blue-gray wood. She wondered aloud, "What *is* this place?"

Stepping closer, Marissa peeked over the stone foundation. A wave of damp, musty air assailed her nostrils. Inside was a pit strewn with rubble, rotted boards and torn shingles.

"The old icehouse," she muttered to herself, and moved back sharply. She grabbed her forearms to keep her hands from shaking.

She'd been here before. Gran had warned her to keep away from the old icehouse. But like any other precocious child, the warning had drawn Marissa to it as a moth to a flame. . . .

What's so spooky about an old icehouse, anyway? Marissa thought scornfully. Sure, Gran had told her to keep away from here because it was dangerous. But she wasn't some dumb six-year-old to fall in the pit and get hurt. She was ten, and braver than that snotty Roger who lived in the big house on the other side of the island. He was the one who'd said that he'd never go to the icehouse, especially alone. There were things there that *hurt* kids.

Whoever got hurt there? she'd asked him. Well, Roger said, Timmy Barker went there, and he fell down on some rocks and broke his glasses. *Timmy*

Barker is a klutz, she'd answered. *He'd trip over his own two feet.*

So, here she was—on a Magical Quest to the Dragon's Lair. Maybe it was like Smaug's cave in *The Hobbit* . . . and there was buried treasure in the old icehouse. That's why it was supposed to be so *dangerous.* . . .

Chilling in the rough breeze, Marissa saw herself, ten years old, dressed in black shorts and a faded T-shirt, once hot pink. Scuffed sneakers on her feet. In her hand she carried a stout, wavy branch stripped of its bark. *Gandalf's staff,* she called it. Her blond ponytail bobbed up and down as she trotted up the path to the dread Smaug's Lair.

When she got to the crumbling icehouse, she felt a swoop of disappointment. It was just a smelly, fallen-down building. Disdainfully, she poked her staff through the rubble alongside the foundation. Her eye caught a glint of gold.

Treasure!

Marissa stooped over and dug a brightly minted golden coin out of the mud. Heavy and shiny, it felt like real gold. She wiped the muddy coin off on her shorts. The front of the coin had the head of a woman on it; she wore a funny sort of squiggly ponytail. There were some words too: *Victoria D G Brittaniar.* On the reverse side, a man on horseback was attacking . . . *a dragon!* She smiled with delight. Maybe it was part of some dragon's lost hoard after all. She saw the year then: 1872.

Could it be an English coin? The date was from Queen Victoria's time, Marissa thought, but the face on the coin looked nothing like the frowning old woman she'd seen in the pictures of the monarch. Still, the coin *was* old: from a hundred years ago.

How did it get here? She felt a quiver of excitement as she held the coin up to catch the sinking sun.

But the sun disappeared behind a bank of sooty clouds on the western horizon, and she suddenly realized how late it was. Gran would be peeved if she was late for supper. If she told her grandmother the truth about where she'd found the coin . . .

She couldn't risk two offenses in one day. Gran might not read with her at bedtime if she did that.

Marissa turned on her heel, her disappointment over the moldering icehouse forgotten in her pleasure of finding the coin. She started back down the path, then stopped abruptly.

A dark-skinned man was coming toward her on the path, carrying a shovel. Marissa ducked behind a buckthorn bush before he saw her.

As the man approached, she got a better look at him. He didn't live on the island, she knew that. The man seemed somehow . . . foreign, that was the word. Short and bandy-legged, he moved with strong purpose. She thought he was dressed funny—in loose khaki trousers and a matching jacket. He stopped at a tree not far from her hiding place and stripped off his jacket, revealing sinewy arms and a strong, thick neck. He began to dig up the earth beneath the tree.

Was he hiding more treasure? Maybe the coin belonged to him. Marissa hoped not. Somehow, he gave her the creepiest feeling. She sidled out of her hiding place and debated whether to try for the path further down, or go the other way. The man had his back to her, so she crept quietly toward the path. If Indians could steal through the forest without making a sound, so could she.

Her foot came down on a dry branch, which broke with a loud crack. Marissa froze. The man's neck snapped around, and his darting glance pinned her in place like a mounted insect.

Below the white scarf wound around his head, she saw one side of his face was smooth and unblemished, his eye bright and piercing. The other side had a hideous, ropy scar that skimmed over his right brow and eye, down to his cheek. His pale, unseeing eye unnerved her as he stared balefully in her direction, muttering something dark and evil-sounding in another language. Then he spat in English, *"You!"*

That single word, spoken with real venom, jolted Marissa into movement. With a high-pitched shriek, she tore through the underbrush, heedless of the scratching thorns and stinging nettles on her bare legs. *Please, God, don't let him catch me. I'll be good, I promise.*

In her wild flight, she tripped over a root and fell, painfully skinning her hands and knees. She whimpered in fright, scrambling to her feet. A protruding branch snagged her long hair, and she yanked it free, tearing the elastic band from her ponytail. Her lungs burned as she ran.

Is he after me? Where did the sun go—why is it so dark here? Oh, please somebody—

Then she broke out of the woods, stumbling into the golden light. She glanced over her shoulder to see if the evil-looking man was behind her.

"Whoa, little lady."

Strong hands caught and held her. She shrieked again.

41

"Child, what is it? What's the matter? Is a banshee after you?"

Marissa sobbed, unable to catch her breath. She looked up at the stranger holding her, wild strands of her hair blurring her gaze. Dressed in white, the tall man had black hair and a nice, handsome face. His English-sounding voice was deep and pleasant. A thin scar traced his cheek, making him look like a friendly Gypsy.

Briefly, his hands tightened on her shoulders. Then, with a light touch, he smoothed the thick, tangled strands of hair off her face. He murmured softly, a foreign word that sounded oddly like an endearment. Yet the intensity of his gaze alarmed her, and she was reminded that he was also a stranger.

"Let me go!"

"All right, child," he said gently, then released her. "Don't be frightened—you simply remind me of a lovely little girl I once knew." He paused. "Do you live here on the island?"

She nodded. "With my grandma, on the north side."

The man bent down to pick up the bouquet of daisies he'd dropped at her feet. Stroking his luxurious black mustache, he asked, "Would you like me to walk you home?"

She took a shaky breath and stared up at him. His dark eyes twinkled with a smiling warmth. She couldn't say why, but she felt comfortable with him. And safe. "Would you, please, sir?"

"I'd be delighted." He presented her the bouquet of daisies with a flourish.

"Thank you. They're very pretty." She gave him a tremulous smile.

"Just as you are, poppet."

The Beckoning Ghost

* * *

A grown-up Marissa Erickson swayed beside the icehouse, reeling with the surge of unbidden memory. It left her feeling cold and sick.

Had she imagined it all back then? Was she having hallucinations when she was just ten? She could have sworn that the man who walked her home was Brendan Tyrell. Impossible.

And that other man—a Bengali by the look of him—who was he? Why did he frighten her so?

Marissa had completely blocked the incident from her mind. She would dismiss it as a childish flight of fancy now except for two things: the vividness of the memory, and the 1872 gold sovereign she kept hidden in her favorite music box—the one that played *Chanson de Shalott*.

She'd almost forgotten where she'd gotten the gold piece. Why did finding the coin here seem suddenly ominous?

The week flew by as Marissa dove back into her work. Her publisher would be pleased that she was on track and should have no problem meeting her deadline next summer. Pulling together her research notes, she started to write the chapters on Brendan's early life on the Continent, his being sent down from Oxford.

As she wrote about Tyrell's youthful fall from grace, she could clearly see the young Brendan, annoyingly individualistic, with a rebellious streak a yard wide. The Oxford students had been forbidden to attend a local horse race. To make a point, Brendan had recruited a small band of followers and gone to the race instead of the edifying lecture they were required to attend.

She pictured him, foolish and brave, facing the

43

gathered dons with a fierce glint in his black eyes, a damning trace of arrogance in his youthful baritone.

Marissa smiled indulgently. "You might have escaped that one, Brendan, if you hadn't brought Professor Hainley's pretty daughter to the race with you."

After that ignominious end to his formal education, he bought a commission in the Seventh Native Cavalry at Lucknow. Last year at an estate sale in Warwickshire, she'd found a cache of original letters to his brother Patrick, written while Brendan still served in India.

Rereading them, she felt the same closeness to her subject that she experienced when she first read the letters. It always gave her a thrill of pleasure to handle them, knowing that Brendan had touched that very paper. The letters were a tangible bond between them, spanning over 100 years.

She saw him bent over his portable writing desk, his dark hair tumbled over his brow as he wrote, the pen moving quickly across the page in his bold hand. When searching for a phrase, he'd pause with a frown of furious concentration. Then he'd run his fingers through his unruly hair, impatiently brushing it back off his brow.

Marissa herself paused, one of Brendan's letters dangling loosely from her fingers. How could she see and hear him so clearly? His mannerisms, the timbre of his deep voice, his flashing changes of expression were all so familiar to her.

Kelsey had remarked on more than one occasion that Marissa had the vivid imagination of a novelist. At least that's what Marissa *hoped* it was, in preference to going balmy.

The Beckoning Ghost

*   *   *

Afraid of losing herself completely in her work, Marissa went to the Humane Society in Golden Valley and adopted two cats. One was a creamy female kitten named Peaches, a cross between a Siamese and an orange tabby. The other was a year-old Russian Blue. She called this svelte young aristocrat "Sasha."

Marissa smiled when she realized that she'd just burned another bridge. Robin simply disliked dogs, but he was *very* allergic to cats.

What's wrong with me? Marissa thought. *I never get up this early.*

At just past six A.M., the pale sun filtered through the kitchen curtains. The forest dripped with dew, and tendrils of morning mist hung from tree boughs like ghostly garlands.

While she brewed herself a cup of Ceylon breakfast tea, Marissa went to the kitchen sink to rinse the conditioner out of her long blond hair. A cool breeze tickled her bare legs as the back of her aquamarine silk robe swished up playfully.

"Sasha," she muttered darkly, "I fed you guys already." Straightening up, she flipped the wet hair out of her eyes and looked out the window. Sasha was outside—stalking a sneaky Peaches, who lay in ambush under a clump of glossy blue-green hosta.

Gooseflesh ran along her arms as she whirled around to face an empty kitchen. Beyond that, the first tentative rays of the sun warmed the oak floorboards of the vacant dining room. No drafts from open doors or windows could explain this one away.

Her pulse racing, she grabbed the towel to dry

45

her dripping hair. Her hands shook as she wrapped the towel around her head. Someone or something had brushed up her silken robe to her knees. She could still feel the silk swishing around her bare calves.

The past few days had been quiet and blessedly uneventful. Just when she thought things had settled down to normal, something bizarre happened. What was it with this house? It couldn't really be haunted . . . could it?

Maybe this morning would be a good time to run into town and have lunch with Kelsey.

Marissa picked up her friend at her loft in the artists' quarter of downtown Minneapolis, and they went to lunch at a little Afghan place with an outdoor terrace near Lake Calhoun.

A forkful of tabouli salad poised at her lips, Kelsey stared at her companion. "You're so quiet today, *amie*. Have you been working too hard?"

"No." Marissa took a bite of chicken, then paused. "Well, maybe a bit. I found it difficult to write about Brendan when Robin was so resentful of this project. But now that I'm here, things are going well again. In fact, it's hard to stop thinking about it." She gave Kelsey a funny, nervous smile.

"Why the inscrutable smile?"

Marissa hunched her shoulders together and picked at the food on her plate. "These dreams I've been having . . . they all have the same theme— almost a continuing story."

Kelsey grinned. "Oh, I see, like the ones you used to have about Mel . . . a nightly romantic farce—er, saga?"

"Poor Mel." Marissa laughed. "Lucky for him that he's got half a dozen kids in real life. Makes

46

him a bit awkward to lust after these days." She paused. "No, it's Brendan."

Kelsey pushed her blue Ray-Bans up into the black curls over her forehead, her perceptive eyes fixing on her friend's lopsided smile. "That's not so surprising, is it, Rissa? He was one hell of a hunk from that portrait you showed me, and you *have* been spending a lot of time with him, in a way."

"I suppose you're right." Marissa hesitated, reluctant to tell Kelsey about her vision at the icehouse, the ghostly footsteps, the way her robe was playfully brushed up her legs. Afraid of worrying Kelsey, she put on a bright face. "So, when are you coming out to meet my new family—Sasha and Peaches?"

By plunging back into her work, Marissa ignored the peculiar events of the past week. Now she was into her notes on Lieutenant Brendan Tyrell's exploits during the Great Mutiny in India, where he'd acted as a secret agent for Sir Henry Lawrence.

Late in the afternoon, she paused over her keyboard. In her mind, she pictured the dusty, pockmarked walls of the besieged British Residency at Lucknow. His uniform long gone, Brendan strode across the rubble-strewn compound in a flowing, belted gray shirt and loose black trousers. The members of the garrison had to make do with whatever clothing they could scrounge up. Looking like a cheerful brigand, he whistled and dodged bullets on his way to his post at Fayrer's Battery.

Marissa shook her head. "You were always too reckless for your own good, Brendan."

47

Catherine Kohman

She could smell the unwholesome miasma from the crowded conditions and the sting of cordite in her nostrils, could hear an 18-pound shell whistle over the walls, followed by the resounding explosion as it hit the upper floor of the Residency.

She felt as if she'd lived through the Siege herself.

Ever since she was a small child, she'd been fascinated by India, though she'd never been there. Only after she finished graduate school in Boston did she make the trip. That journey felt like a homecoming, and provided her with enough ideas and research material for two books, her first one on Jaipur, and this one about Brendan Tyrell.

But her interest in Brendan went back further than that. When she was 12 years old, she found a book about the history of Lake Minnetonka on the cottage's bookshelves. It described Arcadia House and mentioned Sir Brendan Tyrell's residence there, and his subsequent death. For the first time, she saw a copy of Brendan's portrait, and it entranced her even then.

From that point on, she read everything she could find about him. All of his published works, including the translations of Indian erotica. This abiding interest in Brendan shaped her career, since it prompted her to major in history at the University of Minnesota and continue on to graduate school at Harvard. Since she didn't think Brendan's previous biographer had done him justice, she took it upon herself to rectify the situation.

Reminded to get back to work and quit daydreaming, Marissa stretched her cramped arms out to the sides and looked out at the lake to see how long it was till sunset. Leaning against a giant maple tree, his back to her, stood a tall man dressed in white.

Startled by the man's presence, she stared as he knocked his pipe out against the bark of the tree, and replaced it in his pocket. He glanced up at the house, and Marissa recognized Brendan's exotic, handsome face. Her heart pounded furiously, and her throat constricted, making it painful to swallow.

Transfixed by the apparition, she watched Brendan push off from the tree with his powerful shoulder and casually walk down the knoll, toward the dock. When he disappeared over the small rise, she burst into movement and ran out the door, letting it slam behind her. She raced across the lawn until she came to the top of the knoll and looked down at the shore.

Her day-sailer bobbed gently alongside the dock, but no one was there. Across the glassy water, a faint swirling wake led out into the bay, but no other boats were in sight.

Unable to help herself, Marissa shivered uncontrollably in the hot afternoon sun.

Feeling in dire need of human company, Marissa called Kelsey and invited her out to spend the night. Her friend arrived with a feast of Vietnamese take-out and a favorite video, *The Last of the Mohicans*. Comfortably cocooned on the living room sofa, they both enjoyed the lush, romantic saga.

The video over, Kelsey was sighing over the intense, heroic performance of Daniel Day-Lewis, while Marissa could only be reminded of another darkly handsome, larger-than-life Irishman: Brendan Tyrell.

Catherine Kohman

After turning off the lights downstairs, she noticed the living room still seemed bright. Outside the picture window, the full moon made a glissando of light across the water, and Marissa wondered if she was moonstruck. Yet that would hardly explain her seeing Brendan in broad daylight. She refused to believe it was just her imagination run amuck. Something else had to be going on—something damn spooky—but what on earth could it be?

As they headed up to bed, she smiled suddenly at Kelsey, comforted by her company, needful of the anchor to reality.

The midsummer moonlight spilled onto the bedspread, washing the white chenille silver-blue. Marissa turned on her side and felt a wisp of hair brush her cheek. She opened her eyes.

A dark-haired man sat quietly on the edge of her bed.

She froze. The man turned his face into the moonlight, and she saw his high cheekbones, the black slash of his mustache below—Brendan. Her muscles loosened—she must be dreaming.

"Marissa."

The way he breathed her name ... with the faintest hint of an Irish accent ... sent a shiver along her spine.

He said wistfully, "Such a lovely name ..."

Within the languor of the dream, she let her glance slide over him in blissful leisure. His loose white shirt draped a pair of flawlessly sculpted shoulders, and the trim fit of his sailing pants revealed his lean, muscled thighs. With his raven hair tousled by the wind, he looked fresh from a moonlit sail.

50

So close she could feel the heat from his body, smell the spicy scent of sandalwood on his clothes. "Brendan Tyrell . . ."

"At your service, ma'am." The moonlight glinted off his white smile and his dark brows made a sardonic curve. As he bent his head forward in a token of esteem, a wayward lock of hair fell across his brow.

Mesmerized by the way his luxuriant mustache framed his wicked, appealing mouth, she simply stared at him. The loose, open collar of his shirt exposed the clean sweep of his collarbone, and the inviting hollows of his throat. Lost in the potent splendor of the dream, she was amazed by its vivid detail. She wondered what would happen if she pressed her lips to the pulse beating along his throat.

"Marissa . . ." He gave her an indulgent smile.

"What—what are you doing here?" she whispered at last, forcing her thoughts from the intriguing possibilities of his stirring presence.

"I need your help in finding something that was lost to me." He hesitated, a look of painful longing on his chiseled, moon-limned features. "My unpublished work . . ."

"But surely it's been destroyed." She swallowed hard, her throat suddenly tight. It seemed impossible that this beautiful, vital man had perished in that long-ago fire, along with his work. The Fates had been cruel indeed.

"The circumstances surrounding the fire are not what they seem. I believe the manuscripts are still safe, though presently lost." His intense gaze fixed on her face, and Marissa caught her breath as he added, "I want you to help me find them."

She raised herself on one elbow and leaned toward him. Beneath the sandalwood of his shaving soap, she smelled the unique, seductive scent of his skin. Catching her breath, she tried to suppress the dizzying lightness in her head. She focused on what Brendan had said about the lost manuscripts.

"Tell me how I can help."

"You're writing my biography." With long, supple fingers he brushed back the errant lock of hair. "Yet there's so much you don't know...."

Marissa damped her physical reaction as she listened raptly to Brendan. He described the wealth of literature presumed lost in that fire ... translations of the *Mahabharata* and other Sanskrit poetry, the classic Persian poets like Sa'adi and Hafiz. Marissa felt a queer sensation of déjà vu as they shared the magical moonlight and talked about his manuscripts. Though secretly delighted, she finally asked, "Why have you come to *me?*"

"Who better?" He smiled again, a warm, engaging smile. He seemed so real, so wonderfully vibrant, Marissa swept her fingers across the soft tufts of the bedspread, reaching for his hand.

Suddenly he inclined his head toward the door. "I believe your friend—Miss Sheridan—is coming to check on you." He grinned, and his demeanor changed to that of a raffish youth. "I'd better leave now. I don't want to compromise you."

"Wait!" She grabbed for his hand, but with a lithe stretch, he'd already risen to his feet. "Don't go. I need to know—"

"Patience, my dear girl. I'll be back." He opened the veranda door, and winking boldly, silently slipped outside.

Marissa fell back against the pillows as she saw

52

the hall door to her room open slowly. Kelsey peeked inside.

"Are you awake? I thought I heard voices."

Marissa reached over and hugged a pillow to her chest. Her heart beating wildly, she took a deep breath to slow it. "Voices?"

"Just murmurs. Were you talking in your sleep?"

"I—guess so. Must have been all that Vietnamese food," she said with a shaky laugh, "too much garlic." A slightly hysterical thought popped into her head—garlic was supposed to *ward off* spirits and vampires.

"You look pale." Kelsey sat down in the very spot where Brendan had been. "A nightmare?"

"Not a bad dream, no." Marissa squirmed. Could Kelsey tell that Brendan had sat there a mere moment ago? "Just intense."

"Brendan again?" When Marissa simply nodded, Kelsey said, "You're working too hard. Why don't you take a break?"

"I'll see if it will help." Touched by her friend's concern, she added, "Thanks for checking up on me, Kelse."

"*De nada, amiga.*" Kelsey smiled tiredly. "Do you want me to stay in here tonight, to keep you company?"

Though she welcomed Kelsey's presence, she knew Brendan wouldn't return if she wasn't alone. She gave herself a mental shake. *Wake up, Looney Tunes—it was just a dream.*

"You don't have to."

"Well, I will anyway. The cats can sleep on my bed."

"The cats?"

"That's what woke me up. Both of the cats

53

jumped on the bed. Then I heard you talking in your sleep."

"Oh." With an involuntary shiver, Marissa burrowed deeper in the covers.

"Shove over, pal." Kelsey rubbed her sleep-puffy eyes. "Both of us need our beauty sleep tonight."

Marissa moved over to the far side of the bed while Kelsey crawled under the covers and settled in.

"Just like when we were kids, eh, Rissa?"

"Yeah, Kelse . . . just like the good old days."

Kelsey yawned. "Before puberty reared its horny head, you mean . . ."

While her friend drifted off to sleep, Marissa stared up at the shadowy, beamed ceiling. If it was only a dream, it was the most vivid one she'd ever had. Why didn't she remember waking up when Kelsey came into the room?

Could it truly be Brendan? The idea fascinated her. Then she briefly worried: She hadn't lost her mind, had she? *Oh, but if he was really here* . . . it amazed her, an astounding gift beyond anything in her wildest imagination.

Her head whirled with the endless possibilities. All the questions she longed to ask him . . . most biographers would *kill* for an opportunity like that. And she could repay him—she could help him find his missing manuscripts.

Oh, Brendan, this is too wonderful to be true . . .

A tiny voice of reason chimed in: *Are you mad? Of course it's too wonderful to be true.*

It took her forever to get back to sleep.

Chapter Three

*For the sins of your sires albeit you had no
hand in them, you must suffer.*

—Horace

Lucknow, India, May, 1857

On the winding road to Sitapore snaked a line of
mounted Sikhs from the Seventh Cavalry at Lucknow, led by two British officers. The *sowars'* loose
khaki uniforms blended in with the dun fields
along the road, and their horses' hooves kicked up
puffs of fine dust that hung nearly motionless in
the still morning air.

Lieutenant Brendan Tyrell stretched in the saddle, then said to the Englishman riding beside
him, "It's looks to be another scorcher, Tony."

Captain Anthony Seton glanced toward the horizon, where the gray-blue hills shimmered with

heat. Under his sun helmet, his blond hair was already darkened with sweat. He sighed. "It's almost June—I wish the monsoon rains would arrive."

"No, you don't," Brendan answered with a grim smile. "Not until we've finished fortifying the Residency and brought in as many supplies as we have room to store."

He was glad that Sir Henry Lawrence had listened to his intelligence about the disaffection in the native ranks and had taken the precaution of ordering the women and children out of the cantonments and into the relative safety of the Residency compound. If the native troops mutinied, the British garrison at Lucknow could be in for a long siege.

Tony said in a low voice, "You still believe that the mutinies in Meerut and Delhi will spread to Oudh?"

Careful to speak quietly so that the native cavalrymen wouldn't overhear, Brendan replied, "I think it already has, Tony. Why do you think that we've been sent to bring in the Europeans between Lucknow and Sitapore—why I chose the Sikhs instead of the Muslims or Hindus in the regiment?"

While Tony pondered his reply, Brendan looked over his shoulder at the *sowars*, their dark bearded faces below their crisp white turbans. As a group, the Sikhs were tall, brawny, disciplined . . . and in this case, more reliable than the other religious groups in the regiment. He hoped they'd perform their duties faithfully, having partaken of the Company's salt. The British at Lucknow would need as many loyal native troops as they could field in the dangerous days ahead.

"Good God, Brendan," Tony said under his breath, his blue eyes dark with worry, "I should have listened to you and sent Miranda and Sarah up to Simla."

Brendan glanced sideways at Tony, at his upper-class English profile. Though two years older and his superior in rank, his friend sometimes seemed impossibly idealistic. Tony didn't believe that his own troops, his *Baba-log*, would mutiny. Yet surely the officers in Meerut or Delhi had also thought that way, and the sepoys there had risen up against their officers and killed them, as well as their families.

Brendan guessed that Tony was thinking along the same lines. "I'm sure Randie and Sarah will be all right at the Residency," he reassured his friend. "Sir Henry is doing everything possible to ensure their safety."

Brendan knew he and Tony possessed their troops' love and respect. But when others around them began to rage and mutiny, how long would their own soldiers stand true?

Near a somnolent village along the River Gumti, the road passed through a large tope of glossy-leaved neem trees. The forest usually echoed with the chatter of parakeets and the laughing calls of mynahs, but today Brendan thought the tope unnaturally quiet. All he heard was the mournful, cat-like cry of a peacock off in the distance.

The curved tips of his bay's ears snapped forward, and Brendan's uneasiness surged. He murmured a few words to Tony, who called for the *sowars* to close ranks.

"*Din! Din!*" came a ragged, swelling cry from the woods behind them.

Brendan and Tony wheeled their horses, as did the *sowars*. Scores of natives rushed out onto the road, armed with muskets and their curved lethal swords, *tulwars*. From their rumpled uniform coats, Brendan saw that some of the natives were mutinous sepoys from Meerut or Delhi; the rest were *badmashes*—hoodlums from the bazaars. There were well over 100 of them blocking the road back to Lucknow, and who knows how many still lurked in the trees. The cavalry was greatly outnumbered.

As the captain ordered the men to stand firm, Brendan felt his heart race, and the blood pounded in his ears. Tony rode toward the front of his troops. Spurring his horse, Brendan joined him. The British officers coolly faced the mutineers, who milled in front of them, hot eyes glaring.

"You men have broken your salt," Anthony Seton shouted above the mutters of the crowd. Brendan repeated his words in Hindustani and Urdu. "It is bad enough that you are unfaithful to the Company, but now you have taken to the roads like a bunch of *dacoits!*"

Being called honorless thieves made some of the sepoys hang their heads in shame, while the *badmashes* merely raised their swords and jeered. "*Maro!* Kill him!"

At Brendan's signal, the Sikhs raised their rifles and leveled them at the sullen crowd. Brendan drew his pistol while Tony continued to scold the mutineers.

"If you lay down your arms and return to your homes, we will not attack you," the captain warned, "but if you persist in these evil deeds, you will be hunted down and punished. Severely. The Raj will see to that."

"Your *Raj* is finished!" shouted a *badmash*. His face twisted with hate, he raised his stolen musket and aimed it at Tony.

A Hindu sepoy rounded on the man angrily. "Would you kill such a brave man as this?"

The sepoy reached for the musket, but the *badmash* pulled the trigger. The same moment Brendan's bullet hit him in the chest and a gout of blood sprayed across the man's dirty white shirt. Tony jerked in the saddle as a howl rose from the crowd. "Din! Din!"

Brendan shot a glance at Tony, who clutched his shoulder, blood oozing between his fingers. With an oath, he turned back to the mutineers. One of them leapt forward, *tulwar* raised. The Irish officer fired his second shot and hit the man, but the native's momentum carried his arm forward. Brendan tried to block the thrust, but the tip of the *tulwar* slashed open his cheek.

A screaming sepoy rushed forward, but a *sowar* shot him dead as well. The leveled rifles of the other Sikhs fixed the mutineers in place.

Hari Singh, the *daffadar*—or sergeant—of the regiment, spoke urgently to Brendan. "Sa'b, you must take the captain away from here. They are wishing to kill you and Seton-sa'b. You go, and we will hold the faithless ones at bay until you escape."

Brendan noted the pallor of the captain's face. If his friend's wound wasn't bandaged, Tony could bleed to death. But he didn't want to leave the *sowars* to deal with the mutineers alone. The ugly crowd moved and rumbled restlessly, waiting for another attempt to murder the officers. "No, *Daf-*

fadar Singh, I'm staying here." He impatiently dashed the streams of blood from his cheek with his sleeve. "I won't run from these ruffians."

"Please, *sa'b*, go now. It is only *Firinghis* such as yourselves that they want. If anything, these *goondas* will try to enlist our aid in their foul cause. We will be all right."

Tony slumped forward over his pommel, though he remained in the saddle. Splashes of blood stained his mount's sorrel coat even redder. Brendan hesitated, torn in his duty to his regiment and his care for his friend.

The *daffadar* spoke once more. "Tyrell-*sa'b*, for the love your men bear you, and the captain . . . you must go. Save him . . . for his *mem-sahib* and little one."

The image of Miranda's tiny face pinched with grief for her father stung more sharply than the slash across Brendan's cheek. "Very well, *Daffadar* Singh. Look to yourselves, and try to make it back to Lucknow. They'll need you there."

"Farewell, *sa'b*. We will do our duty, never fear."

Grasping the reins of the now-skittish sorrel, Brendan led Tony's mount toward Sitapore.

The *daffadar* saluted them smartly, then turned back to the rest of the *sowars* and the mutinous crowd.

Beyond the village Brendan removed the cloth *puggaree* from his helmet and bandaged Tony's wounded shoulder. The captain was conscious, so he could still ride his horse, but he was weakening fast. A Brahmin from the village told Brendan that the area between there and Lucknow swarmed with bands of marauding mutineers. He wouldn't be able to get Tony back to the hospital that way.

Brendan thought a moment. He knew a *zemindar* who had an estate between the rivers Gumti and Gograh. A *zemindar*'s holding were like a small feudal kingdom, and the man himself had the power of a minor prince. And it so happened that this *zemindar*, Sayed Khan, owed Brendan a debt of honor. He'd once saved Sayed's eldest son from a nasty riding accident while they were out hawking one afternoon. Perhaps now was the time to call on the *zemindar* Khan to collect that debt.

He headed their horses cross-country toward the River Gograh and the *zemindari* of Banthira.

Brendan paced up and down in the airless upper room of the estate's *zenana*. Shuttered to keep out the intense June sun, the cloister was empty of women, but the heavy scent of patchouli still permeated the walls. Sayed Khan's beloved wife had died in childbirth last year. The cloister's now-faded opulence should have rung with bright laughter and light, feminine voices. Instead, it housed two restless British officers, frustrated and eager to be away from their weeks of enforced captivity.

Anthony Seton, clothed in pajamas of turquoise silk, lay on a worn, yellow print divan. His fair hair fell lankily over his pale brow, and lines of fatigue and illness marked his face. He wore a sling that cradled his right arm.

"Sayed Khan has been most generous to let us stay here while I recover from my wound and fever, Brendan." With effort, he pushed himself up into a sitting position. "But we can't stay here indefinitely. One of the servants is bound to talk, and the pandies are sure to come for us then."

Catherine Kohman

Pandy was the nickname that British soldiers had given the mutineers, after Mangal Pande, the sepoy who sparked the mutiny last March, in Barrackpore. Out of his mind with hemp, he'd attacked his officers and been executed for his crime.

Brendan impatiently shoved a lock of black hair off his damp forehead and turned to face Tony. "I know. That worries me."

Sayed had repaid his debt of honor by giving them shelter in his home and providing a faithful woman servant to nurse Tony's wounded shoulder. But Brendan knew that their host's hospitality and patience were wearing thin. When the mutineers came, would the *zemindar* dare risk his home, or his life, simply to save two *Firinghis*?

"Sayed informed me that the native troops in Lucknow itself have mutinied, and bands of mutineers are once again roaming the district," Brendan said. "It's only a matter of time before they reach Banthira. We've got to move, and soon."

Tony offered, "I can ride—"

"No," Brendan said, stroking his glossy mustache, "your wound might reopen and start to bleed once more." He studied Anthony's face, worried by its pallor. Though his friend's fever had subsided, Tony was still weak. Brendan hated the idea of moving him in that condition, but they had little choice. Their only chance of safety would be to reach the garrison at Lucknow, if Sir Henry hadn't closed the Residency, or if it wasn't already besieged.

As he paced the room again, Brendan caught his reflection in a large mirror on the *zenana* wall. He paused. In his borrowed pajamas of claret silk, his dark coloring and tanned skin, he could easily pass as the *zemindar* himself. The thin, healing scar on his cheek only added to his exotic appearance.

That thought led to another: how to safely make their journey across the *mofussil* to Lucknow. "I'm going to see Sayed. I have an idea how to effect our escape from the *zenana.*"

With an amused grin at Anthony's mystified expression, he left the room, whistling a sketchy tune from a Mozart opera.

In the shadowy half-light of dawn, a bullock cart drove across the dry, rutted fields of the *zemindari*. The cart was driven by Jaiji, a brown, wizened pensioner of the Bengal Army. Inside the rumbling cart rode Abdullah, a *hakim* or learned Muslim physician, and his invalid patient, a lady shrouded from head to foot in the black folds of a *burgha*.

They traveled by minor byways, avoiding the main crossroads and villages of the area, pausing only to escape the heat of the day in the shade of a huge peepul tree.

After ascertaining that they were the only ones making use of this cool oasis, the *hakim* spoke quietly to his patient. "Tony, how are you holding up?"

The "lady" in the *burgha* muttered a soft oath. "I'd forgotten how much I hate bullock carts. I think every portion of my anatomy is covered with a bruise." Brendan could hear the smile in Tony's voice as he added, "Still, I daren't complain, or you'll give me some of that monstrous physic of yours to put me to sleep."

"You're right. I will." Brendan grinned. Then he cocked his head, listening to a faint whimper from

63

the underbrush. He drew his pistol and stole around the lantana shrubs.

Cowering in the bushes were a young Eurasian woman and a little girl. Their filthy clothing in rags, they huddled together, and the woman's lovely features contorted into a mask of fear.

"Please, don't hurt my little girl," the dark-haired woman pleaded in English. Tears sprang from her eyes, leaving muddy streams down her cheeks. As she raised her hand in supplication, she continued in Urdu. "Estimable sir, we weren't spying—we were afraid of the *badmashes.* . . . "

Brendan asked softly, "Where are you from?"

"Sitapore," she answered in a rush, relieved at his use of English. She dashed her tears away with the back of her hand, leaving a dirty smear in their place. "My husband was an Englishman, a clerk for the Commissioner there," she continued, her voice trembling. "The sepoys killed him, and I barely escaped with my daughter. We've been trying to get to Lucknow, but I'm afraid to travel the roads."

"We have a cart, and are making for Lucknow ourselves." He paused, observing their ragged, exhausted condition. He'd taken an extra *burgha* along for Tony as a change of clothing, in case the monsoons broke. The woman could wear that. He'd have to find something else for the little girl—perhaps he could send Jaiji into the next village. "You're welcome to come with us. Our food and drink are rather plain, but plentiful."

The woman fell to her knees in front of him and kissed his dusty feet. "Thank you, sir. You were sent from heaven—a true blessing."

Brendan stared at her bowed head in embarrassed perplexity. Then he laughed. "A blessing?

64

Thank you, madam. I'm afraid most ladies of my acquaintance reserve less kind epithets for my person." He held out his hand. "Come, we must get you and your daughter ready for the journey."

The afternoon they finally made it into the city of Lucknow, the monsoons broke. The thin mat of reeds serving as a roof for the bullock cart soon unraveled and left the occupants of the cart exposed to the downpour. Brendan glanced anxiously at Tony, who was shivering in the rain despite the warmth of the afternoon. He wanted to tell Jaiji to whip the bullocks into a trot, but he knew that would only jolt them even more. And they weren't safe in the city. Once they made it into the Residency itself, he'd begin to relax.

The woman, Amelia Morton, and her daughter Juli had been little trouble on their journey. They added authenticity to the two men's disguise, pretending to be Tony's sister and niece. He was glad that something good—the Mortons' rescue—had come from that disastrous excursion across the Gumti.

They passed the massive red walls of the fort, the Machi Bhawan, and turned toward the Baillie Guard Gate. Brendan sighed with relief when he saw the huge, brass-studded doors stood open. A straggling stream of refugees passed under the pillared, stucco gate and he realized that most of them were in rougher shape than they were.

As the bullock cart rumbled toward the entrance, a sergeant of the Thirty-Second halted them with his raised musket. "Whoa, there, fellow. Just where do you think you're going with these native women? How do I know you ain't a bunch of pandies?"

"I'll vouch for them, Sergeant Wilson," Brendan said clearly.

The ginger-haired soldier squinted up at the cart, then his eyes widened. "Well, if it ain't ol' *Sikander* Tyrell himself."

Sikander was the *sowars'* nickname for Brendan. An honorific derived from Alexander the Great, it was used by the Indians as a token of respect. When the sergeant used it, however, his tone was anything but respectful.

"All decked out in your native duds, I see," the sergeant observed with a superior smile. "We heard you were dead."

"Something of an exaggeration, *Sergeant*," Brendan replied amiably, but his dark eyes hardened to flint. "I have Captain Seton in the cart, and he needs the attention of Dr. Fayrer."

A chastised Wilson peeked into the cart, then shrugged. "If you say so, Lieutenant. Dr. Fayrer is at home or over at the Banqueting Hall." He waved them on, and the bullocks pulled the cart through the Baillie Guard into the Residency enclosure.

In the weeks of their absence, the Residency had taken on a bizarre, martial appearance. The ordered beauty of the grounds had disappeared— the trees and tranquil gardens replaced by fortifications, piles of ammunition and stacks of crates full of stores. Uniformed soldiers drilled civilian volunteers, and elephants and bullocks pulled carts or dragged mounted guns across the compound.

Today the rain turned the choking dust to mud, so they made slow progress to Dr. Fayrer's home. Brendan and Jaiji lifted Anthony's limp form from the cart and carried him into the doctor's house

66

as a plump older woman in a fussy pink crinoline came out into the foyer. "You can't bring that native woman in here."

Brendan sent her a withering look, cradling his friend's form in his arms. "This is Captain Seton. He's wounded and feverish. Send for Dr. Fayrer."

A strangled cry came from the top of the stairs. A blond-haired woman stood on the landing, her face white with shock. Her hand to her chest, Sarah Seton whispered, "Tony?"

The woman in pink blushed. "Mrs. Seton, I had no idea. . . ."

Bunching her gray muslin skirts in her hands, Sarah rushed down the stairs. Her delicate features sharply drawn, she pulled the veils of the *burgha* back off her husband's ashen face and touched his cheek. "Tony, love . . ."

He lay still and unresponsive under her caress. She glanced up briefly in her distress, her green eyes searching out Brendan. "Miranda and I have quarters here. Please carry him to my room. Mrs. Curtis, bring the doctor to me at once."

"Of course, Mrs. Seton." Like a schoolgirl anxious to escape her teacher's wrath, Mrs. Curtis fled the foyer.

Sarah Seton looked up at Brendan, her beautiful face lit with gratitude. "Thank you . . . somehow, I knew you'd bring him back to me."

Chapter Four

And all my days are trances,
And all my nightly dreams
Are where thy grey eye glances,
And where thy footstep
gleams—
In what ethereal dances,
By what eternal streams.
                                    —Edgar Allan Poe

Though Kelsey looked rested and relaxed the
next day, Marissa felt like she had a hangover.
She stared at her wan face in the vanity mirror.
Dark smudges around her eyes marred her usually flawless skin, and the brightness of her gaze
was clouded and dim. As for that lush lip line
that Kelsey swore even Michelle Pfeiffer would
envy, she thought sarcastically, no perky smile
there today.

The Beckoning Ghost

A number of times during the morning she wanted to blurt out what she'd seen last night, but she knew Kelsey would either think she was crazy, or simply laugh at her apparent "joke."

After they lunched on seafood at the Blue Point in Wayzata, Kelsey wanted to shop. So while her friend picked through a rack of swimming suits at a boutique, Marissa wandered past a row of antique shops to Aunt Jane's, the bookstore down the street.

She glanced at the displays of new novels and art books in the front of the store, but gravitated toward the back room, which held the used and rare books. Marissa picked up a volume of poetry by Yeats that she'd wanted for some time, then found herself looking at the New Age/Parapsychology section. They had little about ghosts, just a few popular books by Hans Holzer. The lurid blurbs on the covers of those put her off, so she carried her solitary Yeats up to the counter.

"Do you have anything else about ghosts—something a bit more scientific, perhaps?"

The maternal-looking woman behind the counter pushed her glasses back up her nose and smiled. "As a matter of fact, I have a signed copy of Elise Cunningham's respected study, *An Honest Ghost*. She recently retired from Duke University, and lives here with her sister, on St. Albans Bay." The woman reached up to the shelves behind the counter, then handed Marissa the book.

Opening the sedate gray cover, Marissa scanned the table of contents. Scholarly in focus, the book appeared to be a rational exploration of the subject, so she placed it on the counter as well. "I'll take it."

*   *   *

69

Catherine Kohman

Marissa waited in Kelsey's red convertible. The Fiat was totally impractical for Minnesota, for five months of the year at least. So rather than freezing under the rag top from November until April, Kelsey drove her "winter beater," an old turquoise Subaru that made up in reliability what it lacked in beauty.

While she basked in the afternoon sun, Marissa pushed up the sleeves of her ivory cotton sweater. Opening *An Honest Ghost*, she rifled through the pages. Familiar names leapt out of the text—the historian, Toynbee, Jung, and the scenes of famous hauntings . . . Pontefract, Hampton Court, Borley Rectory, Versailles. . . .

"I see you found something to keep you busy while I was maxing out my MasterCard."

At the sound of her friend's voice, Marissa slammed the book shut and inconspicuously shoved it back into the bag. She looked up to see Kelsey standing next to the car with bags from three different boutiques in her arms. With a guilty smile, she reached for two of the bags while Kelse got out her car keys.

"You sure did," Marissa belatedly replied. "What all did you buy?"

"A swimsuit, a Donna Karan blazer, some silk lingerie in the most delicious shade of pink . . . that will probably just gather dust in the drawer." In her yellow Spandex miniskirt and bright green oversized top, Kelsey slipped behind the wheel and pushed a tape into the car stereo. To the low but insistent beat of the latest Peter Gabriel, she smoothly pulled into the traffic on Lake Street. "What did you find at Aunt Jane's?"

"Oh," Marissa answered casually, "a copy of Yeats I've been looking for."

"I've always liked Yeats." Kelsey added with a grin, "In spite of my English Lit professor, who was enough of a bore to put me off poetry for life."

Marissa tried to distract Kelsey's thoughts from the books by asking her about her latest commission. Kelsey had started out in commercial art, but had branched out into selling her own line of prints—the "Sedona" series. The watercolors were paintings with a Southwestern motif, usually Hopi or animal themes. Marissa particularly liked Kelsey's horses. They reminded her of the big-bellied horses in the cave paintings of Lascaux in France, but with a contemporary flair.

With the top of the Fiat down, the breeze ruffled Kelsey's short hair into a tousled mop of raven curls. "You know that I've done covers for some New Age albums and books. Prince was interested in them, and has asked me for a few sample sketches for his next release."

The red convertible skimmed alongside the rippling waters of Smith's Bay. As she struggled to keep her long blond hair from flying into her mouth, Marissa remarked, "From New Age to Prince? That's quite a switch."

"I know," her friend said with a wry smile, "but it would be a big boost for my career."

From the stereo came the driving piano and drums of "Holding Out for a Hero." Kelsey turned up the volume and began to sing along in her best imitation of Bonnie Tyler's intense, rasping vocal. "Come on, Rissa, sing!" Kelsey grinned. "It's our old theme song from high school!"

Catching Kelsey's giddy mood, Marissa joined in on the second half of the chorus. But when the lyrics spoke of a fantasy hero reaching out for her in the dark night, Marissa's voice faltered, and her brief spurt of exuberance faded.

Forgetting the words until she heard them issue from her mouth, she felt her throat suddenly constrict. The song cut too close to the bone, so she let Kelsey sing solo for the rest of the verses.

"Is something wrong, Rissa? You got quiet awfully fast."

"No, I can't sing rock." She rubbed her throat. "My voice sounds like a frog croaking."

Kelsey laughed. "You're *supposed* to sound that way. Gives the tune an edge."

They came to a halt as the busy weekend traffic backed up at the stoplight in Navarre. Marissa despaired of trying to hold back her wind-whipped hair, and while they were stopped, she dug around in her purse for her hair clasp. Kelsey reached over and fished the copy of Yeats out of the bookstore bag.

Marissa almost grabbed for the bag, but caught herself. Don't be ridiculous, she thought. What did it matter if Kelsey saw her other purchase?

"There's a fragment of a poem that's been haunting me for years," Kelsey said, flipping through the pages. "I think it's by Yeats:

A shudder in the loins engenders there
the broken wall, the burning roof and tower
And Agamemnon dead.

"*Leda and the Swan*," Marissa replied promptly.

Kelsey found the proper page and skimmed the poem, smiling with delight. "You're right, as usual. I always envied your excellent recall, especially when it came time for exams. It was bad enough that your family reeked of money. Then you happened to be a whiz kid too." She closed the book and shot her best childhood buddy a fond glance. "I *should* have hated you."

"For sure." Marissa hooted at her. "Whiz kid indeed."

As she slipped the Yeats back into the bag, Kelsey's mouth screwed up into a prunish pucker. "Don't you argue with me, *Ms. Harvard Ph.D.* Oh, what have we here?"

Kelsey removed the ghost book from the bag while Marissa fidgeted, making the leather car seat squeak in protest. "It's a signed copy. The lady at the bookstore said the author lives on the lake."

"*An Honest Ghost,*" Kelsey mused. "Why does that ring a bell?"

"It's a line from *Hamlet.*"

Kelsey sent her an exasperated look. "No, you insufferable scholar." The traffic finally started to move, so she had to look back at the road. "I know. I saw the author on *Good Company.* A sharp, interesting lady. She was talking about haunted houses."

She shot a suspicious, sideways glance at Marissa. "You've been acting rather peculiar lately. Anything weird happen to you out at your new old house?"

"No, of course not," Marissa insisted too strongly. She didn't dare tell Kelsey about Brendan's visit last night.

"I remember you told me long ago that 'the second sight'—or something like ESP—ran in your mother's family. Didn't your grandmother see a ghost once?"

Marissa sighed. Kelsey wouldn't let it drop. She'd have to tell Kelse something—even if it wasn't *everything.* She didn't want her friend to think that her dear Rissa had lost it. Totally.

"Great-grandmother," she corrected. "And not a ghost, to be precise. She saw her neighbor, Mr. Pederson, walk by the dining room window at noon, when he was usually at his job at the mill. She mentioned it to Gran, who was home sick from school that day. Later, she found out that at that exact time Mr. Pederson was on his way to the hospital, after being seriously injured at work. I guess you'd have to call him a *doppelganger*."

"A what?" Kelsey turned to stare at her, then quickly shifted her eyes back to the highway as she rounded the curve onto the road through Enchanted Island.

"A *doppelganger*: the disembodied spirit of someone who is still alive. Some call it bi-location, the ability to appear in two places at the same time."

"Come on." Kelsey shook her head. "Now that really is too weird. It only happens on *Star Trek*, right? The old parallel-universe trick."

"Not necessarily," Marissa explained. "I read about the phenomena in a book detailing out-of-body experiences. There have been cases where people have seen friends or loved ones and interacted with them normally, only to find out later that the person was in another place, even another country, at that very time. It can be a deliberate projection, but usually it happens unconsciously, in times of great emotional need or stress."

Kelsey shivered. "Now that sounds kind of scary." She paused. "So why are *you* interested in that paranormal stuff?" She jerked her thumb at the innocuous-looking ghost book in distaste.

"I like to keep an open mind about things," Marissa equivocated. Still curiously reluctant to mention Brendan, she needed time alone to sort through her thoughts and feelings about last night. Though the bizarre experience had unnerved her, the wealth of possibilities intrigued her and left her feeling an uncanny, almost alarming, exhilaration.

To lighten up the conversation, she said, "I suppose it's those eldritch, mystical genes I inherited." She closed her eyes and intoned in a melodramatic voice, "I come from a long line of seeresses, descended from the Sybils at Delphi. I can divine the future. What would you ask of me, oh, nosy woman?"

Kelsey shook her head in mock disgust. "You're crazy."

Marissa laughed, but a tiny part of her cringed inside. "I *hope* not."

When they reached the drive to the cottage, Marissa said, "Let me off here. I want to pick some lilacs for the dining room, then I'll walk back to the house."

Kelsey stopped the car and Marissa got out. The Fiat purred along the winding drive as she checked the mailbox. A telephone bill, a royalty check from her book on Jaipur, a History Book Club catalog, and a letter with a Los Angeles postmark. Her stomach knotted. It must be from Robin.

Gingerly handling Robin's letter, as if it was written on acid-coated paper, she stuck the mail into the deep pocket of her cotton sweater. In her fragile frame of mind, she wasn't ready to read a letter full of recriminations from her former lover.

She walked over to the late-blooming lilacs along the drive and, with her trusty Swiss Army knife, cut off spikes of the fragrant blooms. Marissa loved the scent of lilacs, though they'd made

75

her feel oddly dispirited when she was a girl. Maybe it was that their perfumed glory was as brief and ephemeral as the spring. Or as fleeting and transitory as love, she thought sadly, feeling the stiffness of Robin's letter in her pocket.

She collected a variety of lilacs: lavender, creamy white and a rich, heavily scented claret. Inhaling their fresh, heady perfume, she slowly strolled back through woods toward the house. The sun filtered through the trees, and the late afternoon breeze teased the thick canopy of leaves into a rustling, restless whisper.

As she walked, a certain heaviness grew in her chest, and a wave of unutterable sadness overcame her. Feeling light-headed, she leaned against the rough bark of a maple tree and dropped the lilacs in the grass at her feet. She closed her eyes, hoping the dizziness would pass. Her fingers dug into the bark as a wave of vertigo swirled through her head.

The forest fell quiet, suddenly swathed in a palpable hush. The cool bark of the tree against her back dissolved into sun-warmed brick. Marissa opened her eyes. To her rising fear and amazement, she saw not the woods behind her house, but a large, brick-walled English garden. The well-tended flower borders bloomed in a riot of spring flowers: purple hyacinths, pink tulips, orange poppies, yellow fritillaries, white and blue anemones.

A wooden gate in the brick wall opened beside Marissa. A girl of 14 or so entered the garden and began to collect flowers for a mixed bouquet. Her blue gabardine school frock hung limply on her gangling form; her face bordered on the point of being gaunt. Her pale blond hair was drawn up to the crown of her head in a thick ponytail, which cascaded down her back in pale, shining waves.

The girl turned toward her, and looked right through her. Marissa caught her breath and stared in blanching horror. The girl's adolescent features were a mirror of Marissa's own at that age. Marissa crossed her arms across her chest in an involuntary gesture of self-protection.

With a dreamy smile, the girl picked a clump of lilacs and added them to her bouquet. The gate opened and shut again. A tall, dark-haired man walked across the lawn with his back to Marissa, his stride loose-limbed but powerful. The girl whirled and her smile became incandescent. She called to the man fondly and rushed into his waiting arms to be hugged.

The touching scene was strangely silent, like a motion picture with the sound turned off. Yet Marissa could smell the hyacinths and pungent evergreen lining the walls, and feel the crisp ivy clinging to the brick and mortar beneath her hands. A rough breeze stirred the boughs of the cedars at the end of the garden; the coolness of the phantom wind caressed her face like a lover's hand. Was she really in the garden or somehow dreaming it all?

The man grasped the girl's waist and spun her around. Marissa recognized him at once. The dark eyes and Gypsy-like cheekbones were as familiar to her as her own. Brendan. Why am I not surprised, she thought, as her fear gave way before fervid curiosity. She had to hold herself back from walking across the grass to touch him; if she did that, he might disappear.

His hawkish features softened by a warm smile, Brendan gazed down at the girl and began talking earnestly. Marissa dared to move closer, straining

77

to hear his words. Oblivious to her presence, they couldn't see her, and she knew then that in their world, *she* was the invisible specter.

While Brendan spoke fondly to his companion, Marissa wondered about the girl's identity. The most logical choice would be his ward, Miranda Seton; the difference in their ages seemed about right. Still, the queer resemblance to herself bothered Marissa. Maybe it was all a fantasy, and she just imagined herself in Miranda's place.

As she listened to Brendan, Miranda's smile faded and her young, mobile face went blank, then suddenly twisted with despair. Tightly clutching her forgotten bouquet, she asked him a number of questions, each one more urgent than the last.

Marissa swore silently, wishing she could hear their conversation during this intensely emotional encounter.

Brendan tried to calm the girl, holding her by her thin shoulders. But Miranda grew vehement and pulled away from him. Her green eyes flashing wildly, she hurled an accusation at him. Stunned, Brendan let his arms drop loosely to his sides. He spoke once more, gently.

Miranda shook her head. *No, no, never!* She turned her back on him with desperate, wounded pride. For a long moment, Brendan stared hopelessly at her back, his dark features a mask of self-disgust and pain. Unconsciously, Marissa took a step toward him, but he turned and left the garden.

In hideous pantomime, Marissa saw Miranda wail and hurl the bouquet toward the gate, then the girl fell to her knees among the scattered blossoms. On the lush green lawn, she wrapped her arms around her waist and began to weep inconsolably.

Drawn to comfort the sobbing girl, Marissa moved across the thick spring grass. Miranda looked up, her streaming eyes coming to rest on Marissa. Her expression of naked suffering gave way to one of alarmed confusion. The girl's face turned ashen.

"I'm so sorry. . . . " Marissa began. As she took another step forward and reached for Miranda's heaving shoulders, a burst of dizziness suddenly assailed her. She sank to her knees while the English garden wavered, then disappeared in a blurred haze. The quality of light changed from bright morning to the slanting beams of afternoon, and the woods came to noisy, sibilant life around her.

Raising her hands shakily to her face, Marissa found it wet with huge, rolling tears.

By the time she walked into the kitchen, Kelsey was there, opening a bottle of LaCroix water. She glanced at Marissa, and her eyes widened. "What happened to you? You look like you just saw one of your *doppelgangers.*"

"Very funny." At that moment, Marissa felt like cheerfully strangling her friend. Dropping the lilacs in the sink, she reached in a cupboard for a vase, glad that she'd taken the time to get over the worst of her fright on the walk back to the house.

Kelsey persisted gently. "Is there something going on that I ought to know about?"

"No, ah . . . just my usual weirdness," she replied, then cursed silently as she shoved the lilacs into the vase of water. She didn't bother to straighten the skewed spikes of bloom since her

79

hands still trembled. "Sometimes my imagination gets the better of me."

"I know that." Kelsey smiled slightly, her blue eyes shadowed with curiosity. "You should try writing fantastic fiction instead of histories and staid biographies."

"Brendan Tyrell is hardly staid," Marissa protested. She could still see Brendan as he strode across the thick green lawn, his dark eyes alight with hope and compassion. She'd grieved deeply at the lost look on his face as he'd left the sobbing girl alone in the garden. The vision of that scene was too vivid to dismiss as a daydream. Should she confide in her friend?

Kelsey shrugged and deftly arranged the flowers. "That's right, dear heart—he's the ultimate *preux chevalier.*"

"Brendan would roar with laughter if he heard you describe him as a 'gallant knight.' " Despite her turmoil, Marissa felt her face soften with an indulgent smile. "He rather enjoys—ah—enjoyed being labeled as 'infamous.' "

Kelsey turned to her with an expression of mock disapproval. "I think you're more than a little in love with him, dearest friend."

Marissa laughed too quickly. "Perhaps I am at that." She brushed her loose hair back over her shoulders and rubbed her neck. What would Kelsey say if she blurted out, *I'm in love with Brendan's ghost. He came to my bedroom last night and* . . .

"Rissa . . ." Kelsey's face held tender concern. "Will you really be all right out here alone? I'm worried about you."

"Of course, I'll be all right," she answered too brightly. "It's much safer out here than the mean streets of Boston. I can definitely promise you that you won't see my story on *America's Most Wanted.*"

Kelsey narrowed her eyes, studying her closely. "Have you been crying?"

Oh, Lord, Marissa mentally swore, *my red eyes must have given me away.* She hesitated. Now was her moment to reveal her deep, dark secret. Yet something held her back. What could she tell Kelsey that wouldn't sound totally wacked out?

The letter from Los Angeles crinkled in her pocket. She'd read it on the way back to the house. *Bless you, Robin Stuart,* she thought, *your letter is just the cover I need.* Though she felt rotten for misleading her friend, she said in a muted voice, "I got a letter from Robin."

"Oh, how sweet," Kelsey remarked acidly. "What does the fair-haired lad want now?" Crossing her arms, she leaned against the counter, a mutinous tilt to her chin. "I hope it's just money or a new car . . . not, God forbid, your body and soul."

Marissa said automatically, "Robin never asked me for any of those things. We were living together, after all . . . and you know I don't like to be selfish. How could I not share my money with him?"

Her friend gazed back at her wordlessly. Then with a wry twist to her lips, Kelsey said, "Yes . . . how could you not?"

Marissa felt a hot flush creep up her neck. They'd had this same argument countless times before. The only difference was that she no longer felt so compelled to rush to her ex-lover's defense. Robin Stuart seemed like a foggy memory in the blaze of Brendan Tyrell's sun.

If she didn't have his letter in her hand, she wouldn't have felt a connection to Robin at all. Still, Kelsey's sarcasm stung her, so Marissa dropped her glance to the offending piece of paper in her hand. "Actually, it's a nice letter. Upbeat, not full of self-pity or recriminations. I think he'll be happy out there."

Kelsey rubbed her right arm with her left hand, as if she felt cool. In that nervous movement, Marissa could see her friend struggling to keep her tongue civil. She almost smiled, noting the fierce protective glint in the other woman's eyes. Kelse had never cared for Robin; she'd always claimed he was too arrogant and took advantage of Marissa's kind and generous nature. Hindsight made her wonder if her friend hadn't been right all along.

Finally Kelsey asked quietly, "So why the tears?"

Marissa thought for a minute before she replied. Though she'd used the letter as an excuse for her puffy eyes, she owed Kelsey an honest answer. How *did* Robin's letter affect her?

"You can't live with a man for five years, then part from him without some sadness." As the words left her lips, Marissa realized that she hadn't told the absolute truth.

Initially she'd grieved at parting from her lover, though she knew it was best for both of them. Yet ever since she'd moved into the cottage, the grief had suddenly waned. Instead she felt a buoyant sense of relief . . . relief that she was free to pursue her interest in Brendan Tyrell without Robin's tense, brooding jealousy. Given the perspective of time, those arguments they'd had over Brendan seemed so pathetic, so juvenile.

Then she remembered the tingling joy she'd felt

when Brendan appeared in her bedroom last night. Perhaps Robin's frustrated jealousy wasn't so ridiculous after all.

"Rissa?" Kelsey moved away from the counter to place a hand on her shoulder. "What else did that damned Scot have to say?"

Marissa sighed. "Robin misses me—a lot. He didn't come out and ask it directly, but I think he'd like me to move back in with him."

Kelsey's brow puckered in an immediate frown. "Tell me you won't even consider it."

"No, of course not. Even if things were perfect with Robin, and God knows they never were, I couldn't live in L.A. Though I enjoyed Cambridge, I've had enough of city life to last me a while." She paused. "And I feel that I somehow belong here."

Impulsively, Kelsey threw her arms around Marissa and squeezed. "Haven't I always told you that?"

Marissa hugged her friend back, relishing the shared warmth of honest, open affection. The cottage, the cats, her dear Kelse and her work with Brendan . . . she truly had a home, at long last.

At the back of her mind rose a niggling, persistent worry. Why *did* she feel so at home here, given all the frightening occurrences at the house? And who truly was the dark, thrilling enigma—man or spirit—she ached to belong to?

Chapter Five

O hard, when love and duty clash!
—Alfred, Lord Tennyson

Two days after Brendan and Tony's arrival in
Lucknow, Sir Henry ordered the rest of the troops
into the Residency, and the huge doors of the Baillie Guard were closed. Tony remained with his
wife and daughter at Dr. Fayrer's, while Brendan
took his quarters with the other officers. He was
pleased to find that *Daffadar* Singh and the other
sowars had returned safely to their post in the Residency.

Brendan learned that Sir Henry planned to lead
a force out to engage the rebels before they could
entrench themselves in the city. He thought it an
ill-advised move, and warned Sir Henry that they
were vastly outnumbered. But the Chief Commissioner had been worn down by listening to Mr.

84

Gubbins and some of his advisors' constant complaints about his inaction, so he intended to go through with the assault. Sir Henry ordered Brendan to remain with the troops left behind to defend the Residency.

Late one afternoon, Brendan stopped by the Setons' quarters upon leaving his post at Fayrer's battery. As he had feared, the journey had taken its toll on his friend. Though Sarah nursed him carefully, Tony's fever had come back.

When Sarah answered his knock and let him into the small room that made up their quarters, Brendan noted the dark smudges around her eyes. "How is he?"

"Worse. He's caught pneumonia." Sarah raised her hand and stroked her forehead. Her translucent eyes obscured with tears as she added softly, "I'm afraid I'm going to lose him, Brendan."

He took her hand in his and squeezed it. "Tony's stubborn. He'll pull through." Then he saw a small, forlorn figure huddled on one of the string beds. "How's Randie?"

"She won't leave." Sarah glanced at her daughter, and another care settled on her brow. "I've sent her out to play with the other children, but she just comes home again. She sits there by his side for hours, as if she's afraid to leave him . . . as if it's her presence that's keeping him alive."

Brendan said, "Why don't you take her out for a breath of air? It will do the both of you good. I'll sit with Tony."

Sarah hesitated for a moment, obviously torn in her devotion for her husband and her worry for her child. "If you wouldn't mind . . . let me fetch Miranda."

"Hello, Uncle Brendan," the little girl said, her

habitual joy at his appearance muted. There were hollows in her tiny cheeks, and her eyes lacked their usual luster.

It tore at Brendan's heart to see her this way. He patted her limp curls. "I've missed you, poppet."

Miranda simply gave him a wan smile, then followed her mother outside. He sat in the chair next to Tony's bed, watching his friend's chest rise and fall with labored breaths. Despite his reassurances to Sarah, he was worried by the bluish cast of Tony's skin.

The man in the bed started to move restlessly, and his eyes opened and fixed on Brendan's face. It took them a moment to focus. Then he smiled and whispered, "Brendan . . . where are Sarah and Randie?"

"I sent them outside for some air. They'll be back in a few minutes. You just settle back and rest."

"Can't." Tony gasped for breath. "I need to talk to you."

"All right." Brendan smiled gently. "What is so important?"

"I know I'm finished this time."

"Tony, stop it. You'll be raising hell again in no time."

With a tired smile, the Englishman languidly lifted his hand to silence Brendan. "You're the hell-raiser, *Sikander-sa'b*." He paused to take a deep breath. "I want you to look after Randie and Sarah when I'm gone. They'll need someone strong. Promise me that?"

Brendan tried to be jovial. "Totally unnecessary, my friend."

Tony's blue eyes glittered. "Promise."

"Very well, I promise. But no more talk about dying, do you hear? Why, next year this time we'll be hawking out on the *mofussil. . . .* "

His voice trailed off. Tony's eyes had closed, and he'd fallen back into his fevered sleep. Brendan lifted Tony's exposed hand and tucked it back under the cotton quilt. *Don't give up now, my dear friend . . . I need you.* Aloud he said, "Rest well, Tony . . . you have your promise."

On the afternoon of June 30th—the same day that Sir Henry Lawrence led his meager force out to attack the mutineers—Anthony Seton died. Sarah and Miranda made their farewells at Dr. Fayrer's house. Due to the gruesome conditions of the makeshift graveyard, no women or children were allowed there. Brendan and *Daffadar* Singh barely had time to carry Tony's wasted body to the burial ground before a dusty and exhausted Sir Henry Lawrence rode back into the compound.

From the grief and strain showing on the Chief Commissioner's face, Brendan knew the battle of Chinhat had been lost. Sir Henry said that they'd been outnumbered, six to one, and that the losses had been heavy. The survivors and wounded were being moved back into the Residency, and the mutineers were arriving in the thousands, swarming over the city. They must prepare for a siege.

In the necessity of the moment, Brendan had to put aside his grief for Tony. The British defenders were forced to retrench. Troops were withdrawn from the Machi Bhawan, and the building itself was blown up to keep it from being used by the rebels. That night, the mutineers trained their guns on the Residency and began a brutal shelling of the compound, underscored with musket fire.

87

Catherine Kohman

Every able-bodied man in the Residency was called to his post.

The second day of the siege, Sir Henry's quarters were hit by a shell, and he was gravely wounded. In terrible agony, he hung on for two days. Then he was gone, buried in a common grave with other casualties of the day. The morale in the compound, already weak because of the intense shelling, sank to a new level of despair.

The day after Sir Henry's burial, Brendan realized that he hadn't been able to visit the Setons since Tony's death. In the blearing haze of his own exhaustion, he hoped they were all right. Dr. Fayrer's house had taken some heavy fire when the mutineers learned that the wounded Chief Commissioner was taken there. But nowhere in the Residency was truly safe. Every day, around 20 men or women were killed from the mutineers' guns.

Brendan promised himself that he'd look in on the Setons the next day, after he caught a few hours' sleep.

"Brendan! I'm so glad that you're all right. We hadn't seen you, and I was worried that . . ." Sarah Seton stopped and wrung her hands in the limp cotton of her apron. Her eyes darted over to the corner of the room where Miranda sat, playing listlessly with her doll.

"How are you, Sarah?" Brendan grasped her two hands in his. Her finely drawn features were even thinner, and lines of sorrow had permanently etched themselves on her brow.

Her eyes filled with tears as she said softly, "I miss him. I still can't believe he's gone. And this hellish noise . . ."

Brendan drew her close to him, letting her cry out her grief on his shoulder. After a few minutes, her sobs quieted. She lifted her head, dabbing her eyes ineffectually with a scrap of a handkerchief.

"I'm worried about Miranda." She glanced at her daughter. "She won't cry or talk to me. All she does is sit and rock in the corner, and whisper to her doll. She doesn't even play with Pippa or Caesar anymore. Maybe she'll talk to you."

"She needs to get out of this room," Brendan said. "I'll take her to a safe spot I know of and see if that will help."

Brendan led a subdued Miranda to a secluded corner near the Begum Kothi, one of the larger buildings in the Residency. There, a small fig tree struggled to survive, its dark pointed leaves coated with dust from the constant shelling. Still, it was alive, and the drab little birds called the Seven Sisters flitted about its branches.

He sat down on a stone bench and pulled Miranda onto his lap. She rested her head against his chest, but said nothing while he rocked her in his arms. "I'm sorry, Randie-*bai*. Your father was the finest man I ever knew. My best friend."

"He shouldn't have died," she said in a tiny voice. "He left Mama and me all alone."

"He couldn't help it, poppet." Brendan looked down at her face, her rosebud mouth compressed in determination not to cry. "Don't be angry at him. He loved you and your Mama—he wanted more than anything else to stay with you and make you happy."

"I—I know you tried to save him, Brendan-ji." Her lower lip trembled. "Papa said you were very brave."

89

Brendan stared up at the newly sprouted, light green fig leaves, a gift of the monsoons. Somehow, life managed to renew itself, even in the midst of all this death and misery. With a catch in his deep voice, he said, "If there's one thing in my life that I'll always regret, it will be that I couldn't do more to save your father, *piara*."

When he looked back down at her upturned face, he had to blink back an upwelling of tears. One of the tears escaped, and slid down his face to splash on Miranda's cheek. Her hand flew to her face as if a drop of acid had fallen there. For a long moment, she stared up at him, her heavily lashed green eyes full of confusion. Then an answering rush of tears filled her eyes, and a choking sob rose in her throat.

Miranda buried her face against his chest and began to sob her heart out. "There now, poppet. That's it—cry it all out." Brendan rocked her gently and stroked her fine blond curls.

"Did you know that each tear you shed for your Papa waters his beautiful garden in heaven? That's my girl, Randie-*bai* . . . that's my darling."

Beyond the worst expectations of those held captive in the Residency, the siege lasted into the fall. Though always hopeful of rescue, the residents grew used to the deprivation and danger, and began to take fierce pride in their very survival. In September, the garrison was roused when Henry Havelock came to relieve the Residency, but he lost more troops than he'd bargained in his assault of the town.

The Residency compound was enlarged to make room for Havelock's troops, so now some areas were relatively safe from musket fire. But no attempt was made to break out, since the combined old and new garrisons still lacked enough men to take on the mutineers. Now, in November, a second relief column under the command of Sir Colin Campbell was approaching Lucknow.

On a cool evening, Brendan came to supper at the Setons' quarters, a habit he'd fallen into in the months following Tony's death. Miranda met him at the door, with Caesar the mongoose perched on her shoulder.

"Mama, Uncle Brendan's here." Her eyes widened at the tins of food he set on their rickety table. "Oh, what did you bring?"

Sarah Seton looked up from the old copper pot she was stirring, a stew made from flour, lentils, a small ration of bullock meat and onions. "Miranda, you greedy child," she scolded, "that's not the way to greet a guest."

"But Mama, Brendan-ji isn't a guest—he's family."

Brendan grinned and swung her up into his arms. Caesar dove onto the bed, his pink eyes aglow as he chattered in affront. "Why, thank you, poppet. What a charming thing to say."

Blushing, Sarah laid three plates on the table and placed a dry piece of the Indian bread called *chupattis* on each one. "Please forgive my hoyden of a daughter, Brendan." She sent a warning glance at Miranda, who smiled sheepishly. "She's been outside with some of the rougher children. Do you know that I actually caught her playing artillery captain this afternoon?"

Brendan hooted with laughter. "Well, daughter of the regiment, did you inflict grave damage on the mutineers?"

"I was smashing them to bits . . . until Mama

91

dragged me away." She smiled again, this time in conspiracy.

Brendan caught the censorious look in Sarah's eye and let Miranda down to the floor. "I know," he said guiltily, "I shouldn't encourage her."

Sarah set the pot of stew on the table and sat down on her chair. Brendan and Miranda joined her. "Thank you for the tinned food, Brendan. I think your constant flow of gifts is what has kept us from becoming ill. What treats do you have for us tonight?"

He displayed his offerings on the table. "Carrots, oranges and," he said with a flourish, "cinnamon sugar biscuits."

Miranda crowed with delight. "Biscuits, Mama!"

Brendan dished out a small portion of stew on Miranda's plate. "Only after you eat all your dinner . . ."

Sarah smiled at her daughter, then cast a wary eye at Brendan. "Dare I ask where these delicacies sprang from?"

"One of the merchants managed to get himself shot," Brendan said casually. "His private stock of tinned and packaged goods was auctioned off, as usual. I'm sorry that I didn't get the chocolate cake, though. Someone outbid me at four pounds."

All three of them fell silent, musing with covetous wonder on the imaginary splendors of that chocolate cake, and each one could almost taste the sweet, rich chocolate frosting melting creamily on their tongues.

Sarah poked her glutinous dollop of bullock stew with her fork. With a deep sigh, she said, "It's no use dreaming of water from the moon. Let's just be properly thankful for our little feast tonight."

"Indeed," Brendan said fervently. Then he winked at Miranda. "When we finally leave here, poppet, I'm going to see that you and your mother have all the chocolate cakes you'd ever want. Just imagine."

With her stew-laden spoon poised in midair, Miranda looked up at him, eyes darkly serious. "I don't know, Brendan-ji . . . I can imagine an awful lot. A whole bakeshop full."

As her mother and Brendan fell into fits of helpless laughter, Miranda watched them in simple enjoyment. She smiled, wondering what she said that was so amusing.

After dinner and an hour of conversation about the promised Second Relief, Sarah let Brendan tuck Miranda into bed. He kissed her forehead. "Sleep well, *piara*."

"Good night, Brendan-ji," she said with a huge yawn. "I love you."

He pulled the quilt up to her chin and smoothed a wayward curl back from her softly flushed cheek. These last months of the siege had melted away the last of her baby fat, refining the delicate beauty of her young face. She was so precious to him—his fey, dearest fairy child.

"I love you too, poppet."

As he got up to leave, he motioned for Sarah to follow him out the door onto the veranda. "I didn't want to say anything in front of Randie, but tomorrow I'm leaving the Residency."

"What?" Her face paled. "Brendan, you can't— we're still surrounded—"

"Listen to me, Sarah. Sir Colin Campbell is

93

nearing the Alum Bagh, on the edge of the city. General Outram has suggested that Sir Colin approach the Residency by way of the Dilkusha, instead of by the canal bridge, as he and Havelock did. It should mean fewer casualties, though Sir Colin will need someone to guide him into the city. I've volunteered for the duty."

"But you could be killed! Can't someone else go in your stead?" She paused, and when she spoke again, her voice was hoarse with emotion. "Brendan, you are so dear to my daughter. If something should happen to you, she couldn't bear it."

"Hush, Sarah." He took her hand in his. How could he explain to her his confidence that he'd survive the mission? Not that he felt invulnerable, but a certainty deep in his belly told him that this wasn't his chosen time. He couldn't bear to leave Miranda and Sarah feeling otherwise.

"Nothing will happen to me, Sarah." He grinned. "Don't you know I'm being saved for the hangman's noose? And I'll be in my native disguise." He paused. "None of the other officers speaks Hindustani and Urdu as well as I do, so it must be me. I'll have a native guide with me, Kanauji Lal."

"Take care then," she said softly, her sea-green eyes grave with worry. "For Randie's sake—and mine—as well as your own."

Brendan kissed her lightly on the cheek. "Don't worry, Sarah. You'll see me again in just a few days." Then he bounded over the veranda rail onto the steps and disappeared into the indigo twilight.

The next evening, Brendan and the native guide, Kanauji Lal, slipped out of the Residency under the cover of darkness. They were both dressed in native costume: simple trousers of less than pristine white cotton, and long matching shirts. Each had a copy of General Outram's dispatches tucked into their turbans.

Silently, the two men stole through the sleeping streets of Lucknow, ever alert for the sign of trouble. They kept to the narrow byways and dark lanes. On a winding, noisome alley by the river Gumti, a drunken *badmash* stumbled along, mumbling to himself. They ducked into a shadowed doorway until he passed.

Furtively, they made their way to the Dilkusha park, through orchards, mango topes, and fields of sugar cane. The scent of verdant earth and mingled smells of the lush vegetation seemed alien to Brendan after the dusty months in the Residency.

Avoiding the slumbering villages, on a dusty path they ran into a small boy in a tattered shirt and an old man in a filthy tunic. The villagers glanced blankly at the two men, without curiosity. Brendan had a moment of fear when the boy's mangy dog sniffed at their heels, but the boy querulously called back the animal to his side.

Brendan experienced a curious mixture of fear and exhilaration. It felt good to be alive: out in the open, walking under the rising moon. Yet at the same time, danger lurked in every shadowed grove and along every rutted road.

In the pale moonlight, their passage over the rough ground was easier, but it also left them vulnerable to unwanted exposure. They decided to cut through a mango grove instead of risking a main crossroads. Quietly, they made for the opposite side of the grove.

"Halt!" came a terse command in Hindustani.

Brendan and Kanauji froze in place as a patrol

of sepoys emerged from the darkness, muskets leveled.

"What is your business in this wood, at so late an hour?" demanded the sepoy in command.

Brendan could feel Kanauji's panic, though the Indian stood over a yard away. He hoped that it was too dark for the sepoys to notice it. His own heart raced as he smoothed his expression to one of mere dismay. Given Lal's nervousness, Brendan decided to answer the question in Hindustani. Instead of his deep, vigorous voice, he used an obsequious, almost abject tone.

"Oh, honored sir, take pity on us, we are but humble men making a sad journey. We bring sorrowful news to a dear friend. His brother has died, and we have been asked to bring him word."

"What of him?" the sepoy asked suspiciously, pointing to Lal. "Can he not speak?"

Brendan glanced at the speechless Lal, who trembled beside him. The words were out of his mouth before he even realized what he was saying. "Worthy sir, the man who died was married to his sister. He was like a brother unto him as well. Most sadly, his grief has overwhelmed him."

"Where does this journey take you?"

Though their lives depended on his words being convincing, Brendan relished the opportunity to fool the mutineers. It was like a deadly game of chess. "Our poor friend resides in a village beyond Bani. We have many miles yet to travel."

The sepoy hesitated, studying their faces, so Brendan bowed his head in an attitude of obeisance. After a moment, the sepoy said gruffly, "Be on your way then."

"Thank you, esteemed sir," Brendan said silkily. "You are most kind."

Brendan politely bowed to the sepoy while Lal did the same. Striving to keep their manner totally calm, they turned their backs on the sepoys and crossed through the towering mango trees. Once out of sight of the patrol, they hurried toward their rendezvous with Sir Colin Campbell.

An hour later, they emerged from a dismal swamp, where the muddy waters had fouled their clothing up to their waists. Exhausted after their struggle through the swamp, they stumbled through a grove of neem trees.

"Halt! Who goes there?"

This time the command came in terse English. They'd finally reached the picket lines of Sir Colin's forces.

"Lieutenant Brendan Tyrell and his native guide, Kanauji Lal. We bring important despatches from General Outram to Sir Colin Campbell," Brendan said with relief.

"Lieutenant Tyrell?" The freshly uniformed soldier doubtfully studied their ragged, dirty attire. "The semaphore signals told us to expect you. Come along, I'll direct you to Major MacIntyre."

They wearily followed after the corporal, though eager to deliver their dispatches. Now that they were in Sir Colin's camp, the reality of the situation struck Brendan. The long-promised relief was really going to happen. There would be a bit of bloody work ahead, but eventually the garrison at the Residency would be freed. The hundred-odd days of the siege would finally be over.

Tony, if you'd only been able to make it until now, he thought sadly. Then his spirits lifted. In a few more days, Miranda and Sarah would be safe.

97

As they walked along behind the corporal, Brendan noticed a rather foul miasma about their persons. No wonder the corporal had looked skeptical at their appearance.

"Made it all the way from the Residency itself, did you, sir?" The corporal glanced at Brendan with a cheeky grin. "I'll wager you'll win a medal for that daredevil piece of work, Lieutenant."

Winning a medal was the furthest thing from his mind at the moment. What Brendan really lusted after was a bath and clean change of clothes, two items sorely lacking in the confines of the Residency. He'd trade any medal for that.

"I was only doing my duty, Corporal," Brendan replied evenly.

The soldier looked at him and grinned boldly. "Whatever you say, sir."

Miranda waited silently at her post on the veranda of Dr. Fayrer's house. Now that Sir Colin's army had fought their way into the Residency, she knew that her Uncle Brendan would be with them. Nothing could have happened to him; to her he was a god, safe in his immortality.

The sun was dropping behind the pockmarked battlements before she heard a clear, familiar whistle. From across the shadowed courtyard she saw him coming, a tall, straight figure in a clean khaki uniform.

"*Brendan-ji!*"

Miranda flew down the steps and raced across the dusty yard. She saw Brendan's tanned face break into a wide grin, and she felt as if her heart would explode with joy.

"My darling girl!" Brendan said, catching her up

in his arms and hugging her fiercely. "How are you, poppet?"

"Oh, *Brendan-ji*, I'm so glad you're home." She nestled her head under his chin and wrapped her arms around his neck. "You won't go away again, will you?"

Brendan kissed her golden hair. "No, *piara*. Not for a while. But we're all leaving the Residency." He set her down then and led her back up the steps toward their quarters. "Where's your mother?"

"Mama is helping Mrs. Quentin. Her baby is sick."

"Then you and I will start packing." He looked around the sparsely furnished room, trying to determine what could be left behind. "I've found a small carriage and a rather tired old gelding to carry you and your mother to Allahabad."

"You're coming with us, aren't you?" Miranda asked, a rising anxiety in her query.

"The Army is going to go with the ladies and children, sweetheart. For protection. I'll be with them and I'll come to see you whenever I can."

"Can't you ride with us in the cart?" Miranda pleaded.

Brendan laughed, teasing her out of an impending sulk. "Now Randie-*bai* . . . can you picture me perching on top of your mountain of baggage? You'll barely squeeze in Pippa and Caesar."

A light footstep and a whiff of lavender heralded Sarah Seton's arrival.

"Brendan! How wonderful!" She stepped into the tiny, whitewashed room, appearing frail and small next to Brendan's masculine form. He grasped both of her hands and pulled her to him, kissing her lightly on the cheek.

99

"You look lovely, Sarah, and smell as fresh as a Sussex meadow."

Sarah blushed and slipped out of his arms. "Thank you." She paused shyly. "I'm so happy that you're here . . . and safe. No more of your excursions across the countryside." She cupped Miranda's shoulder with her hand. "Right, darling?"

Brendan smiled. "I promise. No more gallivanting across the *mofussil* for me, at least for a time. But you ladies will be doing some gallivanting of your own . . ." He went on to explain Sir Colin's plan for evacuation of the Residency to Allahabad. Then he asked Sarah, "What are your plans once you reach Calcutta?"

"Go home to England, I suppose. Anthony's mother is still living near Oxford. She's never seen her granddaughter, and I promised Tony that I'd take Miranda to meet her."

Miranda looked up at her mother. "Can Uncle Brendan come with us to Grandmama's?"

Sarah began, "Randie—"

"Perhaps one day, poppet." Brendan picked up Miranda and sat down on their sturdiest chair, setting her in his lap. "But first let me tell you the story of a wily native and how he outwitted the mutineers in his dangerous journey across Oudh."

With a broad wink at Sarah, he settled into his tale.

Chapter Six

*Oh what can ail thee, Knight at
arms
Alone and palely loitering;
The sedge is wither'd from the lake,
And no birds sing.*
                              —John Keats

Given a few days' respite from supernatural trials,
Marissa relaxed. She fell into a routine—a vigorous walk in the morning, four hours of writing,
lunch, four more hours of work, then a short swim
before dinner. Most evenings she read or watched
a favorite video. It soothed her to put her life in
order; that way she could pretend that everything
was normal.

She started to read Elise Cunningham's study
of ghosts, but she hadn't found any real answers
to her questions. The author pointed out that no

conclusive scientific evidence proved the reality of ghostly visitations, but that the anecdotal evidence was vast indeed. The concept of ghosts wasn't limited to Western civilization . . . a holdover from our dark, primitive past. Almost every culture in the world maintained beliefs in spirits.

Of those who thought that ghosts did exist in some form, there seemed to be two camps. The traditionalists, often maligned because of their past connection to spiritualists, believed that ghosts had distinct personalities. Ghosts were discarnate human entities—the people had died, but for some reason or another, their spirits were earthbound. The traditionalists thought that a person troubled or emotionally overwrought at the time of death was unable to pass into the light.

The other, more recent theory held that a ghost was an electromagnetic recording of strong emotions from the past imprinted on the physical site of the haunting. This was why the ghost haunted a certain rampart of a castle, why feelings of coldness or discomfort were associated with a particular room of a house.

Marissa thought of the lower bedroom of her house, and why she disliked being in there. Animals were supposed to be sensitive to such things, and she noted that her cats never went in the bedroom either. Then there was the ruined icehouse—she avoided that area like the plague.

Other than frightening people, there were no documented cases of ghosts injuring anyone, and Ms. Cunningham reassured the reader that most hauntings were benign.

Reluctant to admit that perhaps her lovely house *was* haunted, Marissa took comfort in that. Yet so many things disturbed her, she tried to sort it out. The bedroom and icehouse seemed to be hauntings of the second kind—a repository of unhappy, tragic emotions of the past. But not Brendan—he had a strong, distinct personality; he had interacted with her, so he couldn't be just a recording. No, Brendan was definitely a Close Encounter of the First Kind.

The fantastic idea that she shared her house with Brendan's ghost both thrilled and frightened her. Frightened her because she was still uncertain whether or not he was a product of her overactive imagination; thrilled her because he seemed so real, so vibrantly alive.

When the nights went by and Brendan failed to reappear, she distinctly felt disappointment and a troubling sense of deep loss.

One evening she took her swim later than usual, and the already cool lake water turned chilly as she swam parallel to the shore. Losing the last warmth of the sun, she looked out across the empty bay.

The other islands and the opposite shore had disappeared into a bank of fog. The mist was alive, moving across the smooth, almost oily surface of the bay in silver-gray billows. Its swiftness surprised Marissa, and soon the curling, outstretched tendrils of fog enveloped her.

The mist swirled around her, and she lost sight of the island shore. Goose bumps raised on her flesh, and the first tinglings of fear tickled her spine.

If a boat skimmed too close to the island, it could hit her. And if she lost her bearings, she could swim the wrong way and tire, leaving herself vulnerable to cramps—and drowning.

Impatiently, Marissa shook her wet bangs out

103

of her eyes. She knew she really shouldn't swim alone, but she was a strong swimmer. She'd even worked as a lifeguard one summer. No need to panic just because of a little mist.

As she turned in the direction she thought was toward the shore, a curious hissing and splashing sound echoed across the water. *God, what was that?* Unpleasant images from Stephen King's novella *The Mist* invaded her mind.

Thumping and puffing, the noise grew louder as it approached. Then Marissa heard the mechanical clank and bang of a steam engine, a boat heading to Arcadia Isle. Feeling dangerously exposed, she feared the pilot would never see her in this mist. The boat cut through the water awfully fast given the conditions. How could he see where he was going?

A sharp whistle sounded, and out of the mist loomed a red and white paddle-wheeled steamer. On a course off to her right, the boat would miss her unless it turned sharply. What was an old stinkpot like that doing out on the lake? An expensive antique, an old wooden steamer, not one of the new gasoline-powered steel replicas in use in the Twin Cities area. Was it the toy of an eccentric millionaire living on the lake?

As it passed by, the mist shifted and she could make out the lettering on its side, the *May Queen*. At the bow stood a tall man in buff hunting jacket and slouch hat. With a broad, enthusiastic sweep of his arm, he spoke to his companion, a young blond-haired woman clad in a summery gown of jonquil yellow. A post-Civil War design, Marissa knew without thinking, since the dress lacked a crinoline. There were other, similarly dressed people moving about the deck. Was it some sort of costume party?

Near the rail amidships, a dark-haired woman in an expensive dove-gray gown of the same period stared out across the water. A heavy silk bonnet shaded her face. Next to the woman in gray, Marissa saw a short brown-skinned man, wearing a turban and a high-collared jacket in khaki.

Startled, she involuntarily gulped a mouthful of lake water, and coughed it up again. The small man reminded her of the man she'd seen near the icehouse. No . . . no, that's impossible.

Gradually, the *May Queen* disappeared into the mist, and the slap of the paddles faded away into eerie silence.

Marissa shivered in the water, and struck out for what she hoped was the shore. After a long minute, her feet brushed the weed-slicked pebbles on the bottom. Relieved, she saw the dark, regular outline of her dock just ahead.

Hauling herself out of the water, she grabbed her towel and vigorously rubbed her arms and legs to get the warm blood circulating in them. Her labored breathing gradually returned to normal as the mist rolled in, slowly climbing the wooded knoll toward the house.

What on earth was an antique steamer doing in these waters? Who were those people on board? They seemed so familiar, but she hesitated to put a name to them. The very idea was absurd. She had enough problems with unearthly visitations; why create more when a perfectly logical explanation existed? A restored steam boat, chartered out for a costume party. She could call the local Chamber of Commerce to find out the name of the *May Queen*'s operator.

105

Catherine Kohman

Marissa wondered if she wasn't spending too much time at home alone. She decided to drive into town tomorrow and meet Kelsey for dinner and a play or movie. The company and change of scenery would do her good.

The next morning, she made three calls, the first to Kelsey to arrange their evening plans. She felt rather foolish making the second call, to the Lake Minnetonka area Chamber of Commerce. She asked the woman at the Chamber about an excursion boat on the lake called the *May Queen*. The secretary said she didn't know it offhand, but she'd find the operator and call back with the information.

Marissa made the final call to an old friend of hers in London, a Civil War scholar with the unlikely name of Owen Rhys Jones. While she'd lived in Boston, Marissa had helped the Welshman with some research on General Phil Sheridan, for his book on the Shenandoah Campaign of the Civil War. He'd offered to reciprocate when she started on Brendan's biography. After briefly exchanging their personal news, Marissa got to the matter at heart.

"Owen, I need your help." Marissa pictured Owen's mop of red-brown hair and impish brown eyes at the other end of the line. "I'm looking for anything you can find on a woman named Miranda Egerton, née Seton." She consulted her notes. "Born Calcutta, July 12th, 1851, died Torquay, September 19th, 1938. Husband Justin, served in India, some time after the Mutiny. I'm not sure if they had any children."

"Got it. What else do you know about her?"

"She was a ward of Brendan Tyrell and later

acted as his secretary, until his death in 1875. After she returned to England she married Justin
Egerton, and eventually returned to India when
her husband was stationed there. She published a
few small works on her own, about India and the
Basques of Spain. Ethnographies of a sort. Oh,
and she edited a posthumous manuscript of Brendan's, a slim volume called *The Art of Falconry in
the Late Kingdom of Oudh.*"

"Strange subject for a Victorian miss. What are
you looking for, precisely?"

"Letters, diaries, photos. Whatever she might
have passed on to her descendants. And any contemporary accounts of her life." She paused. "I
know it's a lot to ask—"

"Stuff and nonsense, my lady scholar." In the
Welsh curl of his words, she heard him smile. "I
owe you at least this much."

"Thank you, Owen. I'll look forward to hearing
from you."

After she hung up the phone, Marissa wondered
why she was suddenly driven to seek out Miranda
Seton's history. She had, in fact, planned to eventually do the research herself. But now she was
struck with an aberrant sense of urgency, unlike
her typically well-ordered research methods.

She looked outside the porch. The June sun cast
a dappled pattern on the green lawn, and the
waves on the lake scattered a multitude of sparkling diamonds across the moving water. *It's too
nice to spend the day inside,* she thought. *That
small bit of work accomplished, I could take the rest
of the day off. And I've earned it, haven't I?*

With a guilty smile, she grabbed her purse and
headed out to her car.

*   *   *

107

Catherine Kohman

After a shamefully fattening dinner at the Malt Shop, she and Kelsey went to *The Age of Innocence* at the Edina multiplex. She'd seen the movie before, but Kelsey had missed it. The movie had been at the Edina for five months straight, but they often held over good films for extended runs.

Kelsey had enjoyed the picture, and Marissa had been able to relax and let her mind be drawn back into the mannered, stifling world of 19th-century society, the tragic love story. As an added bonus, the ever-talented Daniel Day-Lewis was a treat to watch. Almost as lovely a man as her Brendan . . .

Her Brendan. Why she so often thought of him in the possessive, she didn't know. Perhaps he possessed *her*, since she couldn't escape the thought of him for long. She tried to rationalize her fervid interest by telling herself that Brendan was a compelling subject, that anyone would feel the same thing in her position. But it didn't wash—all too well she knew her obsession edged toward the danger zone.

Now, as she drove home alone, a wave of loneliness seeped through her. Unbidden, the vision of a pair of black, Gypsy eyes filled her mind. *Brendan,* she sighed inwardly, *where are you?*

To get her mind off Brendan, she pushed the nearest CD into the player and listened to the opening strains of *The Phantom of the Opera.*

When she reached Enchanted Island, the forecast deluge loomed on the western horizon, jagged bolts of lightning illuminating the roiling, purple clouds of the squall front. The storm first sent forth its shock troops: howling wind and sonorous booms of thunder.

On the stereo, Michael Crawford sang, his rich,

108

seductive voice in counterpoint to the driving music of Andrew Lloyd Weber's score. As she drove along the narrow, winding road, the tall branches above swooped and creaked under the onslaught of the wind. Strong gusts blew a curtain of fallen leaves across the pavement ahead of her, and Marissa hoped she'd make it home before the rain hit.

The dark, haunting music underscored the ominous fury of the rising storm, and shivers raced along Marissa's spine. Abruptly, she punched the stereo button off in mid-note.

"Poor choice of tunes, girl," she said aloud. "Isn't this devil of a storm enough?"

The muscles of her neck and shoulders twisted themselves into knots as she struggled to keep the car from jerking aside in the heavy blow. The first cloudburst hit, and the force of the rain drummed on the car roof like shotgun pellets. The raindrops splashed across the windshield in streams, and danced riotously on the slick pavement.

Then her car rumbled across the bridge onto Arcadia, and the narrow entrance to her drive loomed through the sheets of rain. She turned into the ruts and bounced along the track, while the arching trees swayed above the car, lit by the flashes of lightning. With relief, Marissa saw the white clapboards of her snug, comfortable house gleam in the headlights.

After parking the car, she threw her trench coat over her head and shoulders, and made a mad dash to the house, keys in hand. She wrenched open the door and pulled it shut behind her to keep the slanting rain outside.

In the darkened hallway, she caught her breath, then hung her dripping coat on a hook in the

109

downstairs bathroom. It feels so good to be home, she thought.

Moving down the hallway, she wished that she'd left a light on, not wanting to stumble over the furniture in the dark. A staccato burst of lightning illuminated the living room ahead. In the strobe-like flashes, she saw a man leaning against the mantle, paper and pen in hand. Though he had his back to her, she recognized Brendan's tall, lean form.

In the next flash, he turned toward her and sat down on one of the loveseats in front of the empty fireplace. He began to write, using the folk-painted chest in the center of the loveseats as a desk.

As the rolling boom of thunder shook the house, he glanced up at her. In the ghastly white-blue light, his sardonic smile looked strangely fey, almost sinister. With his upraised hand, Brendan beckoned silently for her to join him.

Muttering a muffled oath, she whirled and raced up the stairs. She didn't stop until she reached her bedroom; then she slammed the door shut behind her. Her back pressed to the door, she shook with nerves and cold.

For a long moment, she stood there, unable to move. Inside her head, a battle raged. Part of her screamed, *Bar the door! Don't let him in!* The other part begged, *But it's Brendan. He won't hurt you. You know you want to see him.*

Unable to decide what to do, she stripped off her clothes and put on a flannel nightgown. Crawling into bed, she found the cats had beaten her to it. The storm raged over the house, the wind tearing at the trees and shrieking around the chimney.

The Beckoning Ghost

She laughed shakily then, huddled in the bed with the cats. Why did she think a bolted door could keep out a ghost? If he wanted to, the spirit could enter the room however he liked. With that comforting thought in mind, she pulled the bedcovers tightly to her chin. Trembling, she listened to the hollow drumming of the rain against the beamed roof overhead.

Awakened by the crazy, gurgling laughter of a pileated woodpecker, Marissa opened her eyes to a sky of pearlescent gray. It was useless to try to go back to sleep, so she got out of bed and slipped into her thick, white terry robe. She walked through the house to see if the storm had caused any damage.

A few thick branches lay scattered on the damp lawn, but the house itself had weathered the storm untouched. In the watery light of early morning, her frightened reaction to the storm shamed her. She must be more susceptible to atmosphere than she thought, to imagine Brendan's ghost in the living room. Totally ridiculous.

Marissa carried her morning tea onto the porch to go over her planned day's work, settling into the chair in her robe. With the blinds still down from the afternoon before, she switched on her small desk lamp and fingered the neat stack of finished manuscript chapters beside her printer. She noticed a folded piece of computer paper on top of the stack. Inside the paper was a note, scrawled in a bold hand with her blue Bic Roller.

My dear Marissa,
I'm sorry if my presence disturbed you last night. I merely wanted to speak to you again.

111

Catherine Kohman

*Bereft of your delightful company, I took the
opportunity to review the completed portions
of your manuscript. I made notes where I
thought the text needed further clarification.
The pertinent sections are marked. I hope
you'll find my remarks useful.*

Entirely at your disposal,
Brendan Tyrell

Marissa dropped the paper as if it were tainted
with the plague. Her glance darted over to the
manuscript, and she noted blue Post-it flags protruding from the edges of some pages—Post-its
that *she* hadn't put there.

Carefully, she exposed one of the marked pages,
chosen at random. The page dealt with Brendan's
arrival at Lucknow on the 22nd of June, and his
reported refusal to accompany Sir Henry
Lawrence on the disastrous attack on the mutineers at Chinhat. In the wide margin, Brendan
had written:

*Not true! I offered my services to Sir Henry but
he declined them, saying he needed me at the
Residency instead. This malicious rumor was
put about by others after Sir Henry's
untimely death.*

Her mind curiously detached, she rifled the
pages, finding similar notes and corrections
throughout the text. This was definitely proof . . .
but of what? That Brendan's ghost was real, *and
editing her work*? The idea unnerved her, but not
as much as the second possibility.

She knew each slashing curve of Brendan's
handwriting—it was nothing like her own, a more

112

even, flowing style with the exception of her flying T's and I's. Where she printed for emphasis, Brendan underscored heavily. Even to the untrained eye, their hands were totally dissimilar.

Could she have gotten up during the night and written these notes herself? She doubted it; to match Brendan's hand so exactly would have required particular concentration. Also, most of the information was new to her. But she might have read it somewhere, then forgotten it; her subconscious could have still retained it.

A memory from graduate school haunted her. At Harvard she'd known a brilliant scholar of English literature—the Romantic poets in particular. Farley Preston . . . a tall, thin, ascetic fellow with a razor wit and a wicked, infectious laugh.

She never realized how tenuous was his hold on reality until the beginning of fall term one year, when an inspector from New Scotland Yard showed up on campus. Over the summer Farley had been collecting precious Coleridge manuscripts from a number of Britain's hallowed archives. Farley's reputation was impeccable, until he started telling colleagues that he *was* Coleridge. Marissa saw his gaunt, haunted countenance as he was taken away for mental evaluation. His mad, dark eyes looked like black holes in a white sheet.

The senseless unraveling of Farley's genius had appalled her. *This* terrified her. Could her own mind be disintegrating? Would she end up a broken shell, empty of all thought but her fixation on Brendan Tyrell?

Her tea rose to the back of her throat, bitter and vile. She stood up. She had to get away from here—away from her work, away from this house,

113

and most of all, away from her perilous obsession with Brendan Tyrell.

Marissa packed warm, casual clothes and left enough dry food and water to last the cats for a couple of days. She'd call Kelsey later to have her check on them.

As she was leaving the house with her bag, she noticed the blinking light on her answering machine. She clicked the button to play and an unfamiliar female voice issued from the tape.

"Ms. Erickson, this is Paula Kline from the Chamber, returning your call. I checked into the matter we spoke of earlier. There isn't a boat like that currently registered on the lake. The historical society in Excelsior told me that a boat named *May Queen* operated on the lake from about 1872 until 1879. Her boiler exploded off Arcadia Isle, and she was never salvaged. I hope that answers your question."

Her face pinched with strain, Marissa stared at the machine as if it held a miniature demon. The tape hissed mockingly at her while it ran out. Mechanically, she shut the tape off and reset the machine. Then she ran out to her car, determined to put hundreds of miles between her and the haunted house.

Chapter Seven

I met the Love-Talker one eve in the glen. He was handsomer than any of our handsome young men, His eyes were blacker than the sloe, and his voice sweeter far. . . .
—Ethna Carbery

Far below her seat on a rocky promontory, the deep blue of Lake Superior rolled eastward, stretching to the distant horizon. Marissa hugged her jean-clad knees and basked in the warmth of the sun.

On such a bright, balmy day, she found it hard to believe that those sapphire waters could turn deadly, but they had. Scores of sunken wrecks attested to the fickle, treacherous beauty of the north shore of Superior.

Yet no maritime ghosts troubled her on the palisades and cliffs of the shore near Grand Portage.

115

Catherine Kohman

To her left, she saw the reddish escarpments and low, greenish-blue mountains of Ontario, while out in the lake lay emerald Isle Royale. The cool, bracing air refreshed her after her long climb. She inhaled deeply, savoring the clean pine breezes.

Hiking in the Sawtooth Mountains proved just the escape she needed, Marissa thought. Their gentle slopes and low altitude provided a taxing, but not rigorous climb. Falling into bed exhausted at the end of the day, she was too tired to even dream. Two days in the pristine north left her feeling almost normal again, not the haggard, specter-ridden creature who had first arrived here.

As the sun lost its strength, dipping toward the hills on the western horizon, Marissa stood up and brushed the rock dust from her seat. Just above her, a chattering squeak erupted. She glanced up to see a peregrine falcon hovering overhead. Its curved black mask and the slate blue coloring unmistakable, the bird folded its wings and dropped into its precipitous stoop. She was awed by the speed and power of the rare bird, her arms raised with gooseflesh.

When the peregrine disappeared into the rocky fastness below her, Marissa turned back onto the path to her lodge. A positive omen, the sight of the peregrine cheered her. She smiled, feeling calm and strong, closer to finding her balance and inner peace.

In her small cabin perched on the granite shelf above the shore of Lake Superior, Marissa slept soundly. Even the bright blanket of moonlight spilling across her bed didn't wake her. Completely worn out by her hike, she didn't feel the warm touch on her hand. Not at first.

116

The Beckoning Ghost

Marissa began to surface from her deep slumber, slipping upward through clinging shrouds of sleep. Wondering what woke her, she felt a light caress on her hand and opened her eyes.

Once again, Brendan sat on the edge of her bed. The moonlight touched his face, revealing its sharp, savage planes. Yet when he smiled at her, she forgot everything but the watchful expression in those raven, piercing eyes.

"What—what are you doing here? I ran away from you."

"I know. I *am* sorry I frightened you the other evening. The storm and I must have been too strong a dose for one night."

Slanting brows over a proud nose and the black curve of his mustache reminded her of the peregrine on the cliffs. *Shahin*—the Indian word for the peregrine leapt into her mind. He was just as beautiful, and just as dangerous.

Her gaze roamed over his face and form. This time clad in dark wool trousers, he wore a heavy sweater, knit in an Aran pattern. She wondered— could ghosts feel the cold?

She noticed how the lavender-gray heather wool clung to his trim, muscular body, showing the broad curving planes of his chest and the breadth of his strong shoulders. How could he seem so solid, so lifelike? She had the insane desire to lean over and draw him down to the bed; real or not, he had the power to move her like no other man could.

Yet his presence here confused her. She sat up in bed, and to damp her wanton thoughts, she circled her arms around her knees like a little girl. "I thought that ghosts haunted houses, not people."

For a moment, he looked taken aback. Then his

117

sardonic brows lifted. "I've never been called a ghost to my face before." His even teeth flashing white, he laughed ruefully. "Yet I suppose that's what I am."

"You seem so real," she said, beguiled by the potent masculinity of his smile. Her voice held a husky note of bewilderment. "You touched me."

"Oh." Again a look of candor, and that suppressed amusement. "Am I overstepping bounds to do that?"

"Don't you know? I've never been haunted before."

Her fingers plucked at the wool blanket as she glanced up at him. How strong and beautiful he was, the fierceness of his Gypsy features softened by the mystic moonlight. Her skin began to tingle, and she felt a insistent rush of desire move through her body. More than anything in this world, she wanted him.

Yet she didn't dare give in to her temptation. It might spoil the miracle. "I just assumed you'd be a more traditional ghost," she said, lowering her lashes to veil her yearning. "You know—wraith-like and transparent."

"This is a novel experience for me as well." His dark, lustrous eyes gazed off into the distance. "You've probably forgotten. I saw you there on the island—when you were just a girl." He sighed once, almost pensively. "I've dreamed away the years in that house, waiting for your return." He looked at her, a faint smile curving his full, wicked mouth. "Then you appeared again, and for the first time I had interest in assuming my worldly shape."

"You gave me a bouquet of daisies—I do remember. . . . " Marissa felt a shiver of pleasure run

118

up her spine at the tender expression in his eyes. "Brendan, I'm not sure I understand . . . why me?"

His face turned solemn, though his eyes sparked with intensity. "We're somehow bound together, you and I. Don't you feel it?"

Catching her breath, she pondered her answer. Could she deny the inexplicable need his presence aroused in her? Marissa envisioned herself walking the edge of a narrow precipice. On the other side, a bright, shining vista of soaring white peaks and sapphire mountain lakes beckoned to her. If she reached this Shangri-la, she'd find a happiness beyond her wildest imaginings. If only she could conquer her fear of the yawning abyss and soul-rending loss it represented. At last, she asked, "Would you prefer me to be honest?"

Brendan leaned forward, a puzzled frown lowering his brows. "Of course."

He's too close; I can't breathe, she thought. He smells of pines and the mountain heather, and most perplexing, the salt tang of the sea. If he comes any closer, I'll disgrace myself by swooning like a ridiculous Gothic heroine. "Would you mind moving to the chair? Your appearance has . . . rather unnerved me."

Brendan looked at her closely, the harshness of his features betrayed by his warm smile. "Certainly. I've no wish to make you uncomfortable."

Rising, he stood in front of the picture window as the waves crashed against the rocks in a timeless, soothing rhythm. Marissa noted that he cast an elongated shadow on the wooden floor. She wanted to go to him, to put her arms around him, but she was afraid . . . afraid of her bitter disappointment if he wasn't really there.

"Brendan, I don't know what to tell you. Until

119

tonight I was almost convinced that I was going crazy. With all the weird things that have been happening to me . . . I've come *that* close to the edge." She paused and twisted a lock of hair around her finger, avoiding his steady gaze.

"Still, part of me—a rather *large* part, I must admit—hoped that you were real, that I hadn't just imagined you." She looked up at him and smiled for the first time, letting her elation shine from her eyes. But that pernicious fear gnawed at her . . . a fear of stupefying loss and hurt that made her dampen her delight. "I mean, what biographer wouldn't jump at the chance. . . . "

Marissa stopped, noting the brief look of pain that the unforgiving moon revealed on his face.

"You're not crazy, Marissa. After my experiences with Rosalind, I should know that." In consternation, he ran his fingers through his jet hair, leaving it in a jumbled disorder that Marissa longed to smooth with gentle, soothing strokes.

"I too must be honest." Brendan's mouth tightened slightly. "I'd hoped that you were interested in me for reasons beyond that of a potentially best-selling biography."

Ashamed of her callous, deliberately off-putting remark, Marissa blushed. Then she pushed back the covers and got out of bed. In her white flannel nightgown, she stood before him in the silver pool of moonlight.

"You must know that isn't my main interest in you. From the days of my childhood, I've been drawn to you. That's why I so feared that I'd imagined you."

Brendan smiled down at her, obviously relieved, and the haunted look in his eyes was replaced by a sudden warmth. "Then you *do* feel it.

You're so like her, I've wondered. . . . "

He caught himself, and his expression closed up. The moment of dulcet, familiar closeness shattered.

"So like who?" she demanded, hot jealousy blossoming inside her.

"You remind me of Miranda Seton. She was—"

"I know who she was." Disturbed by his connection, Marissa thought an undefinable strangeness hovered about the girl.

"I'm sorry," he said, trying to remedy his blunder. "The resemblance is only superficial. You are a unique, enchanting young woman, Marissa Erickson."

The grave beauty in his face as he spoke strummed a deep, sensitive chord of Marissa's psyche, and she instinctively leaned toward him. Forgetting her fear, she reached out and touched his forearm. Beneath her hand, she felt a firm, muscular arm encased in springy wool. Brendan placed his surprisingly warm hand over hers.

They stood close together, and the moon brightened in intensity. Marissa placed her other palm on the rise of his shoulder. He looked down at her upturned face, the pulse in his throat visibly quickening.

"I think that's enough excitement for one night, young lady." He swallowed hard. "You'd better get back to sleep." He stepped away and turned to leave.

"Wait!" Following, she clutched his arm. "How will I know that I didn't dream this night?"

"You have the notes I left you."

"Yes, but," she said with a sheepish smile, "I thought I might have written them myself, in a sort of trance."

121

His brows lifted as he stared down at her. "Hardly likely."

"Brendan, this whole encounter has been 'hardly likely.' "

"I see your point." He grinned then, a grin that melted Marissa's bones with its exotic, seductive charm.

"Well . . . let's see." He idly stroked his mustache with his forefinger. "Do you know any Persian?"

"Just a few words, from my days at Jaipur."

"Tsk, tsk, young lady." He reached out and ruffled her tousled blond hair. "And you a serious scholar of India and the great Moghul dynasties . . ."

Marissa smiled, delighted in his fond scolding, entranced by the way he gently caressed her hair.

"I'll write you a message in Persian, and you can have it translated. That should provide your proof." He reached into the cabin's white pine desk and withdrew a sheet of stationery and a pen, staring at the ballpoint until Marissa took it from him and punched the top button. "Curious writing instrument, this."

He wrote two sentences in a cursive script that Marissa recognized from the walls of Moghul palaces. "What does it say?"

"Ah, now that would spoil the surprise, wouldn't it?" With an inscrutable smile, he folded the note and handed it to her.

"When will I see you again?" she asked too casually, trying to mask her surprising need for his presence.

"After running away from me these hundreds of miles, you're anxious for my company?"

Her pride jettisoned, she warmed under his

teasing grin. "Tomorrow?"

"If you like. I'll tell you my plans for how we shall go about tracing my missing manuscripts."

Marissa's heart lifted at the sound of that *we*. "Good night, Brendan. I'm . . . I'm so delighted that you *are* real."

He smiled softly, his hand on the door. "Good night, Marissa. Sleep well."

After he'd gone, Marissa hugged herself in the chill of the room. Why hadn't she noticed the cold when Brendan was here? *Because his smile heated your blood, that's why,* an inner voice chastised her. She giggled then, feeling young and unburdened for the first time in weeks.

Standing in front of the window, the bright moonlight touching her face, she murmured:

> *O blessèd, blessèd night! I am afeard,*
> *Being in night, all this is but a dream,*
> *Too flattering-sweet to be substantial.*

Shakespeare really knew his stuff, she admitted. With a shiver of delight, Marissa crawled back into bed. Resting her hand on her pillow, she inhaled the rich lanolin smell of unbleached wool. *From Brendan's sweater,* she thought, and curled her fingers over her palm to hold in the scent. This time unafraid of her dreams, she slowly drifted back to sleep.

Sometime later, as the moon slowly circled overhead, the shadows in the corner of her room shifted again with a vital presence. Brendan stepped out into the benevolent moonlight and moved toward the bed. For a long moment, he

123

stared down at the sleeping girl, his soul in turmoil.

Marissa lay on her side, her hand curled beside her face upon the pillow. Curved dreamily in the tiniest of smiles, her lush lips tempted him sorely. Yet he knew he shouldn't disturb her sleep again; he could still see the faint shadows of strain around her fine, lotus eyes. Strain brought on by *his* presence . . . or her anguished worry because of it.

Brendan sighed, a matching line from Shakespeare echoing in his mind.

I've more care to stay, than will to go.
Come death and welcome, Juliet wills it so.

It took all his willpower to restrain himself. He shook with the urgent desire to climb into the bed and just hold her in his arms, savoring the familiar perfume of her hair. From six feet away, the elusive scent of gardenias tantalized him. A piercing need, honed by endless years of waiting, tore into him like a blade, and he forced his gaze from her to stare out at the undulating waves.

Brendan didn't want to upset her, but the very nature of his existence invited disbelief, if not outright distress. What was he to her but a troubling dream . . . or even a nightmare. What right had he to haunt her . . . to drive them both mad with painful longings that might never truly be assuaged?

Come death and welcome . . .

Strangely enough, he didn't feel . . . precisely . . . dead. Yet he knew that he wasn't alive in the traditional sense either. He inhabited a kind of no-man's-land, drifting somewhere in the blurred gray boundary between the physical and spiritual worlds.

Drifting aimlessly . . . until that golden afternoon Marissa blithely entered his presence, rending the veil of gloom with her life-giving light . . . and at last illuminating his dark, somnolent soul.

Reluctant to give up the euphoria of her dream about Brendan, Marissa rolled over in the bed. A shard of sunlight stabbed across her face as she turned, and she groaned. From the heat of the sun, she knew that she'd slept away the freshest part of the morning. What time was it anyway?

She opened her eyes and glanced toward her clock on the nightstand. Obscuring her view was a small white tent, a folded sheet of the cabin's stationery. The bright sunlight turned the paper translucent, revealing inside strange characters in bold, curling strokes.

Brendan's secret message.

Marissa bolted upright in bed. Surely it had been just another dream. . . .

Her hand darted toward the paper, but she snatched it back, afraid to face its dreadful implications. Up here in the mountains, she'd felt free, unburdened. And now *this*—an arcane message scribbled in the middle of the night. She didn't want to think that she'd written the note herself.

What else could it be? Marissa desperately tried to think of another explanation. There was only one—Brendan *had* to be real. *He must be real!*

Trembling, she raised her curled hand to her mouth and bit the tender skin between her thumb and forefinger. Then she noticed a haunting, musky scent on her palm: unbleached wool

125

blended with sea salt and heather. Brendan's Aran sweater.

With a sobbing laugh, she opened her hand and held it flat to her face, inhaling deeply. Her imagination hadn't betrayed her—Brendan had really appeared here last night!

In a sunburst of hot, giddy joy, Marissa jumped out of bed. She grabbed the note and held it to her lips. Then she pirouetted across the wooden floor, her long white nightgown belling out above her bare feet. As she danced, she hummed the tune from her music box, *Chanson de Shalott*.

She stopped, suddenly self-conscious. Her elusive hero had said that he'd come back today, but he didn't say when.

"Brendan? Are you here?"

Dust motes raised by her girlish capers spiraled in the sunlight, which poured in the picture window facing the lake. From outside came the faint, quarrelsome screech of gulls and the soft slap of waves against the unyielding granite.

Her exuberance deflated by the empty silence in the room, Marissa carefully tucked the note inside her portfolio and with a sigh, closed it.

To her chagrin, Marissa caught herself fussing in front of the mirror while dressing. Annoyed with this display of feminine vanity, she pulled on her most comfortable pair of jeans, but weakened when she chose a soft wool turtleneck in a flattering shade of violet. She also brushed her hair until it gleamed on her shoulders like flowing silk.

Then she waited. And waited.

After pacing restlessly in her room for the better part of the day, Marissa still had no sense of Brendan's presence. Her rising agitation made her feel

126

all jittery inside. To use up that nervous energy, she decided to hike back up to the lakeside overlook where she'd seen the falcon.

As she sat on her favorite rocky perch, she stared out over the azure, smoothly undulating surface of the lake. Last night's encounter with Brendan troubled her. She mulled over those vexing thoughts, watching the fitful afternoon breeze send darker ripples of sapphire across the placid water.

If Brendan hadn't left when he did, she wondered what would have happened. She would have gladly welcomed him into her arms . . . and into her bed. How could a mere ghost stir her mind and body with such a potent dose of smoldering sensuality?

Brendan looked and felt like a warm, breathing man. A disturbingly virile and attractive man. A man so seductive, so beautiful he totally possessed her thoughts. Her fierce, dangerous *Shahin*.

Marissa laughed out loud. Was she so sex-starved that she had to conjure up her ideal man in ghostly form?

Another thing puzzled her. He wasn't a chilly, amorphous blob of ectoplasm, but seemed amazingly substantial. She knew that restless souls could appear in a number of guises. Worldwide folklore described an entire litany of the spirit world: phantom, demon, shade, spook, wraith, specter, doppelganger, incubus, and so forth.

Marissa hesitated. Was her Brendan an—an incubus? A lascivious spirit who trysted with mortal females? Her mind filled with the image of Brendan's wicked, brilliant smile. In bemusement, she shook her head. The majority of lustful longings in this relationship were hers, not his.

With a small sigh of regret, she thought she'd have to dig up more research material on apparitions. Then the corners of her mouth lifted. Maybe she should just ask Brendan himself.

A flash of slate blue caught her eye, and she watched the peregrine falcon swoop and soar along the rugged palisades.

"*Shahin,*" she said aloud, calling to her lucky talisman, and heard the word echo off the rocky cliffs.

Marissa turned sharply to see Brendan standing in the leafy shadows of the birch trees behind her. She sucked in her breath, afraid he'd disappear like the last time she'd seen him in daylight. Then, hands casually tucked in his pockets, he moved from the shadows into the glistening sunlight.

Chapter Eight

*What if you slept? And what if, in your sleep
you dreamed? And what if, in your dream, you
went to heaven and there plucked a strange
and beautiful flower? And what if, when you
awoke, you had the flower in your hand?*
Ah, what then?

—Samuel Taylor Coleridge

"*Shahin,*" Brendan repeated as he ambled across
the small meadow behind her, the daisies nodding
as they were brushed by his calves. "That was one
of Miranda's nicknames for me." He laughed,
placing his booted foot on the end of the granite
outcrop where Marissa waited. "One of many, I
might add, though they weren't all that flattering."

She glanced up at him shyly. Today he wore a
hunter green sweater and dark gray slacks, almost
as if he wanted to blend into the surrounding for-

129

est. Her avid gaze noted the way the sun suffused his black hair with metallic highlights of rich copper and cobalt blue. She couldn't believe that she was staring at a man who'd been dead over one hundred years.

Marissa lowered her eyes to her lap, and twisted the amethyst ring on her finger. To regain her composure, she took two deep breaths. Then, protected by the obscuring veil of her lashes, she asked in studied nonchalance, "What was her least flattering?"

"*Chura,*" he said with a grimace.

"Rubbish collector?" Marissa sat up straight in affront, her eyes wide open again, and her hands came to rest on her hips. "Why, that's positively insulting! I hope you scolded her severely."

"Oh, her punishment fit the crime indeed." Brendan's lips curled in a wry manner as he traced the curving line of his black mustache with his forefinger. "I made her muck out the stables."

They both laughed, and Marissa felt her heart lift for the first time in months. Yet something in Brendan's tender expression when he spoke of his ward sent a tendril of jealousy snaking through her.

She dropped her hands into her lap and stared out at Superior's offshore shoals, a shifting pattern of blues and aquamarine. Brendan stood just at the edge of her vision. "Miranda Seton was an important person in your life, wasn't she?" Marissa asked.

"Of course," he said too easily. Rocking back on his extended leg, he lifted his black eyes to the light cirrus clouds drifting lazily overhead. "She was, after all, the daughter of my dearest friends."

She raised her gaze to his face. "And later, your

devoted assistant and secretary. She even published some of your work after your death."

After the words escaped her lips, Marissa quailed inside. How gauche to baldly mention a ghost's demise to his face!

"So she did, by God," Brendan said proudly, ignoring her faux pas. His gaze grew distant and unfocused, and his voice turned bitter. "My wife insisted that all my unpublished work perished in the fire."

Marissa swallowed hard. "You—you remember the fire?"

"Curiously . . . no. I *do* remember the funeral, the posthumous accolades, *and* the scurrilous things written about me in the press."

"I thought it might be too painful for you to talk about," Marissa said, yearning to reach out and smooth the furrow that appeared on his brow. How would he react? Would he respond—or shy away from her touch? Too nervous to find out, she laced her fingers together.

"No . . . I feel remote from the memory of the fire. It's as if I wasn't there." He looked thoughtful as he stroked the thin scar on his cheek. "I remember locking myself in the study with a bottle of brandy that night. It had been a terrible day. . . . "

"Because of your wife's illness, you mean?"

"Yes . . . and no." He glanced at her a moment, then back out at the lake. "True, Ros was in one of her hellish moods, but I had . . . other things on my mind that night."

Marissa could see the pain in his eyes. She wanted to reach out, to console him, to hold him close in her arms until the pain faded, but he held himself aloof, isolated in his grief. Frustrated, she

131

didn't dare jeopardize the tentative bond between them.

"It's rather hazy," he began after a moment passed. "I do recall later on I felt a sharp, tearing pain somewhere in my chest. But there was no heat, no smoke . . . just a numbing sense of cold. That sounds odd, doesn't it?"

Marissa didn't care to dwell on Brendan's death, so she steered the conversation in another direction. "You mentioned that you thought your manuscripts survived destruction. Why?"

"After Miranda and Rosalind returned to England, my wife had my translation of Camoens' poetry published. She claimed it was an earlier translation, but I know it was the *final* version. . . . "

He sat down beside her on the rock, close enough to touch. Leaning forward, he casually brushed a sticky bit of green moss from his black boot. Then he dropped his hand to his lap, his long, lean fingers splayed across the fine wool that stretched over his taut thigh.

"Perhaps she salvaged it before the fire reached the manuscripts," Marissa suggested.

"I was in the same room with my manuscript chest, and the Camoens was stored in the very bottom of it." He turned toward her, a perplexed frown marring his high brow. "Why would she rescue that, yet leave me to burn? She wasn't *that* deranged. . . . "

Inhaling the sandalwood scent of his shaving soap, Marissa felt a thrill run down her spine, and gooseflesh pricked her skin. Unconsciously, she wrapped her arms around her waist, drawing her body inward.

Brendan glanced at her sideways, noting her

movement. With a small quirk of his lips, he gazed out toward the vast inland sea.

"That's *very* strange." She turned to face him. "You're sure it's the final translation?"

"Yes, and there was just one copy."

In her avid curiosity, Marissa shifted her curled body forward. "Why on earth didn't she save *you* from the fire? And how *did* the manuscripts survive?"

"That does trouble me—how I came to die in that fire." His detached tone surprised Marissa; it was quite matter-of-fact. "How the manuscripts were saved, I don't know. Perhaps Rosalind's servant, Biju, dragged the box outside with him."

"But why would she claim they burned?" Marissa asked, mystified by Rosalind Tyrell's motives.

"I have an idea why Rosalind may have wanted them hidden away. My devoted wife . . . and most ruthless censor."

Brendan turned his dark, piercing glance to Marissa's face. "You may find her reasons hard to understand, coming. from your world. As I watched you this past month, I've gleaned a bit about your society. Free sexual expression and content seem to be the norm, rather than the exception. Typically, a woman of your generation isn't offended by overt sensuality."

His level gaze appraised her. "The costumes you young women wear today are enough to try the chastity of a saint."

Placing his palm on the flat granite between them, he leaned toward her and rested the weight of his torso on his hand. "As my biographer," he added with an appreciative smile, "you know that saintliness is *not* one of my most sterling qualities."

133

Catherine Kohman

First inclined to blush and edge away from him, Marissa forgot to be abashed as she absorbed his last comment. Relaxing from her defensive posture, she almost expected him to twirl his mustache or leer and waggle his brows at her like Groucho.

"The ever notorious Major Tyrell." She laughed. "I think you enjoy being a black sheep, Brendan." She held up a warning hand to forestall his protest. "I know your interest in eroticism is genuine and scholarly, but be honest with me. Don't you also enjoy shocking the 'Mrs. Grundys' of the world?"

She dropped her hands to the rock behind her and leaned back, a self-satisfied smile on her face. For a long moment, Brendan stared at her severely, his jet eyes an unfathomable depth.

Worried that she'd been outrageously impertinent, Marissa saw the tips of his black mustache begin to twitch. Sure that she'd scored a minor coup, she let her smile broaden.

Brendan wiped the nascent grin from his face. "Ah . . . yes," he said with a tiny, patronizing smile, "the modern biographer's crystal ball: psychoanalysis."

Marissa mentally gave him credit. Intellectually agile, dangerously urbane, he was one cool customer. She'd have to watch herself with him or she'd be drawn out way over her depth.

"What do you know about psychoanalysis? Wasn't Freud's heyday after your time?"

In a powerful thrust of muscles, he stood up abruptly. "I'm *not* Rip Van Winkle. I do have passing knowledge of what's been happening in the world since my untimely demise. At least whatever *interested* me."

To puncture his pompous stance, she said impulsively, "Have you met Elvis?"

"*Who,*" he asked, his brows raised in total befuddlement, "*is Elvis?*"

"Never mind." She laughed, brushing the thick fall of her hair back, over her shoulders. "I see there are minor areas where you have catching up to do, Sir Brendan."

Looming above her, Brendan shook his head. "You *are* a fey creature, though a lovely one."

The tender, knowing smile on his face sent a wash of heat over her skin, though Marissa tried to blame it on her wool sweater. How much she wanted to explore the heady effect that his provocative presence had on her pent-up hormones, yet she feared what would happen if she tried to touch him in broad daylight.

This strange involvement was still too bizarre for her to react to him as she would any other appealing man. Yet she wanted nothing more than to spend the future in his engaging, if unconventional, company. If only he were flesh and blood . . .

Mentally veiling a number of delightfully sensual but unlikely scenarios, she seized the mystery of the missing manuscripts as she would a life ring. "If you thought your wife had the manuscripts, why didn't you follow her to see where she took them?"

A faint frown of concentration creased Brendan's brow as he looked out over the pristine lake. "I was disoriented, unable to direct my thoughts or movements. By the time I figured out that I could travel about the earth in my present form, Rosalind had already hidden them. And England was not where I wanted to be, in any case."

135

Catherine Kohman

"Where did you go?"

His dark gaze came to rest on her face once more. "India."

"You always felt at home there, didn't you?" Even as she spoke, Marissa knew that he'd kept something back. She remembered that Miranda Seton had married and returned to India after Brendan's death. Had he followed her there, to be with Miranda in spirit, if not in the flesh?

Again, Marissa had to stifle a searing pang of jealousy. She wondered briefly if Rosalind Tyrell had felt the same way about her husband's close relationship with his former ward.

Brendan faced her, his back to the shimmering blue of the lake. The afternoon sun caught his face, turning his skin a rich, burnished gold. Marissa ached to reach up to touch his face, to trace the edge of his thick mustache, to twine her fingers in his glossy black hair and finally, to press her lips to the feathery scar on his cheek.

She shivered. He was Temptation Incarnate, but should she let herself love him when it was so perilous to her peace of mind?

"The sun is setting," Brendan said. "You'll catch a chill in that thin sweater. It's time I left anyway."

"Can't you stay?" Marissa pleaded, hoping that her twinge of panic hadn't colored her tone.

Brendan smiled, a strangely wistful smile. "I don't think that would be wise . . . for either one of us."

In the lambent light in Brendan's black eyes, Marissa saw a mirror of her own unvoiced desires. She stopped breathing. That potent look far surpassed Brendan's natural flirtatiousness. Some stricture in her chest tore loose as she exhaled sharply, and she felt a dizzying lightness of being.

136

The Beckoning Ghost

She rose and stood before him, fighting the painful need to touch him, to press herself against his solid form, to savor the warm strength she instinctively knew he possessed. Instead she asked softly, "I've wondered . . . are you with me all the time, even when I don't see you?"

"Often I am," he replied with a rueful shrug of his broad shoulders, "but even spirits have to rest."

Under the unwavering intensity in his eyes, she felt naked, vulnerable. "When will you come again?"

She could see regret slip over his face in the way his eyes briefly shuttered and the corners of his fine mouth drew inward, an expression quickly masked by one of his cavalier smiles.

"As lovely as it is up here," he said, "I think it's time that you returned to Minnetonka. I believe that someone's trying to reach you there."

She lifted her brows. "Who?"

"My darling girl . . . just because I'm a spirit, do you expect me to know everything?" With a bold wink, he walked away and disappeared back into the trees.

In the growing twilight, Marissa watched the lake shift from luminous sapphire to deep amethyst and faced an agonizing rush of loneliness. She recalled the tender hunger in Brendan's face before he left her, an ardent yearning she understood all too well.

Then her lips curved in a bittersweet smile. *If this be madness*, she thought, *crown me queen of Bedlam*.

"So, *amiga*, you look great. Your mini-vacation must have agreed with you." Kelsey swung the

137

door of her loft wide and pulled Marissa inside, giving her a brief hug. "As a matter of fact, Rissa, I think we managed to put a little meat on those bones of yours." She grabbed a handful of saffron gauze and lightly pinched Marissa's ribs. "You have that sleek and sassy look again."

"Not too much meat, I hope." Marissa groaned ruefully, smoothing her hand down the hip of her turquoise cotton pants. "Blueberry pancakes for breakfast, lake trout and rhubarb pie for supper. You know those little old Scandinavian ladies up north—they always make you eat too much."

Kelsey took off her paint-splashed smock, revealing a bright pink tie-dyed tank top and matching bicycle shorts. She hung the smock on a brass hat stand in front of the huge windows facing the steel blue expanse of the Mississippi River.

"Well, all I can say is that the Norwegian Riviera must have agreed with you." Over her shoulder, she shot a speculative glance at Marissa. "You've definitely lost that haunted look."

Marissa stopped in her tracks. *"Pardon?"*

"I worry about you. You've been working too hard on this book." Kelsey fiddled with the paint brushes, stored in a clear cylindrical vase on the table by the windows. "I don't understand why you're driving yourself so hard. I know you don't need the money, and you said you had plenty of time before your deadline." She paused. "It's as if this Brendan has some sort of hold on you— you're like a woman possessed."

Marissa tried to shrug off the cold prick of unease that settled between her shoulder blades at Kelsey's words. Today she was determined to find out the answer—did Brendan really exist outside of her fevered imagination?

"Thanks for worrying about me, Kelse." Marissa placed her hand on Kelsey's shoulder. "I just wanted to get going on this biography, and I over-did it a bit." She smiled. "I hiked a lot and relaxed by the lake, so I'm okay now. Not so wired."

Kelsey studied Marissa's face in the merciless light pouring in the window. "You do seem differ-ent . . . calmer. I feel a positive energy around you. Almost a glow." Her blue eyes widened. "Have you met someone?"

Marissa stifled her nervous laugh and turned to-ward Kelsey's easel so her friend wouldn't notice her high color. "If only it were so simple. 'I met a man last night' . . . and suddenly, all is right with the world."

"Then that isn't it?" Kelsey asked suspiciously.

"If you mean, have I found a new and satisfying lover? No, it's nothing like that. Much more cere-bral." Mentally, Marissa bewailed, *Too damn cere-bral.*

"Well," Kelsey began in a mildly aggrieved tone, "when you're ready to share your little secret, I'd appreciate it." Then she shrugged. "Now, what brings you in town? Dinner, a play at the Guth-rie?"

"Actually, after all that rich, hearty cooking, my taste buds are screaming for something hot and exotic, like chicken vindaloo." Marissa gave her a cajoling smile. "Want to meet me at the Taj Mahal at six? I have to go over to the U first."

"More research at Wilson Library?"

"Not exactly. I'm meeting Gayatri Kumar, from the Classics Department. She trained at the Uni-versity of Chicago and the Oriental Institute, and she's fluent in Persian." Marissa looked out at the green swath of trees that bordered the riverbank.

"I—ah, have an inscription I'd like her to translate for me."

"For the book?"

"Yes," Marissa lied smoothly, lifting the cover off the painting on the easel. She studied the half-finished oil of an ethereal, white-skinned woman against a shaded indigo and purple sky. "Oh, Kelse—it's superb. Is this for a CD cover?"

"No, this one was inspired by that Yeats poem we talked about, *Leda and the Swan*."

With a patently innocent smile, Marissa commented, "But there's no swan. . . . "

"Idiot Dear," Kelsey said in her most patient voice, "it's not finished yet."

"Oh." A teasing grin split Marissa's lips.

With an exasperated sigh, Kelsey politely directed Marissa toward the door. "If you want to get to the U and the Taj by six, you'd better get moving."

As they reached the door, Kelsey held Marissa back. "I am glad that you're not lost in the Twilight Zone anymore." She hugged her. "Take care and don't get too involved with that silly book again."

"Silly?" Marissa sputtered, then smiled at the protective gleam in her friend's eye. "Sure, Kelse. Don't worry anymore."

With a guilt-laden heart for misleading Kelsey, Marissa slunk down the stairs and out to her car.

In an old Neo-Gothic building on the U's East Bank campus, Marissa knocked quietly on the frosted glass door of Doctor Gayatri Kumar's office. A tall, thin woman with sleek black hair opened it.

"Marissa, do come in. It has been far too long! When did you arrive in Minnesota?"

The Beckoning Ghost

A broad smile lit Gayatri's delicate, youthful features as she swept back her long, silky hair. Though Marissa knew that Gaya was in her late 30s, the Indian woman looked ten years younger than that. She specialized in Greco-Indian culture from the Hellenistic period, but she also spoke a dozen Indian languages. Marissa had become well-acquainted with her during research into the princely state of Jaipur, Gaya's birthplace.

Seating herself in the oak chair opposite the desk, Marissa answered Gaya's warm, personal interrogation. Then she produced Brendan's Persian message. "You've suggested that I learn more Persian, Gaya, and I will one day soon. This is the message I told you about."

Gaya took the note from Marissa's hand. After studying it briefly, she reached for a worn burgundy volume on the book-laden shelves behind her desk. She quickly flipped through a dozen pages before finding the reference she wanted. "That is odd—it's from *The Upanishads*, which should be written in Sanskrit, not Persian. . . . "

She glanced up at Marissa, then quoted:

Lead me from the unreal to the real!
Lead me from darkness to light!
Lead me from death to immortality!

Marissa caught her breath. Noting Gaya's fine brow lifted in inquiry, she said, "It's a private jest from a . . . friend who delights in mystery."

"Anyone I know?" Gayatri handed her the book and leaned back into her chair, her long forefinger delicately placed against her smooth cheek. "His Persian is of a classic style. . . . "

"No, he's from . . . Ireland, actually." Marissa

141

gave her a bemused smile, then bent her head to note the pertinent verses from Gayatri's *Upanishads*. She changed the subject then, moving onto Gaya's latest research in the Oxus River region and other professional chitchat.

As Marissa got ready to leave, Gaya walked her to the door. "And how is your work on the Tyrell book coming along?"

"Oh, well enough. It's . . . quite absorbing research."

Gaya's warm brown glance probed hers. "I have the feeling that this book is very close to your heart. Perhaps you would call it a 'labor of love?' "

For a moment, she gazed into the Indian woman's keen, perceptive face. Just how much of the truth did Gayatri Kumar surmise? She'd grown up in Jaipur, an Indian society much more in tune with the world of the spirit than the West. Perhaps Gaya's intuitive understanding sprang from a deep racial memory.

Marissa answered simply. "Yes. It is a labor of love."

Gaya smiled at her serenely, a warm smile that enfolded Marissa like a blessing.

As she hauled her bag down the hallway of her cottage, Marissa stepped carefully to keep from tripping over the two ecstatic felines who tried to wrap themselves around her legs. She dropped the duffle in the middle of the living room floor and scooped up the impatient cats in her arms.

In greeting, Sasha nudged her nose with his and purred, while Peaches let out a yowling Siamese complaint about Marissa's abysmal neglect. After five minutes of heavy-duty consoling, the kitties were satisfied that their mistress had done her penance for leaving them all alone.

Marissa anxiously checked her answering machine for any unusual messages. Nothing. Brendan must have been wrong about that.

The house looked the same as when she'd left it. But now instead of frightening her, the rustic cottage welcomed her with a soothing tranquility. Though the ceiling vaulted to the peak of the roof, the warmth of the redwood walls, the colorful Navaja rugs and huge fireplace made the room seem intimate, cozy. Marissa ran her hand along the heavy wooden mantel, remembering that the last time she'd come home in the dark, Brendan had stood in that very spot.

Where was he now?

Sorely disappointed to find the house empty, she'd hoped to find him waiting for her. Her fingers strayed to the pocket of her gauze shirt, where she'd tucked his Persian message.

His message hinted that she was the catalyst for some sort of transformation. Could she really help him move from the darkness of his shadow world into the light? Did she have the power to set him free? More to the point, did she *want* to set his spirit free?

Her brow puckered in a frown. If his manuscripts were found, would Brendan still need her? Probably not. Yet she couldn't imagine spending the rest of her life without him—his presence had become her touchstone, her reason for being. The very idea that he was fundamental to her happiness troubled her.

With a self-contained persona, she'd always thought herself a trifle too independent, too reticent in sharing her affections. That inherent aloofness drove Robin crazy, and had sparked most of his jealousy and their fights. How then could she feel this powerful, unsettling need for Brendan?

She turned out the lights downstairs and with a tired sigh, headed up to her bedroom. As she switched on the light beside her bed, she paused.

On the ruffled pillows of her brass bed lay a single red rose, a slip of creamy note paper tucked beneath it. She picked up the rose and, inhaling its heavy damask perfume, read the note. It contained one word in a bold, slashing hand.

Tomorrow.

Chapter Nine

So, if I dream I have you, I have you,
For, all our joys are but fantastical.
                                        —John Donne

Marissa opened her eyes to see the sun spilling through the lace curtains on either side of the bed. From the huge oak tree outside she heard the tuneful, cascading whistle of an oriole, and she stretched dreamily, wriggling her toes under the covers. Two feline heads, one gray and one peachy, reared above the humped bedclothes at the bottom of the bed.

"Good morning, you rotten little beasties," Marissa sang. The two cats eyed her grumpily and settled back down for another long snooze.

With an uncharacteristic burst of morning energy, Marissa showered and breakfasted in record time. Instead of putting on her sloppy sweats, she

145

slipped on a pair of navy blue shorts and a white scooped-neck T-shirt. As a finishing touch, she styled her silver-blonde hair into a French braid. Then she took her second cup of Darjeeling tea to her study out on the porch.

Systematically, she combed her files for notes on Rosalind Tyrell. Over the course of the morning she learned that Rosalind Chenowyth was an orphan raised by her aunt and uncle in India, and that she'd suffered through the Mutiny at Meerut. Biju, the Chenowyths' steward or *khansaman*, had suffered a grave injury while rescuing the young girl from the rage of the mutineers. Because her harrowing experience left her nerves shattered, Rosalind returned to England after the Mutiny, and Biju remained with her as her personal servant.

When Brendan Tyrell came back to England after the Mutiny, British society feted him as one of the heroes of Lucknow. That's when Rosalind first met him and conceived a hopeless passion for him, but Brendan took no notice of her until he brought his ward Miranda to school in England some years later.

Marissa got up from her work station and went to fetch mineral water from the kitchen. Returning to the porch, she decided that she'd be more comfortable on the wicker swing, so she picked up her papers and moved toward it.

She stopped halfway there. Someone was watching her. As she turned, she saw Brendan leaning against the open French door from the living room.

"Brendan! I wish you wouldn't do that. It's . . . unnerving." Beneath her surface annoyance, Mar-

146

issa felt relief wash through her. He *had* come, as he'd promised.

"I'm sorry that I startled you." He smiled guiltily. "I fear that I'm not as practiced as I should be with my entrances and exits."

Marissa simply stared at him a moment, drinking in his appearance. He wore the same sort of costume he'd worn in her dreams. White cotton slacks skimmed his long, muscular thighs and the open neck of his matching shirt revealed the burnished skin of his throat. Though dampened and brushed back from his forehead, his raven hair tended to fall across his brow when it dried. When it did, he usually combed it back with impatient fingers.

Momentarily mystified by her knowledge about the texture and wave of his hair, she let the thought slip by and shrugged. "It doesn't matter; I'm just glad you're here." She smiled shyly. "And thank you for the rose."

"Next time I'll bring you something more unusual . . . an exotic flower to compliment your rare beauty." An amused smile touched his lips.

What a fine mouth he has, she thought, *generous, mobile, sensually full.* His neatly trimmed black mustache curved around it to end at the bottom of his chin. Her pulse quickened as she imagined how his mustache would tickle when he kissed her. *Ah, yes . . .* dangerous thought, that.

Marissa cleared her throat, wondering at the sudden huskiness in her voice. "I was going to sit on the swing. Care to join me?"

"I'd be delighted to." He moved across the porch in a smooth, brisk step that seemed incredibly familiar. She could have imitated his stride quite easily.

147

She sank into the soft chintz cushions and unconsciously waited for the swing to move under his added weight. As Brendan sat down at the opposite end, the wicker creaked and sank just a bit, as it should have. With his longer legs, he pushed off the floor, and the swing swayed gently.

Brendan leaned back into the cushions, throwing one arm along the top of the swing. "I see that you're wearing one of those abbreviated costumes that I mentioned the other day." His gaze slid up her long, bare legs. "Most attractive."

Hot pink rushed to her cheeks. When she'd dressed today, she'd wanted to look reasonably attractive, forgetting that to a 19th-century man, her attire would seem seductive, perhaps even scandalous. Then she remembered the nature of Brendan's harem sketches and relaxed.

Demure compared to the deliberately provocative outfits that Eastern beauties wore, her conservative navy shorts were nothing to blush about. In his time in India, Brendan had been entertained by scores of *nautch* girls and had had the most alluring of concubines lavished upon him.

Damping a twinge of jealousy, she smiled breezily. "I find the shorts comfortable in the warm weather, but for you I'm sure they're a novelty. You're used to women in filmy silk outfits from the *zenana,* or ladies in stiff whalebone and horsehair padding." She made a moue of distaste. "Or those hideous bustles."

With a short laugh, he stroked his mustache. "Believe me when I say that you'd look utterly desirable in whatever you choose to wear—even a bustle."

"Thank you." Marissa dropped her eyes to the papers in her lap. Curiously discomfited by the thrill of pleasure that his admiration stirred within her, she said, "You needn't shower me with empty gallantries. It's charming and romantically old-fashioned, but hardly necessary."

Brendan scowled at her chilly tone. "I never give empty compliments. I thought you knew me better than to think that I ever would."

Marissa looked up, the pinched line of her lips softening. "I'm sorry; I'm a trifle uneasy around you yet."

His frown disappeared, and his mouth relaxed into a gentle smile. "Marissa, you know I would never let any harm befall you. I wouldn't come to you if I thought that you didn't want me here."

Marissa nodded. "I took the message you gave me over to a friend of mine at the University, who translated it for me." She paused. "It's a lovely quotation."

"I chose it with you in mind."

Their gazes met and held. Astonished by the depth of feeling in Brendan's black eyes, Marissa felt her heart skip a beat. He leaned toward her and his hand dropped from the back of the swing. With his thumb, he slowly brushed back a tendril of hair that had escaped her braid, his grazing touch a whisper of movement along her temple.

Marissa sat perfectly still, afraid of her own forceful impulse to take his hand in hers and press it to her cheek. She wanted to smell the scents she knew instinctively would perfume his skin, the

149

sandalwood and leather, the spicy musk that was his alone. She wanted to taste the sun and salt on the tanned warm skin above his wrist.

Paralyzed by a fear of losing control completely, she did none of this, but sat quietly under his light caress. After a lengthy moment, Brendan withdrew his hand.

"Now I'm the one who must apologize," he wryly began. "I couldn't resist it."

Marissa swallowed hard, and tried to defuse the charged mood. "I've been pulling together my notes about your wife. I have a few questions that you could answer for me."

Brendan nodded in generous compliance. Though his face was serious, the knowing light in his eyes played havoc with her composure.

She cleared her throat, saying briskly, "The Minneapolis newspapers stated that after—after the fire, Rosalind came under the care of a prominent local physician, Dr. Winston Heffel. One account mentions that Dr. Heffel was noted for his work on 'nervous disorders,' a nineteenth-century euphemism for mental illness. Granted, your—ah, demise must have troubled her deeply, but the paper implied that Rosalind was his patient *before* the fire. How serious was her complaint?"

Brendan frowned and rubbed his forehead. "She had become unmanageable. Dr. Heffel recommended that I place her in his sanitarium. Rosalind refused, saying that she'd kill herself first."

He let out a long breath. "Curious, isn't it? A bizarre twist of Fate that *I* was the one who died, not Rosalind."

"Rosalind must have been an unhappy woman," Marissa commented. Unconsciously, she leaned toward him on the swing.

"Yes, I'm afraid so . . . most of it due to me." Brendan rubbed his forehead, as if to blot out a hidden pain.

Marissa frowned. "But in my research I found that both depression and schizophrenia ran in her family. Her mother committed suicide within a year of Rosalind's birth, and her father never got over his wife's death. He drank himself to death two years later.

"You probably weren't aware of that, since Rosalind thought her parents were killed in a carriage accident. Her family also kept hidden the fact that Rosalind spent nearly a year in a private sanitarium after her return to England."

Brendan said, "She'd seen horrible things during the Mutiny. Many people never recovered their sanity after that. When I met her, she seemed gay, carefree. That very lightness of spirit first attracted me to her.

"Later, I did find out about her troubled history. Years after our marriage, one of her cousins told me the truth."

Marissa argued her point gently. "I don't see how any of that is your fault. Science has found that both of those diseases can be attributed to physical dysfunctions. Clinical depression often stems from a chemical imbalance in the body, while schizophrenia is frequently genetic in origin. That's why it runs in families. It's nobody's *fault*."

Brendan sighed. "I'm not the hero of a fairy story, Marissa. If she'd married someone else, Rosalind might have lived a perfectly happy life. As it was, my selfishness caused her to become a pathetic invalid." He made a fist and struck the arm of the swing. "I shouldn't have dragged her

151

back to India, where she was unhappy, then on that around-the-world jaunt. I shouldn't have let her see that I . . ."

Marissa watched the guilty turmoil play across his fierce, handsome face. "What were you going to say?"

"Nothing." His expression became deliberately neutral, bland.

"Other researchers have speculated about that last summer, given the unconfirmed reports that you had an affair." She persisted. "Is that why you feel guilty?"

Briefly, he shut his eyes and leaned back his head. When he opened them again to look at her, Marissa wavered under the intensity of his black eyes.

"I cared deeply for another woman, but it wasn't a tawdry affair, by any means. Rather innocent— what you would call platonic." He paused. "Rosalind didn't believe me, and we had a savage quarrel about it, just before the fire."

"Was it Arabella St. John?" she asked, her insides twisting with jealousy. "Rumor had it that you fathered her child before your marriage."

"No . . . after I married, my contact with Arabella was limited to occasional visits to see the boy." His face shadowed, he added, "He never knew of his true parentage, of course."

Marissa touched his hand briefly. "He would have been proud if he had known, I'm certain of that." She paused, the mystery woman's identity still troubling her. "If not Arabella, then who?"

His eyes rested on her for a long moment, as if he were debating something. Then he shrugged. "It doesn't matter now."

A sudden thought hit Marissa and made her

catch her breath. "Brendan . . . you don't think that Rosalind set the fire in a fit of jealousy? She was already seeing that doctor—"

Brendan stood up abruptly, and the swing shook violently back and forth. "I've gone over that in my mind a thousand times, but I don't see how she could have. She was suicidal, not murderous. Yes, she threatened to burn my manuscripts. . . . "

"Burn your manuscripts! Why in heaven . . ."

"Precisely the problem." His scowl looked positively demonic. "She thought I was denying myself a place in her ordered heaven by writing and translating what she considered filth."

"*Oh, Brendan.*" Marissa got up to stand before him, longing to put her arms around him. "That's why you said she had a motive for hiding the manuscripts away. Perhaps she did burn them after all."

Brendan shook his head. "I'm sure the fire was an accident. I don't think my wife could have actually thrown all my years of work into the flames. In a twisted way, she took pride in my talents. It was only after we ran into that crazy Calvinist missionary in Polynesia that she became deranged about her religion."

"That fits the pattern," she said. "Often schizophrenics develop religious or similar manias as a symptom of their worsening dementia."

Again, Brendan rubbed his forehead. "Can we talk about something else? All this talk about Rosalind and her insanity bothers me. I did love her, in my own way."

Marissa nodded. "I understand. I'm afraid that sometimes my puzzle-loving brain leads me into situations where I could be more sympathetic,

153

less clinical. Robin used to call me 'Sherlock' when I got into one of those moods."

"Who is Sherlock, and who is this Robin of yours?"

"Sherlock Holmes—the most famous consulting detective of the nineteenth century. He's still revered today." Marissa blithely neglected to mention that he was a fictional character. "He said that to solve a problem, you must first eliminate the impossible, and whatever remains, however improbable, must be the solution."

"I see." Brendan nodded sagely. "The idea has a certain logic to it. And Robin?"

Without thinking, she answered, "In Boston, we lived together."

"Oh, a woman friend," he said, giving her a benevolent smile, "like your Kelsey."

With a squirm, Marissa wondered how to tackle his misapprehension without offending his 19th-century sensibilities. "No," she began diffidently, "Robin Stuart was a male colleague of mine at Harvard." Hesitating, she debated saying more, then added in a rush, "He's out in California now, so he won't be around to bother us."

Brendan became very still, his jet gaze fixed on her face. She couldn't help but blush under his unblinking scrutiny.

At last he said quietly, "I see. I assume . . . you shared his bed also."

"Yes." Marissa wanted to smooth the tiny lines that formed around his eyes. Why did it matter so much to him . . . and why did she care so deeply about his feelings? Unconsciously, she stepped toward him, but he turned away to face the lake.

In the stiff set of his back and shoulders, Marissa could read his hurt. After a long moment, he

154

asked in a hushed tone, "Do you love this man—
this Robin Stuart?"

"No," she said honestly, moving to face him. "I
thought I did, but I realize now that I mistook
need for love. If I'd truly loved Robin, I'd be with
him now."

She flushed under the scrutiny of his gaze. "I'm
ashamed to admit that as soon as I moved here
and discovered you, all lonesome thoughts of
Robin disappeared." She laughed without humor.
"That makes me sound rather cold and heartless,
doesn't it?"

"No . . . believe me, I understand. Much more
than you imagine." Brendan reached up and
brushed her cheek, the distance in his eyes replaced by deep affection. Marissa swayed toward
him, intent on closing the gap between them. Gently, he caught her shoulders, desire and caution
warring on his expressive face.

"Brendan," she murmured, feeling a spellbind-
ing need to be held close in his embrace.

With a brisk yet rueful smile, he set her away
from him. "What do you say to a sail? I hear the
breeze picking up."

She spoke with difficulty, still mesmerized by
his closeness. "You . . . want to go sailing?"

"Well, yes. That jaunty little craft down at the
dock isn't yours?"

"No—I mean, yes, it's mine." Marissa shook off
the seductive fog that had enveloped her at his
touch. "We can go sailing, if that's what you want."

"You sound a bit dubious. Is there a problem?"

Marissa stared at the toe of her blue Top-Sider.
"Can anyone else see you?"

"To tell the truth, I'm not certain. I've never tried
to appear to anyone, except you." He looked be-

155

mused. "Perhaps they must of be of a particular sensitivity, like you are."

Marissa frowned. She didn't like the idea of being some sort of psi-phenomena detector.

"Where did you get the idea that I'm unusually sensitive?"

"It's very simple, actually. Your great-grandmother Maia Nordstrom told me."

"But—but she's dead." Marissa blinked once. "Oh . . . oh, I see."

"I am glad to find out that you *do* have reasoning faculties, after a fashion." With a gentle shove, Brendan opened the screen door and smiled wickedly. "After you, my dear."

Down at the dock, Marissa quickly rigged the sails and dropped in the rudder while Brendan went over her Laser with amazed interest. He knocked on the blue hull.

He asked, "What sort of material is this made out of? It seems strong, yet lightweight."

Marissa smiled. She'd forgotten that Brendan would be ignorant about modern technology. "It's called fiberglass. Most sailboats are made out of it these days. Even some cars."

"You mean automobiles? I've watched you career around in yours. Is that wise?"

"Mine's steel," she said. "Get in."

He lightly jumped into the cockpit and she sheeted in the main and jib. As the sails bellied out in the stiff breeze, she steered the craft away from the dock with a twist of the tiller. Once they were clear, she tightened the sheets and the little sailboat picked up speed.

They had the bay all to themselves. Marissa relaxed at the helm and enjoyed the simple tranquility of skimming along the surface under wind power, while Brendan perched on the upper rail as they heeled over. He smiled at the same time she did, two souls in blissful communion.

When they reached the far side of the bay, Marissa loosened the jib sheet and made ready to turn the tiller. "Coming about!"

Brendan ducked as the boom swung across the boat. She sheeted in the jib and main, and once again the boat cut through the water.

"You have a deft touch at the helm," he said. "Mind if I try?"

"Be my guest." She moved over and let him take the handle of the tiller from her. She grinned then, wondering what someone with a pair of binoculars would see. A boat steering itself?

"I'm afraid there's no one to race today," she said.

The rough breeze blew Brendan's hair back off his forehead. "Just as well. I'm not used to this boat. She handles much easier than the scows we used to race here. Of course, she doesn't carry as much sail."

Watching him at the helm gave Marissa the queerest sensation—that she'd done this very thing before. Was it déjà vu? Then she recalled the dream she'd had the first night in the cottage. Was it precognition, a past life memory or simply a dream?

"You're so quiet," he said.

"I'm thinking. It isn't often that I go sailing with a ghost."

"Ah. Perhaps you should forget that, and just think of me as a man."

That's the trouble, she thought. *You already seem too real to me. That Persian message made me be-*

157

lieve that I didn't imagine you, but is a ghost any easier to believe in, or more to the point, to live with?

"I think of you as a most fascinating man," she said.

"Why, thank you." A pleased grin played across his face. "And I find you the most charming of biographers."

"Gee. Thanks."

Her lack of enthusiastic response made Brendan look at her. "Ah, I see. Damned with faint praise, eh? Well, let me add that I'd rather be here with you, than anyplace else—on heaven or earth."

Marissa reveled in the sincerity of his voice, and smiled suddenly. "That's sweet of you."

"Surely it's not that 'sweet' of me to speak the truth." His eyes fixed avidly on her face, he seemed about to say something else. Then he let his gaze slide away as he ran his hand along the edge of the cockpit. "So what is this 'fiberglass' made out of?"

Disappointed that he chose to remain reticent, she couldn't remember what fiberglass consisted of. Fibers, obviously, and what else—epoxy? "It's a type of resin, I think. Probably related to plastics."

"So much of your modern world is this plastic?"

"Unfortunately so. It's not biodegradable." She stopped there, unwilling to go into the depressing complexities of mountainous landfills and all the other environmental dilemmas.

Brendan looked thoughtful. "That large box you sometimes watch in the cottage—isn't that made out of plastic and glass? It receives moving pictures and some sort of sound waves."

158

"The TV? Yes, it's a receiver, like a radio." She hesitated. He probably didn't know what a radio was either.

"TV you called it? What does the 'TV' stand for? Terribly vapid? Terminally vacuous? Or The Vacuum?"

Marissa burst out laughing; he'd been teasing her all along. Sure, some things about the 20th century might surprise him, but he knew more than she expected.

"You're right." She giggled. "It's The Vacuum, and it can suck every intelligent thought out of a person's head, if given half a chance."

"I love to hear you laugh," he said. "I hear it far too seldom . . . only when your friend Kelsey is around."

"Well, these days not too many people wander through their own homes cackling maniacally. The men in white suits would come to lock me up if I did."

Suddenly, she remembered that his wife had died in a sanitarium. "Oh, Brendan, I'm sorry. How callous of me . . ."

"It's all right. You meant nothing more than a harmless joke. I'm not *that* sensitive about my wife's illness."

Nonetheless, Marissa felt a cold shadow fall over the boat. She shuddered. Would Rosalind Tyrell cast a pall over her life as she had Brendan's?

When they got back up to the house, Marissa noticed the blinking red message light on the answering machine in her office. She played it back.

"Marissa, it's Owen. Call me back today if you're able. I've got information about Miranda Egerton." Click.

Brendan gave her an odd glance. "What did you want to know about Miranda?"

For some reason, she felt caught. Why *was* she so interested in his ward? "If I located her papers—a journal, for instance—I thought it might give me more information about you."

To her dismay, she sounded lame and defensive.

Brendan just looked at her, a half smile on his face. "I was simply curious. By all means, call your Welsh friend."

He pulled up a chair and began idly rifling through her voluminous notebooks. Itching to snatch them out of his hands, she glared at him. Her notebooks were sacrosanct.

Then Marissa smiled. They covered his life, after all. What secrets did she think he'd find in there? Only her most outrageous speculative comments would embarrass her.

Brendan glanced up at her, his dark hair tumbled across his brow. "Is there something amusing or scandalous in here that you should warn me about?"

"I don't think so," she said mildly, then bit her lip to keep from laughing at the trenchant remarks he'd find therein. "Be my guest. I'm going to call London."

"So, Owen dear, what have you got for me?"

"Not much on this end of the Atlantic. I found a few biographical references here that I'll fax to you, but I think all of her personal papers went to America. She and her husband lost their only son in France during the First World War, so her papers were passed on to the daughter of a cousin. That woman married a Yank during the Second

World War, and she's a widow now, living in Monterey, California."

"Owen, my Welsh hero! You're a sweetheart! Have you talked to her—does she still have the papers?"

"No, I thought it would be better if you contacted her. It's your project." He gave her the name and number.

Marissa thanked him profusely and promised to get together with him in London in the near future. With the slip of paper in her hand, she did a small caper by the phone in the living room. Then she saw Brendan standing negligently by the fireplace, a glint of patient amusement in his eyes.

"Eureka?" he said dryly.

"Owen's found the woman who might have Miranda's papers—in California, of all places." She gave him an excited grin. "I'm going to book a seat on the next flight to San Francisco."

He made a general comment to the cats, who sat hunched on the couch, staring at him. "I quite enjoy San Francisco, a favorite city of mine."

"Oh," she said, nonplussed by his remark. "But how—I mean, do ghosts fly on airplanes?"

"I suppose it would be a novel experience for me. However, why don't I just meet you there?"

"You really want to come with me?" she asked, full of delight.

"Of course. I have as much at stake in this enterprise as you do." His eyebrows arched in a sardonic curve. "Or have you forgotten that, young lady?"

"No, I haven't forgotten." As he looked at her with that devilish gleam in his eye, she noted a tightness in her chest. It was too soon; it couldn't be happening this fast—this terribly unwise, complicated attachment. Feeling like a speeding car about to careen out of control, she smiled weakly.

Brendan smiled back at her, a slow lazy grin that curled her toes.

Chapter Ten

What fates impose, that men must needs abide;
It boots not to resist both wind and tide.
                                        —Shakespeare

The Isle of Ischia, Italy, May, 1872

The ferry from Naples was running late. Brendan
Tyrell opened his pocket watch, and looked at the
clock hands with a jaundiced eye. He muttered to
himself, as if glaring at his watch would make the
Italian ferry system run on a more timely schedule. He smiled then, wondering at his own impatience.

In two years on this sleepy jewel of an island,
he'd come to savor the Ischians' slower pace of
life. The warm, drowsy days had nursed him
through the rigors of the jungle fever he'd caught
in the mountains of Nepal. Today, the sharp resin

of the island's pines, the briny tang of the tiny harbor reminded him of *la dolce vita*, the very sweetness of life.

Sweet indeed, now that his Randie-*bai* was finally coming home. He hadn't seen her since she was a mere child of 14, seven years past. She'd been hurt then, wounded by his sudden marriage to Rosalind Chenowyth. Once he and Rosalind had returned to India, physical distance had compounded the emotional estrangement, and Brendan had felt he'd failed miserably in his duties as a guardian and substitute father.

Eventually, Miranda had answered his letters, but she'd still avoided meeting him in Rome three years ago. Worn out by his prolonged bout with the fever, Brendan had rested there briefly on his way to Ischia. He'd written nothing of his illness to his ward, just asked her to come to Italy from her school in Paris. Miranda had begged off, pleading the excuse of upcoming examinations. Her refusal had hurt Brendan deeply.

Brendan shrugged off his past disappointment. Miranda was coming now. After all these long, lonely years, he'd have his little girl back again.

A piercing hoot of the ferry's horn alerted him to its approach. He leaned over the railing and craned his neck for a sight of the passengers, but the sun glinting off the water obscured his vision. He saw only a dark mass of people and an unkempt pile of baggage on the deck. Under the voluble shouts of the crew and the casting of lines, the ferry nosed its scraped and peeling prow alongside the pier. With a loud clunk, the gangway dropped into place and the ferry began to disgorge its passengers.

A noisy, exuberant crowd of Ischians jostled

past him, eager to meet their relatives debarking from the ferry. Brendan lost his vantage point by the railing. By the time he made his way to the ramp leading down to the pier, a lone farmer was leading a string of beige and black goats down the gangway. In the crowd of passengers collecting their baggage on the dock below him, he saw no sign of Miranda.

A young couple stood off to one side, avoiding the hurly-burly of the family reunion taking place on the pier. Dressed in a summery frock of cool green muslin, the girl conversed amiably with a young man in tight black trousers and a form-fitting jacket. Smooth-skinned, with dark, curling hair, the youth smiled, gesturing up to the hills of the town.

Her back to Brendan, the young woman declined with a shake of her head, causing the pink silk poppies on her straw hat to dance a jig. In polite dismissal, she gave the youth her hand. The lad doffed his hat and with a Neapolitan flourish, raised her hand to his lips in regretful farewell.

The young woman looked up at the ramp. Brendan caught a flash of vibrant gold as a thick ringlet slipped over her shoulder. Stunned, he stared at her face: a fine, patrician nose, long elegant throat, and that delicate English skin so reminiscent of Sarah's.

"Randie-bai?"

He started down the ramp at a dead run.

She caught sight of him, and the easy smile on her lips froze. In an unconscious gesture, her hand rose to the open throat of her stylish gown. Then her eyes lit with a dancing fire as she gathered skirts in hand and dashed to the bottom of the ramp.

165

Catherine Kohman

"Brendan-ji!"

Without hesitation, she threw herself into his waiting arms, to the delight of curious onlookers. Oblivious to anyone but Miranda, he hugged her fiercely to his chest, which expanded painfully. "Randie, I didn't recognize you at first. You're so tall, so beautiful, so . . . grown up."

She tilted her head back to look up at him, her wide-set green eyes sparkling with moisture. "Ah, Brendan-ji, did you think you'd find that forlorn girl of fourteen waiting here on the pier?" Miranda smiled, a lost, wistful smile. "I've had seven long years to grow up."

"Piara, why did you stay away so long?" He stroked her blond curls, feeling a strange, warm peace blossoming within him.

She said nothing, just reached up and gently smoothed back an errant lock of hair from his forehead. For a long moment, she studied his face, as if she were memorizing each character line and crease. Finally, she dropped her hand. "I wanted to complete my education. You had no need of me until I did."

Brendan's grip on her shoulders tightened involuntarily. "No need of you? How can you think that, after our years together in India? Poppet . . ."

Miranda winced. "Please don't call me that anymore." A raw note of pain distorted her clear English voice. "As you can see, I'm not a little girl to be dandled on your knee or bought off with sweetmeats and presents."

Startled, he dropped his hands from her shoulders, and she stepped back, opening some distance between them.

"Please forgive me, Miranda. How foolish of

166

me. I wasn't thinking. . . . "

Regaining her composure, she smiled evenly. "No, I'm sorry for being so churlish. It must be something of a shock for you to see me this way— like Athena, springing fully grown from Zeus's forehead." She paused. "Where's Rosalind?"

"Back at the villa," he said with fond exasperation. "My wife is beside herself. 'What does Miranda eat; will she like the view,' and so forth. She's managed to make herself sick with worry."

"I'm sorry that she's been upset on my account." Miranda touched his arm, and he covered her hand with his. "Are you sure that it's a good idea that I come to live with you? I can easily find a home with friends in Paris."

Brendan felt a stab of dismay. "What? Let that fine classical education of yours go to waste? Nonsense, pop—er, Miranda. You and I are going to work together. Wait until you hear the plans I've made for this trip."

He motioned for the porter to bring her luggage. Tucking her arm in his, he led her up the ramp toward his carriage.

Miranda hesitated at the top. "You're sure that I won't be intruding?"

"Not a chance. I've been waiting for you to come home for seven years, Randie." He squeezed her hand. "From now on, we'll be together . . . a true family again."

Miranda's lips curved, and a sudden warmth glowed in her emerald eyes. "Ah, Brendan-ji . . . you always could make me smile."

Brendan had thought of Miranda as a winsome child, but he'd never expected to find such a stunning beauty on the flagstone terrace of his villa.

167

Catherine Kohman

She stood there now, a slim shape of gilded lavender, silhouetted against the rose-pink of the setting sun.

As he poured the last of their white dinner wine, he studied her in fond tenderness. *Oh, Tony,* he thought, *if you only could see the striking young woman your little girl has become.* Brendan made a silent toast to the spirit of Miranda's father. *Here's to you, dear friend.*

The girl was a treasure: extremely bright, gifted with a ready wit and warm heart, and matchless, ethereal beauty. Brendan sighed with guilty pleasure. He'd have a difficult time keeping the young men at bay. Glad that they'd soon be leaving for the Middle East, he thought Miranda too young to marry.

The threat of her eventual marriage clouded Brendan's sunny horizon. He'd only just gotten his Randie back; he didn't want some callow youth to snatch her away again.

Carrying the wine glasses, he made his way across the terrace to the low wall where Miranda waited. With a small smile of thanks, she grasped the wine goblet by the stem and took a sip.

"Is Rosalind feeling any better?" she asked, turning once again to face the sea.

"No, it's one of her sick headaches, I'm afraid. She should be over it by morning. Rosalind is so anxious to meet you."

"Who is that rather terrifying man looking after her? He seemed none too pleased to find me in residence here."

"Biju Kapoor. He's Rosalind's servant, an old family retainer. Don't let that fearsome appearance and insolent demeanor trouble you. That terrible scar down his face is from a *tulwar*. He got it while saving her life at Meerut, and has been with her ever since."

Miranda glanced back at Brendan, her face a mask of perfect composure. "She must be a fine woman, to inspire such devotion."

"Yes, she is," he replied simply.

With a soft smile, she looked down and touched the shining opal and emerald ring on her left hand. "Thank you again for this beautiful birthday present. You have the remarkable gift to know exactly what will please me, from this ring all the way back to the first present I ever remember receiving from you . . . my lost golden locket."

Brendan smiled down at her. "I remember that too . . . and how furious you were with me on the way to Allahabad when I refused to let you go back to Lucknow to look for it. You would have taken on the mutineers single-handedly if I'd let you. What a brave, impetuous disposition you had for a little girl—still have, I'll warrant. That's why I chose a fire opal for the centerpiece of your ring, to match your fiery nature."

Miranda laughed self-consciously. "You make me sound like some fearsome Amazon, or avenging harpy."

Brendan took her hand in his and raised it to his lips, kissing the delicate knuckle above the ring. "Never, Randie. I know you too well to think that. Like your dear mother, you've a fine, gentle soul, but you've also got your father's courageous spirit." He winked then. "Woe to whoever tries to come between you and yours."

Blushing, Miranda sipped her wine in silence. When she finished the last of it, she set the glass down on the wall beside her. "Why didn't you tell me that you'd been ill?"

169

"I didn't want to trouble you. You were busy with your studies at the Sorbonne at the time." He answered evenly, draining his wine while he smothered his hurt at her past rejection.

In the twilight, her eyes held inky shadows in their green depths. "If I'd known how serious it was, I would have come at once. Nothing would have kept me away."

Though pleased by her declaration, at the same time he was annoyed that she'd think him so old and frail that a mere fever would endanger him. He set his wine glass aside. "How did you find out?"

"Elena, the cook. I spoke with her while you were in with Rosalind. She claims full credit for your recovery."

Brendan laughed. "So she would."

Miranda's chin lifted as she gazed out to sea again. "I'd have never forgiven myself if something had happened to you while I was being so stubborn and silly."

"Randie-*bai*, it was nothing. . . . " He stopped, noting the quiver of her slender shoulders beneath the ruffles of her lavender gown. "Please, don't cry. . . . "

With a flurry of rustling silk, she threw her arms around his neck and buried her face against the soft cambric of his shirt. An anguished sob escaped her.

In spite of his concern, Brendan was secretly delighted. The tall cool beauty of the twilight had melted into someone dearer and more familiar, his darling poppet. His own Randie-bai.

"There, there, *piara*." He gently encircled her in his arms. "I'm fine now. No need for your tears."

Miranda raised her head from his chest, and

dashed the tears from her eyes with the back of her hand.

"Forgive me," she said, "for I have been a spoiled, heartsick child all this time. Because I had you to myself those years in India, I couldn't bear the idea of sharing you with Rosalind. I tried to punish you by staying away. It was wrong and cruel of me; I see that now."

Brendan felt tears prick his eyes, so he closed them. He drew her closer and pressed a soft kiss to her temple, regret lancing through him . . . regret that his marriage had so wounded her. If he'd only known back then the heartache that lay in store for both of them, he'd have never married . . . no, to think that way invited disaster.

"Miranda, I'm sorry that I made you suffer so." Opening his eyes, he placed his hands on either side of her face and tilted it toward him. "Our past hurts don't matter anymore. We need to forgive ourselves for the pain we've caused each other. Then we can laugh and simply enjoy being together again."

She stood pale and mute under his touch, the torment still visible in her lotus eyes. His throat ached as he watched her, feeling that her happiness meant everything to him. "Please, Randie . . ."

Miranda nodded slowly, and the intense pain in her eyes became subdued.

"That's my brave girl." Delighted, he placed a chaste kiss on her alabaster cheek. "Sweetheart, how I've missed you . . ."

Smiling, he ruffled the curls behind her ear. Then, buoyed up by a mercurial shift in mood, he gathered their glasses in one large palm. "I'll go

171

get the maps I've gathered for the trip. Wait until you see the itinerary."

He moved off toward the villa, whistling.

Miranda watched him go in rapt silence, then faced the sinking sun. Her hand lightly touched the spot where he'd kissed her cheek.

From a darkened window of the villa came the secretive whisper of silk and the cloying, sweet odor of violets.

"Miranda, would you mind going down to my cabin and asking Biju to brew me a cup of his headache medicine?"

Rosalind Tyrell looked up from her deck chair on the liner *Maid of Cathay*. She shaded her face from the bright sun with her lace parasol and waited for Miranda Seton to respond to her call.

With the briefest of sight, Miranda closed up her sketchbook and walked over from the rail of the ship. She set the sketch pad on the empty chair next to Brendan's wife.

"Is there anything else that you'd like me to bring you?" Miranda's voice was gentle, yet cheerful as she spoke. Beneath the tight coronet of dark hair, Rosalind's face seemed too pinched and pale for her liking. "One of your novels, or perhaps some fruit from the kitchen? You didn't eat much at luncheon."

Without realizing it, Miranda took an almost maternal care of Brendan's wife. By habit, she pulled the traveler's rug back up over Rosalind's lap.

"One of those Mandarin oranges would be nice, Miranda dear. And my Sophie LaPhonse?" At the mention of her wicked addiction to French melodrama, she gave Miranda a conspiratorial smile.

172

"If you promise to walk around the deck this afternoon with your husband." Miranda smiled, pleased by Rosalind's interest in something besides the poor state of her health.

"Miranda . . ."

"Yes?" With uneasiness, she noted a queer excitement seep into the older woman's tawny eyes. Rosalind's moods changed as often as the weather . . . from dull torpor to frantic gaiety. As Brendan also did, Miranda tried to keep her from bouncing from one extreme to the other.

Rosalind fussed with the lace at her cuff. "I've asked Lieutenant Egerton to join us for dinner tonight. Wear something pretty, will you? Your aquamarine, perhaps? It goes so well with your lovely eyes."

"I'm sure the lieutenant will be bored to blazes with my company at dinner," she said, faintly annoyed with Rosalind's presumption. "I hope Brendan will take pity on me and entertain him."

"He is quite handsome, isn't he?" Rosalind leaned forward in her chair, two spots of pink flushing her cheeks. "That rich chestnut hair, bright blue eyes and manly form. Come, child, you must have noticed."

Miranda had noticed, of course, but she didn't want to encourage Brendan's wife in her shameless matchmaking. "Rosalind, please . . ."

"Well, I've seen him watching you, and a sorrier case of lovesickness I've never witnessed. He's totally besotted, my dear. If you don't have a ring on your finger by the time we're in sight of the Peak, you're a silly fool."

Though Miranda found Justin Egerton to be extremely attractive and personable, she resented Rosalind's determined interference. "Lieutenant

173

Egerton is posted to the colony at Hong Kong. We won't be staying there long."

Rosalind looked up at her slyly. "We can, if you have a mind to."

"I hope you're not planning on having a relapse," Miranda said with a small frown. "Rosalind, you can't . . . you know how your health worries Brendan. He'd be forced either to cancel the rest of his trip or to leave you behind, and you know it would break his heart to do either."

Guiltily, Rosalind patted Miranda's hand. "I'm sorry for being such a burden for the two of you. You'd travel so much faster without me."

Past her moment of irritation, Miranda said gently, "We wouldn't want to. I'll go fetch your 'forbidden fruit' now." She began to walk away.

"Don't forget to lay out your aquamarine. . . . "

With an exasperated wave of her hand, Miranda sighed in chagrin as she headed for the Tyrells' stateroom. Tonight in the dining saloon, she'd feel like a prized heifer on display in her aquamarine finery.

Briefly, she wondered what Brendan thought of his wife's matchmaking. How would he feel if she encouraged this handsome, ardent young officer? Perhaps tonight she'd begin a harmless little experiment to find out. . . .

From atop Victoria Peak, Miranda surveyed the sapphire expanse of Hong Kong's harbor, cradled by a towering ridge of jade-green peaks. The harbor was dotted with tall-masted British clippers and a few gleaming white steamships. In between the anchored ships, bright-sailed Chinese junks darted back and forth, ferrying goods and passengers to Kowloon and Macao.

Below, the city arched up from the substantial brick trading houses along the bustling waterfront streets to the muddy lanes and white bungalows, which topped the crests of the lower hills.

She turned from the view to face her companion, a tall young man in a royal blue uniform. "Thank you for bringing me up here again, Justin. It's marvelous, a sight I'll never forget."

Lieutenant Justin Egerton smiled at her, his vivid blue eyes fixed on her face. "Why let memory serve when you can have the real thing?"

Picking at the lacy sleeve of her pink and green muslin gown, Miranda answered him lightly. "I believe you're teasing me again. You know I can't stay in Hong Kong—the Tyrells and I leave for Bali in three days' time."

"Miranda . . ."

He took hold of her shoulders and turned her to face him, his expression grave. "Every time I try to bring up the prospect of a future with me, you shy away. If I weren't sure that I hold a place of affection in your heart, I'd leave it alone. You do care for me, don't you?"

Miranda looked up. For the first time in their acquaintance, she let herself truly see Justin Egerton as a man, not just a charming foil. He had fine, intelligent eyes, a strong nose and a kind mouth always ready to lift in humor. In addition to his significant physical attributes, he possessed a warm, giving nature as well as a quick mind.

Over the course of their visit to Hong Kong, he'd inveigled his way into her heart without her realizing it.

"Yes, of course," she said softly. "I care very much."

Justin curled his arms around her back and

175

shoulders, drawing her close. "Miranda, I love you." His lips grazed her temple. "Marry me, sweetheart."

Before she could answer, Justin's mouth came down on hers, a thrilling pressure that tickled something hot and giddy inside her. He loosened the ribbons of her bonnet, which dropped down her back, and slipped his hand through her long curls, cradling her head in his large palm.

Miranda closed her eyes, enjoying the way his mouth teased hers, firm then softly tender. Hardly her first kiss, it was the first to deeply affect her. Perhaps she *did* love him after all.

Warm, fervent, his roving lips coaxed a matching response from her. Of their own volition, her hands crept up his chest and slid around the collar of his uniform jacket. His other hand dropped to her waist, pulling her hard against him.

He whispered against her cheek, "Miranda, love, please say yes."

Breathless, she leaned into him. Her questing fingers reached his nape and slid upward to his silky, chestnut hair. A curious sense of wrongness invaded her intoxicated mind. His hair was neatly trimmed in its military cut, not the shaggy, raven curls that she yearned to twine her fingers through.

With a moan of pain, Miranda opened her eyes to stare up into Justin's startled face. Troubled blue eyes met hers, not the fiery black eyes she wanted to gaze at her with love.

With shaking hands, she pushed Justin away. "I can't."

He raised an arm to pull her back, then dropped it. "Miranda, what's wrong? Did I hurt you?"

Mutely, she shook her head no.

176

The Beckoning Ghost

He reached out to smooth her disheveled curls. "I didn't mean to—overwhelm you, sweetheart. I love you so much, and when you kissed me back, I thought you wanted me too."

She took a deep breath, hating herself for what she was about to do.

"I'm sorry, Justin. It was wrong of me to let you think that. Please believe me when I tell you that I do care for you—I just can't marry you."

The pain in his eyes grieved her. Inwardly, she cursed herself for the hurt she was causing him, for the hurt that she knew lay in wait for herself. What a fool she was, to love a man who would never truly belong to her.

With wounded dignity, Justin straightened his skewed collar and looked out toward the sea. He asked quietly, "Do you love someone else?"

Miranda longed to tell him her true feelings, but the serenity of too many lives lay at risk if she did. "No . . . it's not that."

She searched for a form of the truth that would ease his pain. Above all, he deserved some crumb of honesty.

"You've already seen much of the world in the service of your country," she said. "This trip with the Tyrells may be the only chance I'll ever have to travel this far, to see so many strange and exotic places." She let her enthusiasm light up her face. "Brendan is a wonderful traveling companion; I've learned so much from him. More than I ever would from dry, dusty books at the University."

She glanced down at her hands, twisting the opal and emerald ring that Brendan had given her for her birthday. "Besides that, the Tyrells need me. I couldn't abandon them halfway around the world."

"I'm sure you couldn't."

At the edge to his tone, Miranda looked up at Justin. A stormy frown creased his usually clear brow. He'd always been so gentle with her; this change of mood confused her.

He spoke again, his voice husky with suppressed emotion. "Tell me, please, Miranda . . . is it the Major or Mrs. Tyrell that you're so loathe to leave? After all, Mrs. Tyrell has her faithful Biju. What are you to Major Tyrell that he'd find you so . . . indispensable?"

Shocked at the hurt anger in his voice, she couldn't answer, but gazed at him in stunned panic. Had she been so obvious?

To buy time, Miranda pulled up her paisley shawl, which had slipped below her waist, and knotted it carefully. "He—he's the only family I have left."

A muscle twitched along Justin's clean-shaven jaw. "Yet after his marriage, you stayed away at school for seven years without seeing him. I'd hardly say that you've been a close family."

A sharp gust of the mountain wind whipped her hair across her face, stinging it and making her eyes tear. "He's been my guardian since I was eight years old—"

The jealous anger in Justin's face shifted to agitation. "Miranda, don't you see that it's impossible? I've watched you closely, hoping that what I saw between you and Brendan was natural given your relationship as ward and guardian. I see now how deluded I was."

In frustration, he ran his hand through his hair, leaving it to blow in silken disarray. "He doesn't know that you love him, does he?"

"No." She cast her eyes downward, ashamed

178

and frightened at the same time. Now that he'd guessed her terrible secret, what would Justin do?

"And you don't intend to tell him?"

She met his gaze levelly this time. "I can't, not while he's married to Rosalind."

He said, "I know that there are tensions in their marriage, but I don't think that Major Tyrell is the sort to divorce his wife on a whim. She's obviously fragile, and devoted to him."

Miranda winced to think that she'd be a mere "whim" to Brendan. "I don't want to hurt anyone; I just want to be at his side. He does need me. Rosalind . . . she doesn't understand him the way I do, even though they're married."

His face pained and sympathetic at the same time, Justin warned, "You're the one who will be hurt, Miranda. This love you bear will only bring you grief and sorrow."

"It may," she said quietly. "But I cannot choose where I love."

He grasped her shoulders gently. "You can choose whether you follow. If you stay here in Hong Kong, I'll love you so well that you'll forget all about Brendan Tyrell."

Miranda reached up and touched his cheek. "You're making this so hard." She paused. "You've served in India. Do you believe in *karma*, Justin?"

He frowned while stroking the soft Kashmiri wool over her shoulders. "I believe that we are all masters of our own fate."

She laughed, her smile bittersweet. "So manly, so staunchly British." Then she sighed. "I grew up among the hills of India, and I think of it as my true home. Not England, where all I have is a family graveyard full of mossy tombstones. I do be-

179

lieve in *karma,* and that it is *my karma* to be with Brendan."

With a light caress, she smoothed his unkempt hair. "So you see, my dear Justin, I don't have a choice. I must be with him, no matter what hurt it causes me."

Roughly, he pulled her into his arms and hugged her to his chest. He spoke into the wind-ruffled curls at the top of her head. "When you decide it's too painful to stay with them—and I know you will one day—remember that I love you, that I'll be waiting for you, no matter where on this earth you travel."

Miranda curled her fingers into the open lapel of his jacket. Though she loved Brendan, she hated to lose Justin's friendship. "I'll remember."

When he heard the lieutenant's carriage drive up to the house, Brendan suddenly recalled that he'd left his notebook on the dining room table. He casually strolled into the foyer as Lieutenant Egerton escorted Miranda inside, a proprietary hand at her elbow.

Damn if the lad didn't look smart in his uniform . . . disturbingly young and virile, and only six years older than Miranda. Thank God they'd all depart Hong Kong in a few days, leaving the bothersome officer adrift in their wake. Otherwise, he'd have serious qualms about letting her spend so much time alone with the young Englishman.

Her attention fixed on Egerton, Miranda took no notice of Brendan, but the young man saw him lurking in the hallway.

With a curious flash in his eyes (surely it wasn't annoyance) the lieutenant said, "Good evening, sir."

"Lieutenant," Brendan replied with a curt nod.

At the sound of their cool exchange, Miranda turned sharply. In a face pale as a mask, her dark green eyes looked huge with despair. Unthinking, Brendan took a step toward her.

To his amazement, she shrank from him. In obvious distress, she grabbed her skirts and dashed up the steps, fleeing to her room.

Brendan stood rooted to the marble tiles of the foyer, staring up the empty staircase. "What the hell . . ."

Then he turned on the junior officer, eyes narrowed in menacing speculation. "Young man, I've seen Randie this agitated only on one other occasion. If you've done anything to upset her . . ."

"Sir," Justin Egerton said brusquely, "what I did to upset her . . . was ask her to marry me." He stood on a level with Brendan, his carriage stiff and erect, but in his flinty gaze again flared that uncharacteristic insolence.

Taken aback by the young man's words and aggressive manner, Brendan gaped at him. The event he'd dreaded ever since Randie came back to live with him loomed before him. Feeling as if the lieutenant had run his saber through him, he said sotto voce, "I take it that she accepted. Is she upset because she's staying behind in Hong Kong instead of leaving with us?"

In a flash, Egerton's face became haunted, and the implicit threat in his bearing dissolved. "No, sir. She turned me down. She said she'd rather be with her—her family."

In his utter relief, Brendan forgave the lieutenant for his insubordinate behavior. Magnanimous in victory, he even felt sympathy for the young officer. Losing a treasure like Miranda would be

181

hard for any man to bear.

Brendan smiled apologetically. "She's still very young."

Egerton's chin came up and he met Brendan's gaze evenly. "I know. I've asked her to reconsider my proposal after you've finished your trip around the world."

Straining to retain his smile, Brendan asked, "And will she?"

This time, the lieutenant could afford to be magnanimous. With a sure smile of his own, Egerton answered, "She said she would be honored to."

Brendan felt searing pain as the sword twisted in the wound.

The lieutenant turned to go, saying affably, "Please tell Mrs. Tyrell good-bye for me. I wish you all a safe and *speedy* voyage."

Lieutenant Egerton paused, his hand on the door knob. "And tell Miranda I said: *'Au revoir, ma bien-aimée.'*"

Chapter Eleven

My heart, which by a secret harmony
Still moves with thine, join'd in connection sweet.
—John Milton

Mrs. Beatrice Copeland sounded warm and enthusiastic when Marissa called her. Yes, she still
had the trunk with Miranda Seton's papers. No,
she hadn't looked at it for many years, so she
didn't remember all that was in it. Of course, she'd
be delighted if Marissa came out to look at it. She
said it was time that someone showed interest in
Miranda.

Marissa booked an early flight out, then called
Kelsey to ask her to look after the cats. It was
around ten o'clock the next morning when Marissa reached her car in the rental parking lot at
the San Francisco airport. She swung her over-
nighter into the trunk of the Galant.

183

Opening the driver's door, she slid inside the car. In the passenger's seat sat Brendan, a small smile on his tanned face. The way his thin ivory cotton turtleneck stretched over his rugged shoulders and chest, he looked for all the world like a lean, fit executive ready to play hooky.

"Have a nice flight?" he asked politely, examining the crease in his beige trousers.

"Yes," she said, the picture of nonchalance as she put on her seat belt. "Did you?"

He turned to look at her. "As a matter of fact, I did." Eyeing her celadon designer suit with pleasure, he said, "That color looks lovely on you."

"Thank you." Marissa blushed. "Ah, Brendan . . . I have to drive the car, so please try not to distract me."

"Don't trouble yourself, my dear. I'm just here to enjoy the motorcar ride and the California scenery. We are taking the coast road, aren't we?"

Great, she thought, *a ghost who wants to play tourist*. She pulled out of the parking space, toward the busy expressway and the coast highway to Monterey.

As she drove the Galant along the winding curves of Highway One, Marissa relaxed. When he didn't brazenly flirt with her, Brendan proved good company. His conversation was witty, his questions were perceptive, and she experienced firsthand the avid intelligence that made him a traveler, not a tourist, as she'd sniped before.

Below the highway, the ocean rushed to the beaches in long, foamy white rollers, or fountains of spray where the coastline grew more rugged. Enjoying the spectacle, Marissa had a thought.

"Where are you, when you're not with me?

Floating around somewhere in the ozone?"

He snorted with disgust. "Hardly."

"Come on, Brendan—I know nothing about the ghostly life. What is it like?"

After a long-suffering sigh, he began. "It's hard to explain. I feel like I did when I was a living man—I have the same emotions, needs and desires." He glanced at her sideways, with a hint of a smile. "When I'm not with you, you could say that I'm resting. It's an unconscious state rather like sleep."

A distant look came into his eyes as he restlessly drummed his fingers on his thigh. "This sleep does have some strange qualities, like unusually vivid dreams. And at times I have this strong sense of another layer of consciousness, one that I haven't been able to break through to. It's rather frustrating . . . I feel like I'm living two lives, this one and a phantom one."

Marissa smiled. "I'd say that *this* is probably the phantom life, wouldn't you?"

He laughed gently. "I suppose you're right."

"But how do you appear and disappear?"

The drumming fingers paused. "It's a mental process: I simply wish to be wherever you are."

Noting the huskiness in his voice, Marissa shot a quick look at him. His face composed, he stared out the window at the breakers surging against the rocky stacks. Afraid to take her eyes off the road for long, she turned back to watch the winding highway. Perhaps she just imagined the naked emotion in his voice. Wishful thinking . . .

Then Brendan sat upright in his seat. "Didn't you say that your . . . um, former paramour, Robin Stuart, lived here in California? We aren't going to meet him, are we?"

185

"No, I don't think so. He's down at UCLA—Los Angeles. I don't think we'll run into him up here."

He relaxed back against the seat. "Good."

In a fit of deviltry, Marissa decided to provoke him. "Of course, I *should* call him since I'm in California. He'll be hurt if I don't. I'm sure he'd drive up to Monterey just to see me."

Brendan scowled. "I don't think that's a very good idea. We're here to see Mrs. Copeland. This—this Robin fellow would simply distract you."

Inordinately pleased at her petty attempt to make him jealous, Marissa smiled secretly. Let him be off balance for once.

"We don't know if Mrs. Copeland can see you. Why don't you stay somewhere nearby until she shows me the trunk?"

Brendan looked affronted. "You want me to lurk about in corners?"

Marissa smiled pleasantly at him. "Something like that."

She glanced at the address on the pad in front of her. The drive must be just up ahead, through that grove of cypress. Apparently Mrs. Copeland was a wealthy woman; all the neighboring homes were huge and had prime ocean frontage.

"Here it is." She turned the car into a long drive made of gray cobblestone pavers. Curving through the cypresses and down the hill toward the sea, the drive ended before a house that gave you an impression of a French cottage, until you realized the size of it. In front of the house lay an informal rose garden with a small marble fountain bubbling in it.

"Absolutely charming," Brendan said. "This

woman evidently has a discerning eye. In America, it seems that money and good taste so seldom go hand in hand."

"What a chauvinistic thing to say!" Marissa sniffed angrily. "As if Europeans had the market cornered on taste. Brendan, I'm surprised at you."

"I'm sorry," he said with an unrepentant smile. "I don't know what possessed me to make such an unfortunate remark. I'll make myself scarce, shall I?"

Marissa carefully parked the car beside the four-car garage. "Yes, please do—"

Brendan was already gone.

"Miss Erickson, such a pleasure to meet you."

Marissa took the soft proffered hand of her hostess. "Thank you for inviting me into your lovely home, Mrs. Copeland. Especially on such short notice."

A handsome woman with a trim figure, Beatrice Copeland hardly looked her age, which must have been in the sixties. Her white hair gently framed her face, and her soft blue eyes rested on Marissa with kindly interest.

"Tell me a bit more about this project of yours," Mrs. Copeland said.

Over a cup of hot, sweet English tea, Marissa explained about her biography of Brendan Tyrell, and why she was also concerned with Miranda Seton. She briefly ran down the list of her credentials, and gave her hostess a copy of her book on Jaipur.

"Did you know Miranda, Mrs. Copeland?"

"I did, though not very well. I was very young, and she was an old woman by the time she returned to England, after her husband's death.

187

Though sharp-witted, she had a gentle soul; everyone in the family loved her."

Beatrice Copeland's blue eyes clouded with memory. "I always thought she wore a faint air of tragedy about her. My mother said that I was dreaming up romantic nonsense about Aunt Miranda. She'd lost her only son in the First World War, you see. Mother said that if Miranda at times withdrew into herself, it was because of that. I disagreed."

Then the older woman smiled. "Of course, I was sixteen and wildly romantic at the time." Over the rim of her teacup, she scrutinized Marissa. "Please pardon my staring, Miss Erickson, but I keep thinking that you look familiar. It isn't likely that we've met somewhere before, is it?"

"I don't think so, Mrs. Copeland." She smiled. "I'm sure I would remember you if we had."

Beatrice Copeland said finally, "Well, I suppose you're anxious to see Miranda's things. I had my gardener bring the trunk down from the attic and put it the library."

With a surge of excitement, Marissa followed her down the thickly carpeted hall. The older woman opened the library and led Marissa into a spacious room with honey-colored oak bookshelves lining the walls. A matching desk and chair stood in one corner of the room, while a deeply cushioned leather sofa faced the fireplace. By a large window overlooking the English country garden stood a winged armchair, covered in a rich tapestry print.

Near the chair, a large teak chest stood on the Bokkhara carpet. Carved in an Indian fashion, the top was inlaid with mother-of-pearl initials: M.E. Marissa had seen similar pieces in India, but this one served as a fine example of the craft. She itched to dig inside the chest.

"Well, I'll leave you to your task," Beatrice said. "I'd like to know if you find anything of interest." She smiled again, and went out the door, closing it behind her.

When Marissa turned back to face the chest, she saw Brendan sitting in the armchair, his legs casually crossed at the knee.

He raised a raven brow in inquiry. "Well?"

Marissa grinned at him, heady excitement coursing through her. She dropped to her knees on the thick Oriental carpet and ran her hands lovingly over the intricate carvings on the top of the chest. She raised the lid, which slid open smoothly. A faint scent like gardenias and Oriental incense wafted up into the air.

Unconsciously holding her breath, she looked inside.

If she'd expected a jumbled heap of Miranda Seton's personal treasures to spill out of the opened trunk like a pirate's chest, Marissa would have been disappointed. Inside the fragrant chest lay carefully wrapped bundles in white and blue tissue, stacked in neat order.

Marissa glanced up at Brendan, wondering what she should open first. He simply shrugged.

Methodically, she started on the top layer, with its variety of mementoes: a pair of lace gloves, a carved ivory fan, a scrapbook of family photos. The next layer contained more personal items. Tied with a violet ribbon was a bundle of letters from Miranda's son Tony, postmarked from the north of France. Tragically, the last one had a date of July 1917. In the same bundle with the letters

189

was a photograph of a handsome young man in an Army uniform, and a medal for valor.

Blinking back a rush of tears, she studied Tony Egerton's face. "Poor Miranda," she said, "to lose her only child must have almost killed her."

With a look of concern, Brendan took the bundle from her hands and examined it, then set it aside. Marissa brushed away her tears and reached for another package.

This one contained letters from Miranda's husband Justin. The ivory envelopes showed his clear, forthright hand. Since most of the letters dated from before their marriage, Marissa was surprised at the thickness of the bundle. She slid an oversized envelope out of the middle of the stack and opened it. Inside was a pink and white Victorian Valentine with lace cutouts and chubby cherubs. Marissa smiled at its sweet, unabashed sentimentality.

With a growl of impatience, Brendan said, "You don't intend to read all those now?"

Dropping back on her heels, she blinked at him in surprise. "No, but I would like to later." A ray of understanding hit her. "I see . . . I should get to the important stuff at the bottom—the stuff that concerns *you*."

This time, Brendan blinked. "That's not what I meant."

Marissa waved away his protest as she put aside Justin's letters. "Sure, sure. Try to weasel out of that one."

He smiled sheepishly. "I am only human. . . . "

Marissa opened her mouth to dispute that, but she did want to see what else the chest held. Two cream paisley shawls of Kashmiri wool made up the following layer; their silky softness under her fingers amazed her.

Marissa lifted the next object, a hard and bulky one, and set it in her lap to unwrap it. The opened tissue revealed a Kashmiri lacquered box, a black background scrolled with an intricate painting of green foliage and pink and white blossoms. The pattern seemed so familiar to her. . . .

Then she remembered that the families who painted the boxes passed down their designs from generation to generation. She'd probably seen a descendant of this very box in Srinagar. As she lifted the lid, the whirring purr of a Swiss musical movement startled her. The opening notes of *Chanson de Shalott* spilled into the air.

As the bell-like tones of the song filled the quiet library, Marissa felt a cold shiver run up her spine. Her own favorite music box played the same song. Confused, she looked up at Brendan to find him watching her with falcon-like intensity.

He leaned forward. "I had that music box made for Miranda's sixteenth birthday. *Chanson de Shalott* was her favorite song."

Strangely moved by the tinkling music, Marissa listened to the melody. But the more she thought about the coincidence, the more disturbed she became, and she started to close the box.

Brendan spoke up. "There's a compartment inside. Miranda used to keep her smaller treasures in there."

Gingerly, Marissa felt the rose silk lining of the box and found that one side had a false bottom. With her fingernails, she pried off the silk covering. Inside the compartment was a packet of letters in Brendan's hand, and a small green satin pouch.

191

She lifted out the letters with a crow of delight. "Oh, Brendan—your letters! I can hardly wait to read them!"

Bracing his elbow on the arm of the chair, he rested his chin on his palm. A soft smile of indulgence curved his mouth. "Most of them were written to Randie at school, but you might find them interesting."

"Of course I will!" She lovingly traced her finger over the top envelope.

"Aren't you forgetting something?" He motioned to the small satin pouch.

"Oh . . ." It looked like a jeweler's bag, and it felt suitably heavy. She loosened the drawstring and dumped the contents into her hand. On her palm lay a large emerald set in gold filigree; inlaid into the center of the emerald, a heart-shaped fire opal sparkled.

Unable to resist it, Marissa slid the jewel onto her ring finger. It fit perfectly. The opal caught a ray of sunlight and blazed with liquid fire: green and blue, then purple and orange. A thought flashed through her mind: *This is mine.*

The certainty of that thought bothered Marissa.

To cover her dismay, she asked, "Another birthday gift from you?"

"The twenty-first. I—"

"—had it made in Jaipur," she finished for him.

He sat forward, all eagerness. "So you remember. . . ."

Marissa stared at her finger, watching the glimmering play of sunlight across the jewel. "Of course. Have you forgotten I wrote that book on Jaipur? The jewelry makers of the city are noted for these delicate inlays of precious stones."

"What else is in the chest?" he said abruptly.

The Beckoning Ghost

Once more she raised her glance to his in surprise. From the surly slant of his brows, she'd judge his mood to be one of annoyance, not the fond remembrance he'd shown a minute ago.

Marissa moved the music box and Brendan's letters to the side. She removed a small stack of the *Boston Gazette* from the chest. Out of the top copy fell a letter from the editor of the magazine, addressed to Miranda Seton.

As she scanned the contents of the letter, Marissa exclaimed, "Miranda wrote under the name of Mallory Summers! I read these articles when I was at Harvard!"

Glancing up at Brendan's bland expression, she said, "You knew, yet you never told me!" She blew her breath out in a huff, lifting her blond bangs from her forehead. "What else have you neglected to tell me, Brendan?"

Marissa grabbed the next package. As she somewhat hastily unwrapped it, a silver picture frame fell into her lap facedown. She ignored it, all her attention focused on the familiar blue leather volume in her hand. With shaking fingers, she lifted the cover to see what it held.

Inside the cover a Christmas wish from Brendan was inscribed. On the title page it said, *Miranda Seton's Journal, 1875.* The opening paragraph began, "Denver, New Year's Day. It was difficult to celebrate the start of the New Year last night. While I am shut up here in Denver, my heart is with Brendan, up in the snowy Rockies. . . . "

An unremarkable beginning to a year which would bring so much tragedy.

But it wasn't the contents of the page that shook Marissa; it was the writing itself. A smooth, fem-

193

inine hand revealing a quickness of mind in the occasional undotted "i" or flying "t" and with words here and there printed for emphasis.

Marissa's own handwriting.

In a hundred-year-old journal that she recognized immediately.

The journal fell onto the carpet with a muffled thud. Marissa's hands dropped to her lap and unconsciously closed on the silver picture frame. Mechanically, she lifted the photograph to set it inside the raised lid of the chest. With blind eyes, she stared at the two people standing in a ferny grotto.

Tall and darkly handsome in his evening clothes, Brendan's photographic image fuzzily registered on her numb mind. Marissa's gaze drifted to the woman standing next to him, with Brendan's arm gently cradling her waist. The elegant lines of the woman's silvery gown drew Marissa's eye upwards.

Totally focused on her own image in the photograph, she heard, rather than saw, Brendan get up from his chair.

Miranda Seton was her identical twin, so alike were their features. Even Miranda's dreamy, happy expression reflected what Marissa saw in her own mirror.

Shaking uncontrollably, she felt Brendan's arms encircle her. The room began to spin crazily.

He whispered hoarsely, "*Piara* . . ."

The light in the room got suddenly brighter, obscuring her vision. Unable to fight the dizziness any longer, Marissa fainted in Brendan's arms.

He laid her gently on the sofa, and cupped her face in his hands. "Randie-*bai* . . ."

The Beckoning Ghost

The rich California light gilded her ashen, pinched face with a false, healthy glow. Smoothing her tousled hair, Brendan tried to call her back from her deep, somnolent trance. "Marissa . . . wake up, sweetheart."

Her pale stillness troubled him sorely. *Damn it, what had he done*—encouraging her to look through Randie's things without warning her about what she'd find there. Selfish—too bloody selfish, that's what he was.

God, but he'd wanted her to remember who she was . . . to remember what they'd shared together in her past life. Though well on their way to forming a happier, less guilt-ridden union in the present, he'd let his impatience overrule his caution. So he'd dared to risk her fragile peace of mind, with Marissa's collapse the frightening consequence.

Damn you, Tyrell, he cursed himself soundly, *for being such an impetuous fool.*

On his knees next to her, he placed his lips against hers, breathing warmth into her cool, pliant mouth. He felt her stir beneath him, and leaned back to see the lids flutter over her misty aquamarine eyes.

Marissa moaned softly, one word.

Shahin.

"Miss Erickson . . . Miss Erickson, are you all right?"

Marissa opened her eyes to see Beatrice Copeland hovering above her. The older woman's blue eyes were anxious, disturbed.

"Mrs. Copeland . . . I'm sorry. . . . " Groggily, Marissa tried to sit up, but Beatrice pushed her back to lie on the leather sofa. *How did I get over*

195

to the sofa? she wondered. Her eyes widened in alarm. Brendan—where was he?

Half the room was blocked from her view, but she didn't see Brendan anywhere. He must have disappeared . . . hopefully before Mrs. Copeland entered the room.

"I came in to see if you wanted another cup of tea, and found you lying on the sofa," the older woman said. "You didn't wake up when I first called your name, so I was worried." She put her hand to Marissa's forehead. "You do feel a trifle warm, my dear. Should I call my doctor?"

"No . . . no need for that." This time, Marissa managed to sit up. Her brain scrambled for a reasonable story for passing out on her hostess's couch. "I—ah, I had a virus a short while back. I guess I'm still not over it completely, because it makes me dizzy sometimes. I must have fainted."

She ran her hands over her face to brush the last of the cobwebs away. "Don't worry, Mrs. Copeland. I'll be fine."

As she dropped her hands into her lap, she noticed that the ring was gone. Then she remembered the photograph. If Mrs. Copeland saw it . . .

Her eyes searched out the chest. It was closed, all the items put back inside of it. Had Brendan done that as well?

Mrs. Copeland leaned over and patted her hand. "I don't think you should go to a hotel, and I have a small guest house out back. Please say that you'll stay the night."

At a loss to come up with an excuse, Marissa smiled weakly. "Thank you. I'd be delighted to stay."

Beatrice got up from the arm of the couch and

196

went to the door. "Did anything in the chest interest you?"

Marissa's voice caught. "Yes," she squeaked, then cleared the obstacle in her throat. "I found it all . . . fascinating. Tomorrow I'll make an inventory for you, and we can go over it together."

Mrs. Copeland gave her a warm smile. "Lovely."

Beatrice insisted that they have dinner together, so Marissa couldn't escape to the privacy of the guest cottage until twilight. Opening the French door, she saw the chest had been moved to the cottage's living room. She gave it a wide berth as she crossed the room to the rear balcony, which overlooked the small beach below the house.

Marissa stood on the balcony and let the pounding rhythm of the surf soothe her agitated soul. As the last of the light faded, the evening sky and indigo sea blurred at the horizon.

Ever since she'd awakened from her faint, she'd tried to push her connection to Miranda Seton out of her mind. With her New Age wisdom, Kelsey would say that Marissa must be the reincarnation of the dead woman. On a deep, emotional level, Marissa felt the same thing.

So much of what had happened to her in the past month would be explained. The feelings of déjà vu, the curious dreams and visions she'd experienced—it all fit with the reincarnation theory. Yet on a more rational level, she found it hard to accept.

Marissa laughed, a laughter slightly hysterical in tone. She had trouble believing in her own reincarnation, but living her life around a ghost was perfectly normal, right?

Sensing she wasn't alone any longer, she stared

out across the rolling surf as Brendan came out onto the balcony.

He said gently, "Marissa . . ."

"Don't you mean 'Randie?'" She wrapped her arms around her waist to keep her rocketing anger from exploding. "So . . . what other nasty little surprises do you have in store for me?"

Marissa felt him stiffen beside her.

His tone rife with tension, he answered, "I'd hardly call being the reincarnation of the finest woman I ever knew a 'nasty surprise.'"

"Why didn't you just tell me?" She turned to glare at him. "Instead, you encouraged me to look through that damnable chest until it leapt out at me like a horrible, grinning jack-in-the-box."

In frustration, he ran his fingers back through his tumbled hair. "You wouldn't have believed me if I simply told you. You had to feel it for yourself." His tone aggrieved, he added, "You and your friend Owen are the ones responsible for the discovery of the chest. On the other hand, I—how would you say it—I merely came along for the ride."

Marissa angrily tossed her hair. "Hah! You were sitting there in the library like some huge, hairy spider, waiting patiently—no, *impatiently*—for your hapless victim to blunder into your web!"

He opened his mouth for a sharp retort, then looked at her blankly. "What?"

Locked into cruise control, Marissa wouldn't let a measly thing like logic stop her now. No way.

"Don't you see? I don't *want* to be your darling little Randie. I am Marissa Christine Erickson, of the late twentieth century. I have a full, exciting life ahead of me. That—that woman in there had nothing but tragedy in her life. I don't want that—

198

I can't stand all that pain—"

"Marissa, please . . . I don't want to hurt you."
He reached out for her, but she flinched away.

"No, don't touch me. From the moment I saw
you, you've been slowly driving me crazy. Ghosts,
reincarnation . . . next it will be UFO's and seeing
Elvis. Why don't you just leave me alone?"

Brendan pulled in his outstretched hands and
tucked them in the pockets of his trousers. "You're
distraught. I'll come back later." He turned to go.

"Why?" she called after him. "So you can ruin
my life the way you did Miranda's?"

From the reflexive jerk of his shoulders, she
knew her barb had struck deeply. Strangely, it
gave her no pleasure. In wounded silence, he
walked into the shadows and disappeared.

Left alone in her misery, Marissa sagged against
the railing. *God, what had she done?*

Chapter Twelve

The phantom, Beauty, in a mist of tears.
—William Butler Yeats

July 1875

With a metallic screech and the hiss of steam, the morning train pulled into the St. Paul and Pacific depot at Wayzata, Minnesota. It disgorged its passengers onto the platform: hamper-laden picnickers, avid fishermen carrying poles and tackle, weekend sailors, and a multitude of summer vacationers.

The crowd broke up. Some went to the hotels on Lake Street, a pair of shimmering white summer palaces. Others headed down the hill to the harbor, where a collection of boats lay at dock. The fleet consisted of mostly sailing vessels, but a few larger steamboats waited to ferry passengers to various points on scenic Lake Minnetonka.

On her way down to the dock, a newsboy handed Miranda a small newspaper extolling the natural beauty and civilized amenities available to the summer visitor. Its proud headline announced, "Welcome to the Saratoga of the West."

At that rather grandiose claim, Miranda smiled. Still, on the knoll below the station, the lake spread out before her, pristine blue and sparkling in the clear northern light. Fueled by a booming trade, the clamor and bustle of new building surrounded her, proving the popularity of the new summer mecca.

She stopped a porter on his way down the hill. "What boat do we take to reach the Arcadia House?"

"You'd want the *May Queen*, miss. She's berthed at the dock directly below here."

Miranda thanked him, and looked up to see Brendan and Rosalind heading down the ramp. Behind them, Biju and a porter carted their luggage.

The Indian's unusual garb and fearsome appearance made him an object of attention. Beneath his white turban, Biju scowled at a nosy blond-haired boy, who dared to stare at him, wide-eyed and open-mouthed. Closing his mouth with a click of teeth, the youngster scampered away. A thin smile creased the Indian's lips. As he saw Miranda watching him, his face became blank, and he gave her the slightest of shrugs.

After years of traveling together, Miranda found Biju to be a troublesome enigma. Despite her Indian upbringing, no matter how she tried to get on with him, he treated her with an almost distasteful reserve. To Brendan, he showed the utmost respect, to Rosalind, devotion. But his behavior toward Miranda always bordered on the edge of insolence. Miranda never understood what she'd done to earn his enmity, so she found herself trying to avoid him whenever possible.

Once they were all aboard the neat little steamer and under way, Miranda made her way to the bow of the ship. She stood at the forward rail, letting the summer wind blow her curls into riotous disorder. After days of being cramped in the train from Denver, the clean wind felt good on her face.

On the way to the port of Excelsior, they passed a few homes with lush, shady lawns, but most of the land was dense forest, broken by a patch of meadow here and there. With all its islands, nooks and sheltered coves, the lake seemed three times larger than its length of seventeen miles.

She smiled. Perhaps the enthusiasm of the local press had justification. An enchanting, water-blessed playground, Lake Minnetonka beckoned to her. She found it a verdant oasis after the dusty, blistering heat of the Plains.

Miranda felt a light touch as a broad hand came to rest at her waist. Brendan stood beside her, dressed comfortably in his light-weight traveling jacket and cotton trousers. His low-brimmed slouch hat shaded the upper half of his face, but when he smiled, she could see his white teeth framed by his black mustache. When they stood close like this, alone with the wind and the water, she could almost forget that he belonged to another.

"Beautiful country, isn't it, Randie? Lush green woods and rippling, sky-blue water. I think Rosalind will find the setting tranquil and relaxing." The fingers of his free hand drummed on the wooden railing. "I have the name of a doctor here who has experience with nervous conditions like my wife's."

Miranda turned back to the water. "The winter we spent alone in Denver was hard on her, Brendan. She missed you, and Denver itself is a rough, boisterous place." She paused. "I think this the perfect place to spend a quiet, restful summer. You'll have time to finish your book on Polynesia."

"What about you, Randie-*bai*?" He glanced at her fondly. "How do you want to spend your summer?"

Her jonquil-yellow skirts billowed in the brisk wind and wrapped around Brendan's legs. With a practiced hand, Miranda gathered them in again. "I have to organize the notes you took over the winter with the Cheyenne. I also have one or two articles to write for the *Boston Gazette*."

Brendan's brows lowered. "I wish you'd let me speak to my publisher about putting your travel articles in book form. I think you should start writing under your own name, instead of Mallory Summers."

"We've discussed this before," she answered. "For the colorful type of articles that I write, readers would be shocked to see a woman's byline. It's just not done." She smiled up at him then. "I know: 'Damn convention.'

203

"It's much easier for you, Brendan, than it would be for me. Even you have suffered at the hands of a poisoned pen or two." She frowned on his behalf, remembering the vitriol in some of the lesser publications.

Brendan tightened his hand on her waist. "Let's forget about all that rubbish and simply enjoy ourselves. By the time we leave here, I want to see blooming roses in *both* my girls' cheeks!"

Arcadia Island seemed a cool, green paradise. Beyond the long white facade of Arcadia House, a few bungalows lay scattered beneath the towering maples. The Tyrells had rented the most spacious bungalow, an open, airy dwelling with three bedrooms and a large front porch that overlooked the lake. Furnished with new walnut tables, beds and dressers, the bungalow welcomed them with fresh rustic charm.

The occupants each fell into their own daily routines. Brendan worked at his desk or went sailing. Miranda spent half of the day writing; the other half she went for a swim or walk in the woods. Rosalind read or did her needlepoint; sometimes she took the *May Queen* over to Wayzata to see Dr. Heffel, or went shopping in Excelsior. Whatever Rosalind did, Biju followed in devoted attendance.

On a bright July afternoon, Rosalind came home from her appointment with Dr. Heffel to find the bungalow empty. Excited to share her news, she looked for Brendan. The doctor had given her a new medicine for her nerves, one to replace the blue bottle of laudanum, which he'd said was bad for her.

She looked down at the dock. No one was there, but the rowboat was gone. With uncharacteristic energy, she decided to walk along the island's shore to see if she could find Brendan. Leaving Biju behind at the bungalow, she followed the narrow trail that skirted the island's edge. Her confining silk skirts and thin shoes bothered her, but she pressed on anyway.

On the far side of the island, she stopped to rest at a rough-hewn bench placed in a small grassy glade near the water's edge. From the water, she heard the sound of mingled voices and laughter. Rising from her seat, she peeked through the bushes.

Just a little way offshore, Brendan rowed the skiff, the sun shining on his glossy black hair. Rosalind frowned slightly when she saw Miranda seated opposite him in the boat. The younger woman looked cool and dainty in her ice-blue cotton. On her shoulder, she rested a furled parasol trimmed with eyelet lace.

Rosalind wiped her handkerchief down her sweaty neck, loosening the collar of her beige silk. Her own skirts were streaked with leaves and dirt from her trek through the woods. Hot, dirty and tired, she felt a sudden spurt of anger because Miranda sat in her place in the boat, gliding serenely across the water.

A reed bed lay between the island and the mainland. Brendan rowed the boat into the channel by the reeds. Then he shipped the oars and they just drifted, coming close to Rosalind's hiding place. The skiff turned in the water, so she could see Miranda clearly, but only Brendan's profile.

"Why did you drag that parasol along if you

205

don't intend to use it?" he scolded Miranda. "You'll get freckles on that prized white skin of yours."

In response, she made a flourish with the furled umbrella and stabbed him lightly in the chest. "I like the sun—it reminds me of India."

"Fine," he said, "turn into a wrinkled old crone then."

Miranda made a vulgar face at him, then opened the parasol, shading her fair face from the afternoon sun. She sighed blissfully. "What a halcyon day."

"Look." He pointed to the reed bed where two stately birds, one white and one silver-gray, prowled the shallows on long thin legs, their vigilant eyes searching the water. "An egret and a great blue heron."

To see them, Miranda dropped the parasol over her shoulder. The flash of white startled the birds, and they rose up into the sky with a harsh squawk.

"Clumsy wench," Brendan muttered affectionately as he watched the birds take to the air with deep, slow wing beats.

As Miranda glanced away from the birds' flight, her gaze came to rest on Brendan's face. Her expression changed from relaxed amusement to painful longing, and her love for Brendan lit her emerald eyes like a shining beacon.

A rush of outraged betrayal closed Rosalind's throat. When Miranda first came to them in Ischia, Rosalind had distrusted her. Since then, she'd kept a watchful eye on the girl, but Miranda had never done anything overt to arouse suspicion. Now Rosalind stood frozen in place, watching with horror as the girl she'd welcomed into her home made sheep's eyes at her husband.

But as Brendan turned back to face Miranda, the girl's expression changed dramatically. When he finally glanced at her again, she'd composed her wretched, pretty face into a look of companionable affection.

So, Rosalind thought cannily, *Miranda has enough sense to hide her true feelings from Brendan*. And rightly so, for Brendan would send her away if he knew of the girl's forbidden love.

Stung by Miranda's betrayal, Rosalind devised a series of mental tortures for her so-called friend and companion, the would-be Jezebel.

Brendan stood on the front porch of the bungalow, the bowl of his pipe glowing in the twilight. Easing the stiff collar of his white shirt away from his neck, he pondered his submission to the discomforts of evening dress. Rosalind wanted to take this moonlight cruise on the lake. If the evening would lift her spirits, he'd do anything to accommodate her wishes.

A small cough behind him alerted Brendan to Biju's presence. "Yes, Biju, what is it?"

The Indian made a sketchy bow, or *namskan*. "*Sa'b*, the *Memsa'b* wishes me to tell you that to the dancing on the boat, she will not be going."

"What?" Brendan tapped out the embers in his pipe and left it on the porch. He strode back to their bedroom. Still in her dressing gown, Rosalind reclined in the room's chaise, her soft white arm drooped across her eyes.

Brendan smothered his impatience and spoke to his wife gently. "Ros, you're not dressed. Biju said that you didn't want to go on the cruise. I can't believe you'd change your mind; I know how much you were looking forward to this."

With a heavy sigh, Rosalind lowered her arm to reveal sherry-colored eyes marred by shadows. "I'm sorry, Brendan. This headache is enough to lay me low for the evening. You go on without me. I'm sure Miranda will be disappointed if you don't go; she seldom gets a chance to be with young men her own age."

"I'm sure Randie will understand—"

"No, Brendan," she said, a sulky edge to her voice. "If you stay home with me, my headache will only get worse. I just want to sleep. Take Miranda on the cruise . . . she *deserves* it."

"Very well," he said. "Don't overexcite yourself. You know what the doctor told you."

"I'll be fine. Go." She draped her arm over her eyes again.

Thus dismissed, Brendan went out to the living room. Miranda waited for him there, a tall, slender vision swathed in silver satin and lace.

"Rosalind?" Her smooth brows lifted anxiously.

"My wife has a headache," he said flatly. "She said to go without her."

"But the cruise was her idea."

"I know." He stuffed his hands into the pockets of his black jacket. "I didn't think it wise to force the issue."

Miranda moved toward the bedrooms. "Perhaps if I spoke to her . . ."

Brendan caught her bare arm. "I don't think so; she was adamant . . . in one of her strange moods again." He sighed. "We'll go, just the two of us."

He picked up her matching lace shawl and

draped it over her shoulders. With a half-smile, he said, "Come along, Randie. You look far too beautiful to spend the evening at home with only a doddering old gent to keep you company."

The full moon hung overhead, so close it seemed that you could reach up and touch it. The light it cast shone on the tranquil waters of the lake, and the pleasure barge *Nokomis* drifted across a sheet of shimmering silver.

The cruise commenced after an elegant dinner of poached fish, pheasant and champagne at the Minnetonka House in Wayzata. On board the *Nokomis*, ices and fresh strawberries were served as dessert, along with more champagne.

A small orchestra played at the rear, and smartly dressed couples moved across the wooden dance floor in swirling, colorful patterns.

Miranda stood beneath a string of bright, festive lanterns and admired the radiant moon. Brendan was on some secretive errand near the front of the barge. In his absence, she stared out at the luminous water, determined to enjoy the night to its fullest.

"Ah, there you are." Brendan came up to stand beside her, one of his hands tucked behind his back.

"And what was all the mystery about?" she asked.

"I thought you needed a proper ornament for your lovely hair." With a courtly flourish, he presented her with a creamy white gardenia.

"Oh, Brendan . . . how exquisite." Miranda inhaled the flower's sweet, heavy perfume. "Wherever did you find it?"

"There's a bonnie Scotch lassie selling flowers up behind the champagne table. She had lots of pink roses, but just one of these. I knew I had to buy it for you. A rare, delicate blossom is the only fitting compliment for your beauty."

Miranda blinked back a sudden rush of tears. "Would you pin it in my hair? Without a mirror, I—"

"Let me." He took the white blossom and placed it into a curve of her upswept coiffure, above her ear. His fingers stroked the shining wing of hair that cradled the flower. "Perfect."

Miranda closed her eyes and inhaled. The perfume of the gardenia blended with the sharp clean scent of Brendan's sandalwood shaving soap. Both aromas reminded Miranda of the days they'd lived together in India. Totally happy in each other's company, they had needed no one else. If only their lives were that simple now . . .

"Miranda?"

She opened her eyes to find him looking down at her with concern. "Thank you again for the gardenia. I was just thinking of home . . . of Darjeeling."

"Do you miss India all that much?"

"I miss it more the longer I'm away from it." Miranda raised her arms in unconscious supplication. "I wish—I wish we could go back to the hills together to live. Those were the happiest days of my life."

"Rosalind hates India," Brendan said, staring out at the moonlit water. "She says it's a cruel, barbaric country. I'm afraid she's never been

210

able to see the beauty of it. She'd much rather
go back to Italy."

"You must miss India yourself," she said.

"I do—but there's nothing there for me now."
He turned back toward Miranda, his face pensive. "Rosalind tells me that you've had a letter
from Justin Egerton."

Miranda avoided his direct gaze. "He's hoping
that after we leave here, we'll go to England.
He's on an extended leave from the Army, and
will be in England until sometime later next
year."

"He still presses his suit, does he?"

At the annoyance in Brendan's tone, she took
a small, perverse satisfaction. "I think he's been
very patient myself." She laughed gently. "It's
been two years since we left Hong Kong."

Brendan said nothing, just tapped his restless
fingers along the wooden railing.

The sprightly notes of a Viennese waltz
drifted over their heads. With a bold smile,
Brendan took Miranda's hand and pulled her
along with him to the dance floor. He swung
her into his arms and whirled her across the
floor.

Miranda felt capricious, drunk with delight. It
had been so many years since Brendan had
danced with her; surely the moon was working
its potent magic tonight.

She smiled up at him. The stark black and
white of his evening clothes only accentuated
his dark, masculine beauty. Through the satin
of her dress, she felt the heat of his palm
pressed to the small of her back. Luckily Brendan was a strong dancer; if he hadn't swept her
along with him, her feet would have faltered.

211

Catherine Kohman

They danced each dance after that. Breath-less, giddy, Miranda didn't want this magical night to ever end. Brendan smiled down at her, his face full of radiant tenderness.

The orchestra began to play *Chanson de Shal-ott*, Miranda's favorite song. Brendan had given her a music box with that tune in it for her 16th birthday. Once again he drew her into his arms. Throbbing, lushly romantic, the music drove her to lean closer to him. His arms tight-ened around her, then his lips touched her hair above the fragrant gardenia.

Miranda's heart beat so fast, she became light-headed. She depended on the strength of his embrace to get her through the rest of the dance.

All too soon, the dreamy music ended. Smil-ing warmly, Brendan slipped his arm around her waist and led her to a secluded bench under a rose-covered arbor in the middle of the barge.

"Miranda, sweetheart, you look like you need refreshment. I'll be back in a moment."

Before she could protest, he disappeared to-ward the tables near the bow. She took a deep breath to slow her racing heart, then whispered blessings to the gods who were smiling down on her tonight.

Brendan appeared at her side, a small bowl of strawberries in one hand and two glasses of champagne in the other. "Drink this."

She accepted the glass from him and took a deep sip. The cold, bubbly liquid slid down her throat like nectar.

Brendan laughed, a rich chuckle of pleasure. "Not so fast, *piara*, or I'll have to carry you home."

Miranda smiled wickedly at him over the rim of her glass. "A thirst for champagne was a vice I acquired in Paris."

"So I see. Have you any more of these shocking weaknesses that I should be warned of?"

"Oh, Brendan-ji . . . if you only knew . . ."

He plucked a red, ripe berry from the bowl on the bench and held it to her mouth. Delicately, she bit the berry from its stem, savoring its tart sugar before she swallowed it. As fair turnabout, she fed him the next berry, laughing when he had to lick the strawberry juice from his glossy mustache.

In fond retaliation, he picked the largest berry and placed it against her lips. She could only take the smallest half of the berry between her teeth, leaving the other half attached to the stem in his hand. She felt the moistness of strawberry juice staining her lips.

In the shadowed arbor, Brendan stared at her, the moonlight reflecting off his obsidian eyes. Tossing the strawberry over the rail, he leaned over and kissed her full on the mouth, the strawberry juice a cool, sweet contrast to the heat of his mouth on hers. Her lips opened beneath his, pliant and warm. All her life she'd dreamed of this kiss, and the reality proved far, far better than the dream.

His warm hand skimmed up her bare shoulder to cradle the nape of her neck, while his thumb gently caressed her ear. His other arm slid around her back, forcing her body against his powerful chest. Roused by this heady pressure, Miranda raised her hands to curl over his shoulders, making the embrace even more sat-

213

isfying, more intimate. She trembled in anticipation.

Suddenly, Brendan pulled back, his face awash with shame and horror. Without a word, he stood up, and with his back to her, he drained his champagne in one long gulp.

Miranda rose and went to him, placing her hand on the sleeve of his jacket. "Brendan . . ."

"No, Miranda, don't. There's no excuse for what I just did."

"But I . . ." She stopped when he put his fingers to her mouth.

"My dearest, I wish I could blame it on the champagne." With a bittersweet smile, he traced the fullness of her lips with his forefinger. "You're so beautiful, Miranda. Sometimes, it tears at my very soul."

She couldn't stand the naked pain in his eyes. "Brendan, please, don't shut me out of your heart. I need you—"

"No, *piara*, don't. Please don't talk of need. Not now . . . I simply couldn't bear it now." His face shuttered, he turned and walked away.

Holding onto the railing for support, Miranda stared blindly across the smooth surface of the lake. Tears spilled over her eyelids and slid down her cheeks to dissolve into the moonlit waters below.

"Biju, have you seen Miss Miranda?"

The wiry Indian looked up at Brendan from his squatting position on the veranda, his scarred features sly. "No, *sahib*. Missy is not coming this way. Perhaps she is going to the hotel."

Brendan's face darkened into a scowl. First

Rosalind's hysterics and now the servant's mul-
ishness. "Don't be insolent, *goonda*. Where did
she go?"

Biju shrugged. "Perhaps across the water she
is taking the small boat. . . . "

Brendan knew Biju meant the canoe. But
why would Miranda take out the fragile craft
alone when a storm threatened? Turning
sharply on his heel, he strode down to the dock
and quickly rigged his sailboat.

On a rugged promontory overlooking the bay,
Miranda gazed out at the slate-blue water with
unseeing eyes, her fingers shredding the loose
bark of the fallen tree beneath her blue cotton
skirts. Overhead, heavy clouds scudded across a
cobalt sky and the rising wind sighed roughly
through the encircling trees.

"Miranda."

As she twisted on the log at the sound of her
name, she saw Brendan at the edge of the trees,
and her stomach clenched with anxiety. *No, not
now . . . I can't face him now—not when I'm so
weak. Just let him go away unaware . . .
please. . . .*

She turned back toward the lake. "How did
you find me?"

"Really, Randie-*bai*, you didn't make it very
difficult. I remembered that Egret Island was
your favorite haunt, and I saw the canoe up on
shore from the water." He approached her carefully, as if she were a wild creature who would
spook at the slightest provocation. "Rosalind
told me that the two of you had words."

So it had come to this at last; Brendan would
send her away, and she'd never see him again.

215

Miranda fought to control the quaver in her voice. "Did she tell you what we said?"

"Not precisely—she didn't appear very coherent." He came to stand behind her and put his hands on her shoulders. Closing her eyes in anguish at his touch, Miranda fought her urge to seek comfort in his welcoming arms.

"Why don't you tell me what she said to upset you?"

"Oh, Brendan, *I can't!*" Quickly, she rose from her seat and walked away from him. She felt those black eyes of his probing hers, so she averted her face and took a deep breath. "What we argued—talked about, I mean—it doesn't matter. I've decided that I'm going to England, as soon as it can be arranged."

"To Justin Egerton?" he asked, his voice strained.

At another time, she would have been pleased at the raw edge in his tone, but his display of jealousy only wounded her more and made her more determined than ever to leave him. "No. Justin has nothing to do with my reasons for going away."

With a revealing sigh of relief, Brendan moved in front of her and lifted her chin so she had to look at him. "I know that Rosalind can be very hurtful. I'm sure she didn't mean whatever she said—you know she adores you." He added with a wry but tender smile, "As I do."

Brendan's lean brown fingers slid up to cup her cheek, and Miranda couldn't stand her agony any longer. She *had* to know. Deliberately gazing into those dark, smoldering eyes, she asked, "Do you truly, Brendan?"

Brendan's jovial smile faded to a look of tigerish intensity. "Miranda, what did Rosalind say to you?"

She ignored the obvious anger in his tone, knowing it wasn't meant for her. Still, his ire made it hard for her to speak calmly. "Rosalind said—she accused me of—of being your lover."

"What?" Eyes sparking, Brendan dropped his hand from her cheek and clenched a fist. "She's gone too far with her jealous fits this time. Become totally unmanageable! Doctor Heffel warned me—she should be put in a sanitarium."

In his agitation, he turned aside, glowering across the whitecapped bay to the island where the hotel stood in snowy splendor among the towering trees.

"Brendan—no! It's not her fault!" Guilt forced Miranda to place a restraining hand on his arm. "Blame me if you must blame someone."

"You? Why should I blame you?" When he turned back to face her, tender concern overlaid the outrage in his face. "It hurts me to see your innocence abused this way. I won't allow it."

"Through her derangement," Miranda said, drawing in her breath, "Rosalind perceives the glimmer of truth." She paused. *"I do love you, Brendan."*

Briefly, Brendan's eyes held a flicker of uncertainty. Then his gaze became shuttered. "Randie, about the other night—on the cruise. We simply had too much champagne and moonlight."

The muscles in his jaw tightened as he fought some inner battle. "I know you have deep feelings for me," he went on. "I'm your guardian, a

217

substitute for your sorely missed father. Rosalind has twisted—"

"No." Miranda placed a finger on his lips to stop him. "I have loved you all the days of my life. Don't you see? Rosalind knows that I love you as a woman loves a man, and that's why I must leave."

Brendan grasped her upraised hand in his and pressed it to his lips, his eyes closed. For a long moment, he stood silent, unmoving, then sighed regretfully. "Oh, *Miranda . . .*"

Hot tears flooded her eyes. *My God, what a deluded fool I've been—he doesn't love me that way and never will. Wretched, wretched fool!*

"Forgive me, please," she said, blushing with shame, "I never meant to tell you. Of all the stupid, foolish things to say—"

"No, Miranda—*piara*, don't—" As she pushed away from him, he pulled her back and put his arms around her, drawing her close to his chest. Need won over shame and she pressed her face into the crisp cotton of his shirt, her throat aching.

"My darling," he began softly, *"I'm* the fool . . . an older man who bitterly envies the young men courting you, who resents the time you spend with them. A jealous man who brought you halfway around the world with him to prevent a lasting attachment between you and that young Lieutenant Egerton . . ."

Once more he tilted her face toward his. "A married man with no right to claim any of your affection, even though he wanted.nothing else in this world more."

Listening to his gentle. heart-rending words, Miranda felt a surge of sharp, painful elation.

"You *do* love me!" Giddy laughter spilled from her throat. "Oh, Brendan-ji, my dearest heart—"

"God, yes—I love you, my darling Miranda."

A fierce exultation swelled within her as Brendan's lips caught hers in a wounding, desperate kiss. His arms tightened around her until she could feel his heartbeat, pounding and erratic, against her chest.

His soft mustache tickled her chin as he moved his mouth against hers, all heat and urgency. The thirst that had been so long denied raged now for both of them—only a torrent of passion would quench it.

Brendan pressed quick kisses along her jaw, her ear, her temples. Miranda laughed with joyful abandon. "The other night when you kissed me, I dared to hope—"

She stopped to kiss him boldly on the mouth. A long moment later, she continued breathlessly, "How long I've waited for this. Brendan, I love you so much—"

With a groan, he caught her to him again, and kissed her deeply. His hands slid up her back, and one tangled itself in her flowing hair. The other splayed between her shoulder blades and forced her even closer.

The pressure pushed the swell of her breasts above the neckline of her gown, and where Brendan's open-necked shirt gaped, his tanned skin warmed her own bare flesh. She felt a spiraling heat rise from her loins. It spread up through her belly and into her breasts, making her corset and other attire a constricting hindrance. She wanted nothing more than to shed her clothing and lay in the sweet fresh grass with her love.

She sighed. So this was the sensual paradise

that Brendan had studied and written so much about, the sacred mysteries of the Scented Garden. Yet no erotic poetry could prepare her for this rich, swooning pleasure, this intoxicating fever.

Miranda relaxed in Brendan's embrace, and he lowered her gently to the thick meadow grass. Along her slim white throat he laid a garland of kisses, then dropped his head lower, slowly tracing the full, upper curve of her breasts. As Miranda moaned and shuddered under this stimulating assault, he raised his head from his delicious ravishment of her flesh.

Eyes closed, she lay beneath him with a blissful, tender smile. His *piara* . . . incredibly beautiful with her translucent white skin, her lotus eyes that flashed from ingenuous wonder to unconsciously seductive invitation. Lord, but he wanted her more than anything on this earth.

He couldn't believe she wanted him too . . . his sweet Randie-*bai*, so young and vibrant . . . innocent and trusting.

Miranda opened her green eyes in confusion as he took her hand in his, pressing it to his lips. She reached up to touch his cheek. Her voice held an unfamiliar, husky note as she said, "Brendan?"

Chapter Thirteen

Ye gods! annihilate but space and time,
And make two lovers happy.
                    —Alexander Pope

"Brendan?"

Marissa woke abruptly, her hands twisted in the muslin sheets, her heart drumming loudly in her ears. The moon passed from behind a dark cloud and flooded the bedroom with silvery light. She squinted at the clock. Two A.M.

Brushing back her tousled hair, she slid her legs over the edge of the bed. Over her thigh-length chemise, she slipped on her matching silk robe, an Oriental floral print in shades of powder-blue, celadon and rose.

Through the doors that led to the deck, she saw Brendan, casually dressed in jeans and a cotton shirt. Pensive and still in the pale moonlight, he

221

rested his palms against the rail and gazed out at the waves rolling up the beach. She ran across the thick Berber rug to join him.

"Brendan," she said, her hand on his arm, "I'm *so glad* you came back! I didn't mean what I said earlier—I was frightened and upset. Can you forgive me?"

He turned toward her, and his black eyes probed her very soul. "I've already forgiven you, but I haven't forgotten what you said. I shouldn't involve you in this. Look at your life, Marissa . . . chasing around the country on the whim of a restless spirit. I should go and leave you in peace."

"*No, Brendan,* you can't leave me now." Her fingers clung to his arm. "I'm happier with you than I've ever been in my life. And despite what I said earlier, I feel that somehow, everything's happening as it is meant to—that I'm part of it all."

"You said you didn't want to be that woman, yet Miranda is at the very center of all this."

"I just couldn't face it then. I don't know why." She stared out at the sea, her mind still in turmoil. "If I *am* Miranda Seton reincarnated, it would explain why I've felt so close to you all these years, why I instinctively knew your character and strength, even the smallest gestures." She smiled suddenly. "And why my heart sang with fearful joy the first time you appeared and spoke to me."

Lightly, Brendan touched her cheek. "Marissa . . ."

The smile ran slowly from her face.

"What is it?" Brendan dropped his hand to her shoulder.

"I just remembered the dream—if it was a dream. I've seen or drempt so many strange things lately . . . I'm not sure."

"Tell me about it."

Marissa felt pink color wash up her throat, and hoped that the gloom concealed it. "It was about you and Miranda . . . on Egret Island." Haltingly, she described her dream to him. To her amazement, he didn't seem shocked at all.

"That wasn't a dream," he said, "it happened just as you remembered. You said the dream disturbed you. Why?"

"Though moved by your love for each other," she began, briefly unnerved by his intensity, "I was surprised that you *did* carry on an affair with your ward. I know your life with Rosalind was unpleasant. . . . "

Brendan reached out and took her hand, his clasp warm and reassuring. Marissa looked deeply into his eyes.

"I was never unfaithful to my wife. I stopped myself before—before I abused Miranda's innocence any further. That same afternoon, though we declared our love for each other, we decided together that she should return to England alone. The next day she left, and I never saw her again."

"*Oh, Brendan,*" Marissa murmured, wincing at the soul-sick pain in his eyes, "I'm sorry."

Poor Miranda, to lose her love forever . . . Marissa ached for her as well. Without thinking, she held out her arms to Brendan and he moved silently into her embrace. Her eyes filled with sudden tears.

"I love you, Brendan. Desperately."

"*Piara.*" He enfolded her in his arms and crushed her to his chest, stroking her soft hair. A fierce tenderness swelled within him. "I love you, Marissa . . . I love you so much. Don't cry. Please, I can't bear it."

223

Catherine Kohman

Pushing away from him just far enough to tilt her face toward his, she gazed up at him. In the moonlight, her translucent eyes shone like living aquamarine, and her lips parted in provocative invitation.

For a moment, he stared at her soft, tempting mouth, then stroked her petal-smooth lips with the ball of his thumb. "My lotus-eyed darling . . ."

Marissa slipped her hands around his neck, and drew his face down to hers. "Love me, Brendan. Please."

Ignoring every warning ringing in the back of his mind, denying every thought but his dangerous need for this woman, Brendan slid his hand under her long, silky hair and cradled her nape in the palm of his hand. He looked deeply into her jewel-like eyes, and found no fear or hesitation, simply a frustrated passion that matched his own.

His mouth came down on hers, demanding, totally confident. She met him with abandon, moving her lips under his, deepening the kiss and melting against him until her rapid heartbeat became indistinguishable from his own.

Brendan wanted to love her slowly, drawing out the nerve-tingling pleasure until it maddened them both, but a potent force drove him on, urgent and reckless. Slipping his arm down over the curve of her bottom, he picked her up and carried her to the bed. He untied her robe and slid it off her shoulders, never taking his lips from hers.

Yes, Marissa thought, *this is the moment at last*. He knew now that she wanted him—that she had *always* wanted him. How could any modern man compare with him, compare with his bold strength, his charming audacity and outrageous virility?

224

Brendan lowered her onto the bed, then stripped off his cotton shirt. Marissa's gaze took in the smooth, sculpted planes of his chest and she pulled him down on top of her, whispering against his sinfully shaped mouth, "This is what I've waited for all my life—what I've longed for, lived for. *Oh, God, Brendan . . . don't stop now.*"

His face pressed against her neck, Brendan teased the sensitive skin of her throat with tiny bites and fluttering kisses. His hands caressed her breasts through the floral chemise, his deft fingers taunting her, making her gasp as the silk rasped slowly over her puckering nipples.

Brendan delighted in Marissa's soft whimpers of pleasure, but his own frustration mounted. He needed to feel her bare, velvety body beneath him. Suddenly light-headed from the heady desire coursing through him, he reached for the thin straps of her chemise and drew the fabric slowly down over the swell of her bosom.

He caught his breath—her breasts were perfect. Smooth as alabaster and lushly rounded, coral-tipped with pouting, delicate nipples. Letting his breath out in a rush, Brendan dipped his head and explored the inviting valley between her breasts with his lips.

Marissa sighed with quavering need, feeling his warm breath and firm lips on her taut, aching breasts. Tenderly, she ran her fingers through his black, wavy hair, torn between savoring this exquisite moment and craving the most intimate of delights to come.

Brendan hesitated and grew very still. His breathing changed, from deep, regular breaths to shallow, rapid ones.

"Brendan, what's wrong?" Marissa raised her-

225

self on her elbows to look at him.

"Nothing," he muttered softly, shaking his head. Gently, he pushed her back down on the bed and lowered his mouth to plunder her heated flesh once more.

But Marissa felt a spark of fear. When he sagged against her, then with a groan rolled over on his side, she said urgently, "Brendan—what is it?"

Putting a shaking hand to his forehead, he felt disoriented, and the room around him faded. He closed his eyes to stop the room from spinning crazily. Something strong—a powerful force dragged at him to prevent him from consummating his love for this precious, beautiful woman.

"Brendan, please. You're scaring me."

With an effort, he gradually opened his eyes. Her gown drawn back over her fine breasts, Marissa leaned over him. The pupils of her eyes were black and huge, her face white even in the dim light. She touched his cheek.

"Don't worry . . . I'm not done for yet." He smiled gamely and tried to raise himself on one elbow. He failed. Feeling miserably weak, drained of his life force, he said, "I'm sorry, Marissa. To cut our lovemaking short this way . . ."

"I don't care about that," she said fiercely, placing a hand on either side of his face. "What happened to you? Are you all right? You look drawn and tired, almost ill."

He sighed. "One moment I felt potent, incredibly alive, wanting you so desperately . . . then I was dizzy and lost. Drained of all my energy." He tried to smile. "Is there something about California air that causes one to swoon? First you, then me . . ."

She just stared at him, her features sharp with concern.

"I meant it as a joke." He touched her kiss-bruised lips with his finger. "I'm sorry, my love."

Touched by his endearment, Marissa stroked his cheek, tracing his thin silver scar. "Do you think it was our lovemaking?"

"I don't know." His dark brows slanted in a frown. "I hope not."

"And yet," she said, puzzled by his sudden weakness, "this hasn't happened before, has it?"

"No . . . but I've been careful to limit our physical contact." With a passionate yet troubled gaze, he looked into her eyes.

"So lovemaking, or this intense emotion, seems to drain the energy it takes for you to appear." After a moment, Marissa let out her pent-up breath. "It's all right; I don't care about the lovemaking, as long as I have you with me."

"I'm not certain what is really happening to me. And no, it's not all right." Brendan's anger seemed to give him strength again, and he sat up on the bed. "You're young, and beautiful and *alive*. You need a young man who can love you in the flesh. Not some randy old ghost who's impotent, who can only tease you, then leave you frustrated and hurt."

"Brendan, don't." She knelt on the bed and slipped her arms around him. Even if time would prove that they couldn't be joined in the flesh, her powerful love for him would never diminish. "You're the man of my dreams. I'll never find you wanting in any way."

With a kiss on the top of her head, he regretfully set her back on the bed. "Oh, *piara*, what's to become of us?"

227

He rubbed his brow, then shoved back his errant lock of hair. "I thought that since I can touch you, and you can touch me, we would be able to love each other. I never imagined that some strong impediment could hold me back."

"Brendan, it truly doesn't matter."

"I'm not giving up this easily." He got up off the bed.

Worried by his intensity, Marissa followed him. "Where are you going?"

"I need to think." He grasped her shoulders and kissed her lightly on the forehead. "Don't worry, I'll be back. You should try to get more sleep."

She twined her hands behind his neck. "Don't go."

"Marissa, love, I have to be alone to regain my strength." He smiled as he gently removed her hands from around his neck. "You're too much of a tempting distraction. Go to bed."

He turned and went out the door.

Forlorn, her body still hungry for Brendan's touch, Marissa climbed back into her bed. Once again alone.

Marissa woke up feeling out of sorts. The breakfast tray of fresh brioche and raspberries that appeared on her doorstep while she showered made a definite improvement in her mood. She knew she had a job to do, so she spent the morning taking a detailed inventory of everything in Miranda's chest.

She then had the gardener cart the heavy wooden box up to the library in the main house, where her hostess sat at the desk. Dressed in a flowing rose pantsuit à la Kate Hepburn, Beatrice looked up from her correspondence with a warm smile.

"Good morning, Marissa." She gestured to the porcelain tea set on the corner of the desk. "Would you like a cup of tea?"

"Yes, thank you," Marissa answered, wondering about how to approach her hostess about purchasing Miranda's legacy. Nervously, she smoothed her hand over the nubby raw silk of her pants.

Beatrice poured and handed her guest a delicate Wedgewood cup and saucer. The tea tasted the same as the day before—creamy, hot and sweet. Marissa sat in the chair opposite the desk, the detailed list of the chest's contents in the pocket of her beige silk jacket.

"I must say that you look better today, my dear." The older woman's gaze assessed her politely. "Still a little tired, perhaps?"

Marissa smiled ruefully. "Between the virus and jet lag, I am a bit worn out."

"When do you fly back to Minneapolis?"

"I've booked a seat on a flight tonight." Marissa was anxious to get home for a number of reasons, seeing Brendan again the most pressing of them. Ever since he'd left her, she'd been worried about him . . . and lonely.

The Englishwoman took a sip of tea and fingered the *mille fiori* paperweight on her desk. "I hoped I could convince you to stay another day."

"You've been marvelously hospitable, Mrs. Copeland."

Her hostess raised a gentle hand of protest. "Please . . . call me Beatrice."

Marissa smiled in return. "Beatrice . . . I do appreciate your kindness. Most people wouldn't take

229

a complete stranger into their home and treat them as an honored guest, the way you have. I wish I could stay longer, but I can't."

An amused glint in her cornflower-blue eyes, Beatrice set her teacup down in its saucer. "Young lady, I may be old, but I'm not foolish. I knew all about you before you stepped into my foyer. If I didn't feel I could trust you, I wouldn't have given you carte blanche to examine Miranda's things.

"And besides your sterling reputation as a scholar, I simply like you, Marissa. You're going to think me odd for saying this, but in a strange way, you remind me of Aunt Miranda herself."

Marissa blinked. Had Beatrice remembered the portrait in the chest? Or had her hostess gone through the chest yesterday herself and seen the damning evidence?

"I'm not sure precisely what it is," Beatrice was saying, "the similar bone structure, or the shifting hue of your green eyes. . . . " She shook her head no. "Actually, it's more a quality of spirit that you seem to share. Adventurous, curious, yet sensitive . . . I think you're the same sort of woman."

Strangely moved by Beatrice's flattering description, Marissa didn't know how to respond. She could hardly tell the older woman that she suspected that she was Miranda's reincarnation; she still had trouble adjusting to that idea herself.

"From what I know of her, Miranda was all those things." Marissa tried not to look self-conscious. "To compare me to her in any way is a wonderful compliment. Thank you."

Beatrice nodded her head graciously.

Finally emboldened, Marissa drew the inventory sheet from her pocket. "Would you like to go over the list of items and inspect them for yourself?" She slid the sheet of paper across the desk. While Beatrice casually examined the notations, Marissa twisted her amethyst ring.

The Englishwoman smiled as she got to the bottom of the list. "It seems to be quite comprehensive. Down to a packet of postcards from Torquay and a souvenir program from Albert Hall."

Marissa took a deep breath and plunged ahead. "Mrs.—I mean, Beatrice, I'd like to buy the contents of Miranda's chest from you. I hate to ask you to sell your family heirlooms, but I really would like to have—"

A slight frown clouded Beatrice's fair-skinned brow. "I don't think that's a good idea."

Marissa's heart plummeted.

The hint of a smile played at the corners of Beatrice's pink mouth. "You see, I was thinking more along the lines of just giving you the chest and its contents."

Stunned, Marissa sat in total silence for a half a minute. "But Beatrice, these are valuable items: the emerald ring, Miranda's own manuscripts, plus the letters and original notes of Major Tyrell's. Sotheby's or Christie's would be very interested in them.

"I know you're thinking that I'm a poor writer just out of graduate school, and that I have no real idea what the contents are worth. The money isn't a problem, since I have a sizable trust in addition to my earnings, and I'm familiar with the comparative value—"

Beatrice held up her hand. "Let me stop you for a moment for clarification." She raised her brows delicately. "Are you trying to talk me *out* of giving you Miranda's legacy?"

Marissa stared at her hostess in confusion.

231

"No . . . no . . . I'd be delighted—honored that you'd want me to have it. I just don't want to take advantage of you. . . . "

"Look around you, my dear." Beatrice waved her hand to encompass the sumptuously furnished library. "I don't appear to want for funds, do I? My husband and I weren't blessed with children, so this will all go to a charitable foundation when I'm gone." She sighed. "I'd much rather see Miranda's things go to someone who will cherish them . . . than to an auction block at Christie's."

"Still," Marissa said, "I insist on giving you something in return." She paused. "A generous donation in your name to the Women's Studies program at Stanford?"

Beatrice inclined her head. "I guess that I'd find that acceptable. With one small addition . . ."

Marissa grinned. "Name it."

"A promise to visit again when you're on the West Coast, and a signed copy of your biography of Major Tyrell upon publication."

"Hmmm," Marissa said, frowning in mock consternation, "I could live with that, with one small addition of my own: your name in a place of prominence on the acknowledgment page."

"It's a done deal." Beatrice laughed merrily. "It will be the first time such a gift will truly mean something to me."

As the older woman rose from her chair, Marissa also stood. "Would a handshake suffice?"

Beatrice came around the desk. "Actually, the preferred coinage for a transaction involving a legacy of love is . . . a hug."

"Ah," Marissa said with a radiant smile, "my favorite commodity."

* * *

The Beckoning Ghost

On the long flight home, Marissa scanned the early years of Miranda Seton's journals. They started just after she became Brendan Tyrell's ward, in 1860, no doubt because of her guardian's influence. After her mother's death, he became the central focus of her life. He brought her back to her beloved India, and set up a household in Darjeeling.

Though gone for long periods of time on his work with the Indian Survey of the Himalayas, he made certain that Miranda always felt cherished when he was at home. No wonder the girl came to love him. He was a true hero to her—dashing and bold, yet warm and loving to a lost, grieving child.

As much as Marissa enjoyed reading the early journals, she skipped ahead to the one she'd first held—from 1875. Always circumspect in her writing, Miranda couldn't keep her love for Brendan from flowing onto the page with each stroke of the pen. Her words touched a deep, inner chord in Marissa as she read them.

I was born loving you, Brendan, she thought. My whole life has been shaped by my love for you, and I didn't even know it. If only you were here on earth in human form . . .

Marissa shook off that regret before it could become fully rooted and coil around her heart like a parasitic vine.

She flipped ahead in the journal to the time of Brendan's death. As he had said, Miranda left Arcadia Island the day before he died. Her reasons for leaving so suddenly weren't detailed, just that Rosalind was increasingly unstable. Miranda thought if she left Brendan's wife would improve.

233

Catherine Kohman

Of her day with Brendan on Egret Island, Miranda wrote cryptically in Latin,

Sed mulier cupido quod dicit amanti,
In vento et rapida scribere oportet aqua.

Marissa's Latin was rusty, but she recognized enough of it to remember the quotation from Catullus:

But a woman's sayings to her lover
Should be in wind and running water writ.

The day of Brendan's death, Miranda was alone, at a hotel in Minneapolis. Marissa could only imagine her pain and horror when the English girl heard the news. In Miranda's journal on that date, she'd simply written:

My soul is rent in half.

The next entry in the journal skipped ahead to October of 1876, over a year after Brendan's death. Though the occasion should have been a joyful one, Miranda's announcement seemed subdued:

Today I agreed to marry my dearest friend, Justin Egerton. The wedding is to be next June in Epsom. It will be a quiet ceremony, since I have no close family left, and Justin's is not large either.

That was all the mention she gave her engagement. From that point on, the journal lost its most charming quality, Miranda's zest for life. The only

234

real emotion surfaced again in a curious entry from December of that year:

Rosalind came again to call. Having run out of excuses, I was forced to see her. Of all the things in the world, she wants to attend my wedding! She coyly said her matchmaking brought Justin and me together. I believe the woman truly is mad now, though she roams about freely, proclaiming her grief loudly for all to hear. I know one thing: I will not have her there, even if it means running off to Gretna Green.

Marissa knew that Rosalind and Miranda had parted in anger before Brendan's death. Yet before that, the girl had always felt compassion for Brendan's wife. Pictures from Brendan's memorial service showed a heavily veiled Miranda at the widow's side. What had changed her feelings so drastically?

Marissa leaned back into her seat and closed her eyes, trying to reach back for some scrap of inherited memory.

Nothing.

Unless . . . Miranda suspected that Rosalind was in some way responsible for the fire that killed Brendan, as Marissa herself wondered.

It made sense—a madwoman's vengeance turned to fatal holocaust.

Marissa rubbed her eyes. Her Gothic imagination had gotten the better of her once again. Though probably nothing more than a natural falling out between a wife and "the other woman," the quarrel between the two women intrigued her. The most curious thing was Rosalind's determination to remain part of Miranda's life. Out of guilt?

So many questions were left unanswered.

The jumbo jet banked to the left and out the window Marissa could see the welcoming stream of lights on Highway 494, near the Minneapolis-St. Paul airport.

Home again. And Brendan.

After complaints about being abandoned for the second time in a week, the cats expressed their pleasure at her return, but Brendan wasn't there.

Drained by lack of sleep and jet lag, and disheartened by Brendan's absence, Marissa collapsed into her bed and didn't wake until late the next morning. She slipped on her robe and roamed through the house, looking for some sign of Brendan's presence.

The sun danced in shimmering ripples across the lake, and the huge maples sighed and rustled in a light western wind. A lovely day, but still no Brendan.

To distract her mind from worry, Marissa got dressed and spent the rest of the morning safely storing away the items in Miranda's chest. She kept out Miranda's journals, the music box and the emerald ring, deciding to wear it. As she stared at the emerald and opal sparkling on her left hand, she felt an upwelling of desolation.

Brendan, where are you, my love? I need you with me.

She wondered what had happened to him. He'd seemed so drained and pale when he left her in Monterey. They'd only had brief contact before that, and he had appeared strong and vital. It must have been their lovemaking; the experience was too intense for a ghost.

Could she be certain he *was* a ghost? His description of another layer of consciousness, his sporadic knowledge of the modern world intrigued her. What could explain Brendan's shadow life?

For some reason her conversations with Kelsey about the paranormal came to mind. Then she remembered her great-grandmother's vision of her injured neighbor, the *doppelganger* incident. Could some similar phenomenon explain Brendan's experience?

Did it matter? Whatever sort of spirit Brendan was, she missed him terribly.

In desperation, she sat down on the porch swing and once again started reading Miranda's journals. If she couldn't be with Brendan in this lifetime, she'd settle for loving him in the last.

By late afternoon, the handwriting began to blur in front of her eyes. Sorely lonesome, she called up Kelsey and arranged to go to the Guthrie's production of *The Tempest*. She knew she'd go crazy sitting around the house alone all evening, wondering what had happened to Brendan.

To kill some time, she went over to the U's East Bank. Gayatri wasn't in her office, so Marissa wandered over to the shops at Dinkytown. On impulse, she went into an antiquarian bookshop. Browsing the shelves, she came across an old tome called *Phantasms of the Living* which gave 19th-century anecdotes about doppelgangers. She purchased the volume and discreetly placed it in the trunk of the car to avoid Kelsey's notice.

After the play, they went to the Lincoln Del in

St. Louis Park and lingered over chocolate whipped cream cake, talking about the upcoming tenth-year reunion for their class at Kenwood High.

"Let's go together," Marissa said, "that is—if you don't want to bring a date."

"Who would I dare ask? Such a weighty decision can't be made lightly. One disastrous move and I'm stuck with it for the next five years." Kelsey poked her fork around in the chocolate crumbs still littering her plate, a judicious frown on her forehead.

"Now if I could ask Mel Gibson, Kevin Costner or Hugh Grant, that might be a safe choice." She smiled wickedly. "Too bad you can't bring your Brendan Tyrell. He'd put those mincing, retro-Yuppies to shame."

Marissa looked up sharply, a frozen smile on her face. "Brendan?"

"Yes, your late, lamented hero. I haven't forgotten that portrait you showed me. Are you still dreaming about him?"

Treading oh so carefully, she answered, "Sometimes."

"Well, I don't blame you. Who needs Kevin Costner with a hunk like that to dream about?"

Before Marissa could frame a coherent response to that, her friend sped into her next thought.

Kelsey stared down at her plate and said casually, "Speaking of late, lamented hunks, someone came into the gallery the other night and asked about you. A rather intense grilling, I might add. Current whereabouts, romantic status, et cetera, et cetera."

"Who?" Marissa asked with some trepidation.

"Brett Hanford."

"*Oh.*" Marissa's high school boyfriend. Just what she needed.

"You sound less than thrilled." Kelsey's face held amused interest.

"Well, Brett . . . we don't have anything in common." She laughed then. "We never did have much in common except the History Club and a set of raging adolescent hormones."

"*He* doesn't think so, and he's still easy on the eye. If anything, I'd say he's improved." Kelsey leaned across the table, a dangerous glint in her eye as she dangled her bait in front of Marissa's indifferent face. "Body by Oakdale Racquet Club and haircut by Horst himself, Italian suits courtesy of his excellent salary as a rising executive at Carwell."

"Spare me the details," Marissa sighed. "I swear, I have no interest in Brett Hanford. None in the least."

"Methinks the lady doth protest too much."

"*Kelsey Sheridan* . . . you didn't give him my number, did you?"

Kelsey's blue eyes widened in affronted innocence. "Would I do such a thing? I merely said you were back in town."

"Thanks, dearest friend." Marissa glared at her. "*Muchas gracias*, you . . . you foul serpent in the grass."

Kelsey grinned and paraphrased Monty Python. "My mother was a hamster, and my father smelt of elderberry? I get your drift." She shrugged. "He'd find out at the reunion anyway."

"Yeah, but now he's forewarned. Those cogs are already turning in that devious head of his." Marissa frowned absently. "Maybe I should buy a chastity belt before the reunion."

Kelsey patted her hand. "Don't worry, *amiga*. He probably just wants to seduce and abandon you. You know, the lure of the chase . . . the one that got away. . . . "

"Thanks again, Kelse," Marissa said dryly, "for cheering me up."

Kelsey's dark brows disappeared into her tousled black bangs. "Hey, Rissa . . . what are friends for?"

With a mournful gong, the mantel clock chimed midnight as Marissa reached the cottage. She rushed inside to see if Brendan had returned, but the house mocked her in empty silence.

Totally dispirited, Marissa got ready for bed, and once again she lay down with her disappointment. In her mind she went over that night in Monterey when Brendan had told her he loved her. She realized that he had only told her *after* she made the connection to Miranda. Did he really love her for herself, or did he just love the shadow presence of Miranda Seton?

That question and a hundred others whirled around in her brain. After tossing restlessly for hours, she finally sat up.

In the chair by the chimney she saw her ghost, casually dressed in a soft chamois shirt and jeans. He gazed at her calmly, as if he'd been gone an hour or two, not days on end.

"Damn it, Brendan! You frightened me!"

"My dear Marissa, you were agitated in your sleep." He gave her a charming smile. "I merely startled you upon waking."

In her mindless worry, she lashed out at him. "I

240

don't like you sneaking up on me this way. What if I wasn't alone?"

Brendan laughed heartily. "My dear, that's what self-respecting ghosts do—sneaking up on people is a requirement of the job." Then his eyes grew darker as he added casually, "As for entertaining other men in your bedroom, I wouldn't think it proper, given the circumstances."

Marissa hissed derisively. "This is *my* house and I'll entertain whomever I please in my bedroom."

"My, my, we are tetchy this evening." He smiled again, this time a confident, alarming smile, rife with danger. "Let's just say that if you wish to 'tie the true lover's knot' with some young man, I'd suggest you be prepared to explain any untoward happenings to your chosen consort."

Amazed by his coolness, she simply stared at him. "I don't believe it. You're not telling me that you're jealous!"

Brendan scowled at her, a muscle in his jaw twitching. "Hardly. It's just unseemly, that's all."

"Oh, and when did *you* become the model of propriety?" Still angry over his disappearance, she couldn't resist taunting him further. "I've never judged you to be a prude. On the contrary."

Brendan got out of the chair and walked over to the bed. Tall, muscular, he loomed over Marissa as she sat on the edge of the bed, the muslin sheet clutched to her chest. Her heart accelerated wildly.

Grasping her bare shoulders, he pulled her to her feet. He stood close enough so she could feel the heat of his body without actually touching him. His black, Gypsy eyes held a possessive fierceness that at first shocked her, then warmed

241

her, though she still shivered in her thin night-gown.

"I'll show you how much of a prude I really am," he said quietly.

With practiced ease, he slid his hands down over her shoulders to her breasts. He lingered there a moment, and his deft fingers teased her nipples into tight, hard peaks. Satisfied with her quick response, he smiled darkly and dropped his hands to her waist and hips, his fingers a skimming whisper of heat on her skin.

She knew then he was marking her flesh as his own with his expert touch. Perhaps she should have been offended, but she wanted him so much it didn't matter any more.

Marissa leaned toward him, but he held her away from him as he stroked the curve of her bottom, then around to the juncture of her thighs. Through the ivory silk of her gown, his questing fingers caressed her slowly, gently, causing tiny vibrations to move from the core of her belly down into her legs.

When he took his hand away from her most sensitive place, Marissa moaned lightly. With a predatory smile, Brendan ignored her distress and slid his hands upward to her bosom. In his intense, falcon-like expression she saw *Shahin*.

She caught her breath as he cupped her breasts in his palms and squeezed gently.

"Brendan, please—"

"Please what, my darling? Have I convinced you yet that I'm not a prude?" His fingers went to the spaghetti straps of her gown and began to lower them down her shoulders.

"Please," she whispered hoarsely, "stop."

"Stop?" His hands poised at her shoulders, he

242

stared at her in utter surprise.

"No, Brendan . . . the last time we tried to make love, you looked so ill. When you didn't come back for days, I was afraid that I'd lost you forever."

Brendan moved his hands up, burying them in her thick, moon-gold hair. *"Damn it, Marissa, I need you."*

He leaned forward to kiss her, but stopped mere inches from her lips. He saw the erratic pulse beating in her throat.

She was so beautiful and *warm* in his arms; he'd never desired a woman as much as he did Marissa. Yet how could he love her, how could he satisfy her when he was forced to live in this shadowland between her world and the next? Oh, to be flesh and blood again . . .

"Piara," he whispered in quiet desperation, "I want you so much . . . let me love you now. . . . "

Marissa looked up at him, both love and concern on her exquisite face. "If you're sure . . . if you want me so badly, I'm yours. . . . "

Brendan kissed her fiercely, feeling her warmth and softness like a dream in his arms. He pulled her hard against him, releasing her shining fall of hair. The scent of her hair, the smooth heat of her skin under his hands aroused him to aching need. But the intensity of their embrace suddenly made his head spin, and he grasped her shoulders to steady himself.

"Rissa, I don't want to lose you," he said, his voice husky with need. "The idea of you being with another man drives me mad. . . . "

"No other man can hold a candle to you," she murmured, then laughed softly. "My wild Gypsy lover . . ."

"I don't want to let you go." He ran his thumbs

243

along the sweep of her collarbone. As long as he kept his desire in check, his head was clear. But as soon as his arousal reached a fever pitch, the damned dizziness came back. He felt caught, torn between his extraordinary need for Marissa and his very existence on this earthly plane. "What if this night is our only chance. . . . "

"My dear Brendan-ji . . ." She raised her hand to his cheek and stroked his thin scar. "I don't believe the gods would be so cruel after bringing us together." Smoothing his black mustache, she added with a wistful smile, "Perhaps we'll find a way to be together . . . if we're granted enough time."

He cupped her face in his hands and gazed at her long and lovingly. "*Piara,* I hope you're right."

Brendan hugged her close, burying his face in her gardenia-scented hair. He tried to will his arousal away, with limited success. Then, releasing her, he let out his pent-up breath in a rush.

She glanced up and saw his rueful smile. "What's so funny?"

"I'm sorry, Marissa." He leaned over and kissed her lightly on the forehead. "It's just that I had this vivid image of myself, a ghostly Priapus doomed to forever wander the same level of Dante's Inferno as Don Juan and Casanova."

Her brows raised, Marissa thought for a moment, then she too started to laugh. "And so you probably deserve, you wicked man!"

Chapter Fourteen

*Real are the dreams of Gods, and smoothly pass
Their pleasures in a long immortal dream.*
                                        —John Keats

Marissa thought it best to remove them both from
the temptations of the bedroom, so she put on her
terry cloth robe and led Brendan downstairs to the
kitchen. He watched her from his seat at the oak
table as she puttered around making tea and
toasting an English muffin.

"Have you any ideas where we should start our
search for your manuscripts?" She lathered her
muffin with huckleberry jelly. "Sure you won't
have anything?"

"I don't need breakfast, but thank you."

The muffin poised at her lips, Marissa asked,
"Ghosts don't eat?"

245

"I don't feel hunger." He added with a wolfish smile, "For *food*, that is."

"Oh," Marissa murmured, momentarily taken aback. She took a bite of muffin, then gave Brendan a lopsided smile, her lips thinly glazed with sweet huckleberries. "I suppose you don't . . . drink . . . *wine* either."

Brendan simply looked at her, his brows raised in inquiry.

"Never mind, Brendan-ji—it's just a joke from an old vampire movie." She shrugged at his perplexed frown. "What can I say—I grew up on the stuff."

Brendan stroked his mustache. "So vampires are still part of the cultural milieu? Even the ancient Greeks had vampire legends."

"And vampire stories are still on the best-seller lists." She delicately removed a stray muffin crumb from her chin. "Speaking of literary sensations, how do we trace your manuscripts?"

His slanting brows lowered as he concentrated. "Let's piece together what we know about Rosalind's movements after she left Minnesota."

"I'll get my notebook on Rosalind." She fetched a green three-ring binder from her office and laid it on the table in front of her, paging through her notes. "The newspapers said she left here July 20th, bound for England, where a memorial service was planned for you. Miranda went with her, and Biju, of course."

He said, "They held the service August 30th in the regiment's London chapel."

She swallowed a hot gulp of tea. "You were there?"

He nodded matter-of-factly.

"Didn't it make you uncomfortable?"

He leaned back in his chair. "Not by any means. I wanted to hear what the bounders said about me now that I'd passed on. Mostly, they spoke a load of rubbish about my earning the Victoria Cross at Lucknow, my service to the Survey in India. Few mentioned my published work.

"You—that is, Miranda—gave the only honest eulogy. Of course, it was almost unheard of to let a woman deliver a eulogy, especially in a mostly military service. She insisted on it; I was so proud of her—of you."

Brendan reached across the table and lightly touched her hand.

"I'll let Miranda take the credit for now." Marissa smiled, then had a thought. "So you didn't know your wife hid the manuscripts until—"

"After I saw the Camoens published, then I realized that the contents of my writing chest must have survived the fire. By then it was too late."

"Your wife may have burned them at a later date, as she'd threatened," Marissa said gently.

"I don't think so. Though torn between her wretched religion and her pride in my scholarship, Rosalind kept them." Brendan's mouth tightened into a flat line. "Somewhere."

"In England?" Marissa crossed her ankles and swung her feet, totally at ease with her ghostly lover. "Have you looked there yourself?"

"I have, the obvious places. Our friends' flat in London, her father's people in Cornwall. She didn't get on with her mother's family, so I don't think she would have gone to them. I also checked the cottage in Surrey where Rosalind spent the years between my demise and her entrance into that asylum. I didn't find a trace of them."

Marissa stirred her tea, a frown of concentration puckering her brow. "What happened to Biju when Rosalind went into the asylum?"

"He went back to India, but I don't think my wife would have given the manuscripts to him. There would have been no point to it."

Marissa finished her tea, and set the cup aside. She glanced over at Brendan, relishing the easy closeness they shared in her kitchen. "Did Rosalind live anywhere else on her return to England?"

"No, she lived a quiet life. After Miranda left for India with her husband, Rosalind withdrew into herself." He frowned, tracing the grain of the oak table with his forefinger. "Her condition steadily worsened until she could no longer look after herself."

Brendan's last remark reminded Marissa of the strange note in Miranda's journal. "Why would Miranda come to dislike Rosalind so much that she'd refused to invite your widow to her wedding?"

"I don't know." His dark brows lifted. "How did you surmise that?"

She told him about the journal entry. "Could Miranda have guessed that your wife had the manuscripts concealed?"

"It's possible, of course—that would have infuriated Miranda," he said with a fond smile, and Marissa ached to reach out and touch his face. "She loathed people who burned or suppressed writings of any kind. 'Savonarolas' she called them—literary vandals."

Marissa nodded. "To me, burning a book is a heinous crime—the murder of ideas. Most writers feel that way, and I don't think it's just vanity either. Be glad that you didn't witness Hitler and his Nazis torching whole libraries in Germany. . . . "

"I do know about the burned libraries, the dreadful loss of life during that war...." He shook his head. "Sometimes I think the only progress civilization has made is finding more efficient, terrible ways to destroy humanity."

Marissa touched his hand, hoping his knowledge didn't extend to the threat of nuclear holocaust. To lift his melancholy mood, she said with a wry smile, "Well, we've made it this far... in spite of MTV, cell phones, and those godawful infomercials."

She rose from the table. "While I shower and get dressed, make your own notes about possible leads. Today I want to do research in town. Wait— what day is it?"

She glanced up at the Audubon calendar on the wall, noting the luncheon appointment penciled in on the date. Her editor was in town, and she'd completely forgotten about it. Oops.

Marissa paled as she stared at the following day. July 17th—the anniversary of Brendan's death. A superstitious dread overwhelmed her. "You weren't planning on going away again, were you?"

"No." He watched her curiously, then noticed her sideways glance at the calendar. "Ah, the date. Don't let that worry you, *piara*. That day has come and gone well over one hundred times and I'm still here with you."

"Good." Shyly, she kissed the top of his head. As she ran up the stairs, she paused in mid-flight. "I want you to find you here when I come home tonight. Deal?"

He grinned. "Deal."

Marissa breezed through lunch with Karen, her editor, by being charming and forthcoming in all

249

the necessary places and reticent in the others. Carefully she gave the impression that all was progressing smoothly with her biography of Brendan. If Karen only knew what she was really up to . . .

When she walked into the house, a delicious aroma of chicken curry wafted from the kitchen. Brendan stood in front of the picture window in the living room. She came up behind him and touched his shoulder.

"I think you must be a brownie, not a ghost. They're wee folk who steal into your house at night and clean and cook."

Brendan glanced over his shoulder at her, his full mouth temptingly close. If she stood on her tiptoes . . .

"I was born in Ireland, lass," he said dryly and turned back toward the lake. "I know very well what a brownie is."

"Well, I always coveted one; instead I got you. Do you think I came out ahead in the bargain?"

"If we leave the curry to cook on its own," he said, a self-satisfied smile pulling at the corners of his mouth, "perhaps I can demonstrate what an excellent bargain you received in me."

Marissa raised herself on her tiptoes and her lips brushed the shaggy black hair behind his ear. "Watch it, me fine boyo," she purred in his ear, "or one day I may take you up on that boast and wipe that smug smile right off of your face."

Though Marissa recklessly flirted with him, she wondered if they'd ever be able to consummate their love. But she couldn't let that thought dampen her spirits; she'd enjoy each precious hour with Brendan . . . for they had no guarantees how long the miracle that brought them together would last.

Determined to live in the moment, she saw the muscle lining Brendan's jaw work back and forth as he took in her brazen boast. She dropped back down on her heels and sang cheerily, "Right. I wasn't hungry when I drove up, but I am now. How long until it's ready?"

"A half hour," he said tersely.

She reached behind him and pinched him on the bottom. He flinched and brought his head around to glare at her. "Young ladies do not—"

"In this day and age they do." Marissa laughed. "Just checking out my bargain."

"Off with you, saucy wench. You're vexing the cook."

"Yes, *khansaman*." She made a deep *namskan* and left the room, giggling.

From her bedroom phone, she decided to call Owen before it got too late. She dropped her salmon linen jacket on the bed and sat down in her suit skirt and blouse of lacy Irish linen.

Marissa kicked off her heeled sandals and massaged her feet. Thank God she didn't have to dress like this every day. She heard Owen pick up. "Hail the conquering hero," she said.

"Ah, my lady scholar. I take it that the endeavor proved a success?"

"More than you'd ever imagine. She *gave* it to me, Owen . . . all of Miranda's things, even letters of Brendan's." She heard a low whistle from the other end of the line.

"All I can say is that you must have done a hell of a job sweet-talking her."

"That's just it." She went on to briefly describe her encounter with Beatrice Copeland and the items she found in the chest, leaving out her own

251

reaction. "She simply liked me. What can I say?" She paused. "Owen, dear, I need another favor. You know all the dealers in London—has any uncommon Tyrell memorabilia turned up there recently?"

"Not to my knowledge," Owen replied, "but I'll check. You know, of course, that Granger Wilkes has practically cornered the market on Tyrell. He has the most extensive collection that I know of."

"I am quite familiar with Mr. Wilkes," Marissa said coolly. "I barely beat him to those letters of Brendan's I bought last summer. If he hadn't been vacationing in Greece, I wouldn't have had the chance. I'm sure he has an equal fondness for me."

"I still think it would be worth your time to talk to him. If anything unusual is out there, Wilkes will have it." Owen paused and she could hear his smile. "Toss that gorgeous blond hair of yours around and wear a short skirt. He quite fancies himself the ladies' man."

"Owen, you should be ashamed of yourself. I'd never resort to such tactics."

"Sweetheart, if I had your face and figure, *I* would." He laughed heartily.

"Stop being beastly, Owen. You'll put me off Welshmen altogether."

"Ah, well, you never had any time for us Welsh lads anyway," he teased. "It was always the Irish for you."

Brendan appeared in the doorway and leaned against the doorjamb, his dark, saturnine features at odds with the tender, inquiring expression in his eyes.

"It still is the Irish for me." Marissa smiled. "Brendan Tyrell has always owned my heart, you know that. See what you can find out for me, will you? And thanks again, Owen."

"Yours to command in love and war, lady scholar."

After hanging up, she told Brendan what she discussed with Owen, and he agreed it could prove useful.

He presented his arm to her. "Your dinner awaits your presence in the dining room, *Mem-sa'b*."

Marissa joined him at the bedroom door and linked arms with him. "How long has it been since I've tasted your cooking?"

"Oh, I could hazard a guess and say one hundred and fifteen years or more." He grinned down at her, his even teeth white against the black frame of his curving mustache. "My cooking has only improved with age."

"And your other talents—have they improved also?" She sent him a flirtatious glance from under her lowered lashes.

His hand tightening over hers, he glanced down at her, and wished he could ultimately prove the depth of his love and desire to her. "If the gods grant me the chance," he said with a crooked smile, "I'll be delighted to show you . . . my wanton, spoiled darling."

For the rest of the evening, they sat together on the porch swing, fingertips barely touching atop the floral cushions. Marissa drank a glass of Sauvignon Blanc and felt the wine relax her down to her toes. She wanted to lay across Brendan's lap, enfolded in his arms, but didn't think it wise to do so.

Instead, they talked for hours, covering so many different topics, Marissa couldn't remember half

253

of them. Intelligent and easy to talk to, Brendan had a much broader understanding of the world since his death than she thought he would.

Finally, she asked him. "How do you know so much of my world, Brendan?"

"Remember those different layers of consciousness I spoke about in California? My knowledge is filtered through those. I'm not sure where exactly it comes from, though I'd like to find out." He frowned. "It's very frustrating to know something, but not where you learned it."

Marissa shot him a slanting glance. "You're going to think this is a silly question."

"Ask me anything, my sweet one," he said, his frown lifting.

"Where do you get your clothes? They seem pretty modern to me, though some are classic. You could have worn some of them back in your time—like your Irish sweaters."

"I see a closet in my mind and choose what I want to wear." He smiled. "I don't know whose closet it is, but the clothes fit and he does have good taste."

Marissa laughed, then changed the subject. "About your manuscripts . . . tomorrow morning I'm going to start my research into Rosalind's family, while I wait for information to come in from Owen. When it does, I'll have to go to England to search. You'll come with me, won't you?"

"I would be nowhere else than with you."

As she smiled at him, a haunting question rose in her mind. "In California, you said you loved me. Did you mean that you loved *me* . . . or was it Miranda?"

He exhaled sharply. "That's a difficult question for me to answer."

"You just did." To cover her hurt, Marissa tried to maintain a smooth, cool facade. "I understand."

She lowered her eyes, but he tilted her chin so she had to look up at him.

"I love the woman you are now, Marissa. I love *you*." His gaze was honest and tender. "But I see so much of Miranda in you that sometimes it's hard to separate the two of you. Because you aren't separate—you're different facets of the same brilliant jewel. I know you don't feel it yet, my love, but one day you will."

She gave him a tremulous smile. "I truly am Miranda . . . and we're combined in one soul?"

"Yes, *piara*. One of the oldest and most beautiful of souls. We're linked together, you and I, throughout eternity."

That single, moving thought would carry Marissa through the ordeal that lay ahead.

The sweet, fresh perfume of gardenia tickled Marissa's nose and she opened her eyes. In the pale morning light, she saw a delicate blossom lying on her pillow, a note beside it. She reached for the paper and read:

My darling Marissa,
I hate to leave you, even for a little while, but
I must. I promise that I will be back again
tonight. I love you, piara. *Brendan.*

A flutter of disappointment settled in her chest. Dreamily, she picked up the white flower and held it to her nose. Closing her eyes, she inhaled the gardenia's heady fragrance. A sharp, clear image invaded her mind—she and Brendan danced together under a lantern-lit canopy. Around them

255

shimmered the moonlight waters of the lake, and she realized that they were on a cruising boat.

Her silken petticoats swirled around her legs as Brendan led her in the dance. Wrapped tightly in his arms, she felt a wave of blissful happiness wash over her. When at last he kissed her, bliss turned to ecstasy. . . .

The vividness of the image startled Marissa out of her reverie. It didn't have the hazy glow of a dream; the immediacy and clarity of the scene possessed the quality of a real memory. She swallowed hard. Miranda's memories were bleeding through to hers. Brendan said that it probably would happen, but she wasn't comfortable with the situation yet.

Where was he? She'd gotten greedy and wanted him there with her 24 hours a day. Yet she knew that he needed to rest, and he *had* promised to return tonight.

Tonight. The anniversary of his death in the fire. The idea didn't trouble Brendan, but it bothered Marissa. Already planning a busy day to keep her mind occupied, she got up out of bed and grabbed her robe.

Marissa spent the morning in her office, cross-checking her notes on Rosalind with Brendan's. The notes meshed pretty well, so they had ascertained Rosalind's movements from her arrival in England until her commitment to the asylum in 1880. A three-month gap showed up in the spring of 1876, between the time Rosalind left London and when she rented her cottage in Surrey.

Intuitively, Marissa felt that they should concentrate on the time period when Rosalind had disappeared. At that time, Brendan had more interest in staying near Miranda; he didn't pay much attention to his widow's absence from London. Only after he realized that she must have his manuscripts did he become suspicious of her whereabouts.

In Miranda's journal of 1865, the year that Brendan married Rosalind, Marissa found a reference to a maternal cousin of the bride's.

Miranda had refused to attend the wedding in July, and after the wedding, Brendan and Rosalind returned to India. Feeling abandoned at the beginning of the new school term, the girl made friends with Lucy, a fellow student from Cheltenham. Lucy knew Rosalind's mother's family, the Keatings. She told Miranda that after Rosalind came back to England after the Mutiny, she stayed with her mother's brother and his wife in Cheltenham. Rosalind and her cousin Johanna became good friends.

But the horror of the Mutiny had affected Rosalind's mind, and she started acting strangely. Remembering her mother's suicide, the family put her in a sanitarium. Her uncle John found the stigma of another case of madness in his family too much to bear, and once Rosalind was released from the sanitarium, John effectively cut her off from his family. Lucy knew that Johanna and Rosalind continued to secretly correspond after she returned to live with her father's family, the Chenowyths.

So, Marissa thought, Miranda knew that Rosalind had suffered a mental breakdown long before Brendan did. Yet she didn't say anything of it to Brendan; at least not until a much later date. What a heavy burden for Miranda to bear at 15. She had her own objections to Brendan's marriage, but to find out that he'd married a woman with a history of madness in her family troubled her deeply.

Setting aside her own sadness at the tragedy of the Tyrells' lives, Marissa fixed on that cousin's name. Johanna Keating. She'd probably married, but the genealogical records in the Mormons' vast repository in Salt Lake City might give her the name of the man Johanna married. Then Marissa remembered that the local branch of the Genealogical Society Library in Golden Valley had computerized access to some Salt Lake records through the International Genealogical Index, or IGI.

It might be worth a trip into town to check it out . . . better than waiting at home all day for Brendan to return when her nerves were on edge. Rising from her chair, she noticed that her back felt sweaty, and she saw the thick curtain of humidity that hung across the lake. Not a breath of air moved in the sultry heat of the day.

Uh-oh, she thought. *Tornado weather.*

Through the sticky brooding weather, Marissa drove to the Golden Valley Genealogical Library, where the elderly woman clerk showed her how to use the IGI index. Nervously, she typed in the name "Johanna Keating" and waited for the computer to track the appropriate English records, if any existed.

Two records came up on the screen: Johanna's birth in 1843 and her subsequent marriage in Cheltenham to an Edward Hensley in 1864. Johanna Hensley! But where did the couple live at the time of Brendan's death and Rosalind's secretive visit?

The Beckoning Ghost

The IGI scan came up with five sons born to the Hensleys, all christened in the village of Cassington in Oxfordshire. The computer also listed a number of Hensleys of later generations, still in the general neighborhood. It would certainly be worth a visit to Oxfordshire to track down Johanna's descendants.

As she printed copies of the pertinent records, she glanced at her watch. Almost three . . . she'd better get on the road home before the rush hour traffic peaked. She didn't want to be late on this of all days.

Driving west on Highway 15, Marissa turned on the radio to pick up the weather. The station reported a tornado watch in effect for central and southern Minnesota until midnight. Even without a tornado, the system could produce a line of severe thunderstorms. Normally, storms didn't worry Marissa much, but because she was already on edge today, the preternatural stillness in front of the approaching weather bothered her. As she turned off the highway onto the winding road through Island Park, she stepped on the accelerator.

At home, everything had remained quiet and calm. She stood at the living room window, and through the trees she could see a bluish-black line of clouds lurking on the western horizon.

Power outages from storms were common in the Minnetonka area because the large trees often took out power lines. Marissa unplugged her sensitive electrical equipment to protect it from lightning strikes, then closed the heavy blinds on the porch to keep rain from blowing in.

A rough gust of wind shook the house, rattling the windows. As Marissa came back into the living

Catherine Kohman

room, the cats suddenly appeared from snoozing on her bed upstairs. She petted them and set them into their cat beds in front of the fireplace. They watched her anxiously as she turned on the radio to the station her grandmother used to call Panic Radio.

Whenever foul weather threatened, they canceled regular programming, filling the air with live listener reports of nature's havoc and dire warnings from the National Weather Service. Marissa found their almost gleeful reporting on the storm to be a bit obnoxious, but they usually had the first reports of severe weather warnings.

The Panic Radio announcer said urgently, "Our state-of-the-art Doppler Radar has picked up a hook echo northwest of Glencoe in McLeod County. Ground reports from the sheriff's office also report a possible circulation. A tornado warning has been issued by the National Weather Service for the counties of McLeod, Wright, Carver and Hennepin until 5:30 P.M. Persons in those counties are advised to seek shelter if threatening conditions occur in their area."

The door under the stairs led to the basement. If necessary, Marissa and the cats could take shelter there. But the storm hadn't really hit them yet; she'd wait and see if it got that bad. A tornado cloud had passed over the island in 1965, so this storm could follow the same path.

She went to the living room window again and stared outside. The sky was a sickly green color to the west, and roiling masses of low black clouds swept overhead. Thunder boomed and streaks of lightning darted from cloud to cloud. With a howling screech, the wind buffeted the old house, and sheets of rain pounded on the cedar roof.

260

The Beckoning Ghost

The raw, elemental fury of the storm raised the hair on Marissa's neck, and she moved away from the window when another blast of wind shook the house. As the clouds moved in, the ensuing gloom made the inside of the house dark as night. Just as Marissa turned on a lamp by the couch, she heard a popping crackle from outside. The light flickered, then died.

Great. There went the power.

Marissa tried to remember where she stored her emergency supplies. That was dumb of her—she should have located her flashlight and candles *before* the lights went out. The closet in the downstairs bedroom—that's where she'd put them.

As she entered the bedroom, a chill passed over her. Since she'd bought the house, she'd tended to avoid this room; it made her feel uncomfortable. Just why, she couldn't explain . . .

Through the gloom, she groped her way to the closet. Inside a shoe box on the shelf she kept her candles, batteries and flashlight. Wait—the flashlight was gone. Damn! She'd used the flashlight in the basement last week. Where could she have left it?

Well, the candles would do for now. She placed one of the tapers in a brass holder and lit the wick. A small flame burned steadily, giving her enough light to see, so Marissa grabbed the shoe box and turned to go back into the living room.

What she saw made her freeze in place.

Where on earth was she?

Chapter Fifteen

If I must die,
I will encounter darkness as a bride,
And hug it in mine arms.
                    —William Shakespeare

Though the room seemed vaguely familiar, Marissa couldn't imagine where she was—certainly not her house on the lake. Her muscles tensed as she realized that she must have slipped into another vision, perhaps brought on by the storm.

Roughly furnished as a study, the room also contained a narrow single bed and nightstand. A full bookcase and laden desk filled one corner of the room; a stack of packing crates and a smooth wood and brass-bound chest stood in the other. This room had a fireplace, and a large winged chair pulled up close to it. In the grate, the embers of a dying fire lit the room with a rutilant glow.

Then she noticed a movement. Someone was sitting in the chair. Unconsciously, Marissa moved forward to see who it was.

"Brendan!" she cried with relief, taking a step toward him.

He remained still, staring deeply into the fire, a glass of brandy cradled loosely in his hand. With his other hand, he ran his fingers back through his unruly hair. Shocked by his appearance, she could see the pain in the ravaged lines of his tired face. Even the fire's ruddy glow failed to light the dullness in his dark eyes, which usually shone like polished obsidian.

"Brendan, what is it? What's wrong?" She placed the shoe box and candle holder on a table, then moved next to the chair. When he didn't answer her, she dropped to her knees on the Turkish carpet beside the chair.

"Brendan, my darling . . ." Marissa touched his hand.

His hand flinched, but he just stared into the fire, lost in his misery.

Thoroughly frightened now, Marissa came around to stand in front of the chair. *"Brendan!"*

He stared right through her, as if she was invisible.

Maybe she was—if what she saw was a vision of the past.

A sharp knocking at the door caught Marissa's attention. Brendan apparently heard it too. He said, "Go away."

A female voice came from the other side of the door. "Brendan, you've been locked away in there ever since Miranda left this morning. Let me in. I want to talk to you."

Brendan's face darkened. "Leave me alone, Rosalind. I have nothing to say."

She rattled the doorknob in frustration. "I'll be back."

Marissa heard Rosalind's heels click down the wooden hallway of what must be the Tyrells' bungalow. It was the night of the fire. She had to warn Brendan to get out. . . .

"Brendan, can you hear me? It's Marissa. Please, if you can, give me a sign." She touched his shoulder, but he just rubbed it idly with his hand.

The sound of a key in the lock made Marissa turn her head toward the door. Dressed in a violet silk dressing gown, Rosalind Tyrell came inside and closed the door behind her. Her dark brown hair fell over her shoulder in an unkempt braid. On her way to Brendan's chair, she looked right through Marissa.

Neither of them can see me, Marissa realized. How can I warn them about the fire if they don't know I'm here?

Rosalind faced her husband, who slumped in the chair in a wrinkled white shirt and khaki pants. Her face was white and pinched, with bruise-like shadows around her tawny eyes. Marissa didn't like the high-strung, skittish look in Rosalind Tyrell's eyes.

"So you intend to lock yourself away in Miranda's room," Rosalind spoke sharply. "I can't believe that you're actually pining for that girl—that impudent hussy!"

Brendan looked up for the first time, his gaze hardening as he faced his wife's ire. "Don't bait me, Ros."

"I thought once I got rid of her, you would talk to me again." The note in Rosalind's voice sounded both plaintive and angry. "She's gone, Brendan, and she's never coming back."

With a lithe movement, Brendan rose from the chair and threw his glass of brandy into the fire. The shattering glass and alcohol sent up a blaze of sparks. Rosalind shrank from the dark violence on her husband's face.

"I know damn well that she's not coming back," he said, his voice taut. "Now, what did you want with me?"

Marissa felt like a walk-on character in a play, a tragedy that would soon spiral out of control. Desperately, she grabbed at Brendan's arm, but he had no awareness of her. She could only watch and witness what was about to unfold.

Rosalind's eyes widened, and her lower lip began to quiver. "You do love her after all. I thought you sent her away because of me—because you loved me. Now I see that it's Miranda you love—it's always been Miranda."

Brendan walked away from his wife and sat down behind the desk. "I didn't want to hurt you, Ros—you're still my wife, for God's sake. Miranda's gone now. Can't we just leave it at that and go on with our lives?"

Rosalind confronted him, her fingers plucking at the sash of her robe. "No . . . no. I demand to know why you married me if you've always loved Miranda."

Marissa could tell by the tenseness in Brendan's jawline that an interrogation from his wife was the last thing he needed. She was amazed and proud of him, when he simply sighed and said, "I married you because I loved you then. I still do . . . though I find it hard to tell you when you're always raging at me for one thing or another."

Catherine Kohman

Rosalind bit her lip. "If I've been upset with you, it's because you were always in here with Miranda, working on those . . . filthy poems and stories. No wonder she thought of becoming an adulteress, reading those wicked, wicked tales you translate about concubines and . . . *fornication* in gardens."

Marissa could see him losing patience with his wife, and she prayed that Rosalind would have the sense to leave him alone with his grief.

Brendan's dark eyes flashed. "You may have your narrow-minded opinion of my work, but Miranda was *not* an adulteress. I don't ever want to hear you speak ill of her again."

"If you can write that—that lewd vileness you call your work, I can call her a wanton Jezebel or whatever I please."

"Not in my presence, nor to anyone else." Brendan sat rigid in the chair. "I'm warning you, Rosalind. Don't push me."

Defiant anger drove the hurt from his wife's face, and she turned to the bookshelf beside her. "This is what I think of your accumulation of filth."

She casually tipped the shelf forward until the books spilled out, crashing to the floor. Brendan got out of his chair and grabbed the bookcase. "Quit acting like a spoiled child."

"Oh, but I thought you *liked* children." Rosalind's piercing voice rose higher. "You've loved Miranda since she was a little girl; I'm surprised you didn't marry her instead of me. Of course, she was only fourteen then . . . most people would have thought it sordid to marry a girl young enough to be your daughter, a girl under your protection."

"For God's sake, stop it!"

Marissa's throat ached from the wincing pain on Brendan's face as he turned away. In high dudgeon now, Rosalind followed him back to the desk.

"That's why you brought Miranda to school in England. Her young, nubile flesh had started to interest you. You just married me to have an acceptable outlet for your base lust."

Brendan shot a dark, lancing glance Rosalind's way. "You didn't always feel that way about sex, did you? *You* were the one who pursued me, the one who didn't want to wait. As I recall, your dress was white, though by wearing it in your sacred church you perpetrated a bald-faced lie."

Rosalind's face paled and her thin body vibrated with holy outrage. "So I was not a virgin on my wedding day." Her eyes took on a sharp, feral gleam. "I'll warrant Miranda isn't one either. I'm sure that Justin Egerton thinks he'll be her first lover, but he doesn't know that you've already beaten him to it!"

Brendan clenched his fists. "Shut up, Ros! *I mean it!*"

His wife smiled, fox-like, her teeth pointed and glinting in the fire's glow. "Was that why Miranda refused to come to our wedding? Only fourteen and you'd bedded her . . . no wonder she couldn't stand seeing her lover marry someone else. *The stupid little slut.*"

Brendan's flat hand lashed out and caught Rosalind's cheek. The slap rocked her back on her heels. With a choking cry, she raised her hand to the stark-red imprint on her cheek. For a moment she stared at him, her eyes burning and hot.

On the edge of Brendan's desk lay a stack of

papers weighted down by a *kris*, a sacred dagger with a wavy edge used by the Nepalese. Rosalind snatched it off Brendan's desk and unsheathed it. She held it to her breast, the point making a small splotch of crimson on the bodice of her white nightgown.

Brendan edged toward her. "Rosalind, put the knife down," he said, his voice smooth and coaxing.

"No, you hate me. You never loved me, it was always her. I can't stand living anymore, knowing that you hate me and love her. I want to die."

Before Marissa's riveted gaze, Rosalind drew the dagger back to plunge it into her chest. Brendan leaped for her hand and caught it just in time.

"No, no," Rosalind pleaded, "I want to die."

Brendan struggled with his wife, but her madness gave her unusual strength. She pulled her hand free and hit him with her fists. "No, you won't stop me."

Like a slow-motion scene from a horror movie, Marissa saw the knife in Rosalind's hand, saw the wicked, sharp blade enter Brendan's chest. A thin gout of blood sprayed across Rosalind's face.

Brendan looked down at his bloodied shirt, a bewildered expression on his face. "Ros?"

Then he collapsed onto the carpet.

Marissa's heart froze as she saw Brendan's life-blood ooze out onto his chest. With a choking sob, she dropped to her knees beside him and pressed her hands to his chest. But she knew instinctively that the wound was too deep, too close to the heart. *Oh, God, no . . .*

Beneath her cold hands, his chest rose and fell in weakening, shallow breaths. She leaned forward, and her blond hair was tipped with scarlet.

The Beckoning Ghost

Please, Brendan, stay with me.

Behind her, she heard Rosalind shriek. Biju opened the door and rushed into the room. "*Mem,* what is it?"

Marissa heard him come to an abrupt halt as he saw Brendan on the floor, Rosalind with blood on her face and a knife in her hand. A strangled moan came from the Indian's chest.

"Oh, *Mem,* what have you done, what have you done?" He sobbed. "You have done and murdered the good *Sa'b.*"

Rosalind looked at Biju blankly. "He's not dead, tell me he's not. . . . " She collapsed into the Indian's arms.

Marissa touched Brendan's face, and to her surprise, he opened his eyes. "Randie . . . you came back."

"Yes, Brendan, I'm here." She didn't know why he could see her now, when he couldn't before. Maybe it was because he was slipping into the realm of the spirit. Whatever the reason, she didn't care; she thanked the gods for letting her be here for him.

With trembling fingers, she smoothed the dark hair from his forehead. "I'll be with you forever, my darling; I promise."

"I love you, *piara.*" He smiled gently. "One day soon, we'll go back to the hills, back to Darjeeling. I know you've always wanted to return there, where we were so happy."

"Hush, love . . . save your strength." She lifted his warm brown hand to her lips, and she thought her heart would burst from the pain. "Brendan, I love you so much."

"Don't go back to England, Randie. It's cold there. Ever since we left India, I've missed the heat

269

of the sun. Even now I miss it. . . . " He closed his eyes again, but kept breathing.

Marissa heard Rosalind's shaky whisper. "Who is he talking to?"

"The *Sa'b* thinks the Missy has returned, *Mem*. It is kinder to let him think so."

Marissa felt the tears rolling down her cheeks to splash onto Brendan's bloody shirt. "Don't leave me, Brendan, *please*."

Brendan's dark eyes opened again, filled with concern. "*Piara*, don't cry. I won't leave you . . . ever. We're fated to be together, you and I—it's our *karma*."

"Yes, my love. I know." She leaned down, putting all her love and need into one single embrace. "Take this kiss with you until I can hold you in my arms again."

"I will." He raised his hand to stroke her cheek. "I love you so much . . . my darling Miranda." His eyes drifted closed, and he sighed as he lowered his hand to her hair.

"Brendan?" Under her hands, Marissa felt his breath stop, and his heart stilled. A fresh wave of hot tears flooded her eyes and rolled down her cheeks.

Then she felt a sudden sick dizziness spin through her, like vertigo. The orange glow in the room flickered once, and then thick, soft blackness surrounded her. In that smothering cocoon, she gave up her fight and spiraled down into the deep, waiting darkness.

Chapter Sixteen

*Life is a dream . . . we waking sleep and sleep-
ing wake.*
                                    —Michel Montaigne

"Marissa . . . Marissa, sweetheart, can you hear
me?"

A feathery touch across her forehead—Brendan's mustache?

Marissa found herself looking up into Brendan's worried face while lying in her own brass
bed upstairs. Joyous relief made her sit up and
throw her arms around Brendan's neck and hold
tight. *"Oh, you're here—you're all right!"*

He drew away so he could hold her face between his hands. "Marissa, are *you* all right? Darling lass, you gave me such a fright! I came back
to find the house completely dark, a terror of a
storm howling outside and you, lying on the floor

271

downstairs, as cold as ice. I carried you up here and warmed you up as best I could, but you still didn't wake."

He stroked her hair. *"Piara,* I worried so . . ."

"I'll be fine, now that you're here with me." She hugged him fiercely.

"What happened to you?"

Marissa held onto his shoulders to support herself as much as to comfort him. "I—I saw your death, Brendan. I witnessed your murder."

"Murder? What—what do you mean?" His face went blank with disbelief.

"You didn't die in the fire, Brendan; I suspect that was just a cover-up for your wife's crime. Rosalind stabbed you in a fit of jealous anger."

His dark eyes troubled, he asked, "You really saw . . . this?"

Marissa explained in detail what she witnessed. "I'm sorry, Brendan, but I think what I saw was real. Don't you remember any of it?"

"The memories I have of my death have always been somewhat hazy. I do recall the argument, but that's the last thing . . ." He looked at her with amazement. "I thought I remembered Randie being there, but it must have been you that I saw. Miranda was in her hotel that night. *You* were my angel in need."

"If it's any comfort to you, I think Rosalind stabbed you by accident. She hit you with her fists, and forgot the knife. Though who can say . . . furious with you, she may have wanted to kill you subconsciously."

"So you think Biju covered up the true manner of my death—that he did it to protect Rosalind?"

"It would explain why they never found your body. You weren't in the fire at all. Biju must have

272

been anxious about the fire being put out before enough of your remains were destroyed. I think you're buried out by the ruins of the old ice house. When I was just a girl—the same day I saw you on the island—I had a vision of Biju digging out there. And I found an 1872 gold sovereign—it could have fallen out of your pocket when Biju carried you there."

Brendan looked thoughtful. Glad that her revelations hadn't upset him too much, she stroked his arm.

"That would also explain how she saved my manuscripts," he said with a wondering smile. "It's ironic, isn't it? She called them filth just before that."

"Perhaps Biju saved them. He always had great respect for you." She shivered. "It was me he didn't like."

"I think somehow Biju realized, even before I did, that *you* were the love of my life, not Rosalind. He spent his entire life protecting her."

Marissa sighed. "I wish there had been some way for me to warn you, but you couldn't see me until you were dying."

Brendan ran his hands down her arms and held her hands. "You know all things happen for a reason. I had you with me when I needed you most."

She asked, "Do you think Miranda suspected Rosalind?"

"It's possible she learned something later. Perhaps that's why Rosalind tried to remain on good terms with her. We may never know."

Marissa went into his arms again and laid her head on his shoulder. "I don't ever want to lose you."

"My love," he said with a poignant smile, "if the Fates allow it, I will never leave you."

The next morning, the air was rain-washed and perfectly clear. With Brendan around, Marissa went about her business, humming lightly. Eager to get on with the quest for Brendan's manuscripts, she slipped upstairs and made reservations to London for the following day without telling him. Then she arranged for Kelly, her vet's assistant, to come over and "cat-sit" while she was gone.

Marissa also decided to give Owen a call and warn him about her imminent arrival. She asked him to have his source at Somerset House see what other records existed for Johanna Hensley, such as her death records. Marissa wanted to know who might have inherited her possessions.

After dinner that night, she and Brendan sat in their customary places on the swing, he in his jeans and white cotton shirt, Marissa in a pink sundress. She asked casually, "Do you have anything planned for tomorrow?"

His Gypsy eyes alight, Brendan said, "No, I think my schedule is open."

She looked at him in frank assessment. "How extensive is that wardrobe of yours—got any tweeds in that closet?"

"Tweeds?" His brows quirked in puzzlement.

She stretched out her legs the length of the swing and wriggled her bare toes invitingly. "Yes, I have a yen to go motoring in the country: Oxford, the Cotswolds, even Bath . . . wherever strikes my fancy."

"Ah . . . England." Brendan smiled. "When do we leave?"

"I'm flying over on Northwest Airlines tomorrow afternoon. Shall I meet you in London—at the Montclair?"

"As you wish." With a mischievous smile he added, "I'll be glad to show you around my old haunts . . . or explore some new ones with you." He dropped his hand down from the back of the swing and massaged her foot, then slowly ran his fingers up her calf.

"Of course," she said evenly, though her heart began to race. "Ever the intrepid adventurer."

"I'm always interested in charting new territory, especially lush, rolling hills . . . and vales." His hand skimmed her bare skin, up under her cotton skirt to her thigh.

As his long, cool fingers stroked the warm, smooth skin inside of her thighs, Marissa felt a core of sweet, molten heat rising from her loins. In a teasing way, his hand grazed over her silk panties, then found that particularly sensitive spot between her waist and her hip.

Marissa closed her eyes and made a low murmur of pleasure in her throat. Holding her breath, she knew she should stop him before their desire became too heated. Just a moment longer . . .

Then he started tickling her.

"Brendan!"

She tried to twist away from that terrible tickling monster, but he pinned her down on the swaying swing. She shrieked again, and in between laughter and yelps of distress, begged him to stop.

Finally, the wretched man decided that he'd tortured her long enough. Panting, Marissa lay on her back, her skirt twisted up around her waist, her lower body completely bare to his eyes except

275

for the wisp of white silk across her hips. Leaning back for a better view, Brendan ran his gaze down her body with an appreciative grin.

He laughed. "Had enough, pet?"

Marissa lowered her lashes and seductively pursed her mouth before Brendan's amused gaze. In her best Mae West, she drawled, "Hardly, my boy. When are you going to stop fooling around and get serious?"

Brendan's eyes darkened and the edges of his mouth tightened. His intense gaze sent a shiver of fearful anticipation through her. Then his lips curved in a wicked smile. "Don't tempt me, you minx . . . or I'll tickle you again."

"You wouldn't." Marissa sat up and moved closer to the edge of the swing, ostensibly to pull down her skirt. She didn't know how long they could play this sweet, dangerous game without giving in to their yearnings. Then what price would they have to pay?

"You know better than to dare me, Rissa." He raised his hands, poised for another devilish attack.

"*Hah!*" Marissa leaped up with a huge push that sent the swing flying, and Brendan tumbled backwards into the cushions.

Giggling madly, she ran into the living room and up the stairs. She heard Brendan pounding after her, and felt a rush of air as he dove for her ankles at the top of the steps. He missed his catch and she flew down the balcony to slam her bedroom door behind her.

Her chest heaving with her exertion, Marissa rested against the heavy wooden panels. She heard Brendan's purposeful footsteps outside the

276

door. "You can't come in. I don't allow ticklers in my bedroom."

"What about lovers?" came the husky reply.

No, no, Marissa thought, *I can't give in, no matter how much I want him.*

"None of those either." She smiled to herself, a half-smile that spoke more of heartache than joy. "Especially not tall, dark Gypsies with a gorgeous mustache and a scar."

"You know, you can't stop me, if I want to." Again, that deep seductive timbre.

Marissa's knees felt like Jello, and it wasn't from her dash up the stairs.

"Go away," she said with wavering determination. She had to remind herself that to give in to her treacherous desire now would be a mistake. Brendan's search for his manuscripts must come first.

She cleared her throat and said firmly, "I have to pack for the flight to London."

"If you insist . . ."

She heard the regret in his voice. Then he added, "You and I will have a rematch in London, young lady. And there will be no strategic retreats there."

As his footsteps faded away, Marissa heard him whistling an old Irish ballad called *Slievenamon*. She relaxed her tense muscles. *Be strong and prosperous in this resolve,* her conscience quoted to her.

"All right, I get the message." She blew out her breath, fluffing the bangs on her forehead. "It isn't going to be easy. . . . "

Then an echo of Brendan's voice from ages past—from Miranda's memory—rang through

Catherine Kohman

her mind. *There's no happiness without a measure of sorrow in it.*

Frowning, she went to the closet and dragged out her suitcase, then threw it on the bed. For a frustrated moment, she glared at the innocuous suitcase, hands on hips. Then, sending an exasperated glance toward the door, she muttered, *"Irishmen!"*

On the flight over, Marissa took her carry-on from the overhead, and wondered why it seemed heavier than normal. Digging to the bottom, she extracted the weighty tome *Phantasms of the Living*. Not exactly light reading . . . odd that she didn't remember packing it.

Since she'd lugged it aboard the plane, she decided to read some of it. The anecdotes sent chills up her spine, and she snuggled deeper into the wool blanket as she read. One man deliberately projected himself into his fiancée's bedroom at midnight. The girl's married sister slept in the same bed, and the man had taken the woman's hand in his before he left the room. So not only did the man's astral double *look* real; he also had a physical presence.

The number of cases recorded in the book astonished Marissa; of course they weren't under scientific conditions, but the sheer volume of the anecdotal evidence gave the theory of bi-location some weight. *Astral doubles*, now there's an intriguing theory—in some ways it could be useful. Why fly to London when you could just "beam" yourself over there?

Marissa smiled then, a bittersweet smile, as she thought of her own beloved spirit. She bet the psychic researchers would *love* to get their hands on

The Beckoning Ghost

Brendan . . . *and so would she. . . .*

Setting aside the thick book, she pulled the blanket up to her chin. She still had a few hours to nap before they landed at Gatwick.

Marissa checked into a suite on the top floor at the Montclair, a small gem of a hotel overlooking Green Park. After a long, relaxing shower, she came out wearing a thick terry robe with the hotel's gold crest on the pocket.

In the peach lounge chair by the window, Brendan sat with his long legs casually crossed at the ankles. "Well, where are we off to first?"

"Brendan, you didn't listen when I told you about jet lag. I need to sleep for a little while. This afternoon, we'll go see Owen."

He smiled in apology. "I'll make myself scarce, shall I?"

She yawned. "I would like a few hours of *uninterrupted* sleep."

"I'll go explore London on my own, and see what damage one hundred-odd years has done to the old girl. I'll be back at 3."

Marissa curled up on the turned-down bed and answered groggily, "Mmm-hmm."

Brendan pulled the covers up to her chest as he left, pressing a light kiss on her moist cheek.

Owen had a flat over a Greek restaurant in Kensington. As Marissa climbed the stairs, she could hear bazouki music and smell roasting meat, rosemary and oregano from the kitchens. Brendan followed behind her, and she caught his glance lingering on the sway of her denim-clad hips.

"This reminds me of a little place I knew in Cyprus," he said. "The owner's name was Pericles and he had the loveliest dancing girls in the Eastern Mediterranean."

"Brendan."

"Sorry, love." He grinned sheepishly. "The bazouki music brought back memories."

Here she was, standing outside Owen's flat and talking to a ghost about bazouki music. Marissa shook her head in disbelief as she knocked on the door. She didn't think Owen could see Brendan, but she wasn't sure. . . .

Owen flung his door open and pulled her inside. Brendan barely got in as her friend slammed the door behind him. Obviously, her ghostly lover was invisible to her host.

Owen gave Marissa a big, long hug. "Lady scholar, you're here at last."

Marissa basked in the warmth of his musical Welsh voice. "Owen, it's great to see you again. How long has it been?"

She took in the jumble of furnishings in her friend's crowded apartment. Books, more books and over by the window, a diorama of the Battle of Sharpsburg. There were, however, a number of chairs pulled up to a table holding a Civil War chess set.

Owen answered, "Ah, well . . . since that encampment at Fredericksburg, summer before last. Too long."

Marissa found herself staring over the Welshman's shoulder into Brendan's watchful eyes. She glanced back at Owen's thin, long face, which was overshadowed by his mop of russet hair. He didn't sense Brendan, so she relaxed as they caught up on the events of the past two years.

Brendan started pacing back and forth in his impatience. "This is all very cozy, but could you please ask him about my manuscripts?"

Marissa frowned at him and motioned for him to sit down.

"So, Owen dear, have you found anything new for me?"

"My friend Jackie at Somerset House said she doesn't have a death record for Johanna Hensley, but she's checking to see if Johanna remarried before she died. It's their busy season, so it may take a few days' time for that record."

"Thanks, Owen. I appreciate all your efforts."

Owen smiled, his hazel eyes lighting with pleasure. "Think nothing of it, lady fair. It would help if I knew what you were looking for."

Out of the corner of her eye, she saw Brendan shake his head no. "I'm not sure exactly; I just have the feeling that there might be a few more pieces in the Tyrell puzzle. A letter or two that may have been overlooked, an article or poem. Why, remember those folios of Shakespeare's that recently turned up? It's a vast, undiscovered territory out there."

"I can arrange an appointment for you with Granger Wilkes. You really should see him." Owen grinned. "Remember what I told you—lots of leg, and a little cleavage wouldn't hurt either."

Marissa blushed, afraid to turn and see the black look on Brendan's face. "Owen, you're a terrible influence on me. I'd better leave before you corrupt me altogether. And I think I'll pass on seeing Wilkes for now, since I have some promising leads up Oxford way."

"You can't stay for dinner?" His mop of hair dipped forward in disappointment.

"You mean you actually have a kitchen somewhere under all these books?"

281

Owen sniffed in mock annoyance. "Most amusing, wretched girl. I remember your flat in Cambridge—even the bedroom was lined with bookcases. So don't condescend to me, lady scholar."

The storm cloud on Brendan's brow looked about to burst, so Marissa hugged Owen briefly and said her good-byes, with a promise to have dinner after she returned from Oxfordshire.

Once they were out on the street, Brendan took her arm with punctilious courtesy. "How, pray tell, does that scruffy young Welshman know the furnishings of your bedroom?"

Since they were alone on the street, she replied, "Brendan, don't be ridiculous . . . I was living with Robin then. Owen is just a dear friend. We had a party when he came to visit and the crowd spilled over into the bedroom."

She paused to look at him. His brows still slanted dangerously.

"You seem on intimate terms with this fellow," he said. "He calls you 'lady scholar' and 'lady fair' . . . and what's all this talk of showing leg and cleavage? Does he fancy you're some sort of *fille de joie?*"

Marissa stopped and dragged her arm out of his grasp. "I can't believe you're jealous of Owen. He's a sweet, gentle fellow who's been very helpful to me . . . and to you. He's Welsh and given to flowery language, so he teases me, I tease him back. It's all very innocent."

She took a deep breath. "And as long as we're on the subject, his references to showing leg and cleavage were a joke. He didn't insult me, the way you just did."

Brendan's brows raised in perplexity; then he

had the grace to look ashamed by his outburst. "I'm sorry, love, if I offended you. I simply don't understand this modern bantering back and forth between the sexes. It's too new to me. Will you forgive me this time?"

Marissa relented with a smile. "You really ought to stop scowling all the time. I know you're not as fierce as you pretend to be."

"Ah, but I can be." He grinned then. "Especially in the boudoir."

"Brendan Tyrell," she said with a wry smile, "you're incorrigible."

Early the next morning, Marissa drove her rented Jaguar up into the English heartland. Once beyond the London traffic, she relaxed behind the wheel and enjoyed the rustic charm of the English countryside with Brendan beside her.

As they passed a particularly garish entrance to an RV park on the outskirts of Oxford, Brendan asked, "What in God's name is 'New Shangri-la?' "

Patiently, Marissa explained the reference to Hilton's mythical Himalayan kingdom and the function of the resort.

Brendan shook his head. "Well, I traveled all over the Himalayas for the Survey, and I never saw anything as grotesque as that—what did you call it? Ah, yes . . . 'holiday camp.' "

"Don't be disheartened, Brendan-ji." She patted his hand consolingly. "The twentieth century hasn't ruined quite everything."

As if to make her point, the countryside proved relatively unspoiled as they neared the village of Cassington. From a distance they could pick out the tall spire of a Norman church, and the road led them past thatched-roof cottages built from cut stone to the neat village green.

After parking the car near the green, Marissa consulted her blue notebook. "The Hensleys used to live at 20 Larkspur Lane. Come on, love, it's a beautiful day for exploring."

As she gathered up her purse, Brendan leaned over and kissed the tip of her nose. "My adorable Sherlock, what ever would I do without you?"

"Oh, you'd probably wind up in *Ghost Six: The Return of Groucho*." She winked at him boldly.

"I beg your pardon?" His raven brows lifted.

"*Ghost Six*—a movie sequel," she said sunnily, "and Groucho . . . well, you do remind me of him sometimes, when you get that certain devilish gleam in your eyes."

"He's from the cinema then? Has he any relation to this much lamented Elvis person, or that 'Mel' hero you and Kelsey often talk about?"

Marissa laughed softly. "No, he was a great comedian, a funny, sharp and intelligent man. I grew up on Marx Brothers videos and reruns of *You Bet Your Life*." She sighed in fond remembrance. "I *loved* Groucho."

He gave her an indulgent smile. "If you loved him, that's good enough for me. I'll be your Groucho, whenever you'd like."

"That's sweet of you . . . now all we need is a pair of glasses with a fake nose and bushy eyebrows." She opened the car door and slipped out as Brendan made a grab for her wrist. Chuckling, she turned to lock the car door, then heard a voice murmur in her ear.

"If it's dress-up and frisky games you have in mind, my dearest, I can assure you that I have quite an extensive wardrobe as well as a fertile imagination."

With his warm breath tickling her neck, Marissa felt a chill of anticipation run down her spine as playfully erotic illustrations from a private Victorian edition of Brendan's *Scented Garden* leapt into mind. Her skin flushed suddenly, and she thought, *Please, not now*.

"Brendan, not here," she muttered. "I can't talk to you out in public without looking like the village idiot."

She smiled sheepishly as an elderly gent on a bicycle passed by, giving her an odd look. "See what I mean?"

"Very well . . . a temporary truce then. Lead on, Sherlock; let's find the Hensleys' former residence."

Ten minutes' walk along winding lanes brought them to a sizable stone cottage at the edge of town. Marissa ducked under a massive pink rosebush that hung over the wooden half-door and knocked politely. As approaching footsteps sounded from inside the house, she shot Brendan a nervous smile.

A gray-haired, matronly lady came to the door, an inquiring smile on her lips as she dried her hands on her apron. "Yes?"

After introductions were made, Marissa explained that she was doing research on families from this part of the county. "I believe a family named Hensley once resided here. Do you happen to know if the family still lives in the area?"

The woman, Mrs. Derham, said, "Oh, my, the name is familiar, but I can't really recall . . . wait a moment. When we were doing some restoration on the house, I remember seeing their name on the old deeds. I believe when they sold the house they moved to a farm near Eynsham. It's not very far from here."

"When would that have been? Have you any idea?"

Mrs. Derham pursed her mouth. "I'd say it was before the 1880s. The house has been in my family since then."

Thanking the woman profusely for her help, Marissa headed for the Norman church with Brendan following in her wake. She glanced up at him as they crossed the empty green. "Don't look so glum. It would have been a little optimistic, even for me, to expect to find the manuscripts all boxed up and tied with a neat bow back in Larkspur Lane."

Brendan sighed. "I suppose you're right. I merely hope this isn't one of your 'wild-goose chases.' "

"I'll check with the vicar. He may have records that would give us the name of the farm they moved to."

While Marissa admired the beautiful old stained glass in the roundels and Brendan lounged in a centuries-old oak pew, the young vicar consulted his dusty tomes. Fresh-faced and blond-haired, he didn't look at all like Marissa's vision of an Anglican clergyman.

Brendan said, "The vicar looks like he should be in short pants instead of a cassock."

Marissa found herself smiling in agreement, then hastily sobered as the young man came around the screen, volume in hand.

"Ah, here we are," he said. "Chalgrove Farm, Eynsham. Does that help you?"

Marissa smiled at him warmly. "Yes, Vicar, it

does immensely. Thank you again."

As she turned to leave, the vicar asked, "Are you sure you wouldn't care to stay and have lunch?"

"I'd love to, but I really need to come up with some concrete results for this project today. Perhaps another time."

The blond-haired man smiled back, a touch of regret in his eyes. "Yes, well . . . do stop in again whenever you're in the area. I'd like to buy a copy of that book when it's finished."

Marissa gave him her hand in farewell as Brendan looked on, a cynical smile on his face. "I'll be sure to send you one."

As they walked back to the car, Brendan remarked, "Shame on you, young woman. Misleading that cherubic young clergyman, using your enticing smile to charm the information from him."

"He was sweet, wasn't he?" Marissa added guiltily, "I hope he's not too disappointed when the family history fails to materialize." Then she smiled. "Chalgrove Farm, Eynsham. Come on, Watson, the game's afoot." She raced him back to the car.

Brendan trotted easily up behind her, muttering to himself, "*Groucho . . . Watson . . .* whatever will she come up with next?"

Chapter Seventeen

Is there no bright reversion in the sky,
For those who greatly think or bravely die?
            —Alexander Pope

For the second time in a day, Marissa knocked on
a stranger's door. This time she found herself in
front of a rather ugly brick farmhouse of indeter-
minate parentage, though obviously late Victorian. Had the Hensleys built this house when they
moved to Chalgrove? If so, she lamented their
taste.

A young woman with disheveled brown hair
and a squalling baby in her arms answered the
door. At the harried expression on the girl's face,
Marissa diffidently asked after the Hensleys, then
glanced up at Brendan for further guidance. With
a small smile and a Gallic shrug, he left her to fend
for herself.

288

The young woman looked blank for a moment, then turned and shouted into the house. "Granddad! Come out and chat with this American lady, would you? I think Ned has a soggy nappy." She smiled sheepishly and disappeared into the dark recesses of the hallway as a white-haired gentleman shuffled to the door, a pair of reading glasses perched on his forehead. "Oh, a Yank, and a pretty one too."

Marissa put the same question to the grandfather.

"No, sorry, my dear. No Hensleys live here, nor anywhere else near about as I can tell. When the old farmhouse burned down, the Hensleys pulled up stakes and moved to South Africa. That's when my father purchased the farm and built the new house."

With a sudden plunge into dismay, Marissa repeated, "Burned down? *South Africa?* When?" She felt Brendan's hand touch her back.

"Oh, I'd guess around 1880," the grandfather said cheerily. "That's how old the house is."

Brendan watched the misery blossom in Marissa's eyes as the old gent went into an enthusiastic description of the fire and the Hensleys' departure for Capetown. Though his own sense of defeat nearly overwhelmed him, Marissa's obvious disillusionment pained him more. He loved seeing the excited eagerness in her eyes during their search, and would have given anything to have it back there again.

"Come on, *piara*. He's a garrulous old man with no one to listen to his stories. Don't let his relish of old disasters discourage you. It sounds like the house was only damaged, not destroyed, and we

289

don't have proof that my manuscripts were ever here."

Marissa looked up at him. "But I was so sure."

The grandfather paused in his recital of doom. "What was that, miss?"

"Oh, nothing important," she said to the old gent with a covering smile. "I really must be going." With a gracious thank-you, she backed her way down the walk toward her car while the old man kept talking. Finally he went back inside and she could escape to the privacy of the Jaguar, where her shoulders slumped in dejection.

Brendan took her hand in his. "Listen to me, lass. Would Sherlock Holmes give up this easily? Surely not."

The moisture in her eyes at the brink of becoming tears, Marissa shook her head in mute agreement.

With a reassuring squeeze to her shoulders, he said, "I saw an attractive wayside by a stream just back the road a bit. I think we should buy you some lunch at the nearest pub and have a picnic. That should refresh your little gray cells."

The trembling of Marissa's lush lower lip stopped. "Little gray cells? Have you been sneaking a peek at Agatha Christie when I'm asleep?"

"Agatha Christie? I don't recall anyone by that name."

Her glance skeptical, she probed further. "Hercule Poirot, the Belgian detective?"

Brendan shrugged. The name meant nothing to him . . . or did it? For some peculiar reason, a vision of an elegant train popped into his head—the Orient Express? Another one of those frustrating fragments from that other layer of consciousness.

"Well, that's certainly odd." Her despondent

mood seemed to abate as a tiny smile curved her lips. "Perhaps we ought to stop at a chemist's and buy you some mustache wax and hair pomade, *eh bien?*"

The nearest pub provided Marissa with a substantial ploughman's lunch, though she opted for a serving of crudités in place of the boiled egg. Drinking a cool cider instead of warm ale, she sat on the picnic blanket that the rental company had thoughtfully provided with the car.

Brendan entertained her with outrageous tales of his days in India, while he worked for the Survey team. Danger, mind-boggling luxury, spiritual wonder, the remarkably resilient people and the splendor of the Himalayas—he'd seen it all.

Brushing a drowsy fly off her cotton slacks, she said, "I bet Miranda never heard half these stories."

"Oh, I think she heard most of them, though censored to a small degree." Brendan smiled up at her from his reclining position on the blanket.

Marissa hugged her knees and sent him a sidelong glance. "But I get the unexpurgated versions?"

He rolled over onto his side and squinted up at her, the filtered light from the oak tree above them dappling his face. "I don't respect you any less, Marissa. You've had a different upbringing than Randie did—what she might have found scandalous, you find mildly amusing."

"I think you underestimated her worldliness. In some ways, she was always a woman-child to you."

"Does that bother you?" With a pensive look, he sat up and slid closer to her, disturbingly close. "If

291

it does, I want to assure you that you're the most captivating *woman* I've ever known."

A beam of sunlight slanted across his eyes, reflecting off flecks of gold deep within them, like precious metal streaked through obsidian. She saw herself mirrored in their dark depths, and felt a queer sense of submersion, akin to drowning. Shaking off the eerie sensation, she said, "Well, we ought to start back for London before it gets too late. Maybe Owen will have news."

Brendan kept his silence as she packed up the remnants of her picnic and stowed them away in the trunk of the car. She hoped she hadn't hurt his feelings, but sometimes his intensity scared her; she was afraid of losing herself to him. If she opened up completely, she'd be so vulnerable . . . like Miranda. Of all things, she didn't want to end up like Miranda, a sad, tragic figure.

Alongside the road where she'd parked the car, a lovely cottage garden bloomed in rich profusion. Pink stock, a riot of sweet peas, blue delphiniums and white lilies crowded the gray wooden fence. Marissa saw an old woman in a frayed straw hat tending one of the rose beds and on impulse, decided to speak to her. "Pardon me, could you tell me the name of these pink flowers? They look like miniature hollyhocks."

The old woman came up to the fence, carrying a basket of peach roses. Under the hat brim, a pair of clear blue eyes peeked up at Marissa. "Some people call them that, but their botanical name is *sidalcea*."

Marissa smiled. "I've never seen them before." Always interested in flowers, she asked more questions about the garden. She enjoyed talking to the old woman, Margaret, who seemed proud and pleased to discuss the fruits of her labors. Marissa thought about asking the villager about the Hensleys, but the prospect of another dismal recitation of the family's exodus to South Africa kept her from mentioning it.

Brendan waited patiently nearby, an amused smile on his face. When she bid Margaret a reluctant good-bye, the older woman pressed a small bouquet of the roses upon her. Marissa asked, "What are these called? The peach color is exquisite."

"I don't know the true name," Margaret said thoughtfully, "something French I'm sure. They're very old. A friend of my grandmother's gave her a cutting, and all my plants sprang from that. I simply call them 'Johanna's roses.' "

Something fluttered in Marissa's chest. "Johanna?"

"Hensley, though that wasn't her name after she remarried and moved away."

Marissa felt like kissing the old woman, but settled for sending Brendan a quick, triumphant glance. He grinned back at her and gave her a thumbs up sign. In a barely controlled tone, she said, "What a coincidence! I'm researching the Hensley family line and I thought I'd lost track of Johanna, since I'd heard she moved to South Africa. What was her second husband's name?"

Margaret looked chagrined. "Now, isn't that silly? I can't remember the name of the fellow she married—when she lived here, she was known as Edward Hensley's wife, you see. But you are mistaken about one thing . . . only the oldest sons went to Capetown after their father's death, and the fire. Johanna moved with her new husband back to his village in the Cotswolds."

293

Marissa felt like a puppet on a string, yanked up and down with the twists of fate. "Can you remember the name of the village, Margaret? It would be so helpful to me!"

The old woman thought another minute. "I'm sorry, m'dear; I can't recall his name or that of the village. Perhaps my grandmother never told me."

"She's a very old woman, Rissa," Brendan remarked. "Give her some time and she might come up with the information. It's our only lead."

Obviously reading Marissa's crestfallen face, Margaret added, "If I do remember something, I can call you, and I'll ask around the village to see if anyone else knows the names."

Subdued, Marissa gave Margaret her card with the Montclair's number written on the back. "Please call, Margaret, if you remember *anything*."

The Englishwoman gazed at her steadily. "This is very important to you, isn't it, child?"

With a heartfelt glance at Brendan, Marissa smiled gamely. "More than you can ever imagine."

"What a roller-coaster ride!"

As they drove through the twilight back to London, Marissa shook her head in frustration. "The new Eynsham vicar wasn't too helpful either, was he? I suppose he wearies from all the amateur genealogists plaguing him with questions in the summer. A rather dour fellow after that nice young Mr. Hood at Cassington."

"What do you propose now?" Brendan asked, admiring the way she skillfully maneuvered the Jaguar around a narrow curve. Her smooth coordinated movements as she shifted and turned the wheel fascinated him. Somehow, driving a motorcar seemed much more sensual than driving a carriage, with the powerful purr of the engine under the hood. He tried to dampen the erotic urges that always lay just beneath the surface whenever he was near her.

Marissa sighed. "I'm afraid it's time to see Granger Wilkes. Owen's right—I shouldn't let my personal prejudices interfere with the search. In the meantime, Margaret may come up with something for us."

Granger Wilkes's housekeeper ushered Marissa into the library of his Neo-Gothic mansion in Guildford. Unseen by the older woman, Brendan followed in behind them.

He glanced at the bookshelves with their neat sets of leather-bound volumes, chosen for their display qualities, not their contents. Obviously not a true scholar's library.

Glass-topped display cases and upright cabinets stood along the wall in front of the windows, hung with swags of a hideous puce velvet. On the farthest wall sat a massive mahogany desk, and over the mantel hung a large oil portrait of Brendan himself.

"What the devil am I doing here?" he exclaimed as the housekeeper left the room.

Marissa moved over to the painting, the same portrait she'd shown to Kelsey. "It's a recent copy. The original hangs in the National Portrait Gallery, unless Wilkes has managed to buy his way into that treasure trove as well."

Prompted by the sarcasm in her voice, Brendan asked, "What sort of fellow is this Wilkes? It appears that there is little love lost between the two of you."

"You can determine that for yourself. He's com-

295

ing down the hallway now."

The double doors opened and Granger Wilkes made his entrance into the room. Of slim build and medium height, he was dressed in a camel suede jacket and a silk turtleneck, along with beige slacks. His dark hair—a flat black with no life to it—swept back from a brow that Brendan judged too low. Dyed, Brendan decided with disgust.

"Ah, Miss Erickson." As Wilkes reached for Marissa's hands and patted one, Brendan noticed his nails were polished. "So delighted to hear that you were in London. How is your biography of Brendan coming along?"

Brendan frowned at the man's use of his personal name.

Marissa removed her hands from Wilkes's grasp and shoved them into the pockets of her heather tweed jacket. "It's coming along very well, Mr. Wilkes," she said with a thin smile, "but I had to check with you for any crucial bits of information that I may have missed in my research."

"Please, my dear, call me Granger. And may I call you Marissa in return?" He smiled ingratiatingly. "After all, we share a passionate interest in our unsung hero."

Granger's eyes strayed to Brendan's portrait. "I'm sure your biography will bring him the fame and glory wrongly denied him in this life."

Though he ought to have been flattered by the man's words, Brendan felt distinctly in need of a bath. To Marissa he said, "Who *is* this unctuous toady?"

The corners of Marissa's mouth twitched briefly, and she shot a warning glance in Brendan's direction. "I'm primarily interested in any letters or manuscripts that you have in your collection."

Wilkes led her over to a glass case by the windows, and from a drawer in the cabinet extracted a number of acid-free manuscript protectors. "I'm afraid even my collection is pitifully weak, Marissa; we lost so much in that holocaust in Minnesota."

Granger set the boxes on a table in front of the window and drew up a pink damask-covered chair for Marissa to sit in while she worked. She took off her jacket and draped it over the back of the chair, revealing an ivory silk shirt tucked into the waist of her gray slacks. Marissa seated herself in the chair and opened the first box.

To Brendan's dismay, he saw Wilkes stare at the way the silk clung to the enticing swell of Marissa's bosom, the neat curve of her waist. As the man leaned over her shoulder to make a comment about the contents of the box, his hand rested on the arm of the chair, just inches from her breast. Wilkes was positively drooling over her, and he had to be 50, at least.

On a low cocktail table in front of the library's leather sofa sat an arrangement of yellow and white lilies. With a nudge of his booted toe, Brendan sent the crystal vase spilling onto the Oriental rug.

Both Marissa and the toady turned around in surprise. Wilkes said, "What the . . ."

As Wilkes walked over to inspect the damage, Marissa glanced up at Brendan, who tried to look guileless and innocent. Her eyes narrowed in suspicion, but she said, "Perhaps the arrangement was a bit top-heavy. That's happened to me a number of times."

Catherine Kohman

Frowning, Granger picked up the vase and flowers. "I'll speak to the housekeeper about it. If you'll excuse me, my dear."

After Wilkes left the room, Marissa said, "You did that deliberately."

Brendan folded his arms across his chest. "I had to get his attention off your feminine charms before he started pawing you. His hand was just—"

Marissa's green-gray eyes sparked dangerously. "I know where his hand was, and if he'd moved it an inch further, I would have nailed him. I can take care of myself, Brendan. Wilkes is a dirty old weasel, but relatively harmless."

"Well, if he tries it again he'll have more to deal with than a damp carpet."

"Really." Her mouth tightened in exasperation. "Why don't you do something more useful than protecting my virtue? Take a look at these and tell me if any of them should have been in that fire."

Together they studied the assembled manuscripts, mostly translations of poems, articles and letters. Marissa had seen the majority of the items, or copies of them, before this. They were working on the last box when Brendan laid six sheets of thick paper in front of Marissa.

"Do you recognize these?" He gestured to the sketch-pad pages. Four of the pages contained notes; the other two had sketches of decorative patterns and garments.

"No." She skimmed the pages quickly. "The sketches appear to be costumes and beading patterns from a northern Plains tribe, but I don't recognize the language."

"Absarokee," he answered. "A handsome young man from their tribe came into our winter camp in Wyoming, and I used the time of his visit to

298

record some of the basic vocabulary."

Marissa looked up at Brendan, her irises darkening. "But this had to come from Minnesota . . . unless you sent it to someone, or gave it to Miranda."

"No, I'm sure that it was in the chest with all the other manuscripts. We hadn't started work on the Plains book, so I would have had this with all the other notes."

With a sputter of laughter, Marissa pushed herself up out of the chair and flung herself into Brendan's arms. She pressed a joyous kiss on his lips. "We're on the trail! Oh, Brendan—"

The doors to the library swung open and Granger walked back into the room. Marissa glanced at Brendan in dismay and stepped back, dropping her arms. She blushed furiously as Wilkes approached her.

"That high color suits you, my dear, but I won't flatter myself by thinking that I'm the cause of it." He paused a moment as if waiting for her to contradict him. When she didn't, he self-consciously cleared his throat. "Have you found something of interest then?"

"Of *minor* interest . . ." Marissa briefly glanced at Brendan. "These pages with the sketches—do you know what they are? I'm not familiar with them."

"Hmm . . . I'm not sure myself," Wilkes answered. "American Indian, I believe. Navajo, perhaps?"

Brendan laughed out loud. *"Navajo?"*

"Of course." Suppressing a smile, Marissa asked casually, "Do you remember where you found them? I don't have many notes on Brendan's research on the . . . Navajo."

299

Granger sighed. "The provenance on this item is not very good, though I bought it from Arbuthnot's in Belgravia. There weren't many items in the lot: just this and a photograph. I didn't need the photograph, of which I already had a copy. Yet I'm positive these notes are Brendan's."

"Would you be so kind to send me a copy of these pages when it's convenient?" With a dry smile, Marissa reached into her jacket pocket and gave him her card.

Wilkes stared in rapt fascination at her pink mouth, then licked his lips. "Uh, certainly, my dear."

Brendan made a choking noise of disgust. "Let's leave . . . before I hit him."

Marissa pulled on her jacket. "Well, ah— Granger, thank you so much. You've been *such* a help," she said breezily. "I'll send you a copy of the biography when it's finished."

"Won't you stay for lunch?" Wilkes took her hand in his and stroked it. "I know you're interested in India. I could show you my collection of Moghul miniatures; they're very unusual. . . . "

Brendan said, "*Now, Marissa.*"

She yanked back her hand as Brendan pulled at her sleeve. "No, sorry—simply can't. I really must run."

Leaving a crestfallen Wilkes behind, Marissa escaped out the door. Brendan followed her out to the Jaguar, hands shoved in the pockets of his black trousers.

"What a vile piece of work he was," he muttered. "You know, of course, what sort of *unusual* miniatures he was talking about. They certainly aren't fit to show a respectable woman."

Marissa laughed. "I've seen a good number of

those erotic miniatures. I found them quite charming, actually."

Brendan's brows lifted in a sardonic curve. "Young lady, will you ever cease to shock me?"

"God, I hope not!" Marissa smiled sweetly at Brendan.

She started the Jag, and swung the car through the courtyard gate. In moments, the smooth purr of the Jag's engine sped them along the tarmac to Belgravia.

Chapter Eighteen

And there I shut her wild, wild eyes
With kisses four.
                              —John Keats

The brass letters on the sign overhead proclaimed
this to be the establishment of Harry Arbuthnot,
purveyor of rare books and maps. As Marissa
opened the door, a bell tinkled in the rear of the
shop and she and Brendan went inside.

Instead of the disorderly jumble of its humbler
cousin, the used-book store, this shop displayed
its wares in glass-fronted walnut bookcases and
softly lit glass cases. From the small office in the
rear came a tall, older man dressed in a black
sweater and trousers. His thinness gave his hawkish nose prominence in a face topped by a thick
mane of gray hair.

"How can I be of service to you, miss?" he asked

in round, mellifluous tones.

"Mr. Arbuthnot, I presume?" Marissa said. "Granger Wilkes gave me your name. He recently purchased a small manuscript of Brendan Tyrell's from you; I wondered if you had any more items from that source, and where it came from."

Arbuthnot shook his head sadly. "I'm afraid that's all there was, except for the photograph, which Mr. Wilkes declined to purchase. As for the items' origin, they were found in the store-room of an old country house scheduled for demolition."

Marissa's anxious glance briefly touched Brendan's. "Where was the building? Has it been torn down?"

"I think the house has been demolished."

Marissa blanched, and felt Brendan's hand come to rest on her shoulder.

Arbuthnot was saying, "Located in Surrey, for some years it operated as the Briarhurst Private Sanitarium." He paused. "I believe the items belonged to Mrs. Tyrell herself, since she was in the care of the sanitarium when she died."

"May . . . may I see the photograph?" Her heart sank under the weight of this development.

"Of course." Arbuthnot went over to a display case and removed a large photograph framed in mahogany with silver trim. He handed it to her.

With dismay, Marissa saw that it was Brendan and Rosalind's wedding portrait. He stood tall and erect in his dress uniform, outrageously handsome and youthful, his bride dainty and radiant in a white gown with a voluminous skirt and train. Rosalind's face glowed with happiness, while

Brendan looked into the camera with a forthright, confident smile.

Staring at the picture, Marissa could hardly believe that only ten years later that fragile, pretty woman would murder her beloved husband in a fit of jealous madness.

Brendan looked down at the photograph with an expression of hurt mingled with distaste. "Come on, Marissa," he said, his deep voice flat and emotionless. "You don't want that. This is useless. If my manuscripts were hidden at Briarhurst, they're gone now."

He started for the door, his broad shoulders weighted down in dejection.

She said, "Wait."

Arbuthnot glanced at her curiously. "Miss?"

"Um—yes, I'll take the photograph." She pulled out her billfold. "How much?"

Marissa could see the pound signs rolling up behind Arbuthnot's pale blue eyes. How stupid of her to say she'd take it without even asking the price.

"Since it was most likely Mrs. Tyrell's, and the heavy frame is especially fine . . . fifty pounds?"

"Sold." Marissa handed over the pound notes. "Would you please wrap it for me?"

"Certainly." Arbuthnot disappeared into his office.

Brendan stood by the door, staring out into the busy street. "I don't know why you wasted your money on that . . . abominable photograph. It's simply another reminder of the biggest mistake of my life . . . and I'd think it would be painful for you to look at."

Marissa moved beside him and spoke softly. "It's not something I particularly want to own myself, but the photograph is the only tangible link we have to the missing manuscripts." She paused. "Trust me, Brendan. I think that if we can track down the elusive Johanna Hensley, we'll find your manuscripts."

"Here you are, miss." Arbuthnot handed her the wrapped photograph. "Thank you for your custom."

Marissa nodded politely and they left the shop. On the walk back toward the car, Brendan said, "Well, *Sherlock*, what do you propose we do now?"

As they moved along the street, Marissa glanced idly in the shop windows. "I'll call the Montclair. I want to see if Owen left any messages for me."

She came to a stop in front of an exclusive dress shop, and her mouth lifted in a secretive smile. "Why don't you go on ahead to the hotel? I want to do a little shopping."

Brendan's eyebrows lifted dubiously. "You want to shop *now?*"

"Why not? I could use the relaxation."

"I've never understood why shopping is the preferred leisurely pastime for women. To me, it's nothing but a bother." He frowned. "I suppose the men of your generation think otherwise."

Marissa smiled up at him fondly. "No, most men I know feel the same way you do. I guess some things never change."

Back at the hotel, Marissa was surprised to find the suite empty. There had been no further word from Owen, and Brendan hadn't left her a message either. She made a call down to the hotel restaurant, then went in to run a bath.

Up to her neck in gardenia-scented bubbles, she soaked in the warm water and felt the tension in her shoulders melt away. Letting her head drop back onto the bath pillow, she closed her eyes in bliss.

A short while later, Marissa opened her eyes to see Brendan perched on the edge of the tub. With a soft, languorous smile, she said, "I didn't hear you come back."

"I went for a long walk. You looked so peaceful, I didn't want to disturb you." He dabbled his fingers in the perfumed water. "Very nice."

He traced his wet finger along the skin of her exposed shoulder, down to the slick upper curves of her floating breasts. He smiled slowly. "Would you like company?"

All the soft, pliant muscles in her body sent her a yearning message. *Yes, oh please, yes.* But her damnable brain short-circuited it as Marissa sank in the bubbles up to her chin. "I would love to, but . . ."

A persistent gleam shone in his black eyes. "But?"

He reached over and lazily stroked the damp tendrils of hair behind Marissa's ear.

"Well . . . that is, I ordered dinner sent up to the room. It will be here at seven-thirty." She grinned sheepishly. "I forgot to warn you . . . it's strictly black tie."

"Ah." His Gypsy eyes filled with amused regret. "I'd better leave you to your ablutions then. I know from experience how young ladies like to linger over their preparations on such momentous occasions."

With a smooth stretch of muscles, he rose from the edge of the tub and paused at the bathroom door, a dark promise in his eyes. "Until seven-thirty."

The Beckoning Ghost

*   *   *

Marissa let in the waiters, who set up a table for two and a serving cart on the small terrace overlooking the lights of London. She dismissed the waiters with a large gratuity, telling them that she'd prefer to handle the service herself.

Candlelight shone on the gold and white porcelain service set on pristine table linen. The flickering candles made prisms of light dance on the crystal, the silver gleamed and in the center sat a fragrant bowl of gardenias.

Marissa stood in front of the full-length mirror, anxiously running her hand along the soft, shirred velvet of her strapless gown. Superbly cut, the red dress displayed her bare shoulders, the curve of her waist—she'd never worn such a daring, provocative gown.

Well, that was the point, wasn't it? To take Brendan's mind off the setback that they'd suffered this afternoon.

She pulled on a set of elbow-length lace gloves in a matching shade of red and slid Brendan's opal and emerald ring over the glove. Her hair was swept up into an intricate French braid, revealing the shimmer of diamond earrings. Satisfied at last with her reflection, she went to stand at the terrace wall, looking out over the twinkling carpet of lights spread out before her.

"*Piara* . . . you look ravishing." Brendan appeared beside her and took her gloved hand in his, raising it to his lips. "I don't think there's a woman anywhere in the world tonight who could compare with you."

Marissa smiled tremulously. He looked so tall and elegant in his black evening clothes. Above the winged collar of his white shirt, his skin

307

glowed with a burnished, golden tan. His thick black hair, brushed back from his noble forehead, curled intriguingly at his nape.

"I could say the same for you, Brendan-ji." She touched his cheek. "You're so beautiful it pains me to look at you."

For a long moment, Marissa's misty gaze melted into the molten obsidian of Brendan's, and they needed no words to convey their timeless love for one another.

He reached out and caressed the line of her jaw with his thumb. The luminous oval of her face captured the moonlight, while her lotus eyes held a special sheen that hinted to him of profound, erotic secrets. The smooth sweep of her pale shoulders and the lush upswelling of her cleavage beckoned to him, a siren song of seduction. Only by summoning all his powerful reserve could he offer her his arm. "After you, my dear . . ."

Reluctantly, they moved over to the table. Brendan pulled out Marissa's chair for her and handed her a fluted glass of the golden, bubbling champagne.

"Isn't this revelry a bit premature?" he asked.

"No . . . we're simply celebrating the fact that we're here together."

"Then let me propose a toast." He sat down across from her and touched his empty glass to hers. "To my darling Marissa," he began, a huskiness creeping into his tone, "for you I've breached the boundaries of time and space. Yet that feat is insignificant compared to the love I bear for you . . . a love I hope we'll share for eternity."

Marissa clinked her glass against his, her eyes sparkling. "To eternal love."

* * *

The Beckoning Ghost

Though the food was excellently prepared, Marissa found she could eat very little of it. She toyed with the fresh raspberries and white chocolate shell on her dessert plate. Across the table, Brendan watched her with a pensive look on his face.

"What is it?" she asked finally.

"Nothing for you to trouble yourself about. Enjoy your dessert."

"I'm not that hungry." She pushed her plate away and rose from the table. Brendan followed her into the suite.

She turned to face him. "I don't know why I'm so restless tonight. About the manuscripts . . . I keep feeling that there's something I've overlooked, that the answer is staring me in the face and I just don't see it."

"I thought you didn't want to dwell on the problem of the manuscripts tonight," Brendan said. "It's too lovely an evening to waste in useless speculation." He turned to the radio in the room. "Doesn't this box produce some sort of music? Why don't we dance?"

"Why not?" Smiling, Marissa switched on the radio and soft, slow music issued from it. "This should do in lieu of an orchestra."

As Marissa moved close to him, Brendan said, "I'm not sure I know how to dance to this."

"It's simple enough . . . just put your arms around me and sway with the music." As he slid one arm around her waist and the other around her back, she nestled her head into the hollow between his neck and shoulder.

Gradually Brendan got the hang of it and they moved across the floor together, slowly swaying to the beat. He dropped both hands to her waist. "This is wonderful," he said, "much more intimate than those whirling waltzes and country dances."

"Mmm-hmm," Marissa said, tightening her hands on his broad shoulders.

Chris DeBurgh's *Lady in Red* came on the radio. Halfway through the song, Marissa felt a rumbling chuckle spread up through Brendan's chest.

"Did you somehow order this song to be played?" He brushed his lips against her temple. "It's the perfect expression of how I feel tonight. You *are* utterly gorgeous and amazing."

Marissa raised her head from his chest and smiled dreamily. "How terribly sweet and romantic for you to say so." She pressed a soft kiss along his jaw, then laid her head back on his shoulder. His chest firmly muscular, he smelled of clean soap and sandalwood.

Brendan lowered his head and placed his warm lips on the sensitive spot at the base of her neck where it joined her shoulder. A racing chill sped down Marissa's spine. Brendan lingered at that spot for a minute, then traced his lips up her neck to her ear.

"*Piara*, I want you so much. . . . "

Marissa shivered as his hands went to the back of her dress and lowered the zipper. She kissed the strong, tanned column of his throat and held onto his shoulders to keep herself from stumbling.

Brendan's firm hands moved inside the open back of her gown to encircle her bare waist. Inexorably, he guided her toward the large bed. As the back of her knees hit the bed, Brendan lowered her to a sitting position. His hands rested briefly on her naked shoulders before they slid downward, drawing the red velvet bodice to her waist. Her lacy white brassiere did little to hide her breasts.

310

The Beckoning Ghost

Brendan smiled down at her and stroked the lace covering her nipples, which furled into hard little buds at his touch. Placing one knee on the bed beside her, he took her shoulders and gently started to lower her to the satin bedspread. In a moment, his hard body would cover hers and she would be lost . . . they would both be lost. . . .

"Brendan, no." Marissa struggled to sit up, drawing her dress up over her breasts with shaky fingers.

Brendan stood up straight, a frustrated scowl rampant on his face. "What do you mean, no? I know you want me as much as I do you."

"I—I'm sorry. This was a bad idea. I never meant to let it get this far; I just wanted to distract you. . . ."

"Well, you did an excellent job of it," he said with a low snarl. "I've never been so easily or thoroughly seduced. Though I will say that no other woman has dared to stop me so close to the brink."

He stared at her, his eyes black hollows. "So beautiful, so artlessly sensual . . . you would have made an admirable courtesan in another time, my dear."

"Brendan, don't do this." She stood and zipped up her gown. "My love, I don't want to risk losing you forever. The last time, in California, you became so dizzy and ill, and then you went away for so long. I couldn't take that chance."

"*Marissa,*" he said plaintively, turning away from her. His glance, snapping with frustration, came to rest on the wedding portrait. "What is this doing in here?"

"I unwrapped it and set it there when I got back."

311

Catherine Kohman

"I told you that I didn't want to look at the damned thing." He slammed the heavy frame facedown on the table.

Marissa heard the glass shatter and the wood frame cracked sharply. She pushed past Brendan. "Now see what you've done."

As she gingerly lifted the frame off the table, the backing came loose and shifted downward. In the open gap near the top of the frame, Marissa saw a yellowed sheet of paper. Her glance lifted to Brendan's face.

With a letter opener, she pried up the felt backing and extracted the page of paper, which was covered in a brown, spidery hand.

"That's Rosalind's writing," Brendan said.

Marissa scanned the page. "It's dated from 1880, and addressed to Miranda."

Together, they read the letter.

So, Jezebel, you've come this far. How much you must want those manuscripts of Brendan's, to send that sniveling priest to my door in search of them. Can a woman lust after books like she would a man—another woman's husband? Are the rewards of pornography as gratifying as the pleasures of adultery?

Whore! Brendan died in the midst of his sins, thanks to your wickedness. Shall I send this letter to your poor, deluded Justin, so he can learn the truth about your depravity? Or shall I wait a bit, and let you stew in your vileness, never knowing when the axe will fall?

Those books are all I have left of Brendan, my dearest love, my very life. Disgusting as they are—you were right, I couldn't destroy them. I have hidden them away in a safe place—my cousin Johanna's house at Wind-rush, the Darland farm.

Why tell you this, you wanton harlot? I'm going to give you a copy of my wedding portrait, and hide this letter inside it. Either you'll have to look at it every day, tortured, wondering what I meant by it. Or, silly slut, you'll destroy it, and with it any hope of finding those filthy books you harangued me about.

How wonderful, fitting that you lose what you most want in this world, just as I did, but it will be your own malicious handiwork that causes it.

Marissa dropped the letter on the table and ran her hands up and down her arms as if she felt a chill. "I knew there was some reason why I had to buy this blasted photograph!"

Brendan poked the letter with a grimace of distaste. "Lord, what a horrible letter. How could Ros write such a thing?"

"Brendan . . . she stabbed you to death in a fit of rage, and you wonder how she could write a twisted letter like that? She was a madwoman! Thank God she never sent me—Randie, I mean—that portrait after all, or I would have destroyed it as she guessed I would."

Marissa tried to shake off the sick feeling Rosalind's letter left behind, and focused on the information instead. "At least we have Johanna's name; even better, the name of the farm."

"Rissa, my darling!" A warm smile on his face, Brendan picked her up by the waist and twirled her around. "If it hadn't been for your dogged persistence, we would have never found this." Dropping her lightly to her feet, he said, "Windrush . . . Windrush. Where is that?"

She went to the suite's desk and found her map. Checking the index, she spread the map across the desk top. "There." She pointed. "It *is* in the Cotswolds. We can drive up there first thing in the morning."

"What if it's another dead end," Brendan said, "and the family doesn't live there anymore? Or this house also burned? I can't bear to wait until we get there to find out."

"Sometimes modern technology is a blessing." Marissa grabbed the telephone and dialed information for the Cotswolds. "Yes, please . . . do you have a listing for a Darland family in the village of Windrush?" After a moment, she grinned. "*You do?* And the number . . . thank you."

Marissa scribbled the number on the pad by the telephone. Then she picked up her velvet skirts and capered across the floor. "It's too late to call now; those villagers retire early. Let's just go—up at dawn to beat the traffic."

Brendan watched her with a tender smile. "I think you've never looked lovelier than you do this very moment, flushed with sweet victory. I love you, darling girl."

With Brendan beside her, Marissa guided the white Jaguar up a winding slope toward the Cotswolds village of Windrush. The bright morning light turned the verdant summer countryside to patches of emerald set amongst the deep forest green of the hedgerows. Overhead, the azure dome of the sky arched with only a few puffy clouds on the western horizon.

She'd stopped at a wayside rest to call the Darlands and make sure they were home and amenable to a visit. The older gentleman on the phone sounded a bit puzzled, but cordial.

Going by his directions, Marissa drove up the cobbled main street of the village, which sat atop a crest of a hill. Small, elegant gray stone houses and shops perched alongside the steep roadway and its adjacent narrow lanes. If she hadn't been on a matter of pressing concern, she would have stopped in the village square at the top of the street and explored the hamlet's charming environs.

After passing through the square, she found the proper lane and turned off the main road. The lane curved around the crest of the hill and dropped a hundred feet from the top into a copse of beech trees. Nestled into the side of the ridge sat a substantial stone farmhouse, its slate roof gleaming like polished steel in the sunlight.

"We're here," she said with a slight smile, parking the Jaguar in the courtyard between the house and the barn. As they got out of the car and began to walk up toward the house, Marissa nervously adjusted the scarf at the neck of her ivory cotton sweater and shook out the soft pleats of her powder blue skirt.

Along the paving stone sidewalk, pink and red roses bloomed in profusion, perfuming the air with their rich, damask scent. Over the door, a massive white climbing rose thrust its arching canes, heavy with blossom.

Before they got to the front door, a man Marissa took for Will Darland opened it wide. He looked to be in his mid-60s, with a fine head of silver hair and a sunburned, outdoorsy face.

"Miss Erickson, please come in." He showed her into a small foyer, its walls painted white to reflect

315

the light from the stairwell. "My wife is in the kitchen. I'll tell her to bring in a spot of tea to the parlor."

Her host directed her into a large, airy room. Outside the window, the view stretched for miles over the river valley to the abutting hills. Two comfortable-looking chairs and a matching sofa upholstered in a sunny chintz floral faced each other on either side of the fireplace. In the corner stood a curio cabinet filled with Staffordshire ware jugs and other collectibles.

"Here's Miss Erickson, Emily."

Marissa turned from the view and introduced herself to his wife. The rosy-cheeked matron smiled and offered her a cup of tea from the tray that she'd carried into the room. Marissa noticed that both of the Darlands had put on their Sunday clothes for the meeting. The three of them seated themselves near the hearth.

Marissa stole a glance at Brendan, who gave an ineffective impression of casually inspecting the furnishings in the room.

Will Darland cleared his throat, taking her attention away from Brendan.

"Now, miss, what did you want to ask us about?"

"I have reason to believe that a woman named Rosalind Tyrell may have left some of her husband's papers here, with her cousin, Johanna, back around 1880. I wondered if you know whatever became of them."

"Tyrell, you say?" Mr. Darland scratched his temple thoughtfully. "It doesn't ring a bell. Johanna now—that was my great-grandmother. She died not long before I was born."

His wife Emily spoke up. "I believe we have

316

some of Johanna's things stored up in the attic. None of the Darlands ever were much for throwing things out."

With a rueful glance at her husband, she smiled. "I don't even know what is up there—a few chests and boxes, I think."

Brendan stopped his pacing of the room behind the Darlands. He raised his brows and twitched his head toward the stairs. "Come on then."

Marissa tried to ignore him and inquired politely, "Would you mind if I took a look at them?"

Will Darland glanced at his wife for approval. In response, Emily gave her another smile. "Why ever not?"

Will showed them upstairs to the part of the attic where Johanna's things were stored. He took down a stack of boxes for Marissa and set them beside a large chest and a leather-bound trunk. An overhead window cast slanting beams of summer sunshine into the area so she could see without artificial light.

"Well, miss," Will said, "I'll leave you to look through these yourself. Just give a shout if you need any help with those heavier boxes." Then he took himself downstairs to his tea and cozy chair.

Marissa smiled at Brendan, anticipation making her fingers tingle. "Where do we start?"

"My wooden writing chest was rather large. Why don't we look in the trunks first?"

Marissa opened both of the trunks, which were piled high with old clothing. If she'd been interested in 19th-century costumes, the trunks would have been a real find, but she closed them in disappointment. "We'll have to look through the

317

boxes. Maybe Rosalind broke the collection into smaller lots."

One by one, she and Brendan checked the contents of the smaller boxes. One by one, they found nothing but papers and trinkets of Johanna's and other members of her family. As she closed up the last box, Marissa sat down on it and rested her head on her hand.

Brendan reached down and stroked her hair. "It's all right, poppet."

"I can't believe your writing chest is the *only* thing the Darlands ever threw away," she murmured dejectedly. "They kept *everything*." She sighed. "I'm going to look through the trunks again. Maybe there's a clue in there somewhere, hidden in the clothing."

She sank on her knees in front of the leather trunk and opened it. Carefully lifting out a thick layer of the clothing, she gently shook it to see if anything fell out of the folds. Finished with those, she reached for the next layer. Her hands touched something solid.

"Brendan! There's something in here!" With careless regard for the old clothing, she swept it aside to reveal the varnished surface of an oak chest. In black lettering, the top read: *R. Tyrell, Household Accounts.*

Chapter Nineteen

O, lost, and by the wind grieved, ghost, come
back again!
                                   —Thomas Wolfe

Eagerly, Brendan leaned over the trunk and
helped her lift the wooden box out. "My God, Marissa—you found them!"

"Eureka!" With a wide smile, she started to raise
the lid. "No, it's your work, Brendan . . . *you*
should open it."

Catching his breath, he opened the chest and
looked inside. He removed a layer of bound books
from the top and handed them to Marissa. With a
start, she recognized the French melodramas that
Rosalind had been addicted to. A puzzled frown
crept across Brendan's face as he dug deeper into
the box, only to come up with more old novels.

Finally, in outraged frustration, he tipped the

box over and dumped the remaining books onto the attic floor. A thin blue sheet of paper floated out in a capricious swoop and skidded across the floor to land at Marissa's feet.

Heart in her throat, she picked it up and they read the spidery handwriting together:

Jezebel, you have more wit than I credited you with, though I always thought you a sly creature. What a pity for you that I changed my mind. I don't want you to find Brendan's treasure trove after all. The books are hidden in a secret place you'll never find, where only I can touch them and Brendan is with me, ready to light his pipe and read them aloud, as he did before you came and spoiled it all with your wanton witchery.

You don't deserve to have his books. Circe, your foul sorcery can't touch them—they belong to me and before I die I'll see them blaze in a pyre in the sacred wood, purifying Brendan's soul with cleansing flames.

How do bitter ashes taste in your mouth, Hecate's spawn?

With a sharp cry, Marissa let the paper drop to the floor. "No—no, she couldn't have . . . not after we've come this far." Feeling nauseous, she began to shake. "My God, she's had her revenge—even though it took her a hundred years."

Brendan pulled her into his arms and stroked her hair. "Marissa . . . please, love, don't let her hate wound you like this." His lips brushed her temple. "She can't hurt us anymore."

"How can you think that?" She shivered in his arms. "Don't you see—*this* is her vengeance, the

320

knowledge that we'll never find your work." With a bitter laugh, she added, "Rosalind chose her poison well."

Brendan turned her face up to his. "Easy, my darling. We don't *know* that she burned the manuscripts; she didn't even send Miranda the portrait. In all likelihood, my books are still stashed away in a forgotten place in this very neighborhood."

Marissa pushed away from him, agitation replacing the revulsion of a moment ago. "Even if they are—which I doubt—how will we ever find them? Mad she may have been, but she certainly retained all her guile and spite."

Brendan took her by the hand and sat her down in an old mahogany rocker. "Calm down, *piara*."

She dropped her head into her hand, then shot him a perturbed glance. "How can you be so—so relaxed about this? It's *your* life work after all."

Brendan perched on the trunk beside her. "You dare to ask the famed hero of Lucknow, *Sikander* Tyrell, how he stays so cool under fire?" He grinned at her. "Practice, my impassioned beauty, practice. How else do you think I survived all those years exploring the Himalayas—by dressing in a morning coat and simply presenting Her Majesty's calling card? The Raja of Banpur would have had my liver served to his tigers for breakfast."

At that preposterous image, Marissa had to laugh, and with the laughter came perspective. "I'm sorry, Brendan. Rosalind's letter shook me up even more than the last one. Her writings give the term 'poison pen letter' a whole new slant."

Brendan stroked his mustache and sent her a thoughtful glance. "That's the second time you've

321

used that word—*poison,* and I'll warrant you
didn't even realize it."

Marissa shivered again. "Must be the tone of
that letter—all that vitriol."

"Precisely." He stooped over to pick up the letter, and read it silently. After studying it a moment
more, he said, "Read it again, Marissa, this time
with an analytical mind, not your emotions."

With an air of repugnance, she re-read the letter, once quickly, the second time with more
thought. Finally she said, "She makes four references to witches in the text. Was that part of her
dementia—a fear of sorcery?"

"Not particularly so, though it may have been
in her later years. Yet when she wrote that letter,
it obviously preyed on her mind; I doubt if she
realized the words she used gave us the final clue."

Startled, Marissa looked up at him. "What
clue?"

Brendan smiled at her, a vibrant smile that
warmed her chilled blood. "You're forgetting your
county geography, sweet one. What famous
beauty spot lies over the hill?"

"I don't know," she grumbled. As she slumped
back, the chair rocked, creaking alarmingly. "I
didn't memorize the Blue Guide, and there are so
many.   Stow-on-the-Wold?   Bourton-on-the-
Water? I give up."

The rocker groaned again in protest as she
bolted up right. "*Wychwood Forest!* Her *sacred* forest!" She scowled. "But it's so huge."

"Not to someone who spent two weeks of his
honeymoon," he said, his dark Gypsy eyes alight
with triumph, "in a cottage in the Evenlode
Valley."

Marissa wrapped her arms around her waist,

322

afraid to give in to this exhilarating rush after the past bitter defeats. "Pure conjecture."

"It makes as much sense as anything else. Her unconscious use of the witchcraft imagery, her references to a hidden place where she once felt happy . . ." Brendan's dark eyes clouded with bittersweet memory. "I'd prefer to think of her as that woman, rather than the harpy who wrote these letters."

"Brendan, we're only speculating. I don't know if I can stand to be disappointed again."

"Trust me, Marissa." Pulling her to her feet, he held her close. "My sweet, sweet sorceress . . ." He kissed her eyelids. "Here's a devoted subject most appreciative of your enchanting arts."

When Marissa described the cottage to the Darlands, Will gave her the name of a realtor in Ascott-under-Wychwood who could locate the owner and perhaps show her the secluded house. Wasting little time, they drove up over the hill into the Evenlode Valley and met the realtor in the tiny village.

The owner of the cottage, a woman named Letitia Pennyroyal, would meet them there just after tea. Mrs. Pennyroyal owned a large farm nearby, and used the cottage as a retreat. When Marissa anxiously asked the realtor about the condition of the house, the agent reassured her that it retained all of its Victorian charm.

After a sinfully rich tea in the village, Marissa drove the Jaguar along the winding road to the cottage. The way took them over rushing streams and past water meadows, through woods echoing with cheerful birdsong, a place not at all like the dismal sound of its name.

323

Catherine Kohman

As they bumped along a narrow lane arched over by trees, Marissa watched Brendan carefully, hoping the setting didn't bring back too many memories. Yet it seemed that his interest in the prospect of finding his manuscripts outweighed any maudlin memories of his honeymoon.

Around a sharp bend a shining meadow appeared, and the thatched cottage stood at the edge of it, nestled in a bower of sheltering oaks. Marissa marveled at its rustic beauty, spoiled only by the modern Austin parked in front. "Has it changed much?"

For once, the devilish glint in Brendan's jet eyes was subdued. "No, it looks the same as the day we left it."

Parking under the trees, she got out of the car. Brendan met her and squeezed her hand as they walked up the cobbled path to the door, through a flower and herb garden full of lavender and fragrant verbena. Mrs. Pennyroyal, a tall, thin woman of about 40, met them at the door. With dark lustrous hair and a bright smile, Letitia Pennyroyal was far from the little old lady Marissa expected.

After Marissa introduced herself and explained what she was looking for in vague terms, Mrs. Pennyroyal led her inside. "Please call me Tish, and feel free to explore all the corners. I'm thinking of selling the cottage anyway, since I'm in the process of getting a divorce. My husband and I spent our honeymoon here, so I don't come very often."

"I'm sorry to hear that." Obviously, as lovely as it was, the cottage had provided an inauspicious start to at least two marriages. Marissa stole a glance at Brendan, who was gazing around the cottage with interest, not really listening to their hostess.

Just when she was wondering how to discreetly rid themselves of Mrs. Pennyroyal's presence, the older woman said she'd rather wait for Marissa in the garden than remain inside.

Once Letitia left the cottage, Marissa and Brendan examined all the obvious places—the tiny attic, the Welsh dresser and cupboards in the quaint kitchen, the carved oak armoire in the sitting area, the huge cherry wardrobe in the bedroom. She even poked into the bright chintz draperies behind the large raised bed, hoping for a hidden closet, even a priest's hole. Though undeniab y charming with its antique furniture and beamed ceiling, the cottage proved another disappointment.

Sitting on the lofty edge of the platform four-poster, Marissa tapped the solid wood sides of the bed with the crepe heel of her shoe. "You stayed here, Brendan . . . do you remember any hidey-holes or secret places? We've looked everywhere else."

Up to now, Brendan had avoided the area of the bed, but he came to stand next to her. "No, I can't recall anything unusual about the cottage, except for the bed, of course."

"The bed?" She studied the large expanse of floral bedspread, a Laura Ashley print. "It is rather large for a cottage—more like a bed of state. I wonder if it came from one of the country houses around here; it looks familiar. It must be very old—at least seventeenth century."

As once more she softly tapped her heel against the solid oak, a niggling thought poked at her consciousness. But the wounded look in Brendan's eyes alarmed her, and she saw the sight of his marriage bed bothered him. Reading the first sign of defeat in the droop of his mustache over his fine mouth, she offered him solace.

"We can't give up now . . . not after coming all this way. Everything in Rosalind's note pointed to this place. Do you think your wife would have buried the manuscripts here, or perhaps burned them as she'd threatened?"

Brendan shook his head and ran a distracted hand through his raven hair. "I doubt she did either. The damp in the ground would ruin the manuscripts, and for some reason, I refuse to believe she burned them after all. In a way, her mental condition may have proved a blessing for us, because she never had the opportunity to come back here and carry out her threat."

"Then where do you suppose they're hidden?"

"I wish to God I knew," he said with an exasperated sigh. "Maybe someone cleaned house one day and simply threw them out."

Marissa leaned back, studying the carved canopy overhead. "I suppose it's possible, but I can't believe that they'd do that without reading them, or trying to find out what they're worth."

"Works more precious than mine have been wantonly discarded before." He stroked the scar on his cheek. "It seems there's always a story about someone buying a lost work by Van Gogh or even an old master at a flea market."

"Flea market?" With a small smile, she asked, "Have you been reading the tabloids again?"

"I beg your pardon?" he asked, frowning.

She smoothed a hand along the intricately shaped bedpost. "Still, it's a thought—we should check out the London book markets."

"Marissa, would you please get off that *damned bed*," Brendan stormed without warning.

At the raw emotion in his voice, Marissa jumped down off the bed, and her heel struck the frame with an odd clunking sound. She turned and stared at the bed for a long moment as that niggling thought came back in all its blistering clarity.

She reached for the bedpost and swung on it, laughing. "That's it—the damned bed! Brendan, love, remember my joke about a priest's hole? There *is* one here, but not in the walls—they're not thick enough. I once saw a bed like this in a stately home—it's part of the frame! All we have to do is locate the opening. . . . "

Dropping to their knees, they hurriedly examined the sideboards and ends of the bed, pressing carvings and knocking on the sides. After a few minutes' search, Brendan said tersely, "It's here."

Using delicate finesse, he swiveled the top of a carved pineapple and with a clicking sound, a panel in the side slid open. It revealed a dark yawning space, large enough for a man to lie in comfortably, if he didn't mind the coffin-like atmosphere.

"Be my guest," she said, gesturing to the opening.

"It's your discovery."

"No way." She grimaced. "There could be spiders in a dark, dusty place like that."

Brendan looked at her blankly. "Spiders—you have a fear of spiders?" He laughed then. "So you're human after all, my pet."

Marissa waved an impatient hand at him. "No time for analysis now, Doctor—check the bloody priest's hole!"

Catherine Kohman

With a heart-stopping grin, Brendan slid his upper body into the space. For a moment he said nothing, and kept very still. Then he pivoted his torso and Marissa heard the joyful sound of wood rasping on wood.

Emerging with a dusty wood and brass bound chest, he grinned again as he set it carefully on the thick bedroom rug and wiped off the pall of dust. "This is it—my manuscript chest!"

He pulled her into his arms and kissed her fervently. Marissa thought she would faint from the intensity of that kiss, from the sheer excitement of discovery. Brendan released her and she sank dizzily back on her heels.

Brendan stared at the chest, holding his breath.

With an exultant smile, she touched his arm. "Go ahead. Open it."

With a rough exhalation, he undid the latch and lifted the wooden lid. Inside were stacked bundles of manuscripts, each securely tied with string. Brendan took them out of the chest, and after carefully inspecting each one, he handed them to her to neatly stack aside the chest.

The depth of the material astonished Marissa. First came the Sanskrit texts in translation: the *Ramayana*, the *Amarusataka*, the *Subhasitavali*, the poets Kalidasa and Vijika and other love poetry. Then the Persian: The *Gulistan of Sa'adi*, the great poet Hafiz of Shiraz, and Assar. From China: the poets Su Tang Po and Li Po.

Those were just the classic texts that Brendan had translated. There were also ethnographic monographs from India, Bali, China, Polynesia and the American West. The sheer quantity of the material staggered Marissa.

When they finally reached the bottom of the

chest, she asked, "However did you write all these texts? There's more here than most men can write in a lifetime, and you were cut down in your prime."

Marissa and Brendan began to replace the manuscripts in the chest, satisfied that they were all there.

"I translated the Sanskrit and Persian texts while still in India. The rest I collected on our trip around the world, and I simply worked on them every day, with your—I mean—Miranda's help."

The last manuscript safely stored away inside the chest, they stood up and gazed at each other in rapt contentment.

Brendan said, "Well done, Sherlock."

Marissa shrugged. "Elementary, my dear Watson."

He raised his left brow in inquiry. "Just who *is* this Watson?"

"Never mind." She laughed. "I'll tell you later. What are we going to do with them now?"

Brendan tugged the ends of his mustache wistfully. "I would like to see them published . . . would you edit them for me?"

"Me? I—I would be honored to do it, but your expertise outshines mine in so many areas. I'd need to bring in some top guns—that is, expert help."

"Get it then. But beware of stuffy scholars— they'll strangle the beauty of the verse every time with their bloody literal-mindedness."

She smiled. "I'm delighted to hear that you're as jealous of your work as the rest of us lowly authors are." She paused. "I suppose the first step is to have these authenticated by the British Museum staff."

329

Catherine Kohman

"I believe the *first* step is to get Mrs. Pennyroyal to release the material to you," Brendan said.

"You're right. The manuscripts themselves are worth a lot of money. I wouldn't want to have her think I was trying to cheat her of anything that was rightfully hers. Perhaps the cottage isn't such a jinx after all."

She gave a tired sigh. "I should go talk to her; I'm sure she's wondering what I'm up to." Glancing up at him, she said, "But first I need a hug."

Tenderly, he enfolded her in his arms. "Thank you, Marissa. Because of you, my life has had its meaning restored. It was lost to me, but you gave it back to me again."

Marissa held onto him tightly, as if she was afraid he'd vanish into thin air now that their search was over. Brendan stroked her hair and kissed her temple to reassure her, but that thought gave him pause. How long would he be able to stay and love her? After all, he didn't really exist in her earthly plane. . . .

He squeezed his arms tighter, molding her body to his, wishing he could give her as much happiness as she'd brought to him. His lost manuscripts! Only one thing would bring him greater joy—to love Marissa, physically and spiritually, without any fears or constraints, to promise her that he'd never leave her and be certain he could keep that promise.

Oh, piara, he thought, *how can I bear to exist without you?*

After talking it over with Mrs. Pennyroyal, Marissa loaded the chest into the trunk of the Jag. Marissa had said that she was only interested in being the literary executor of the papers, and had

330

promised that any monies derived from the sale of the manuscripts themselves would belong to Tish—Mrs. Pennyroyal.

By the time she left, the older woman was bewildered but happy. Marissa left Wychwood Forest with a warm glow in her own heart.

On the drive back to London, Marissa and Brendan talked in greater detail about the publication of his manuscripts. He had some particular ideas about format and commentary that she was interested in seeing. When they finally drove up to the Montclair, Marissa's adrenaline rush had run out.

Once she and Brendan and the chest were safely deposited in the suite, Marissa crashed. Barely able to keep her eyes open in the bath, she fell into bed and slept late.

Over juice and croissants the next morning, she chattered on happily about the manuscripts. She noticed Brendan's silence, but she didn't question him about it until he declined to accompany her to the Museum.

"Why not?" she asked.

Brendan stroked the scar on his cheek, a gesture she'd noted when he was anxious about something. "My part in this is all but finished— I'm just a phantom lurking in the background. All the credit and glory should go to you."

"But we discovered the manuscripts together. I never would have found them without your direction."

"Marissa . . . what are you going to say to the press? Tyrell's ghost led me to them? Do you have any idea how they'll paint you if you even *hint* something like that?"

Her face fell. "All right, you've made your point. I'll go without you this morning, but I want to see

331

you here when I get back."

In a strangely somber mood given the circumstances, Marissa picked up her purse and briefcase. The bellboy had already taken the chest out to her car.

Brendan stopped her at the door and placed a kiss on her forehead. "We'll spend a quiet afternoon together, if that's all right with you."

"That would be lovely." She smiled bravely and went out the door.

"Brendan? Brendan—oh, there you are!" Marissa found him out on the terrace. "The staff at the Museum raved over our find—we ought to have authentication in no time. I hope you're ready for some long, hard work."

He turned to face her and smiled. "You'll manage very well without me, darling lass. The literary world will soon be at your feet."

"I don't want to own the literary world. All I want is for you to be at my side, working with me. Oh, Brendan, together we can—"

"Marissa, darling . . . I need to talk to you." Taking her by the hand, he led her inside the suite and sat her in one of the peach lounge chairs.

A tendril of fear curled in her stomach at the serious expression on his face. "Brendan, please—what is it?"

His eyes sad and gentle, he began. "I've had this feeling for a few days, but I didn't want to spoil your joy at our discovery."

The tendril blossomed into a monstrous growth that ate at her very core, and she started to shake. *"Tell me."*

"Darling, I can't stay with you any longer. Now that the manuscripts have been found, I've accomplished the task I was sent here to do. I have to go back—back to wherever I came from."

A drumming beat pounded in her ears and she distantly recognized the sound of her own heart. "No . . . no, that's not true—you can stay if you want to. Please, Brendan, tell me you will."

"I wish I could, love, but the energy it took to come back, to stay with you and love you . . . it's all used up." He paused. "I first noticed it at your charming little dinner party. That's why I desperately wanted to love you that night—I was afraid it would be our only chance to be together."

The sight of his sorrowful, troubled face nearly killed her. Hot tears flooded Marissa's eyes and spilled down her cheeks. "Oh, my God, please— this can't be happening . . . it can't." Her voice rose in wounded desperation. "Brendan, you said you loved me . . . *that we'd be together forever!*"

"And we will, my darling. At least in spirit."

"No, it's not enough!" Her voice cracked with emotion. "I want you here and now!" The aching in her throat threatened to choke her, but she spoke anyway. *"Brendan, you can't leave me alone again. If you go this time, I'll die."*

"No . . . you'll live and write more marvelous books, growing older but more beautiful with every year. I simply won't be here to share it." He sighed brokenly, the clogging of unshed tears in his voice. "I'm sorry, my love. I can't stay with you. Though I thought somehow I could, it just isn't possible."

Through her tears, she asked dully, "When?"

"Now." He paused. "It took whatever I had left to wait for you to come back."

"No, I won't let you go." She stood up and threw

333

her arms around him, a ragged sob escaping her swollen throat.

"Please, Rissa, don't. You're tearing my heart out as it is, my darling. I have to go—now."

"Oh, God . . ."

Brendan hugged her tightly and she felt tears from his eyes drop softly on her hair. Sobbing, she ran her hands over him, memorizing the shape of his head, the way his hair curled under her fingers, his strong shoulders and narrow waist . . . all of him.

Brendan held her face between his hands and brushed her tears away with his thumbs. *"Piara* . . . I want you to listen to what I say—it's very important. Tomorrow or the day after, I want you to go to Ischia."

"Oh, Brendan, *no.* Stay here with me." She pressed her lips to the thin scar on his cheek.

"I can't, love. If I could, I would *at any cost."* He paused. "Marissa, please—go to Ischia. I can't tell you *why* it's important, or even *how* I know it, but it is. You must go there, to my old villa. Perhaps . . . perhaps you'll find peace, or even a bit of my soul there, if that's any comfort to you."

He kissed her full on the lips, all his love, his soul fused into one melting touch of his mouth. She closed her eyes, feeling his heartbeat blend with hers. Desperate to hold on to him, she kissed him back, reckless with fear and heartache.

He suddenly released her. She stumbled back a step and opened her eyes in wild, racing panic.

Brendan was gone.

Chapter Twenty

My heart aches, and a drowsy numbness pains my sense.

—John Keats

Marissa spent the next day alone in her room. The entire night after Brendan went away, she cried in long, gulping sobs, and in the morning felt as if her eyelids were lined with ground glass. She lay on the bed with a cool cloth on them to take away the sting, her mind sick and paralyzed with loss.

By afternoon the phone in her suite started to ring as word leaked out about the discovery she'd made. Asking the front desk to hold all her calls gave her a few hours of peace and quiet, but in the evening a reporter showed up at her suite.

Marissa begged off, saying she was too ill to talk. From her puffy eyes and ravaged face, the

335

man must have believed her, because he left after the briefest of statements from her.

Go to Ischia, Brendan had said. But why? Wouldn't it just open the wounds deeper?

Another reporter tried to barge in for an interview. That being the last straw for Marissa, she called the airlines and made a reservation to Naples early the next morning.

At the hydrofoil dock on Ischia, a car from the Grand Hotel Excelsior waited for her. As the driver gave her a quick travelogue, Marissa stared out the window. Pastel and blinding white, the town's buildings climbed the high, rocky cliffs. A romantic, crumbling castle perched on an islet out in the sparkling blue of the Tyrrhenian Sea, and gaily painted fishing boats lay like shells on the beaches. Among the fragrant pines and palms bloomed a riot of tropical flowers: bougainvillaea, jasmine, gardenias and hibiscus.

The scenery looked familiar, but she'd probably seen pictures of it. She felt a deep ache in her chest. *Oh, Brendan, why did you ask me to come here?*

Its imposing entrance softened by whimsical ironwork and lush, trailing greenery, the creamy yellow facade of the Grand Hotel Excelsior welcomed her. Even in the heat of the Italian summer, the pale walls and smooth marble surfaces of the lobby gave an impression of cool serenity. With warm and personable service, the bellman brought her up to her room on the top floor.

Rather than compete with the glorious ocean view, the room itself was decorated with understated elegance, its walls a glowing celadon and the furnishings in soothing shades of ivory and

336

palest peach. The long day of traveling had worn her out, so Marissa stripped to her underclothing and laid down on the huge, four-poster bed, which reminded her painfully of Wychwood.

The pine-scented breeze blew in the open window and soon lulled Marissa to sleep. For the first time in days, she dreamed.

In the first dream, here on Ischia, she and Brendan rode in an open carriage, dressed in 19th-century clothing. On their way to visit the cemetery, they planned to place a bouquet of gilly-flowers on the grave of an obscure Roman poet. She could smell the sharp spicy scent of the flowers and feel the ocean breezes lift her hair in the wind. In her sleep, she wondered, *Is this Miranda's memory?*

The second dream sent her back to India. She and Brendan walked down the side streets of Lucknow, but in modern dress. As Brendan stopped her and pulled her into a cluttered shop, she saw something strange about his face . . . he didn't have his scar or mustache.

She held onto the dream as long as she could, but it slipped away.

Waking with tears in her eyes, she felt more refreshed than she had been in days, yet curiously restless at the same time. She decided to join the other guests on the terrace for dinner, rather than spend the evening alone in her room. Unable to face another evening alone, she hoped the music and holiday mood would lighten her bleak spirits.

In the morning, Marissa went to the cemetery. Rosalind Tyrell had had a monument erected there in Brendan's name. When the taxi dropped her off at the cliff-side cemetery, she experienced a flash of déjà vu. The neat graves with marble headstones and the whispering pines were in her dream of last night—she *had* been here before.

Making her way to the corner where Brendan's monument stood, she remembered that Brendan himself was actually buried in the woods behind her house on Arcadia. This fall, she'd plant hyacinths, anemones and daffodils on his grave. A quotation from Pope drifted into her mind:

Yet shall thy grave with rising flow'rs be dressed
And the green turf lie lightly on thy breast.

That thought gave her cold comfort at best.

The monument, a large white marble sculpture in the shape of the Taj Mahal, was expertly crafted. Carved in relief in a niche, Brendan's face gazed coolly out at her, an inscrutable smile on his lips. Below the portrait, a verse from the *Mahabharata* had been inscribed.

Marissa suddenly realized that *she*—as Miranda—had chosen the quotation for Rosalind. That, more than the cold, lifeless portrait in stone, made her feel close to Brendan. Below his marble image, she placed a wreath of gardenias and jasmine.

The immensity of her loss hit her like a breaking wave. As grief engulfed her, she dropped to her knees on the flagstones and sobbed softly, praying desperately to God to send Brendan back to her. After that prayer, she invoked the name of Allah in her supplications, and lastly, with bowed head she begged the Hindu gods Krishna and Laksmi to take pity on two lovers wrenched apart by the gulf of time.

Kneeling on the hard stone until her joints

burned, she begged any of the gods to heed her prayer. Stiffly, she rose on trembling legs and wiped the cold tears from her cheeks.

Brendan's villa on the island had been turned into a charming little museum. It clung to a promontory overlooking a vast blue stretch of the Tyrrhenian Sea, a modest villa by modern-day standards. The bedrooms all opened out onto the terrace, as did Brendan's study, while the back of the house contained the kitchen and former servant's apartment, now the museum office.

Marissa wandered through the house, getting tiny flashes of memory. She knew the light, airy bedroom with the white curtains and pine furniture was Miranda's room. The larger room with a huge antique oak bed belonged, of course, to Brendan. She refused to think of Rosalind sharing that room with him.

The study contained a reconstructed version of Brendan's library, most of which had perished in the fire. That was Miranda's doing as well, since she knew the contents of his collection better than Rosalind did. When she began to look closely at the volumes and the small mementoes scattered through the study, other touches of verisimilitude in the museum struck her. It was designed by someone who knew Brendan's habits well.

Marissa approached the middle-aged caretaker as he sat reading a newspaper in his office. He glanced up from his paper, a day-old copy of the *Herald Tribune*.

"What can I do for you, signorina?" he asked politely.

"Good morning, *Signor* Ponci. I have a question

about the founding of the museum. Could you answer it for me?"

He put aside his paper and smiled. "Ah, *bella signorina*, I'd be happy to."

She asked him when the museum first opened, if he knew who designed and funded it.

"Sure, *signorina*. It opened in the 1920s. An English lady came here to find the villa empty and in poor repair. This *signora* designed the museum and donated the funds for the restoration."

"And her name?"

"I'm sorry, *signorina*," he said solemnly. "She didn't want recognition for her good works. She preferred to be known as 'an admirer of Major Tyrell's work.'"

"But *you* know her name, *signore* . . . it was Miranda Egerton, wasn't it?"

His black brows lifted in surprise and he stared at her with his mouth agape. "How do you know that?"

His glance strayed back to his newspaper. "Wait a minute, I know who are. You're the young American lady in the paper!"

In dismay, Marissa watched him turn his *Herald Tribune* back a page. The caretaker's thick finger jabbed at the brief article titled, "Lost Manuscripts Found in Country Cottage." Below the headline ran a thankfully blurred copy of Marissa's old publicity photographs alongside one of Brendan.

"My cousin who works at the hotel gives me these," he said, "because I like to read in English. So I can talk to the tourists when they come here." He beamed. "*You're* this Marissa Erickson, discoverer of the major's lost books! Wait until I tell Girolamo—"

"*Signor* Ponci, *por favore* . . . I came here to Ischia to get away from all this." She pointed at the paper. "Could you try to keep my stay here on the island a secret?"

His face fell. "You want me to say nothing?"

"*Signore* . . . you would earn my deepest gratitude if you told *no one* I was here." She gave him her brightest, heartfelt smile.

"Okay. For you, *signorina*, I will do this. Not just because you have found my major's books," he said, a grin creasing his sun-burnished face, "but because you are . . . *bellisima!*"

"*Grazie, signor,*" she said, blushing, "*mille grazie.*"

Because of who she was, *Signor* Ponci gave Marissa free access to everything in the museum. She spent the afternoon at the villa, sitting in Brendan's chair, lying on Brendan's bed—anything to feel closer to Brendan's spirit, or perhaps even make contact with him again.

When the sun began to sink into the sea, casting dark purple shadows in the interior rooms, Marissa sat quietly under a rose-covered arbor on the terrace. Looking out to sea, she felt nothing but emptiness inside her.

The caretaker found her at last. "I'm sorry, *Signorina* Erickson . . . I have to close the museum now."

"Oh, *mi scusi, signore.*" She stood up. "I must be keeping you from your family and dinner. Thank you for letting me spend the afternoon. It's—it's been very helpful."

"For you, *bellisima*, anything." His brown eyes twinkled in the slanting sun. "You will come back again soon?"

She smiled sadly. "I don't know. . . . "

"Please, *signorina*," he pleaded, "you must visit one more time before you leave the island. The major will be insulted if you don't."

Marissa glanced at the caretaker sharply. "The major?"

"Just a little joke between us," he said, lowering his voice in a conspiratorial manner, "I talk to the major sometimes."

"And," she asked carefully, "does he ever answer back?"

"Ah, no," he said, his face crestfallen, "to my regret. I'm sure he'd be a most interesting man to talk to."

Holding her breath, Marissa looked at *Signor* Ponci a long moment. If there was a chance that this man could help her contact Brendan . . .

But no, her love was gone, beyond her reach. She smiled once more in farewell. "Yes, he would be, more than you could ever imagine, *signore*."

A week later, Marissa stood still on the heated flagstone terrace of Brendan's villa, all her senses alert, expectant. But there was nothing, just the sounds of the bees droning around the scarlet bougainvillaea behind her, the mournful whistling of the wind through the cypress trees, and the faint boom of the surf on the rocks below.

Staring out at the impossible blue of the Tyrrhenian Sea, she felt cheated. She'd come to Ischia hoping to capture Brendan's essence, and she'd only found another drowning wave of loneliness. *Oh, Brendan . . .*

For the past week she'd visited all of Brendan's haunts on the island, hoping that his last words to her had some meaning after all. Yet she'd found only lush, tranquil beauty and rich Mediterranean light. Of Brendan's essence, she felt no sign.

What am I doing here? she thought. *I should be back home, trying to get on with my life instead of brooding over my loss. Brendan was wrong. There's nothing for me here. Nothing.*

Still, she dreaded her return to the empty house on the lake. She'd have to face it one day . . . perhaps she ought to go now, and face it squarely.

The elusive scent of sandalwood wafted up from the cliff below her. The spicy fragrance pierced through her, and her longing surged anew, fresh and agonizing.

Hesitantly, she stepped over to the wall and looked over the edge. A dozen steps below the terrace hung a hidden balcony, and silhouetted against the slanting sun stood the figure of a man.

Dressed in a flowing white shirt identical to those Brendan wore, he stared moodily out to sea. The man's pensive stance drew her eye—for a moment she thought it could have been *him*.

Frozen in place, she stared at him, her heart pounding painfully. But closer study made her realize that he was all too real. From the modern cut of his hair and the way his stylish slacks clung to his lithe form, she guessed him to be an Englishman or American in his early 30s.

The lowering sun infused the tall man's dark hair with copper. Glancing away from his perusal of the view, he turned toward her. She saw his face then—a handsome stranger's face, yet the oddly familiar lines of his visage troubled her. His hair fell over his forehead in an impetuous tumble, and his eyes seemed very dark. *Not American,* she decided, *probably British*.

He piqued her interest further as he moved up the stairs, whistling *Slievenamon*—one of Bren-

Catherine Kohman

dan's favorite Irish ballads. The jaunty smile he
gave her as he reached the top step made her catch
her breath as he extended his hand in welcome.

"Another pilgrim to visit the shrine of St. Brendan?"

Marissa stared at him, listening to the rich,
modulated tones of his Oxford accent; then she
belatedly gave him her hand. "A rather devoted
pilgrim, I must confess." She smiled back. "Marissa Erickson."

He held her hand a moment longer than necessary, the strong, firm clasp of his hand decidedly
pleasant. While she waited for his introduction,
she gazed up at him, studying the planes of his
face: the high cheekbones, proud nose and chiseled chin. She felt a jolt of recognition, but before
she could put a name to his face, he introduced
himself.

"Philip St. John."

Of course, Marissa thought—the television host
for that BBC series on ancient Near Eastern civi-
lizations. She'd been an ardent admirer of his for
some time, yet she thought the camera hardly did
him justice. You didn't feel the potency of his dark
gaze, or the provocative warmth of his smile.

"Ah, *that* Miss Erickson," he said with relish.
"The caretaker told me about you. You're Sir
Brendan's biographer, the one who just unearthed
his missing manuscripts. I'm truly delighted to
meet you.

"Haven't we met before?" His gaze focused on
her face. "I can't believe that I'd forget a face as
lovely as yours, but you seem so familiar. . . . "

"I don't think so, Mr. St. John." She smiled politely, but a tiny chill raced up her spine. His last
name—St. John—what was she forgetting?

"You feel it too." His words stated a fact, rather than a question.

Confused by her galvanic response to him, she shied away from his directness. "I don't know what you mean."

"I don't think I've developed sunstroke," he said, "yet I feel as if I know you."

She laughed lightly, attempting to divert him. "I would like to tell you how much I enjoyed your series on Palmyra, Petra and the Medes. I found it fresh and original."

"Why, thank you, Miss Erickson." He sketched a slight bow. "I bask in the heady warmth of your approval."

Marissa searched his face for the taint of sarcasm, but saw only a teasing glint in his eye. With horror, she felt hot blood rush to her face. "I take it you're an admirer of Brendan Tyrell's work."

"Yes, I have been ever since I could read. One of my friends said that I resembled him." He hesitated. "To be honest, I'm not surprised. A certain ancestress of mine was quite enamored of the illustrious Major Tyrell."

Though clean-shaven, he did have a strong look of Brendan. The intensity in his black eyes was startlingly similar. If he had a mustache and scar, the resemblance would prove remarkable.

Of course—*St. John*—the connection her distracted brain had missed. Brendan's only offspring was his love child by Lady Arabella St. John. Was Philip truly Brendan's descendant? The balmy Mediterranean breeze suddenly felt cool.

"My friend Robert has teased me about being the modern incarnation of Tyrell ever since I took a First in Asian Languages at Oxford." Philip laughed ironically. "I always thought it a capital

joke, with the family skeleton and all. Now I don't
find it quite so amusing. . . . "

At his rueful words, Marissa felt a curious shimmer of hope. No—the very idea was mad. Still, she
had to ask, "What do you mean?"

With a disturbed smile, he ran his fingers
through his windblown hair, brushing it off his
brow . . . a gesture so familiar it made her throat
ache.

"It's all rather unsettling." Philip shook his head
slightly, as if to clear it. "For the last few months
I've had the strangest dreams about Brendan
Tyrell, but though the dreams are very vivid, I
can't recall them in any detail after waking. So this
summer I've been doing a bit of detective work
about Tyrell, trying to learn where these odd
dreams have been coming from. That's why I'm
here."

Philip glanced across the terrace and out to the
wine-dark sea. When he turned back to face her,
his Gypsy eyes darkened with perplexity. "I've always found reincarnation an interesting theory,
but just that—a theory. I never believed it would
affect me personally. Yet since arriving here, I've
had the strangest feelings of déjà vu. And now,
meeting you . . . I'll *swear* that we've met before."

Suddenly, he took her right wrist and slid her
coral silk blouse up over her elbow. She was taken
aback by the pleasant warmth of his fingers on her
skin, and her immediate response to his touch
surprised her. Her arm raised with gooseflesh as
he traced the small crescent scar in the bend of
her elbow.

"You got that scar climbing through a barbed-
wire fence when you were only eight years old.

346

How do I know that about you, Miss Erickson? Tell me—please."

Marissa pulled away from him, avoiding the daunting question in his black eyes. How could he know that? She *had* cut her arm on barbed wire on her grandparents' farm when she was a little girl. Brendan knew it of course. . . .

Oh, God, could it really be him?

With the rush of hope came a staggering fear that paralyzed her. What if she was wrong . . . the disappointment might truly be the end of her. More than once she'd thought of taking her own life, to be able to join Brendan again. If her feelings about Philip St. John proved another fantasy, the sheer drop over the terrace wall might be too tempting for her to resist it any longer.

"Really, Mr. St. John," she joked in panicked desperation. "What sort of parlor tricks are you practicing on me?"

"Parlor tricks?" His reflexive smile didn't reach his eyes. "Then you didn't get the scar that way? Still, I knew it was there."

"Perhaps the breeze blew up my sleeve." Driven by the pressing need to put some distance between them, she added archly, "I will admit it's a novel approach. Has it worked before?"

His jaw tightened. "As a pick-up line, you mean?"

She hated to see the vulnerable curiosity on his face turn into chagrin, and the idea that she'd somehow hurt him made her insides clench painfully. Why did she deliberately push him away when there was a chance that . . .

No. She closed her eyes, unable to put herself through that mental torture. When would she finally accept the truth? *Brendan is gone.*

Catherine Kohman

Compelled to face the living, she forced herself to look up at her quiet companion. Philip St. John stood before her, wounded male pride clearly written on his face. "I'm sorry, Mr. St. John; I didn't mean to sound so cynical. It's just that a woman traveling alone, especially in the Mediterranean, hears a lot of bizarre come-ons."

He shrugged, and his shoulders loosened. "Well, since you seem to think that I have treacherous designs on your lovely person," he said with a challenging smile, "perhaps I should oblige you. Will you have dinner with me this evening?"

He'd graciously provided her with a chance to make up for her slight. "Throwing down the gauntlet, sir? Very well. I'd be delighted to dine with you. The Hotel Excelsior?"

"Actually, I have a villa." He smiled ruefully. "It's got an amazing view from the terrace. Of course, if you'd feel safer at the Hotel . . ."

Marissa laughed, touched by his gallantry. "No, your terrace sounds divine."

"It's a date." He looked at his watch. "I should give the cook fair warning. Villa *Soave* . . . at eight o'clock?"

"That sounds perfect."

Chapter Twenty-One

Twice or thrice had I loved thee,
Before I knew thy face and
name.
                              —John Donne

Marissa dressed with unusual care for the evening, choosing a romantic dress with a scooped neck and small puffed sleeves. An Oriental-style print of lavender flowers and pale green foliage scrolled across the peach silk of the background. She liked the way the silk flowed around her bare legs as she moved.

With her blond hair swept up off her neck into a shining cluster of curls, she pinned a gardenia above her ear for remembrance. She noticed her fingers shook.

Why was she so nervous? Was it because she teetered on the edge of madness? She *must* be

349

mad to think Philip St. John was connected to Brendan in any other way besides genetics. No matter how bizarre, her desperate mind latched on to the merest thread of an idea.

Marissa glanced at the clock. Lord, how did it get so late? She grabbed her purse and dashed for the elevator.

When Marissa knocked on the heavy oak door, Philip himself answered it. His dark eyes lit with appreciation. "Miss Erickson, please . . . welcome to my abode."

Marissa noted that Philip had taken pains with his own selection of attire. He wore a jacket of ivory raw silk over a shirt of the palest blue; through his open shirt collar, she could see the strong, clean lines of his throat.

"Thank you for inviting me." She smiled.

As they walked through the casually elegant villa, he kept turning around to steal glances at her. For her part, she watched him move easily across the flagstones with barely disguised delight. He towered a full six inches over her own considerable height, just as Brendan had; and without being muscle-bound, the two men also shared a lithe, trim athlete's physique.

When they reached the terrace, he said, "I'm sorry. It's rude of me to keep staring at you. You do look incredibly lovely in that dress, but . . ."

Marissa lifted her brows slightly. "But?"

He gave her an apologetic smile. "We've been over this ground before. I'm certain that I know you from somewhere else."

"I'm afraid I can't help you there." She smiled innocently, though her heart beat faster. "Perhaps it will come to you later."

350

The Beckoning Ghost

"I hope so." He led her over to a beautifully set table at the edge of the terrace, next to a low wall so they could see down to the rocky cove below. From this height, the water cascading over the rocks made a wistful, sighing sound. Behind the table, an arbor covered with white jasmine blooms perfumed the air around them.

Philip pulled out Marissa's chair for her, and once she was seated, handed her a glass of champagne. He sat down across from her with his own glass.

Marissa took a sip of the dry, bubbly wine. "How did you know about my weakness for champagne?"

Philip's eyes lit with puzzled laughter. "I seem to know a great number of curious things about you. Some of them are obvious guesses, like the champagne, and your love for Eastern cooking. Others—like that scar—are a bit more difficult to explain."

Marissa felt that bubble of hope rise up in her chest, and tried to force it down. She didn't dare risk being premature and scaring him away. "Such as?"

"You have two cats, correct? A Siamese and a Russian blue. I believe their names are Sasha and Peaches. And you have a best friend named Kelsey who is an artist."

Marissa sat back in her chair, stunned. Only Brendan would know that. . . .

Again, with rising hope came that not-so-irrational dread of terrible hurt.

Wait, wait . . . there were other explanations. Maybe Philip had read about her in the press. She'd avoided all the British and American papers since she arrived here, but one of the tabloids could have dug up such simple facts as those.

She gave him a tremulous smile. "Are you practicing those parlor tricks again, Mr. St. John? Or has there been something about me in the newspapers that you might have read? I left London to get away from the press."

Philip shook his head. "As much as I would like a simple explanation, that won't work either. I haven't been keeping up with the news, either in the papers or the other media. I only recognized your name because the caretaker told me who you were."

"Ah, *Signor* Ponci." She toyed with the stem of her glass. "And he promised me that he'd keep my secret."

Philip laughed at her dejected expression. "Don't blame the man too harshly. When he found out I was a scholar with similar interests, he couldn't resist bragging about you."

She laughed softly in response. "He is a sweet, funny man."

"You have a delightful laugh, Marissa. That is, if I may call you Marissa." He paused, his dark gaze resting on her face. "Why do I get the feeling that you haven't laughed much lately?"

Marissa stared down into the bubbles rising in her glass and twisted the stem in her fingers. "I lost someone very dear to me." She paused, choking back the swell of emotion in her throat. "It's been so . . . difficult to accept."

Philip reached for her other hand. As his long, lean fingers curled around hers, Marissa felt a tingle of heat run up her arm.

"I *am* sorry," he said. "You have this aura of deep sadness about you. If you'd like to tell me about it . . ."

"No," she answered faintly, "not yet."

"I understand." His glance dropped to her hand, and his finger touched Brendan's ring. "I've seen this before . . . it's beautifully made. Is it a copy from a museum collection?"

"No," she said, clearing her throat. "I believe it's an original design, made in Jaipur . . . over one hundred years ago."

"That's strange. I *know* this ring, and yet . . ." He frowned for a moment, deeply lost in thought. "You bought it in Jaipur while you were there doing your research?"

"No, it was a gift. Part of a legacy."

"Ah . . . I must be mistaken again." He regretfully released her hand and stood up. "I'm shamefully neglecting my role as a host. I'll see if dinner is ready to be served."

On his way back from the kitchen, Philip paused in the doorway leading to the terrace. Marissa sat alone at the table, the lamplight gilding her silver-blond hair, an expression of unveiled grief on her lovely oval face.

So beautiful, with that air of mysterious tragedy about her . . . the hypnotic kind of beauty that snared a man's unwary soul.

Why *was* he so drawn to her? He'd never known this mesmerizing need for any woman before, and he'd only met her a few hours ago. More than a physical attraction, he felt beguiled by the very essence of her soul, a connection so powerful it shook him with its intensity. Did it spring from his certainty that he'd known her somewhere before?

That evening before Marissa arrived, he'd been leafing through the previously published biogra-

353

phy of Tyrell and had come across a picture of Brendan's memorial service. To one side behind the grieving widow stood a tall young woman, heavily veiled in black. The photograph's caption simply identified her as Brendan's former ward and secretary, but the obscured lines of her face and her air of mourning reminded him strongly of Marissa Erickson.

Philip had recognized his own physical similarity to Brendan Tyrell some time ago, blaming it on a genetic fluke. Surely it had to be more than coincidence that Marissa bore such an intriguing resemblance to an important figure in Brendan's life.

Now Marissa wrapped her arms around her waist and stared into the candles glowing in front of her. Feeling her slip away from him into her world of private torment, he put aside his troubling speculations. Somehow, he'd pierce that cool shell of reserve and find out the mystery behind the sorrow of his captivating guest.

Just then Rosa the cook came out, pushing a small serving cart. She spoke little English, and with Marissa's meager Italian, the two women communicated with smiles and gestures.

As Philip rejoined them, Rosa peppered him with questions while she served them a crisp, cool salad and warm, buttery bread. With a satisfied smile, the voluble Italian disappeared back into the kitchen.

"My cook heartily approves of you, Marissa. She says you're 'a most beautiful young lady,' only a trifle thin. Rosa wants me to bring you back here every day so she can fatten you up to her standards."

Marissa smiled. "Thank her for the compliment,

but I'm afraid tonight is the only chance she'll have to feed me." She paused. "I'm leaving the island tomorrow."

A cloud settled on Philip's brow. "Must you go so soon?"

Distractedly, she picked a piece of bread apart with her fingers. "I've been here over a week. I have my biography to finish, and the daunting task of finding the right publisher for Brendan's manuscripts."

Despite the smile on his lips, Philip's eyes were darkly serious. "Is there anything I can say to convince you to stay a while longer?"

She felt a flutter of movement in her chest. They'd only just met, and he'd asked her to stay. Normally, things didn't move that fast in a relationship . . . unless their connection really did go deeper than it appeared on the surface. If she said yes, what was she committing herself to? But could she walk away now, never knowing the truth?

She answered honestly, "I don't know, Philip. . . . "

Seeing her hesitation, he leaned forward, a contagious excitement in his rich, mellow voice. "Now, this isn't simply a ploy to keep you here . . . but I would like to discuss with you the idea of doing a documentary program on Brendan Tyrell's life, plus a segment on how you found his missing manuscripts. We could tie it in with the publication of your biography, which would be a bonanza for your sales. Look what happened to Beryl Markham's book after that one-hour program on public TV. I thought perhaps a four-part program. . . . "

Every time Marissa glanced at Philip, she

thought of Brendan, but to keep talking about him only poured salt in the wound. She gave him a faint smile. "Yes, I would be interested in discussing it with you, but . . . not this moment. Could we talk about something else?"

He leaned back into his chair, a puzzled look on his face. "I see. There I go again . . . talking shop over dinner. Will you forgive me?"

"Certainly."

Over the pasta and the main course of poached lobster, they talked about a safe range of topics: how he got started in television, her book on Jaipur and his days at Oxford compared to her days at Harvard. They both shared a love of the lands of Asia, and India in particular.

Marissa noticed that his eyes lingered on her while he thought her attention elsewhere. Not that she had vast experience in such matters, but his fascination with her face could be a sign that he was falling in love with her. It could also mean that something about her truly did baffle him.

In return, she watched every little gesture and expression of his. The way he brushed back his hair and drummed his fingers on the table, those were Brendan's. So was the animation in his features whenever he talked about his work. Some moments Marissa even thought she heard Brendan's manner of speaking. Then Philip would make a completely contemporary remark, and she felt the slight dissonance between the two men.

A thought entered her mind. *Was this how it was for Brendan—this peculiar blending of my personality and traits with Miranda's?*

Was Philip's similarity to Brendan based solely on shared genes? Or was the intimate connection what Marissa secretly hoped for, but was afraid to admit even to herself?

Could Philip and Brendan be two halves of the same soul? She'd finally come to accept Miranda as part of herself. What would Philip say if she told him that she thought he *was* Brendan?

Yet how could Brendan be with her, and still be Philip? Was Brendan really a *doppelganger*, not a ghost? Marissa remembered studying the unusual phenomenon known as bi-location: the ability to be in two places at one time. To the human recipients of such visits, the doppelganger seemed real and substantial: a living breathing human being.

Could the projection of part of one's soul be done unconsciously? Philip seemed to be unaware of Brendan's presence, except for his troubled dreams and sense of déjà vu.

That theory would explain a number of things. Why Brendan came and went as he did . . . the different levels of consciousness he talked about in his frustration . . . his limited energy . . . why he was unable to physically make love to her . . . and lastly, why he had to leave her.

Brendan had insisted that she come to Ischia. He must have known on some level that Philip was here.

"Marissa? Would you care for another glass of champagne?"

She glanced at Philip, who loomed over her. How embarrassing. They'd finished dinner and she was off in the realm of spirits. "Yes, I would."

"You looked like you were off in a strange world of your own," he commented with an indulgent smile.

"Something like that." She rose from the table. "You know how flaky writers are. . . ."

Catherine Kohman

Laughing, he poured her another glass, then re-filled his own. They stood next to each other and looked over the wall across the undulating, moon-lit sea. The soft ocean breeze swirled Marissa's silken gown around her knees.

"It's curious that men used to think you would go blind or mad by staring at the moon," she murmured. "The moon's rays are magical . . . but I've never thought of it as anything but beautiful."

"To people in the ancient world," he answered, "anything that magical and powerful had to be dangerous as well."

Philip paused, and from the way the line of his jaw tensed she knew he was about to ask her a troubling question.

"Marissa, I know that Brendan Tyrell has con-sumed a major part of your life. With the biogra-phy and now his literary legacy to take up your time, you must feel overwhelmed by his person-ality at times."

He ran his fingers along the flute of his glass, then drained it. "I'm interested in Brendan myself, for a number of reasons, including these curious dreams I've been having. But every time I bring up his name, I can feel you withdraw from me. This sadness of yours—what does it have to do with Brendan?"

Marissa couldn't look at him, afraid he'd see the truth in her eyes before she was ready to tell him. She gazed out over the water. "Tell me about these dreams of yours."

He laughed softly. "You're evading my ques-tion."

She quirked her lips. "I know."

Philip let out his breath in a long sigh. "They're mostly just fragments. I see a quaint white house set in a wooded glade, surrounded by sheets of water—fresh water. Brendan is there. He's sailing, walking in the woods, sitting on a swing and conversing with a woman. I can't seem to see her face; I only know that she's younger than he is. The strangest part of the dream is that it isn't set in the past—it's today. And I'm there . . . inside him."

"Philip, I . . ."

Marissa stopped. How could she tell him what she only suspected? He'd think she was crazy. If she could only show him, so he'd see the truth for himself . . .

She remembered her own physical response when he touched her. Did he feel the same current pass between them? If he did, could she somehow tap into his unconscious memory?

She smiled shyly. "Philip, I feel like paying homage to this lovely moon. Would—would you dance with me?"

His brows raised slightly, but he smiled back. Slowly, he ran his forefinger down her arm, from her elbow to her wrist. To Marissa, it felt like a shimmering brand of heat on her bare skin.

With a thrilling promise in his obsidian eyes, he said, "I'll be right back."

Philip came back with a portable stereo and a thick stack of CDs. "I think there may be danceable songs on these. Choose whatever pleases you."

Marissa found some light instrumentals and the song she was looking for, *Lady in Red*. To her delight, another CD contained Miranda's favorite song, *Chanson de Shalott*. She loaded them into the CD carousel and turned the music on.

Marissa held her breath as Philip drew her into his arms. He felt so much like Brendan, it made her tense in his embrace. But he was such a

359

smooth and agile dancer, she finally forgot to be nervous and relaxed to the soft, soothing music.

Philip's touch was light on her back; he held one of her hands in his. Marissa could feel a tingling flow where their skin pressed together. As they danced to the second song, Philip bent his head forward, and his breath stirred fine tendrils of her hair.

Marissa wanted to rest her head against his shoulder, but she didn't want to seem too forward. Instead, she stared up at his lean, long throat and the masculine curve where his jawline swept back to his ear. The lines of his face were so like Brendan's; he even smelled like her lost love, of sandalwood and a hint of piney sea air. She ached to trace a line of warm, soft kisses up the side of his strong neck.

Lady in Red came on next, and Marissa prayed that some shred of Brendan's memory would stir in Philip's mind. At first he did nothing, just held her a little tighter. Marissa decided to gamble. She rested her head against his shoulder and slid her hands across his back, entwining the fingers of one hand in the long hair that curled at Philip's nape.

Then she felt his lips brush her temple. A quiver of anticipation ran through her body.

"Sweet, beautiful Marissa," he murmured into her hair, his voice gently baffled, "why do you move me so much? I feel incredibly close to you."

Marissa raised her head to look up at him. She saw a flicker in his black eyes, but nothing more. She wanted to answer him, but didn't dare say too much.

"Philip, I feel the same way." She gave him a

winsome smile. "Maybe we're moonstruck after all."

"No, it's more than the moment...it's so strong. I can feel it pulling at me and yet..." He shook his head as if to clear it. "I don't know what it is."

Philip drew her close against his chest. She felt the warm, hard length of his body pressed along hers. *Please,* she thought, *please let it happen now.*

The music changed, and the lilting strains of the *Chanson de Shalott* came on the stereo. Marissa suddenly had a flashback to the dream of Miranda and Brendan dancing to this song on the boat deck. If only Philip shared the same memory...

"That gardenia in your hair smells incredible," he said softly, "the perfume is so intoxicating. It almost makes me dizzy."

"Gardenias have always been my favorite flower." Marissa knew she spoke for Miranda as well. "In India, we used to wear chaplets made of them."

"This song seems hauntingly familiar," he asked. "What is it?"

She told him and Philip let go of her hand, placing his own hand just below her waist and above her hip. "You have a tiny mole right here, don't you? It marks the spot where you're the most ticklish." He shook his head again in bewilderment. "How do I know that? We were never lovers—"

Marissa pressed her lips to the underside of his jaw line. Now was her moment, or it would be lost forever. "But we wanted to be, Brendan. Oh, how much we wanted to be."

He missed a step and came to a jarring halt. *"Piara?"*

Philip swayed on his feet, his hand raised to his

forehead. Her heart in her throat, Marissa slid her shoulder under his and led him through the nearest doorway. She sat him on the loveseat and turned on the small, pink-shaded lamp beside it.

Philip slumped forward, his head in his hands. Marissa sat next to him, tears stinging her eyes. What had she done?

After a long moment, he looked up at her. His face filled with a desperate longing, but his eyes were still puzzled.

"You called me Brendan. . . . "

"I'm sorry . . . I couldn't help myself."

"And I called you *'piara.'* That's an Indian endearment, isn't it? I've never called anyone that in my life. Yet with you, it sprang to my lips as if it was the most natural thing in the world."

Again, Marissa saw that deep flicker in his black eyes, almost like a spark waiting to burst into flame. She put her hand on his arm, and he covered it with his.

"You know, don't you?" he asked, his face haunted. "You know what's wrong with me."

"Nothing's wrong with you, my dearest. Please believe me." A single tear spilled over her eyelid and traced a slow path down her cheek.

He caught the flowing tear with his forefinger. It sparkled like a jewel on his fingertip. "Why are you crying then, poppet?"

What had Brendan said, *On Ischia, you'll find peace, my love, and perhaps even a little bit of my soul.*

A fearful joy swept through her. "I don't know *why* I'm crying . . . *Shahin.*"

The confusion clouding his brow brightened into incredulous wonder. As his dark eyes widened in astonishment, he started to raise his hands to her shoulders, then dropped them in his lap. His eyes searched her face, and the intensity in them burned through her like a living flame.

For a moment, he held his breath. Then he whispered, his rich, resonant voice now broken and hoarse. *"Randie-bai?"*

Marissa nodded silently, her throat tight with tears. She took his limp hands in hers and held them tightly.

Philip stared down at their linked hands, and his lips moved once, but no sound came out. He gave a long, soft exhalation and when he spoke, his voice shook. "My God, it is true then . . . I *am* Brendan."

"You must be," she said fiercely. "You *are* Brendan . . . I feel it with every fiber of my soul."

"And you are my beloved Miranda," he said in a voice heavy with emotion. "It is you, isn't it? Or should I call you Marissa?" He laughed then, a deep laugh rife with pleasure. "My heart is beating so hard, poppet."

Her tears splashed onto their joined hands. Letting go of her hands, he reached over and brushed the tears away gently, exploring the bones of her cheeks with his thumbs. She trembled under his touch.

Philip leaned over and pressed his forehead to hers, cupping her face between his hands. "I remember now—all of it. Good God, *Rissa!* You're the woman haunting my dreams. Not only now, but back beyond childhood. My darling Marissa, I've loved you forever—I just couldn't find you until now!"

"Brendan, I was so afraid that I'd lost you forever. Is this happening, or is it another dream?"

"No dream any longer, my beloved." He drew

363

her up with him and pulled her into his arms, smiling at her with Philip's face, but Brendan's soul. "I love you, *piara*."

Inhaling his sandalwood fragrance, a scent she'd come to relish, she stood on her tiptoes to press a kiss against his lean, tanned throat. "I can't believe that we're really here—together."

He chuckled, a resounding laugh full of happiness. His arms tightened around her. "Believe it, Randie-*bai*."

"At last, Brendan—Philip." She laughed too, absolutely giddy with joy. "I don't know *what* to call you."

"It doesn't matter—just call me your one and only love."

He bend down and kissed her then, a deep, soul-stirring kiss filled with yearning. So firm and thrilling, she thought, and she wrapped her arms around his neck, savoring the press of his solid warmth against her. She already knew the particular taste and feel of his lips, and it was a sweet homecoming to be in his arms again.

Her fingers curled through the shaggy hair at his nape as she felt his tongue lightly graze her lips. As she opened her mouth, their tongues mingled with slow, stirring caresses, and shivers of raw pleasure ran down Marissa's spine.

Philip's fingers found the zipper of her dress. Unzipping it all the way, as Brendan had, he encircled her waist with his hands and stroked her sensitive skin.

Marissa wanted to feel his body bare under her hands, so she pulled off his raw silk jacket. Then, drawn to the dark vee of skin above his pale shirt, her fingers went to work on the small pearl buttons. With a playful nip of his lower lip, she stripped his shirt from his wide shoulders to reveal his powerful, sculpted torso, and held her breath in awe.

"Philip . . . you're so perfect." She slid her hands up his smooth chest, then gave a throaty laugh. "My wild Gypsy lover . . . I have you at last."

"You will have me, provocative woman that you are," he growled lightly, "as many times and as many ways as you have the inclination and desire."

Drawing the silk gown down over her shoulders and past her waist, he let it fall to the polished marble floor. Marissa barely had a second to step out of the dress before he pulled her into his arms again. As their mouths met hungrily, they ran their hands over each other in slow, grazing exploration.

Philip released her mouth to cover her face and neck with quick, joyous kisses. Incredibly tender, he nuzzled the hollow between her neck and shoulder. Feeling a warm flush spread across her chest and shoulders, Marissa trembled with sheer need.

His hands cupped her breasts, finding the buds of her nipples through the lavender lace of her brassiere. As his thumbs traced a slow lazy arc around the crests of her breasts, her nipples raised into erect, tingling peaks.

Marissa caught her breath sharply, swaying into him, and Philip laughed deep in his throat. "My lotus-eyed darling, so sweet, so unbearably beautiful."

He deftly undid the clasp of her bra and slid the straps over her shoulders, dropping the bra to the floor. Philip gazed at her breasts lovingly, then brought up his hands to savor their lush, alabaster perfection. He cupped, then squeezed them gently, and Marissa let out a low whimper of pleasure that set off an answering shiver of response within him.

Reaching for the belt of his slacks, she unbuckled it with impatient fingers and let him step out of them. Marissa then loosened the waistband of his briefs, peeling them down over his narrow hips. Her loving touch made him feel light-headed, so he grasped her shoulders as she slid the briefs down over his thighs to drop at his feet.

On her way back up, she pressed her soft, round breasts against him, the hard little buds of her nipples grazing the responsive skin of his thighs. He gasped with delight as her warm hand encircled his erect, aching shaft, and she placed a moist, fleeting kiss on the rounded tip.

Impatiently, Philip drew her up against his chest. Between kisses against the delicate skin of her throat he murmured, "I've waited an eternity for you."

His roving hands stripped the wisp of lavender silk from her hips and thighs. Now, both fully naked after waiting a hundred years for this moment, they stopped to share a rapt, loving glance, each one deeply moved by the splendid beauty of the other.

Then Philip picked her up in his arms and carried her to the wide bed, which lay in a pool of moonlight by the open window. Placing her in the middle of the bed, he stared down at her, running his gaze over the delicate hollow where her ribs dropped to her flat belly and the long, elegant curve of her legs.

With a slow exhalation of pleasure, he dropped on one knee beside her, leaned across her to reach up and unpin her hair. Removing the fragile gardenia, he spread her long, shining hair across the bedspread like a silken silver fan. In the half-light, Marissa's misty green eyes glowed up at him like dusky jewels.

Philip stroked her satiny hair and murmured, "Marissa . . . how long I've hungered for this moment, to be able to tell you how much I love you. I've waited so long to hold you in the flesh."

He dropped his head down to bite her neck, tiny nips that tickled her and made her arch her neck like a swan. Then he lowered his mouth to tease the sensitive peaks of her breasts with his pliant lips and tongue.

Marissa dropped her head back against the bed and whimpered with delighted abandon. Philip's expert touch moved her in a way no other man had ever done. This thick, honeyed delirium coursing through her veins could only be inspired by the touch of one man . . . this man, her beloved.

She ran her hands up and down his back, his long, sinewy thighs, asking for more and receiving it from Philip's questing mouth and hands until she thought she'd die from sheer wanting.

"Love me, my darling," she pleaded. "I can't wait any longer. . . . "

Philip slid his body over hers, his velvety skin pressed against her entire length, from her throat all the way to her knees. Carrying most of his weight on his forearms, he moved between her open thighs. She caught her breath sharply as she felt Philip's warm, hard shaft against her soft, sensitive center.

His ebony eyes glittered darkly in the moonlight, his gaze riveted to her face. As he pressed into her, he sighed deep from his heart and captured her lips with his, slanting his mouth across hers with a ferocious hunger.

At the piercing sweetness of Philip's entry, her body welcomed him into her with a shudder of mindless, dizzying pleasure. Then he moved deeper, opening the thin, furled petals of her womanhood as he would a rose . . . with delicate finesse. When she was fully ready for him, her flesh dewy with moisture, he touched her deeply.

With a heartfelt moan of delight, Philip murmured, "God, you're beautiful, so warm, like silk inside. Stay with me always . . . through a hundred lifetimes."

"Always," she whispered, her voice tremulous, "I've loved you so long. Don't leave me—ever."

"Never," he whispered back, his lips brushing the skin beside her ear. "Never . . . we'll never be parted again."

Then his mouth touched hers, lightly at first— a sweet kiss that changed a moment later, deepened and became hotly possessive.

And they moved as one, entwined in passion, hearts and souls forever bound together.

As she felt her tumultuous release rushing upon her, Marissa tried to hold back the torrent, afraid to surrender too soon, greedy for more of him. But the flickers of heat licking at her very core fused into a tongue of flame that seared her flesh and left her sobbing helplessly.

Philip felt her small shudder beneath him, her body taut around him. With a deep moan, he met her, spilling into her heated, welcoming flesh.

Pulling his full weight upon her, Marissa wrapped her arms around him tightly, and curled her silken leg up over his thigh, bringing him even closer, deeper. For a moment, his heart seemed to stop, and he gazed down into his beloved's soft, glistening green eyes. *"Piara...."*

"Shahin ..."

Under his pleasurable weight, Marissa raised a trembling hand to his face, and he turned his head to kiss her warm palm. Then they collapsed into each other's arms, clinging together, and their bodies shook with matched, pounding heartbeats.

As their breathing softened, he moved beside her and pulled her close, her head tucked into the hollow between his neck and shoulder. An overwhelming peace filled Philip, more powerful than any physical satiation. He'd waited over a hundred years to love this precious woman; his incredible feelings of tenderness for her, their amazing closeness astonished him.

With a light kiss to his jawline, Marissa sighed in utter bliss. That deep void in her soul, a void that she'd felt her entire life and beyond, had disappeared, replaced by the healing, all-consuming love of this man. In her mind's eye, the hopeless dream of the two of them sharing their love amid the shining splendor of the Himalayas became reality. Her fear of hurt, of mortal loss, had vanished too, exorcised by Philip's love.

He swept her long, moon-silvered hair off her neck. "My beloved, we're so lucky to have finally found each other. I shudder to think that you were going to leave the island tomorrow. If we both hadn't decided to go to the villa—"

She placed her fingers to his lips. "But we did, as we were meant to. You told me more than once to trust fate, Brendan-ji."

"So I did, sweetling, so I did." He hugged her fiercely. "All that matters is that we have each other now. And not simply for this lifetime, but forever, love."

Smiling, Marissa traced her fingers over the sharp, chiseled bones of his dear, familiar face. "Yes, my one and only love. This time forever."

Epilogue

For a spur-of-the-moment wedding, it turned out remarkably well.

At sunset a week after they met, Marissa and Philip were married on the terrace of Brendan's villa. Kelsey served as her maid of honor, while Philip's childhood friend Robert acted as best man. Besides the bride and groom's families, Owen Rhys Jones and Beatrice Copeland attended the small, private ceremony.

As a wedding gift, Kelsey gave the bride a Victorian lace wedding gown that she picked up at a vintage clothier's during her brief stopover in London. Deeply touched, Marissa thanked her dearest friend.

Wearing Kelsey's gift and a chaplet of fragrant stephanotis in her hair, Marissa carried a bouquet of her beloved gardenias and jasmine. Tall and darkly elegant in his wedding suit, Philip waited

371

for her beside the priest. The overwhelming delight in his eyes at her appearance thrilled her.

As they exchanged their vows in the rich, golden Mediterranean light, Philip said, "I do." Then he whispered so only she could hear, *"Randie-bai."*

Awed by the heartfelt tenderness in his tone, Marissa blinked back a tear as the priest queried her. In a soft voice, she answered, "I do." Then, looking up at her husband, she smiled and murmured, *"Shahin."*

Down a narrow winding lane off the Hazrat Ganj, Marissa and Philip walked side by side, his arm draped around her shoulders, while hers circled his waist. In the distance they could hear the clamor and noisy hubbub of Lucknow's main bazaar.

Here in the lane it was quiet. The afternoon light suffused the buff stucco walls of the street to a rosy shade of pink, and single pedestrians stole shy glances at the couple.

As Westerners, they were dressed unremarkably in jeans and light cotton shirts, so Marissa couldn't understand the smiling nods they kept receiving.

She glanced up at Philip, her eyes warmed by love. "Do you think we still have that newlywed aura around us?"

He laughed, tightening his arm around her. "Because complete strangers smile at us on the street? They don't know we're married . . . but I'm sure they can see that we're truly, madly, deeply in love."

Marissa touched the delicate wedding band of gold filigree below the emerald and opal ring on her left hand. "Mad, certainly. Can it be only three weeks ago that we met?"

He gazed down at her with a fond, teasing smile. "Do you find married life so tiresome, my sweet, that the days drag by for you?"

"No," she said with a light pinch at his waist. "I meant only that so much has happened in that short time. Our wedding, that splendid, dreamy week at the floating palace in Udaipur . . ."

Philip sighed. "Ah, 'that purple-lined palace of sweet sin,'" he said, quoting Keats in a voice heavy with wistful longing. "Come, my wanton beauty, let's return there anon 'to make delicious moan upon the midnight hours.'"

He turned around and pulled her with him, but Marissa dragged her heels until he stopped short. Glancing around and finding the street empty, she wrapped her arms around his neck and kissed the tender spot below his ear. He grabbed her by the waist and drew her even closer, lowering his head to hers. With a playful smile, she put her finger to his lips.

"Philip, we have locations to scout here and in Darjeeling, books and scripts to write." She placed her hands on either side of his fiercely handsome face. "Husband dearest, as much as we'd like to, we can't spend our entire life in blissful abandon."

He kissed her mouth gently, toying with her lips. "And why not, sweet wife?"

She stared up at him, feeling that honeyed weakness only he could inspire seep into her knees. "Yes, why not?"

Marissa kissed him back, then lightly slipped out of his embrace. "All of a sudden, I'm starving."

She turned him in the direction they were originally headed, and they strolled along the street arm in arm.

"Where did you want to have dinner?" he asked.

She sent him a long, languorous glance. "Who said anything about dinner?"

Philip grinned.

As they passed an antique store window glittering with gold, old bejeweled carvings and other objects d'art, Philip stopped abruptly. Before she could say anything, he dragged her inside the close, cluttered shop.

Philip asked the shop owner to see a locket displayed in the window. Marissa looked up at her husband, perplexed by the curious excitement in his face.

Then the brown, grizzled shopkeeper laid the locket upon a piece of blue velvet and switched on a display light. Marissa caught her breath as she stared at the locket's finely carved gold face.

It looked like the locket Brendan had given her—that is, Miranda—just before the Mutiny in Lucknow. In the hasty retreat to Allahabad, Miranda had lost the locket, and it had broken her heart.

Philip said, "Open it, *piara.*"

With trembling fingers, she released the catch and the locket fell open. On either side, the locket held painted miniature portraits—one of Brendan, the other of Miranda as a young girl.

Her very own locket . . . found again after a hundred-odd years. Tears sprang into her eyes as she gently lifted the locket into her hand.

She looked up at Philip and saw the faint sparkle of tears in his black eyes. To the shopkeeper's amused interest, she kissed him tenderly, savoring the warmth of his mouth on hers.

Then Philip asked the shopkeeper the cost, and cheerfully paid the exorbitant price. His face filled with love, he fastened the locket around Marissa's neck. She turned it over and read the engraved inscription on the back: *To my dearest Randie-bai, Love, Brendan.*

Marissa let the locket drop inside her shirt, and she felt the heavy gold rest safely near her heart. The wheel of *karma* had turned full circle.

As they left the shop, Marissa stepped on her tiptoes to kiss Philip again. "Thank you, my love. I can't believe that we just stumbled across the locket all these years later."

"*Piara* . . . we were meant to find the locket, just as we were always meant to find each other again." With a smile, he added, "Now, promise me you won't lose it this time."

She slipped her arm in his to nestle in the curve of his elbow. "Now that I have you both back, I swear I'll never lose either of you again. *Never.*"

Hearts and bodies touching, they moved off into the rosy Indian sunset.

Dear Reader,

Like the heroine of this book, I have long been fascinated by the life of a notorious author/explorer, Sir Richard Francis Burton. His adventures provided a loose framework for the life of Brendan Tyrell, with some notable changes.

Sir Richard Burton was not murdered by his wife, but lived to a fairly venerable age. After his death, his widow Isabel burned most of his unpublished works, notebooks and diaries. A deeply religious woman, she thought she was doing a noble thing, but posterity has not forgiven her for that tragic holocaust.

Though he once served in India, Burton was not present at the siege of Lucknow. The dangerous trip from the Residency to the approaching British lines was taken from the heroic exploits of a real-life Irishman, Thomas Kavanagh. Christopher Hibbert's book *The Great Mutiny* was my indispensable reference for the Indian Mutiny of 1857.

For more information about Sir Richard Burton, I recommend the biographies written by Fawn Brodie, Byron Farwell and Edward Rice. The film *Mountains of the Moon* is a fictional account of Burton and Speke's search for the source of the Nile.

Colin Wilson's recent work *Beyond the Occult* is an exhaustive survey of all things paranormal; I found it a most valuable resource. While the book of astral doubles, *Phantasms of the Living*, is a real work, the Cunningham book *An Honest Ghost* is an invention of my own.

I spent my childhood summers in the lakeside cottage Marissa owns, and it really was haunted. Those experiences inspired this book, though I never had a ghost as appealing as Brendan Tyrell

376

appear to me under a midsummer moon. . . .
I love to hear from readers. You may contact
me at: www.whitetreepress.com

Catherine Kohman

Catherine Kohman spent her childhood in a haunted lakeside summerhouse. Her first memory is of her grandfather telling spooky tales in front the fire. This influence sparked her fascination with storytelling and the supernatural. Her first novel, *The Beckoning Ghost*, won the Golden Heart Award from Romance Writers of America. A life-long *Lord of the Rings* fan, Catherine also published a fan appreciation anthology, *Lembas for the Soul: How the Lord of the Rings Enriches Everyday Life*. She continues to be active in Tolkien fandom while working on her next novel.

Minnesota natives, she and her husband have lived in Milwaukee, Chicago, Utah, Miami and the Florida Keys. They currently share their woodland home with two whippets, the latest in a long line of rescued sighthounds.